# BLOOD AND DUST

F. M. Parker

# BLOOD AND DUST

WHEELER PUBLISHING, INC.
ROCKLAND, MA

★ AN AMERICAN COMPANY ★

Published in Large Print by arrangement with Kensington Publishing
Corp. in the United States and Canada.

Wheeler Large Print Book Series.

Set in 16 pt Plantin.

*Library of Congress Cataloging-in-Publication Data*

Parker, F.M..
   Blood and dust / F.M. Parker.
      p. (large print)  cm.(Wheeler large print book series)
   ISBN 1-58724-089-0 (softcover)
   1. United States—History—Civil War, 1861-1865—Veterans—Fiction.
2. Ex-prisoners of war—Fiction. 3. Physicians—Fiction. 4. Texas—
Fiction. 5. Large type books. I. Title.

[PS3566.A678 B56   2001]
813'.54—dc21
                                                        2001026364
                                                             CIP

A man who has no woman sleeps with
   the wind.
A woman who has no man has only a
   blanket to protect her.

—Author Unknown

# Prologue

*The Making of the LLano Estacado,*
*Staked Plain.*

The broad sea, ancient beyond imagination, had been created so long ago that even the sun had forgotten it had ever shone upon its birth. The sea had come into existence when the breast of the continent had subsided and the great oceans of the earth flooded in to fill the depression.

Seventy million years ago, the sea was shoved away to the south as a tremendous force lifted and buckled a broad section of the earth's mantle. The force continued to torture the crust of the earth, thrusting the rocks upward until a mighty mountain range with a north-south axis pierced the sky.

On the west side of the mountains, a grand river came to life, fed endlessly by the countless streams pouring with awesome violence down the mountains' steep flanks. The strong current of the river rushed away to the south until it reached the far-off sea.

On the east side of the mountain range a myriad of streams tumbled down from the high ramparts. As the grade flattened on the lower

1

reaches of the streams, they slowed to wander in meandering courses, dropping their load of eroded mountain debris. The valleys of the streams became choked with swamps and shallow lakes as thousands of cubic miles of sediment were spread in ever-thickening layers over the land.

The millennia passed, score after score, adding to millions of years. During the long epoch a broad plain was built at the base of the mountain and extending to the east and south for hundreds of miles. So flat was the land surface that the larger animals could see each other for great distances, to the limits of their vision.

Twenty million years ago on the bank of the grand river, and near where it entered the sea, a hungry lizard raced down the bank to capture a fish that was stranded and floundering in a shallow pool of water. The lizard's tail left a small scratch in the mud. From that tiny scar in the dirt during the next rainstorm, an incipient streamlet was born.

The rivulet had inherited the hunger of the beast that had created it. Within a foot, the rivulet cut into the course of another trickle of water and beheaded it, adding that miniature flow to its own body. Then it captured another streamlet, and another. Swiftly the rivulet grew to become a creek.

The new creek greedily ate its way north across the plain, in its journey encountering the channels of many streams. A battle was fought each time to determine which stream would die. The hungry offspring of the lizard won every battle.

The creek grew to become a river flowing in a wide valley. Its headwaters had reached the very summit of the mountains far to the north. Now there were two large rivers, with a mighty mountain range rearing high into the sky between them.

This is the way a tribe of men, migrating from a distant place far north of the mountains, found the land when they arrived twelve thousand years ago. The people liked the flat plains and the two rivers, and the abundant buffalo, elk, and antelope, and they stayed, their numbers increasing.

Thousands of years later, barely a tick of time as measured on the geologic clock, a second tribe of men arrived, moving cautiously up from the south. They also found the land of plains and the rivers most pleasing. These men called the flat land the LLano Estacado, and the rivers the Rio Grande and the Rio Pecos. They settled there with their women and children.

Time ticked again, and a third tribe of men came hurrying onto the land. They came from the east and their numbers were many. They made savage war upon the first two tribes. They made even more terrible and bloody war between factions of their own tribe.

The events of this story happened during the days of the third tribe's civil war.

# One

Ben Hawkins reined his horse to a halt on the bank above the Rio Grande. The string of four stolen horses he led, tied nose-to-tail with short lengths of rope, came to a stop behind him. The animals stood sweat-lathered and lungs pumping.

Ben dug a telescope from a saddlebag and twisted in the saddle to look south behind him. He extended the brass tube and with the aid of the magnified field of vision, scoured the land he had raced across. There was no sign of his pursuers, only the desert baking under the burning sun and a faded blue domed sky arching high above. He hadn't expected to see the Mexican riders, not yet, for he had changed mounts four times since sunup, rotating among the horses and pushing them hard. In four days he had traveled three hundred miles.

Ben collapsed the spyglass and stowed it away. He began to examine the dense stands of huge cottonwoods growing on the floodplain along both sides of the river. The Mexicans

5

might be miles behind, but this was Comanche territory and he didn't want to stumble into a band of those fierce warriors.

He saw nothing of concern from his location; still, there were sections of the woods that he couldn't see into and he wanted a closer look. He tied the Mexican horses to a tree and then rode his gray mount, Brutus, down to the river's edge. Ben studied the far shore for a time, checking the openings among the cottonwoods, and the border of the Llano Estacado, the Staked Plains, that showed beyond the trees. Seeing nothing threatening, he crossed the river on a sandy-bottomed ford where the water ran clear, and came onto American soil.

Ben searched for the presence of other men. He found only the tracks of buffalo, deer, wolves, and smaller wildlife. He returned to the south shore.

All the horses had now caught their wind and cooled, and Ben allowed them to drink. The Mexican horses were again fastened to a tree. Ben brought the saddled Brutus near the water with him and dropped his reins to ground-hitch him. The cool, clean water had enticed Ben to bathe. He thought he had time before his enemies arrived, but still he wanted his guns and horse close.

Ben hung his belted Colt pistol over the saddle horn and quickly stripped down to his skin. He was two inches above average height and rawboned. He had gray eyes and his hair was black. His beard, now some two weeks long,

6

was a reddish black. The dusty, sweaty clothing was swiftly washed, the water wrung out, and the clothing hung on a low limb of a cotton-wood. He took one last keen look all the way around, and then dove into the river.

Ben came up spouting water. He flung his long hair back across his head and squeezed the water from it. With long, easy strokes, enjoying the grand feeling of the water upon his skin, he swam across the thirty yards of river and back. In the shallow water just above the ford, he scrubbed his dirty body with the fine sand of the river bottom. Then he lay down by the riffling ford and let the cool, gentle fingers of the river current wash over him and carry his weariness away.

A hawk come from somewhere in the north and with its head turned down and telescopic eyes hunting, began to circle in the sky above Ben and the horses. After half a dozen circles, the bird drifted away downriver, still hunting.

"Brutus, I think Mr. Hawk must have decided we were too big to eat," Ben said to the gray.

The long-legged brute looked down with gold-flecked brown eyes at his master, lying in the water with just his head showing like a big river turtle. The horse snorted once to show it had heard the man's words. Then it lifted its head and rested watching the far shore.

Ben felt a wind come alive, and heard the leaves on the cottonwoods begin to stir. At the sound, he sat up, for a feeling had come over him that he had spent too much time in the water. He waded to the shore and hastily pulled on his damp clothing and stomped into his boots. He swung astride Brutus, reined him up beside the other horses, and untied them.

The cavalcade of horses splashed across the Rio Grande to the north shore, and onward through an opening in the cottonwoods to the broad, flat Llano Estacado.


Ben found what he needed, a place where the limestone rock beneath the plain had been leached away, leaving behind a sinkhole deep enough to hide the horses. He took the animals down into the house-size depression and tied them to a stunted oak bush.

Carrying his telescope and rifle and a bandoleer of cartridges, he went back half a hundred paces toward the river to a slight rise of land. He lay down in the knee-high buffalo grass. Through a break in the trees, the river crossing was in plain view a couple of hundred yards distant.

He rested the telescope and rifle upon the bandoleer to keep them out of the dirt. Both the rifle, a Spencer seven-shot repeater, and the telescope had been taken off the dead body of a Union sharpshooter he had killed in the battle of Cedar Mountain in Virginia this past August. It had been during that battle that his life had changed forever and he had fled back to Texas.

The Spencer was a fine weapon. With it Ben

could shoot thirty aimed shots in a minute. Even if his enemies came in a large number, he should be able to fight them by himself. That was good, for all he had was himself. He was a thief who walked alone.

Now there was only the waiting. He hoped the Mexicans didn't cross the Rio Grande and come into the States chasing him.

He made himself as comfortable as possible on the ground, and with eyes hammered down to a squint by the bright sun, kept watch south. Frequently he raised the spyglass and scanned the great, level plain. After a time, the hot wind began to blow more strongly, whispering the reeds of grass together with a sibilant, snaky sound.

His pursuers would be several of Ramos Valdes's toughest *pistoleros*. How many, or who would be leading them, Ben could not guess. They would have orders to kill him on sight and reclaim the stolen horses. Should he make one mistake, he would die.

This was the third time he had made the journey south to steal Valdes horses. They were famous throughout northern Mexico and south Texas for their speed and endurance, and for their brilliance and purity of color. They were worth the risks to go upon the rancho and take them from under the noses of the guards that were always posted. The Valdes brand, V Bar V, was burned into the left hip of each horse. In most parts of Texas, a horse stolen in Mexico and brought north of the Rio Grande was totally acceptable. If it carried the

9

Valdes brand, that added much to the value. Sometimes, though, the more law-conscious Texan would modify the brand to a Diamond Bar Diamond, fooling nobody.

The four horses Ben had with him would sell for many hundreds of dollars, an amount several times the yearly salary of a working cowboy. He could make the trip from Abilene and back in three weeks, or a little longer depending upon the trouble he encountered. The time was very profitably spent. He intended to steal enough of the Valdes horses to acquire the money necessary to carry out his plan.

Ramos Valdes was wealthy, owning more than 200,000 acres and controlling twice that many by the use of force and through the connivance of Mexican federal officials to whom he paid bribes. Scores of peon families labored at barely survival wages to care for his large number of horses and vast herds of cattle. The man would not miss the few horses Ben stole. Still, he would kill Ben if he could catch him.

Ben lay in the heat and wind-tossed grass and sweated. He wiped at the salty brine trickling down through his black beard and flicked a droplet off the tip of his nose. He waited. He was a patient man.

Ben frequently scanned the land, for his enemies could appear at any minute, and most probably would come from the south. But he also kept a close watch to the east and west along the American side of the river.

The Mexicans might suspect an ambush, and veer off his trail, cross the river someplace other than the one he had chosen, and strike him from the side or rear.

Ben halted the sweep of his spyglass and focused it more sharply. Something was moving far off. He had spotted the band of men, six miniature riders upon six miniature horses. They were dogging his exact trail. That fact told Ben that old Ramos Valdes was not leading. He was too foxy to come straight at Ben and fall into an ambush.

The band of men drew ever closer. They moved as a tight group, a large hunting animal in swift pursuit of its prey. The band reached the river and stopped on the south bank. One man dismounted and began to examine Ben's tracks. Ben recognized Carlos Valdes, the older of Ramos's two sons. Ben wondered what Carlos thought about him taking time to have a swim.

Carlos called his men together and they began to talk among themselves. Ben saw two men, nervously eyeing the north shore, shake their heads in disagreement with what Carlos was saying. Then Carlos spoke, giving an order, and all the men swung astride their mounts. They rode down the bank and into the water of the ford, and crossed the river onto the American side.

"Damn you, Carlos," Ben exclaimed, his mood turning ugly at the man's action. He wasn't going to allow the Mexicans to chase him across Texas.

11

"Carlos, you should've stayed in Mexico," he whispered, and raised the Spencer to his shoulder. The .52-caliber lead bullet the rifle fired was a real man-killer. He put the sights of the weapon on Carlos's broad chest and took up the slack in the trigger.

# Two

Ben held the rifle aimed at Carlos, but halted the squeeze of his finger on the trigger. He considered the Valdes wealth to have been gotten largely by illegal means. Further, a great uncle of Ben's had been killed at the Alamo, and another at the battle of Goliad, so stealing from the Valdes did not trouble his conscience or cause any regrets. Still, Ben understood why Carlos and his *pistoleros* were trying so hard to take back the horses; they considered them to rightly be Valdes property. Also, they wanted to catch and punish him to set an example for other thieves. The fact the men were trying hard to kill Ben was bothersome; however, he would make that feat a very difficult task to accomplish.

He shifted the aim of the weapon from Carlos to the black horse he rode. A cold chill went through Ben at the thought of killing the splendid animal. He moved the point of aim back to Carlos. Shoot the man or the horse, hurry and decide, for the band of *pistoleros* was spurring their mounts up the north bank and directly at him.

Ben couldn't bring himself to shoot the man without warning. He settled the sights of the rifle on the black horse and fired. The animal staggered back at the punch of the big bullet and sank to its knees. Carlos sprang clear as the horse toppled to its side on the ground.

Ben levered another bullet into the firing chamber of his fine killing weapon. He pressed the trigger and sent the bullet into the horse of the rider to the left of Carlos. Immediately he shot a third horse.

He lowered the rifle. He felt revolted at what he had been forced to do. *Carlos, you son of a bitch, go back to Mexico now.*

The three remaining riders spun their mounts, and lashed them back down the bank and into hiding among the cottonwoods by the river.

Carlos rose to his feet and faced toward Ben, lying unseen in the grass. He raised his fist and shouted out in English, "You ugly bastard, I'll kill you for this."

"Not right now." Ben lifted his rifle again and fired. The bullet struck the ground between Carlos's legs and clods of dirt and fragments of lead stung him. The man jumped, and in his hurried action, stumbled and fell to his knees. He straightened, and stood aiming his eyes in Ben's direction.

After several seconds, Carlos slowly and deliberately turned his back to Ben. He spoke to the other two men who had lost their mounts, and all three removed their canteens and rifles from their dead horses. Carlos bent down and started to loosen the cinch of his saddle to remove it. Ben fired a warning shot close above Carlos's head. He had once seen the saddle and knew its high value.

Carlos jerked back from the saddle. Ben could see the man shaking with anger. Without looking again in Ben's direction, Carlos stood erect and went down the bank toward the river. The other two men went with him, throwing nervous looks behind as they moved.

Carlos shouted out angrily ahead. His three mounted riders came out of the woods to meet him.

Ben rose up from the grass and stood watching the Mexicans, riding two to a horse, cross the river and go south. He chuckled to himself. By trying to catch him they had lost three additional horses and a very valuable saddle, and had a long distance to travel riding double back to the Valdes rancho. When the riders had become lost to sight and none of them had dropped off a horse to stay behind to trail Ben, he snapped his spyglass closed and turned away.

Carlos would know that Ben could have killed him; still, that would do nothing to lessen the Valdes family's desire for revenge. Ben took the saddles and bridles from the dead horses and fastened them upon the backs of three of his. Carlos's riding gear was heavy, with beautifully sculptured silver ornaments, and the most valuable Ben had ever seen.

Hardly a section of the equipment was free of decoration by the precious metal. The saddle and bridle were worth as much as all the horses.

Ben mounted Brutus, and the fall of hooves carried him and his prizes north into the awesome emptiness of the Staked Plains.

The sun had rolled down its high-sky trajectory and lay flaming on the far, flat horizon when Ben drew close to the spring he had guided his course toward. While still out of sight of the spring, he left his horses behind and stole forward. He wanted to be certain no enemy had laid claim to the water ahead of him.

He reached the lip of the valley and peered over. The valley, shallow and narrow with a dry watercourse in the center, lay deserted. The spring, its location marked by three trees clumped together, was on the far side of the valley directly opposite Ben. He felt an increase of his thirst for he knew the water, coming from some deep subterranean reservoir, was sweet and cold.

Ben gathered his animals and went down into the valley. After hobbling the front legs of the stolen horses with short lengths of rope, he turned them loose to graze the wild grass. Brutus was left free for he would always hang close to Ben.

Ben spread his bedroll on the thick mat of leaves beneath the trees. Taking his canteen, he went to the spring. The water came to the surface on top of a layer of sandstone, poured down into a pool some five feet across, and then flowed away for a few yards before disappearing into the ground. He knelt and leaned over the pool of water.

A devil's face rose up out of the depths of the water to look at Ben. The reflection was of Ben's face, a face mutilated and scarred and, God, so horribly ugly. A Union cannonball had struck him a hard, glancing blow on the face and ripped the flesh from the skull. A Confederate surgeon had attempted to restore Ben's face to a human appearance, but so torn and mangled was the flesh that the surgeon had failed, failed horribly.

When Ben returned from the war to El Paso, he had asked for his old job back as deputy sheriff. The sheriff had been his friend, and reluctantly returned the badge to him. He'd quickly learned that he could not take up where his prior life had ended. The world had changed most drastically for him. Men he met on the street would take one look at him and then turn hastily away, for they were unable to endure the sight of his grotesque features. Women and children ran from him in horror. Within hours of receiving his badge, he had returned it to the sheriff. He bought a broad-brimmed hat and kept it pulled low, and also held his head slanted down so that his face was mostly hidden from the people he encountered.

Once he had gone to a brothel to satisfy his twenty-three-year-old body's needs for a woman. No amount of money could persuade one to lie with him. When a woman finally offered herself if he would put a pillowcase over his head, he ran from the whorehouse in heartrending humiliation.

He had often reflected during this past year on how it would be to have a loving wife and several children, and how at his death they would be gathered around him. That was not to be, for his ugly wounds had changed the rules of the world. He was an outcast and would be alone forever, and would die, and his body would rot and waste away, in some wild and lonely place.

He leaned closer to the gargoyle face in the spring. He shivered in revulsion at his own image. He was overwhelmed at the unjustness of such a wound. He should have been killed outright; that would have been so very much better than this. Now all he had was a bleak, empty life stretching out ahead of him. A burning anger seized him. He closed his right hand into a fist and smashed the face in the water.

The reflection shattered, vanishing in a turbulence of waves. But the water quickly quieted and his image reassembled itself, thrusting itself before him with its twisted features screwed into even greater ugliness by his raw anger.

In a paroxysm of violent blows, he began to beat at the repugnant face. The water jumped and splashed under his driving fists. Beat the damn thing. Destroy it. He hammered and hammered at it.

Finally Ben controlled his crazed outburst of swinging fists. His arms lowered to hang by his sides. He hunkered there by the spring, breathing through his ragged slash of a mouth.

The reflection of his mutilated face came together again as the water stilled. He cried out, the anguish-filled voice rushing out across the plain. A sob escaped him before he could trap it in his throat.

He pulled his pistol and placed the end of the barrel against his head at the temple. There was a way to end all his suffering.

On the plain not far from Ben, a young female wolf halted her smooth, fluid lope and froze into a gray statue when the cry of suffering reached her. She cocked her ears in the direction from where the sound had come, and heard the human sob of anguish that followed after the cry. In her wolf's way, she sensed the other creature's deep pain. Earlier this day, the male wolf she had journeyed with since being a pup had been killed by a bull buffalo, and her feelings of loss and aloneness were still tormentingly fresh.

She raised her head and howled a long and lingering cry full of her own sorrow. She breathed and again howled, a mournful sound flowing out through the dusk of the evening.

Ben lowered the pistol from his head and listened to the plaintive wolf call. He tried to pinpoint its source, but it had no origin, seemingly coming from nowhere and everywhere. He was struck by the similarity of the sound to his own voice raised in lament. Why had it responded to his cry, and at the exact moment when he was prepared to send a bullet crashing into his head? A wolf had saved his life. For what purpose?

Ignoring the face in the spring, he lowered his canteen into the water and filled it. The canteen was laid aside and he lowered himself to drink straight from the pool. He blew against the water to break up his image, and drank, the water sliding down his throat cold and delicious. There was always tomorrow to use the pistol.

The black wave of the night came stalking, and Ben went to his bedroll and lay down. He couldn't sleep, and lay watching the full moon come up, a huge yellow sphere that faded to a silver dime as it rode higher in the sky. Later he was still awake when the star-filled sky, whirling about its axis, swept the Seven Sisters of the Pleiades right up overhead. Brutus finished feeding and came to stand close to Ben. The horse lowered his head to be petted, and Ben stroked the long, bony jaw.

"Brutus, old horse, it's just you and me. I'm damn glad that you don't care how ugly I am."

# *Three*

General Grant took a long pull on his cigar and blew the smoke out into the morning air. His heart was beating nicely. He had won the battle, wresting Vicksburg from the rebel Confederacy after a bitter siege of forty-eight days. This victory more than redeemed his defeats at Belmont and Shiloh.

Grant stood on the top-floor balcony of the two-story house he had commandeered for use as his headquarters. The house was located on the highest point of the town and two hundred feet above the Mississippi River. From here he had an excellent view down over the cannon-shattered city, and beyond that some quarter-mile distant to Commander Porter's flotilla of ironclad ships, gunboats, and river steamers tied to the wharfs on the Mississippi. Commander Porter had held the water side of the siege line and prevented the Confederate army from escaping or receiving supplies by boat.

The general savored the quietness after weeks of constant cannon fire, and the air was sweet, cleansed of its sulfurous stink of burned gunpowder. Today there were no battle plans to devise. All the deadly forts, the strong redoubts, salients, and bastions of the enemy-fortified city, had been surrendered the day before and were now occupied by his troops. Squads of Union soldiers patrolled the city streets to enforce his Orders of Occupation.

Within but a few minutes after the Confederate forces had surrendered the city, the news had made a quick passage through both armies. Then a strange and moving sight had occurred. Brothers and cousins and uncles and nephews who had minutes before been enemies had come out from the opposing armies and into the narrow no-man's-land between the trenches, and laughingly shouted out greetings to their kin. Every man, happy to be alive and glad to see his relatives were also among the living, had embraced without constraint.

The fourteen thousand enemy soldiers, stripped of their weapons, had been allowed to leave the city. Grant had no way to hold them prisoners, so he had paroled them upon their sworn oath that they would never again take up arms against the Union. Of course, Grant knew that many would immediately break that oath. Left behind were three hundred Confederates too badly wounded to travel. They were being cared for in private residences in the town.

Heavily armed Vicksburg, with its strategic position on the high ground overlooking the Mississippi, had controlled that vital artery of transportation and denied the Union its use. Jefferson Davis, President of the Confederacy, had called Vicksburg the Gibraltar of

21

the West and the lynchpin that held the South together. General Grant had knocked that lynchpin loose. All the machinery of the factories and mills of the town was salvageable and would be quickly put into operation for the Union. The full length of the river now belonged to the Union, and its soldiers and cannon, all the necessities of war could move freely. Texas, Louisiana, and Kansas had been severed from the Confederacy. Grant knew his victory would substantially shorten the war.

"General, sir, may I speak with you?" Colonel Crowley, the chief surgeon, said from the top of the stairs at the end of the balcony.

"Come up and share the view with me, Colonel Crowley," Grant replied.

"Thank you, sir," Crowley said. He came to the railing of the balcony and looked west across the battered town toward Louisiana on the far side of the river.

"A much more enjoyable view this morning than the ones we've had these past many days," Grant said.

"Yes, sir."

"Victory does that, changes the complexion of everything," Grant added.

"It's sad that men have to fight and kill each other."

"At times fighting is necessary. And fighting means killing." Grant's tone was sharper than he wanted. Still, many Union and Confederate soldiers had been killed in the battle for Vicksburg, and Crowley shouldn't have brought that into the conversation and ruined a glorious day. "What did you want to see me about?" Grant asked, still angry at the chief surgeon.

"Captain Payson has requested to be released from duty and discharged," Crowley replied. The general's tone had stung.

"Discharged? He can't even stand on his feet." The young captain hadn't recovered from the injury he'd received when the Confederates had tried to break out of the siege three weeks earlier. The enemy's attempt to breech the encircling Union lines had been near the hospital, and in the bitter fighting, a pistol bullet had struck the tent where Captain Payson had been operating on the wounded. The bullet had entered his right chest, penetrating his lung, and lodged against the spine.

"He can get better treatment from you and your staff than from any civilian doctor," Grant added.

"He's very ill and wants to go home to Texas."

"Do you think he'll die?"

"The odds are greatly against him, for lung wounds are almost always fatal and his was an especially serious one. He survived the injury and the operation to remove the bullet because he has such a strong will. But the internal bleeding won't stop and he continues to cough up blood. I believe the injured lung has adhered to the side of the chest and simply his breathing keeps the wound open and bleeding."

"What does he say?" Grant wanted the captain's opinion, for he judged him to be one of the best surgeons in the medical corps, even though he was the youngest at twenty-five years.

"We've discussed the wound, and though he hasn't said so, I think he agrees with me. He appears to have accepted the likelihood of dying and now just wants to choose his burial place."

Grant considered most of his officers likeable fellows. He found Captain Payson the most pleasant of all. In the evenings he would assemble his staff and discuss the results of the day's fighting and the plans for the following day's action. After the meeting he would frequently invite Payson to stop by his tent and they would talk, sometimes play chess, and sip a little bourbon. Grant sorely missed the man's company.

"Sounds like foolishness. But let's go and hear the captain's plans," Grant said. He led off with the colonel following him down from the balcony to the ground. Grant's two orderlies, armed with rifles and pistols, came to attention at the foot of the stairs. They were also his bodyguards, for there were thousands of men in the city who wanted him dead. They fell in behind Grant and the colonel and went off along the street with them.

# *Four*

"What's the Johnny Reb doing there by the officers' hospital?" Grant asked Colonel Crowley. He pointed ahead at the man in faded gray uniform leaning against a tree in the front yard. "All of them that can travel should be gone."

Immediately upon capturing the city, Grant had evicted the occupants of half a hundred houses and moved his wounded officers and enlisted men from tents east of town and into houses. He had chosen the houses on the highest ground so that any breeze that blew would find and cool the injured soldiers and make the July heat more bearable.

"His name's Davis, Corporal Davis," Crowley replied. "He's agreed to help Captain Payson get to Texas."

"Why would a Reb do that?"

"They're both from El Paso and knew each other there. But more than that, the corporal feels he owes the captain. He was seriously injured in the leg when we took him prisoner in our first attack on the city. Most of the surgeons thought the leg too badly damaged to save and wanted to amputate it. But Captain Payson didn't agree and did some excellent work. The corporal will always limp but he's got his leg."

"Your own leg, even if you limp, is certainly better than a wooden one," Grant said.

The Confederate corporal, a short, stocky man with a wide face, came to attention as

Grant drew close. The general thought the corporal was going to salute, but the man just stood rigid, with his eyes cold, and watched him pass.

Grant continued on into the hospital. His head lifted as his nose caught the biting odor of disinfectant and the morbid, ugly stench of gangrene that came from the rotting flesh of living men. The smells were all too familiar to him after two years of heavy fighting. He shut them off from his thoughts.

Grant had kept track of Captain Payson's condition and had come a few times to visit him, but not so many that the other wounded officers would think him too much a favorite. He went directly to Payson's room on the main floor. The captain lay motionless upon his cot with his eyes closed. He was gaunt with his bones sharply etched against skin the gray hue of the dead. Grant felt a deep sorrow for the young captain. He was a gentle man. Grant ordered men into battle to be killed or wounded, while this man used his remarkable skill to save their limbs and lives.

Grant had first seen Evan at the end of the battle at Fort Donelson in northern Tennessee. He had gone to the hospital area to visit his wounded, and there had been a stranger in civilian clothing, fearfully splattered with the blood of his patients, operating alongside the army surgeons. Grant had stopped to observe the man at work and noted his great skill, and an amazing swiftness that was very important in the absence of anesthetics. A man could stand just so much pain before he died.

Grant learned that Evan, fresh out of medical school in Philadelphia and on his way home to Texas, had come upon the scores of wounded soldiers lying on the ground and awaiting treatment. He had stripped off his jacket, laid out his private surgical instruments, and waded in to help. Grant needed surgeons badly, and had persuaded Evan to join his army.

"Good morning, Captain Payson," Grant said.

Grant's familiar voice reached Evan Payson through the haze of the pain-deadening laudanum circulating in his blood. He fought his eyes open, pulling the heavy lids apart, and looked up at the general. He tried to speak, but failed, his throat clogged with mucus and blood. He coughed—God, that hurt—and tried again.

"Good morning, General Grant," Evan said, his voice frail.

"How are you today?" Grant asked, staring down into the captain's brown eyes, appearing huge in his gaunt, bony face.

"Wanting to travel, sir." Evan mustn't show his weakness.

"That's what the chief surgeon tells me. Says you want to go to Texas."

"Yes, sir. El Paso."

"I'd estimate that to be about twelve hundred miles. You up to that?"

"Yes, sir."

"Can you trust the corporal to stick with you all the way?"

"John Davis is a good man. He said he'd help and he will."

Evan knew he had to show his determination to leave. He mustn't die here in Vicksburg, for then he would be buried with the other slain soldiers in the military cemetery north of the city. The cemetery was but a few weeks old, yet it already contained more than 3,700 dead, counting both Union and Confederate casualties. The call of home was a drumbeat in his heart. Home was where he must be buried, close to his kin, who were the very best comrades for the long journey through eternity.

The wound and the many days lying on the cot had drained him of his strength. Could he make his crippled body rise and show his ability to travel? He willed his right leg to move, and slowly it slid to the edge of the cot. Then it was over the iron rail of the cot and he felt the touch of the wooden floor against his bare foot. Fighting a sharp lance of new pain, he rolled to his side and brought his left leg to the floor.

With a supreme effort, he sat up, a scarecrow man straining to move. He swayed with dizziness, and coughed. Fresh blood came into his mouth and out onto his lips. He brought a trembling arm up and wiped the blood away with the sleeve of his shirt.

"Lie back down, Captain," said the chief surgeon. "You're killing yourself by trying to stand."

Evan laughed, a hard and bitter sound. "You're probably right, Colonel, but I don't intend to lie here and die in this bed."

He shifted his bloodshot eyes and fastened them on Grant. "General Grant, I'm no longer of any use to your army and I request a release from duty. I may not live long enough to even cross the Mississippi, but I want to start for home."

Grant reached out and clasped Evan's hand in a firm grip. He felt the long slender fingers, the fingers of an artist who was a surgeon and could do such magnificent work. Grant was losing his very best. Also, he was losing a man who was closer to being a friend than any other in his army of tens of thousands. Grant continued to hold the captain's hand. His friend was dying, and never again would he see him. Death was an old acquaintance to Grant. It always journeyed with his army, and now had chosen Evan Payson. The place where it finally claimed the man wasn't important. He released Evan's hand and stepped away.

"Yes, Captain, I'll release you from the Army so that you may go home."

The world around Evan felt fragile, as if it could shatter into nothingness at any moment. The pounding pistons of the engine of the river steamboat transporting John Davis and him across the Mississippi River seemed muted to but a fraction of its usual noise. The splash of the big stern paddle wheel was far away. Was his inability to hear the full volume of the sounds around him a sign that he was dying?

Evan believed he could well be dying from his wound, for he had come close several times before. He wanted to delay that eventuality for as long as possible. He opened his eyes. Perhaps looking at the world would strengthen his hold on it. At the thought, he laughed sardonically to himself. His mind must already be going.

He looked out from the bed of the surrey where he lay on a pallet made of the cotton mattress from his hospital bed. He judged the steamboat to be midstream in the three-quarter-mile-wide river. The docks on the Louisiana side of the river could be seen ahead. Half a score of Union gunboats were tied up there. Closer to him and upriver, a big fish roiled the surface of the greenish-tan water. The world still existed and the journey home was beginning.

Evan had drawn his mustering-out pay and given John money to purchase a vehicle to carry them to El Paso. John had secured a strongly built surrey with soft springs. Evan's riding horse and a second one bought from a fellow surgeon had been paired to form a team to pull the surrey.

The vehicle had a leak-proof top of canvas, and side curtains of the same material that could be raised and lowered. John had removed the rear seat and created space for Evan's pallet, and his personal belongings consisting mostly of a trunk of clothing. John had no possessions except the garments he wore. Evan had told John that he would share what he had.

At General Grant's orders, Evan was provided food from the officers' commissary, and also the authority to cross the river on one of Commander Porter's riverboats. The army had recently received a shipment of provisions from Cincinnati. John, with the general's order in hand, had loaded the carriage with a wide variety of foodstuffs: canned corn, pears, peaches, salmon, sardines, ham, and a lucky find, bottles of wine. Colonel Crowley had given Evan a supply of laudanum.

Evan had refused to allow his surgical instruments to be loaded on the surrey. He had asked John to take the full set of fine steel instruments—saws, scalpels, lances, needles, all the paraphernalia of a surgeon—to the Army hospital. Evan had become revolted at the carnage done to fine, young men. Too many had come under his knife and saw, never to be whole again. He could only guess how many arms and legs he had amputated. Many hundreds for a certainty in the battles of the past year and a half. Then there were the lesser wounds to men's bodies from bullets, bayonets, and bomb fragments. He was sick of it all and wanted never again to cut the flesh of a man's body.

John came and stood beside the carriage. "Need anything, Captain?" he asked.

"No, thanks, John. I suggest we call each other by our names for our soldiering days are finished."

"That's a fact. It'll be good to get home."

"We haven't had much time to talk, and now

31

I'd like to make a request of you. If I die along the way, see that I'm buried in a cemetery and my grave is marked so that my mother and father can find it."

"I'll surely do that. But don't you go and die on me. We're all set for traveling and in a couple of months we'll reach El Paso. But there's something else we need."

"What's that?"

"Guns. There's all kinds of rough men running loose now that the good ones are off fighting. We may run into some who'd take our belongings. We'd be safer with a couple of pistols, maybe even a rifle. Then we could give them a hot time."

"You're right. We'll buy some at the first gun store we see."

The sound of the engine decreased. The big stern paddle wheel stopped and reversed. A moment later the steamboat nudged against the dock, and deckhands threw lines to men on the dock and she was made fast.

"Looks like we've reached Louisiana," John said. "You just rest easy and I'll get us headed west."

He climbed up in the driver's seat and took up the reins of the horses. The ramp was lowered to the dock and he drove onto the shore.

# Five

Brutus bugled a shrill, challenging call. He stomped the ground with his iron-shod hooves and bugled again.

Ben snapped awake at the horse's warning. He scooped up the pistol that lay by his side on the blanket and pointed it in the direction the horse faced. He expected to find his Mexican pursuers or Indians ready to attack. But there were neither, and for an instant he missed seeing the wolf standing in the morning dusk.

The gray pelt of the female wolf blended almost perfectly with the half-light. She sat quietly, ignoring the troubled Brutus and the Mexican horses grouped nearby, and looked at Ben. She appeared unafraid, merely curious.

Ben could shoot the wolf for she was in range of his pistol. Instead he lowered the gun and returned the stare of the wolf. He had no way to truly know; still, he believed that this was the same wolf that had howled so mournfully the evening before. Now she was here. Damn strange behavior for a wolf.

Brutus, not liking the presence of the wolf, moved closer to Ben. He nickered down at the man.

"She's no danger," Ben said. "Just looking us over."

He rose to his feet, expecting the wolf to leave at his movement. She remained in place, eyeing him, ears pricked in his direction.

"Hello, Lady Wolf," Ben said in a friendly tone.

The wolf bobbed her head once and then went back to being a statue.

Ben grinned at himself for talking to the wolf, and for even wondering if she could really have acknowledged his greeting.

He locked stares with the wolf for a moment, and then turned away to gather up his blanket. There was more than two hundred miles to go to reach Abilene and he should be riding. Breakfast would have to wait, for he had eaten the last of his food the evening before. That wasn't a problem. On the Llano Estacado, food was but a rifle shot away.

He saddled Brutus and three of the other horses. Tow ropes were fastened. He mounted Brutus and reined him north. The horse broke into a gallop with the other horses following nose-to-tail.

The wolf came to her feet and took a tentative step forward. She stopped and whined. Then she broke into an easy lope after Ben.


Ben crossed the Pecos River when the sun had climbed a third of the way into the sky. He allowed the horses to drink, and then rode up out of the valley and onto the north bank. He turned in the saddle to look back at the wolf that had trailed behind. Would she cross the river and continue on with him?

The wolf had halted on the far shore and was standing looking in his direction. Her territory, the land where she knew every water hole, the favorite places of all the other animals, lay miles to the south. As Ben watched, she barked twice, then turned to the rear and broke into a ground-devouring lope that quickly took her from his view. He felt a loss at her going.

He looked back to the front and lifted the horses to a trot, a rough gait for the rider, but one the horses could hold for miles.

Near noon, Ben saw a broad swath of land ahead that was unnaturally dark. As he drew nearer, he saw the land seemed to be undulating as if the surface of the earth was moving. He recognized what he saw. A herd of tens of thousands of buffalo were migrating north. Their migration was late this year. Usually by mid-July most of the animals would have been near the Red River in north Texas, or beyond into Oklahoma.

He pulled Brutus down to a walk and rode closer to the big herd. The nearer buffalo looked up and inspected the approaching horses and rider. A young calf, still retaining its tannish-orange color and not dark like the adults, ran in a frolicking, quick-stepping way out to examine Ben. The cow sounded a warning whoof. The calf watched Ben a moment longer, and then wheeled and dashed back to the side of the cow.

Ben came to the edge of the herd and the buffalo drew back both left and right from him, parting in a great black surf, to let him ride through. Two large wolves, part of the large pack that followed and fed off the buffalo, watched him from a distance. The horses warily eyed the buffalo and the wolves.

For more than three hours, Ben rode through the countless thousands of buffalo. Both to the left and right of him, the moving herd extended to the horizon. He had never seen the huge beasts allow a man to approach so close, some of them but a few feet away as he passed.

The buffalo gradually closed in behind Ben. The wolves again took station on the perimeter of the herd, their keen eyes searching for an unwary calf, or an animal weakened by injury or disease.

Reaching the border of the herd, Ben pulled the rifle from its scabbard. Hunger growled in the pit of his stomach. The tender meat of the hump of a buffalo's back would quiet it. He chose a yearling bull and raised the rifle. At the crash of the gun, the bull fell.

He brought Brutus up beside the carcass and stepped down from the saddle. With a few strokes of his skinning knife, careful to keep hair off the flesh, he laid back the skin from the ridge of the yearling's back, then sliced five to six pounds of meat from the hump.

Ben cut off a big bite of the dark meat and shoved it into his mouth. He chewed contentedly as he peeled a section of the thinner hide from the buffalo's belly and wrapped the meat in it. He climbed upon Brutus. In the evening, he would make jerky.

The Comanche warrior was standing on the plain and crying. Damn strange, thought Ben.

Several minutes before, Ben had spotted the strongly-built Indian. After hiding his own animals, he had taken his rifle and crawled forward. Through the spyglass, he saw the man was wearing buckskin pants and naked above. He held a musket in his hand. Close by were two horses. Ben had examined them, found them fine-looking animals, and had decided to take them from the Comanche.

The man had all his attention focused upon something on the ground and had not once looked around him. Ben had tried to see what attracted the Comanche, but the object lay in tall grass and out of his sight.

Ben drew within two hundred yards and raised the spyglass to his eye. In the magnified field of the spyglass, he saw the man's bare brown shoulders were shaking. The man lifted a hand to wipe at his face, and in the action turned his face partially in Ben's direction.

Ben saw tears, and something even more astonishing, and his pulse jumped. The Comanche's features were gruesomely ugly. The full side of the face that Ben could see was heavily scarred, as if it had been cut and ripped by a saw blade.

Ben was seeing the second ugliest man in Texas.

Was the Indian crying because of his mutilated face? Or was the unseen object on the ground the cause?

The thoughts of stealing the Indian's horses left Ben. He sensed the uniqueness of this convergence of the paths of two men inflicted with such unhuman features. An irrestible need to talk with the man came over Ben. He lowered the spyglass and shoved it under his belt out of the way.

Ben wanted to talk, but the Comanche could have different ideas. Ben cocked the rifle and held it in his right hand. He had but to tip the barrel up and fire if the Indian wanted to fight.

Ben went forward, walking upright and in plain view. He drew within a score of steps.

The Comanche stiffened. He raised his head and smelled the wind flowing over the plain, and his tongue ran out as if tasting it.

Ben coiled for action. He raised his left hand with palm out toward the man, and with his right aimed the rifle to point at the man's chest.

The Comanche spun around and at the same time lifted his musket.

Ben kept his left hand raised. He would give the man a fraction of a second more to see his open palm. If the peace sign didn't stop the man from trying to shoot Ben, then the rifle would.

The Comanche halted the movement of his gun. His scarred face showed surprise, and the realization that Ben could have easily killed him before now. The man lowered the musket. His eyes became hooded, and he began to chuckle, the harsh guttural sounds coming from a long gaping tear in his left cheek.

Ben's gash of a mouth opened and he laughed a devilish laugh of his own.

The two ugliest men in Texas greeted each other.

Ben looked past the Comanche and saw the reason the man had cried. An Indian boy of nine or ten lay dead on the ground. He had a very handsome face and a lean, long-legged body. He had been a lad of whom a father would be very proud. Now the jagged ends of splintered bones protruded from the boy's chest, and fresh, red blood pooled beneath him.

"Your son?" Ben asked in Spanish and nodded at the boy.

"Yes. Son Of Moon." He pointed at the horse standing close by. "That worthless mustang fell and rolled on him."

The Comanche jerked up his musket and fired. The top of the mustang's head exploded, showering skull and brains upon the ground. The animal fell with a thud, kicked a few times, and lay still.

Ben started to say something about the uselessness of killing the horse, but stopped himself. The man had felt the need to destroy the horse and it wasn't Ben's right to find fault.

"I'm sorry for the boy's death," Ben said.

"It will be a lonely life without him. But he now goes to live with the Great One."

*If there is such a being*, Ben thought. "I have no son," he said. He slid his hand down across his mutilated face. "I can't get close enough to a woman to make one."

"Neither can I, not anymore."

"We've both had bad luck."

"My name is Black Moon."

"I'm Ben Hawkins. May I help you with your son? I would be honored to do so." He felt a growing kinship with the ugly Comanche.

"I accept your help. We will bury him here where he died. And very deeply so the coyotes can't reach him." He laid his musket on the ground and pulled a knife from his belt. He began to dig at the sod of the plain.

Ben knelt beside Black Moon and began to dig with his skinning knife.

When the grave was deep, Black Moon wrapped his son in a blanket and gently placed him in the earth. Then the two men silently filled the grave with soil. From a source nearby, they carried flat slabs of rock and piled them on top of the grave.

Black Moon pivoted slowly around as he surveyed the land. Completing the full rotation, he spoke to Ben. "I will always remember this place and the wonderful son that is buried here."

"I shall also remember it," Ben said.

Ben heard tears in the Comanche's voice. But then he saw the man change, his body straightening and head lifting, as he struggled to pull back from his loss.

"Which way do you go?" Black Moon asked.

"That way," Ben said, and pointed north. "To Abilene."

"I will go partway with you and we can talk of our bad luck."

"Good."


In the dusk of the evening, the two men made camp on the bank of a steam, a tributary to the Pecos River coming in from the north. While Ben built a fire and began to cook buffalo meat, Black Moon caught grasshoppers for bait, and with a hook and line snagged two fair-sized bass. In the flickering light of the campfire, they ate hugely of the buffalo meat and topped it off with a fish for each. The remainder of the buffalo meat was cut into slices and hung over the fire to make jerky.

"Why do you go to Abilene?" Black Moon asked.

"To sell my horses."

"They are Mexican horses. Valdes horses."

"You know the Valdes brand?"

"Yes, I know it. Once I went there and took two horses." He touched the scar of a bullet on the side of his ribs. "They gave me this. Still, I kept the horses."

Black Moon fastened his eyes on Ben, and smiled, his scarred face twisting with humor. "You are a thief. I am a thief."

"Sounds like it."

Black Moon nodded at Ben's face and asked, "What bad luck caused that?"

"A cannonball fired from an enemy's big gun

hit me." Ben wasn't certain there was such a thing as luck. More likely things happen by the cold lottery of chance. "Do you think there is such a thing as luck?"

"Yes," Black Moon said with conviction. "You had bad luck. But the cannonball missed other men so they had good luck."

Ben shrugged. "How it came to hit me and not somebody else isn't important, not now."

Black Moon regarded Ben for a moment in the light of the campfire. "Luck is important. Mine was very good for a long time. I had a pretty woman and she gave me a strong, handsome son. Then a friend, knowing I am a good hunter, asked me to go far off to the mountains and kill one of the great grizzly bears that live there. We found the bear and fought it. Before we can kill it, my friend is slain, and the bear's long claws did this to my face. That was very bad luck." Black Moon ceased talking, turning inward, remembering the fight.

He spoke again. "When I returned to my village, my woman is frightened by my ugliness and will not come to my blanket and lie with me. Soon she sees a handsome man and goes to him. He should have sent her back to me. When he did not, I killed both of them. That made me an outcast among my people. I take Son Of Moon and go away. Now Son Of Moon has been taken from me and I have nothing. Except this face that I don't want. So you must believe there is bad luck."

"I can understand why you believe it."

"Would you like to have good luck with a woman?"

"How? By hiding my face?"

"I know a village that has many pretty women. We can go there and take two of them."

"Whether they want to go with us or not."

"What they want wouldn't be important."

"Kidnap and rape, that's what you're talking about."

Black Moon looked puzzled. "My mother was a Kiowa. My father rode into their land and killed two of their warriors and carried her off. I never heard her complain of what he did."

Black Moon studied Ben for a moment to see how he was reacting to the proposal. "Perhaps it isn't the white man's way to steal a woman. Only another man's horse."

Black Moon's eyes bore into Ben's with fierce intensity. "Do you want a woman? Want one badly enough to take her by force? To kill anyone who would try to stop you?"

Ben knew he should be telling Black Moon that he wanted nothing to do with his proposal. Instead, a hot craving for a woman was rushing through him and he was actually considering the possibility of joining the man. A god-awful long year had passed since he had touched the soft, smooth skin of a woman, had enjoyed the full depth and pleasure of her body. He recalled the night spent with the last girl he had known, the beautiful redheaded Charlotte in Cincinnati, whom he had met when passing through that town on his way to join

43

the Confederate Army. There would be no other women, not with a face that even men could not look at. The Llano Estacado was far from Cincinnati, far beyond the edge of civilization and the white man's laws. The laws that he had once enforced did not exist here. Do as Black Moon suggested, his body urged him. The tribes had been stealing each others' women for thousands of years. What did it matter that this time a white man joined in the theft?

"I'll go with you," Ben said. "How far away is this place?"

"Two days if we ride from sunup to sundown."

"We have nothing else to do but ride."

## Six

"Hold on, Evan, there's another section of corduroy coming up ahead," John Davis called from the driver's seat of the surrey.

"Slow the horses down and take it as easy as you can," Evan called back from where he lay on the pallet in the bed of the vehicle. He groaned at the thought of the jarring that he must again endure as they pounded over the logs of the corduroy road. He uncorked the bottle of laudanum and took a swallow.

The two men were on the military road that ran west from Vicksburg to Monroe, Louisiana, some eighty miles distant. They were still on the floodplain of the Mississippi River and the road was frequently forced to cross swampy ground. To provide a means to pass over these watery, muddy areas, the road-builders had felled trees from the dense stand of oaks and birches and walnuts and cut the trunks into lengths that were laid side by side crosswise on the road. Dirt had been thrown upon the logs to provide a somewhat smooth surface. The dirt had been mostly washed away by recent storms, and for yards at a time the round logs were exposed.

The surrey rolled onto the corduroy section of road. Frequently a wheel fell into the hollows between the logs and Evan was given a rough shake. The seepage of blood into his mouth increased, and he coughed and spat over the low sideboard of the vehicle.

"Almost off the corduroy," John called. "Just a few feet more and there's dry ground as far as I can see through the woods."

"That's damn good," Evan replied.

The right front wheel of the surrey fell into a hole and landed a foot down with a crash. The sudden, unexpected movement flung Evan crashing against the sideboard. With the surrey towed on by the horses, the wheel immediately bounced up out of the hole. Evan was thrown hard in the opposite direction.

His lung exploded, and fire burned and raged within his chest. Blood came pouring up from his lung and into his mouth. The fall had ripped open his wound.

"Sorry, Evan, I didn't see that last log had rot away," John said.

"Stop, John, stop! I'm bleeding bad."

John pulled the horses to a halt as the surrey rolled off the corduroy. He sprang down from the driver's seat to the ground and ran limping to Evan.

"What do you want me to do?" he asked quickly.

"Put me on the ground. Hurry."

John reached into the bed of the surrey and lifted Evan's thin body. He carried him a few steps to a big oak tree, and kneeling, placed him gently on the bed of leaves that had collected there.

"Damn, Evan, I sorry," he said, his face taut with worry.

"A bad road isn't your fault."

"What else can I do for you?"

Evan spat bright-red blood. Then looked at John. "Nothing. This is just between God and me now."

The words brought a bloody froth to Evan's lips. He shuddered, coughed, and spat blood out onto the leaves. He felt an icy doubt that he was going to live. He had come to death's threshold half a score times in the weeks since he was wounded and he had made somewhat of a peace with death. Still, he didn't want to die. He didn't want to die!

He must do something to save himself. But what? *You're a surgeon, so think. Think.*

His right lung was filling with blood. The left must be kept free so he could breathe. How could he accomplish that?

He saw the mat of leaves upon which he lay

was thicker nearer the tree, and thus there was a downsloping surface in a direction away from its trunk. Evan twisted around until his head was lower than his feet. He rolled to lay on his right side with his cheek against the ground.

Evan knew the blood leaking from the wound in his right lung would overflow into his left. Should that happen, he would drown in his own blood. He pulled air into his open lung, and then forced it vigorously out to carry the blood up into his throat and onward to his mouth. Then he spat it onto the leaves. He breathed, coughed, and spat again.

Evan held his position on his right side and concentrated on two things, breathing air in and out, and spitting blood.

The minutes passed as Evan fought his battle. He felt his strength draining away, his senses fading. The huge blood loss was weakening him. He struggled against the blackness that hovered on the borders of his mind.

John squatted beside Evan and listened to his ragged, wet breathing. Every breath sounded as if the man was strangling. The ground near his face became horribly splattered with blood. John had failed to protect the man who had saved his leg when all the other surgeons had wanted to cut it off. That failure was a heavy weight to bear.

He batted away a lone mosquito that was hovering over Evan's face. The day was ending and soon the insects would be out in full force. Evan's face was a bloody specter, and the blood would draw the insects by the thousands. He must be shielded from them.

"Hang on, Evan. I'll be right back." John wasn't sure the man heard him. He rose and pulled his jackknife.

He cut slender lengths of willow and returned to Evan. The willow stems were bent into a bow and shoved into the ground so that they made an arch above Evan. Over this framework, John stretched a piece of netting he had obtained from the Army stores in Vicksburg.

He unhitched the horses from the surrey and staked them out on picket ropes to graze. He returned and sat down beside Evan. Immediately he recognized the man's breathing was weaker, the strangling sound more pronounced.

"Don't die, Captain," John whispered.

He sat in the darkness and listened to the man struggle to live. Around him, the mosquitoes came and sang their vampirish songs.

# *Seven*

In the dark before the dawn, when man's vitality is at its lowest ebb, death came for Evan. Unconscious and never knowing of the raging battle, he fought death to a standstill. With the dawn, the blackness in Evan's mind lifted and one by one, his senses flicked back to life.

His breath made a raspy sound in his throat, yet never had the air tasted more sweetly. He thought he might even be breathing a little with his damaged lung. Maybe, just maybe, the lung had pulled free from its unnatural adherence to the ribs. He felt himself drawing back from death and the gulf widening between living and dying.

He opened his eyes and found he still lay on the leaves beneath the oak tree. Light came in through netting stretched over an arch of limbs above him. That would be John's work.

He lifted a hand that felt immensely heavy and pushed the netting aside. The sunlight was at a low angle, and that told him he had lain under the tree all night. Not far away, John slept on a blanket with his head covered by netting. John came awake and sat up at the sound of Evan's movement. A big smile swept over John's face.

"By God, Captain, you made it," John said happily. He had always thought the captain was the kind of man who would fight to the last heartbeat.

"Would seem so. I can breathe better now than I could yesterday."

"Damn glad to hear that. I felt bad about running the wheel into that hole."

"Forget that. You might have done me a favor. Hand me a canteen. I'm awfully thirsty. I've lost a lot of blood and must have water to rebuild it."

"Do you want something to eat?" John asked. The captain looked like a skeleton man.

"Maybe later. What do you say to us resting here for a few hours?"

"Whatever you want, Captain—I mean Evan." John picked up a canteen and handed it to Evan. "We're both crippled up but we're alive. We'll get to El Paso when we get there."


Ben and Black Moon lay on the bluff and spied on the Comanche village of seventy tipis strung along a creek below them. Black Moon had led them to this location for this was the village of Black Moon's wife, the woman he had slain. Ben thought the man had returned to this particular place to take revenge upon the people for the unfaithfulness of his wife.

Through his spyglass, Ben surveyed the Comanche encampment. Downstream a quarter mile or so, half-grown boys watched over a herd of at least three hundred horses. Upstream from the village, in the flat ground between the creek and the foot of the bluff, was a thick stand of trees. In the afternoon of the sweltering July day, most of the people were lazing about and talking in the shade of several trees growing among the tipis. Five boys were laughing and playing in the creek. He saw no lookouts to call warning of an attack by enemies.

"Men coming from the north," Black Moon said.

Ben put his spyglass on the men. Six horsemen with twice as many packhorses were approaching the village. "Hunters," Ben said. "They've got buffalo quarters hung on the pack animals."

The hunters crossed the creek and came into the center of the village. The women quickly gathered to share in the meat. Ben heard an argument begin between two women, apparently about the equality of the division. One of the men called out sharply and the women fell silent. In a surprisingly short time, the meat had been divided and carried away.

"The women will go for wood now to cook," Black Moon said. He nodded in the direction of the woods. "We can catch two of them there."

Ben looked at the Comanche and saw his eyes had the menacing look of an animal of prey. Did *his* eyes have the same expression?

"All right, let's go," Ben said.

They took up their rifles and crawled back from the lip of the bluff. Out of sight of the people below, they went parallel to the creek until opposite the woods. Finding a gully that would hide them when they crouched low, they descended to the woods and hid in a dense brush thicket.

"We take only the prettiest," Black Moon said. Ben nodded. He felt deep misgivings about what they planned. Could he really do it? Had he misled Black Moon, and now at the last minute must he back away from doing the deed?

"One comes, but she is ugly," Black Moon said. A squat, broad-faced woman was walking toward them, now and again stooping to pick up a dead limb that had fallen from the trees. She veered off around the thicket where the men hid, and was soon out of sight. A woman and two little girls of six or seven came into view. The woman was scolding the girls, telling them to stop chattering and gather wood. Other women, often with children, wandered past. Then the woods became empty. None of the women were acceptable, and Ben was relieved. The decision of whether or not he would steal a girl didn't have to be made.

"Our luck has changed," Black Moon whispered in a pleased voice.

Two young women dressed in buckskin skirts and bright red blouses had come into view and were walking slowly toward the men. Both were very pretty and hardly more than girls. They were talking and laughing, and occasionally picking up a piece of wood as they ambled closer. They were much more interested in their conversation than in wood gathering.

Comanches did little trading with the whites, so Ben judged the red blouses meant the boyfriends or husbands of the women had been on a raiding party, either south to Mexico or north to one of the American settlements. The women who had owned the garments before, were they now dead?

"I want the one on the right," Black Moon said.

Ben said nothing. He wondered why Black Moon had chosen that particular girl since she was the least pretty of the two.

He focused totally on the girl on the left. She moved with easy grace, the skirt swinging and caressing her legs. The mounds of her young breasts pressed against the red blouse that was cinched in with a leather belt. Her hair was as black as a slice of midnight. The perfect oval face was constantly animated in a delightful way by her thoughts and reactions to the words of the other girl. Now that Ben saw the prize that was within his grasp, his reluctance to steal a woman evaporated. He would certainly do it, gladly do it. A woman was glorious in her beauty; however, her beauty was a very great danger to her.

"Don't let them make a sound," Black Moon said.

Ben knew Black Moon was ready to act, and so he quickly looked around for anyone who might see them. The woods were empty within the area he could see.

"Ready?" Black Moon said.

"Let's do it."

Black Moon leapt from the thicket. He crossed the few paces separating him from the girls with a burst of speed that left Ben in the rear.

Ben increased his speed and rushed upon his girl. Her eyes widened in surprise. In an instant her expression was one of pure terror. Her mouth opened to scream. Before the scream could come, Ben sprang upon her and bore her to the ground. The jarring impact upon the earth tore the breath from the girl in a hissing burst of air.

Ben dropped his rifle, clamped his hand over the girl's mouth, and straddled her. Swiftly he gagged her with his bandana and tied her arms and legs with lengths of rawhide. He swung the girl's slender body across his shoulder, her head on his back, and held her there by the legs. He scooped up his rifle from the ground and left that hazardous place at a run.

As swift as Ben was, Black Moon was equally swift. They ran through the woods carrying their trophies. The girl kicked, and squirmed, and pounded Ben on the back with her bound hands. He hardly felt the blows as he bent all his strength on the race, and on hoping the kidnapping had not been seen and pursuit begun too soon.

Ben broke from the woods and entered the gully leading to the top of the bluff. He was now ahead of Black Moon. He charged up the steep grade with the girl. He reached the top of the bluff with his breath a hoarse saw in his throat. He ran on with the girl bouncing on his shoulder.

He heard Black Moon's thudding footfalls close behind, and a strange feeling came over him. It was grand to do something dangerous with a man who was equally strong and daring, and almost as ugly.

In a stand of low-growing, barely waist-high, shinnery oak, the only hiding place the men had been able to find on the flat plain, he lowered the girl to the ground. She immediately scooted away from him on her rump, her black eyes full of fear and horror.

"I know I'm not a handsome knight carrying you off," Ben said in English and with a sardonic smile. "And my horse isn't white. But I'm not going to do anything to you that you wouldn't naturally do."

The girl cringed back even more at his words, and her white teeth chewed at the bandana wedged between her teeth. He saw the revulsion in her eyes and felt her hatred. Ben knew that even if she had understood his English, the reaction to him would have been the same.

He stepped to his two horses, which lay on their sides in the shinnery oak. He and Black Moon had thrown their horses to the ground to hide them from view of any enemy on the flat plain. The animals' legs had been tied to prevent them from standing. Now he jerked the tie ropes loose and brought the horses to their feet.

He untied the girl and lifted her astride. He tied her hands to the pommel of the saddle.

"Don't fall off or you'll get dragged," he told her in Spanish. By her expression, he knew she understood.

Ben swung up on Brutus. He looked at Black Moon and saw him mounting, his girl already astride the horse Ben had lent him to carry away what he captured.

The girl spoke to Black Moon in a scornful way. He snapped back, and an angry conversation began between the two. Ben didn't understand the rapid Comanche. It seemed odd the man would be arguing with the girl.

"What's wrong?" Ben called out, interrupting the heated debate.

"Nothing of importance," Black Moon replied.

Shrill shouts from the village below came to the men. Both men fell silent and turned toward the sound to listen.

"They'll be after us in a few minutes," Ben said.

He looked west at the chain of towering black thunderheads on the horizon. He and Black Moon had observed the storm building as they arrived, and had decided to use the rain to hide their tracks. He estimated the distance to the edge of the storm to be eight or nine miles. He wished it was shorter.

"Best we get riding," Ben said.

"They can't catch us for our mustangs are fresh," Black Moon said.

"Something can always go wrong," Ben said.

He kicked Brutus into a run. The girl's mount followed behind on a tow rope.

Black Moon and his captive took station on Ben's right.

# Eight

The threatening black thunderhead hung, spilling rain. Lightning flared within the boiling cloud mass, lighting it with an infernal purplish glow. Thunder crashed, shaking the Llano Estacado. Frigid wind poured down from the miles-high center of the storm. The wind was deflected outward upon striking the ground, and rushed over the plain to violently pummel the four riders racing to meet it.

Ben and Black Moon and the two women plunged into the thunderstorm, a twilight world drained of all color. Thunder boomed and jarred the ground beneath them. The cold, wind-driven raindrops slapped them stinging blows, and wet them instantly. The horses staggered under the onslaught and tried to veer away, but the men held them to the course and straight toward the center of the storm.

Ben looked to the side for Black Moon and the woman. They were there in the wind and rain, a shadowy mixture of man, woman, and horses.

Ben signaled to Black Moon and they slowed their horses. They were safe now, and would be for the breadth of the storm that extended for miles across the land. They would leave no trail for the pursuing warriors to follow. Nor could their enemies guess where Ben and the others would emerge from the protective cloak of the heavy rain.

As they rode nearer the center of the storm, the rain became an icy waterfall deluging them. Ben looked at the girl. She seemed to have grown smaller, almost childlike, with her clothing plastered to her slender body. He reined Brutus in close to the girl and started to put his hat on her to protect her head. She gave him a hard look and swung her head, dislodging the hat. It would have fallen to the ground had Ben not caught it.

*Have it your way,* Ben thought. He put the hat back on his head.

Black Moon had pulled ahead while Ben had tried to help the girl. He let the Comanche lead. This was his land and he should be able to find his way through the storm to their camp. Should Black Moon not be able to, Ben could with ease. The camp was in the middle of the Llano Estacado, with no landmarks of significance, nothing that could be seen beyond a couple hundred yards. Yet unerringly, no matter how far he traveled from it, Ben could once again return. Without fail he could return to every distant spot he had known since he had been old enough to travel alone. Once Ben had tried to analyze the instinct that guided him. However, as he'd cast about through his mind searching for that unique sense, he'd felt it slipping away. The desire to understand the gift, indeed the mere quest for it, could mean destruction. He had immediately ceased his mental probing. It was enough to possess the knack.

Ben and Black Moon and the two women came out of the storm wet and cold and ten miles from where they had entered it.

Black Moon cast a measuring glance up at the sun, now low in the west, and then pointed out across the plain. "Our camp is there," he said to Ben.

Ben nodded in agreement. "About an hour's ride."

He turned to the two girls slumped in the saddle. Both had turned to face the sun. They were shivering, and he felt sorry for them. He saw them look at each other, and he wondered what signal had passed between them. Immediately he knew, for in unison they controlled their shivering bodies and straightened to sit erect, their faces proudly raised. They were Comanche women and proud. Their bound hands only added to their show of courage, and Ben's respect for them.

The men, with their captives, reached their destination in the dusk of the evening. The camp was in a meadow beside a small stream. Ben's two Mexican horses that had been left behind staked out on long lariats watched them ride up.

Ben dismounted from Brutus. He went quickly to the girl and untied her hands. He started to lift her down, but she ignored his outstretched hands and slid from the saddle to land on her feet on the ground.

Ben heard Black Moon curse in Spanish, and turned. Black Moon's girl had, upon his releasing her hands from the saddle horn, jumped off the opposite side of the horse she had ridden. She was running strongly off over the plain, her flapping skirt sounding like a bird's wings in flight.

Black Moon stretched his legs and gave chase. He swiftly overtook her, and reaching out, caught hold of her long hair streaming out behind and pulled her to a stop. He returned, shaking her roughly by the shoulder at each step.

Upon reaching the girl's horse, Black Moon took the rawhide thong from the saddle horn to retie her. When she saw what he intended, she whirled and struck at him.

Black Moon blocked the blow and captured her hands. Holding both of hers in one of his, he slapped her harshly across the face, rocking her head to the side.

She screamed something at Black Moon that Ben didn't understand, but he knew she had to be cursing him. Black Moon struck her again, even more savagely. He drew back to hit her again.

Ben leapt forward, grabbed Black Moon's cocked hand, and prevented the blow. "Don't hit her again," he ordered.

Black Moon spun on Ben. He jerked his hand free, his eyes fierce. He snarled something in his own language and readied to strike Ben.

"Don't try that," Ben said roughly. "I'll make your face a hell of a lot uglier than it already is."

"She's mine and I can do anything I want to her," Black Moon said angrily, but the fire of his anger was dying.

"Don't ever hit her again."

Black Moon laughed cynically. "We steal them and now you want to protect them."

"Why be mean to her?"

"She's Swan Woman, my wife's youngest sister."

"So what? She's not responsible for what your wife did."

Black Moon smiled without humor. "What are you going to do if that one you have won't lie with you?" he asked.

Ben did not reply. The question bothered him. Would he force the girl to lie with him if she resisted? He moved away from Black Moon and the girl.

"Do you want to know her name?" Black Moon called after Ben.

"No."

Ben didn't want to put a name on the girl he had stolen.

"It's Morning Dew." Black Moon gave a knowing chuckle.

The fire had burned down to a bed of red coals when Black Moon rose to his feet and reached for Swan Woman, sitting beside Morning Dew. She drew back from him. He stepped and caught her by the arm with a firm grip. When he pulled on her, she came stiffly to her feet. He led her into the night.

Morning Dew's presence near Ben was a living force pulling at him in the darkness. She did not move, made no sound. What were her thoughts now that she had been carried away by a man with a monster's face?

Ben was shamed by his deeds this day. He was but a ghost of the man he had once been. Still, there was enough of him left that he wanted a woman. But there was no place on earth where a woman would accept him, and so he'd been led to this.

The girl, Morning Dew, was lovely and he wanted to touch her, to hold her in his arms, but only innocently. He took her hand from her lap and drew her upright. She stood silently beside him with her eyes still on the red coals of the fire and gave no sign that she was aware of what was happening.

"Come with me," Ben said gently. "I'll not hurt you."

They reached Ben's blanket, spread on the ground. At Ben's slight pull, she lay down alongside him. He drew her close and wrapped his arms around her. *Just hold her innocently like you promised yourself you would. Enjoy the pleasure of the nearness of a woman.*

His hands obeyed him for a moment and held the girl tenderly. But then they moved of their own accord, as if they had a mind of their own, and they explored her body, feeling the soft, rounded female form of her.

The needs of the man betrayed him, stripping away the thin veneer of civilization, and he felt himself enlarging, becoming hard. The urgent now of it prodded him powerfully. But he wouldn't do it if she fought him, or pleaded, or cried.

He rose to his hands and knees and moved over Morning Dew. She was facing him and her features looked frozen in the ice-pale glow of the moon. He tried to see her eyes, to read them, but they were hidden in the shadow-filled caverns of their sockets. He leaned more closely to see, and he felt the breath of the girl on his face. He breathed deeply of the sweet air the Indian girl breathed into the night.

Ben waited for Morning Dew to resist him in some manner, to utter a word, to make a movement to fend him off. However, she continued to lie quietly beneath him. The only detectable change was her breathing, which had become more rapid.

Ben inserted his knees in between Morning Dew's legs and spread them, and there was no resistance. He began to tremble at what that meant. He lowered himself onto her and merged their bodies together.

# Nine

Ben awoke with Morning Dew sleeping close beside him. Not having wanted to tie her up during the night, he had slept lightly, always alert to her movements. He climbed quietly to his feet.

He glanced down at the girl. She had wakened from sleep and was watching him. Ben thought there was more than merely watching him in those intelligent black eyes; she seemed to be evaluating, measuring him in some manner. He would have liked to know what she was thinking. He felt he should say something to her, but what could he say to this stolen girl that would lessen his crime?

Taking his guns from under the blanket, he walked a short ways from camp and out into the tall, untrod grass of the prairie. The morning sky was a brilliant blue, swept clean by the passing storm. The air coming over the green land had a pleasing smell. The day was beautiful, but spoiled by his conscience gnawing at him.

The voices of Black Moon raised in anger and Morning Dew's sharp reply came to Ben from the camp. He hastened back for he didn't want Black Moon to hit the girl.

As soon as Ben reached the camp, Morning Dew pointed at him and spoke rapidly to Black Moon. The man shook his head.

"What did she say?" Ben questioned Black Moon in Spanish.

"She just wants to complain." Black Moon replied in the same language.

"Tell me exactly what she said." Ben was certain Black Moon was keeping something from him.

"I can settle this," Black Moon said firmly.

*"Tres dias,"* Morning Dew said urgently. *"Tres dias."* She pointed at Swan Woman and herself and then at Ben and Black Moon and down at the ground. She then pointed at Swan Woman and herself and made a walking motion with her fingers off in the direction of her village.

"I understand that part of it," Ben said to Black. "Now tell me what else she said."

Black Moon reluctantly replied, "They say they will stay with us three days and not try to run away if we will then turn them loose to go home. They say they will give us much pleasure."

Ben saw the pleading, the hope for his approval of the proposal in Morning Dew's eyes. She was bargaining with him, trying to make a trade. The only coin she had was her body, and she was offering that to him.

The question of what he was going to do with the girl had been nagging him. A girl, Indian or white, wouldn't fit into the life he must lead. Why not agree? Three days of willing love from the pretty girl would be a grand gift. He nodded at Morning Dew. She gave him a quick smile and hurriedly looked away from his face.

Black Moon saw the exchange between Ben and the girl. "I don't agree," he said.

65

"Are you going to keep Swan Woman permanently? Someday she might catch you sleeping and cut your throat."

Black Moon considered that for a moment. "She would be much trouble. And besides, I can always steal another woman."

"Then tell them we both accept their offer. Also tell them I will give them a horse to ride at the end of the three days."

"Let them walk for it's not that far. Maybe one day if they hurry."

"Just tell them what I said. If they return with a good horse, they can say they stole it and escaped. Their people will accept them back more readily that way."

Black Moon spoke rapidly to the two young women. They cast a short, pleased look at Ben. Morning Dew said something to Black Moon.

Black Moon looked at Ben and grinned. "She wants to know if you want to take a walk with her." He gestured at the plain covered with the tall, concealing grass.


Black Moon held his musket and watched the five white men sitting their horses off a ways on the plain. They had been there for a short time silently evaluating his camp, and his and Ben's horses. They were enemies, as were all white men to the Comanche. All except for Ben, and that was only because he had a face even uglier than Black Moon's.

They were far out of range of his smoothbore musket, and he wished Ben was here with his long-range rifle. However, Ben was off hunting for meat. Black Moon would have to fight the men by himself.

One of the men dismounted and took something from one of the two packhorses the men had with them. He sat down on the ground with just his shoulders showing above the tall grass.

Black Moon recalled that once he had seen a white man who had been shooting buffalo sit in that same position. That man had erected a type of rest of forked sticks from which he could shoot his rifle very accurately for a long distance. Even as Black Moon recognized his danger, a puff of smoke blossomed from in front of the man. Instantly a mighty blow struck Black Moon in the chest, and a great pain erupted as he was slammed backward to the ground.

He attempted to rise. He must get up and fight the men. But he couldn't get control of his muscles, and lay on the ground sucking at the air, trying to breathe. He knew he had been shot with one of the large-caliber buffalo guns and was seriously wounded.

He felt hands upon him, tugging at him, and he slowly, laboriously turned his head. Swan Woman and Morning Dew were kneeling beside him.

"Get up and fight!" Swan Woman cried. "They are coming."

"Set me up and give me my gun," Black Moon said.

The two girls propped Black Moon up in a

sitting position. Morning Dew handed him his rifle. Black Moon brought the gun to his shoulder and shoved it out through the tops of the waving grass. The gun weaved about in his weakening hands. He fought it steady and brought the sights to bear on the white man in the lead. They were within range now. They thought him dead. They were correct. He was a dead man, but hadn't yet died.

Black Moon began to squeeze the trigger of his old, familiar musket. This would be the last enemy he would ever slay. The gun fired. At the strike of the bullet, the white man rolled onto the back of his horse, and then off onto the ground.

Black Moon saw the remaining white men jerk up their rifles and begin to shoot. He heard Swan Woman and Morning Dew screaming. Then they were silent.

A bullet struck Black Moon in the throat. Time stretched out for him, long enough to feel the sorrow of knowing the pretty women were dead and his own death was very near. He was greatly troubled that his enemies were still alive and there was absolutely nothing he could do to make them pay for the deaths of the women or for his death. Darkness closed upon Black Moon and engulfed him completely.

"Hello, the camp," Ben called.

He was some two hundred yards away from his camp and riding Brutus slowly closer.

Four white men were standing near his stolen horses and Black Moon's mustang, alertly eyeing him as he approached. He saw nothing of the three Comanches. Something awful had happened to them, he knew it.

"Can I come in?" Ben called. The men looked dangerous and they were four to his one. But he must learn where Black Moon, Morning Dew, and Swan Woman were.

"Sure, come on in," one of the men shouted back, and made a motion with his hand to back up his words.

At fifty yards, Ben could look over the crotch-high grass and see the trod and matted-down grass of the camp. He saw what he had desperately hoped not to see. The slack, bloody bodies of Morning Dew, Black Moon, and Swan Woman lay close together on the ground, so close that they were touching each other.

He felt as if a picket pin had been hammered into his chest. His blood cascaded through his veins in a storm, and hate flared so hot it seemed to burn. "You sons of bitches, I'm going to kill every one of you," Ben silently raged.

# Ten

Ben brought Brutus to a stop a few feet from the bloody bodies of Morning Dew, Swan Woman, and Black Moon and looked down at them. Tears pricked his eyes. That wouldn't do, for he mustn't give a sign that he knew them. He blinked his tears away and focused on devising a plan that would give him a chance to kill the four men.

"Looks like you killed some Indians," Ben said, fighting the tightness in his throat.

The four men remained silent, staring at Ben's mutilated face. The sight of him had thrown some confusion into the group.

Finally a tall man with a full beard spoke. "We didn't mean to shoot the squaws, but they were too close to the buck and got in the way. Ruined the fun we could've had."

Ben saw a man lying on the opposite side of the camp. By his posture and a trail leading from him off through the grass, it appeared he had been dragged in from some other location and dropped on the ground.

"Looks like the buck got one of you," Ben said. *Good for you, Black Moon.*

"A tough son of a bitch. That Sharps bullet should'a killed him straight out."

"He's dead now," Ben said. "A bad-luck Indian."

"And sure an ugly one. Don't see how a man that ugly could have two such pretty squaws." The man was smirking as he looked into Ben's ugly face.

Ben read the man's insult. But that was nothing as compared to his hatred of the men for killing the Comanches. "Were some of those horses his?" Ben asked.

"Yeah, those five there. Fine animals too."

"Those are Valdes horses," Ben said. "That's their brand, all right."

"That means the Indian was down south robbing the Mexicans. He must've killed a rich Mex, for that one saddle has a lot of silver on it. I bet he got more than just the horse and saddle. Did you search his pockets for gold coin? Even the squaws could have gold on them."

"Didn't think of that. I've never found coin on an Indian I killed." He motioned at the other men. "Have a look."

Three of the men went to the Comanches and began to search through their clothing.

The tall man seemed mesmerized by Ben's face. "Did you get that in the war?" he asked.

"Yes," Ben replied and grinned, his face twisting into a horrible mask with the action. "Would you like a souvenir from the war?" He moved his hand toward his hip pocket as if reaching for some object back there. His hand stopped at the holstered pistol on his side.

The man looked perplexed by the question. "What do you mean?"

"There was a hell'uva lot of death there." Ben pulled his pistol and shot the man in the forehead. Ben pivoted toward the remaining three men. He must quickly identify the man who would react most swiftly to the shot. A small, skinny man jerked around. In a fraction of a second he took in the situation and grabbed for his pistol. Before the man could touch his weapon, Ben shot him through the heart. He shot the third man as he looked up from Morning Dew's body.

The fourth man hastily stabbed his hands up above his head. "Don't shoot! Don't shoot!" he cried.

"Why not?" Ben asked, holding his pistol pointed into the man's face. "Why should I let you live?"

"I ain't done nothing to you. Nothing a'tall. Let me get on my horse and ride out."

"Why didn't you ride on by and let them safe?" Ben moved his free hand to indicate the three Comanches.

"They were just Indians."

"Yeah, they were. I knew them and was getting to like them. And I don't like you." Ben shot the man through the right eye.

Ben buried Black Moon, Morning Dew, and Swan Woman close together in graves he dug in the prairie sod. The bodies of the white men he left for the coyotes and buzzards.

He gathered the horses, now numbering thirteen counting the packhorses, and tied them in a line. He mounted Brutus, and sat looking down at the three graves. The Llano Estacado was a place where living things died by violence, and he had added to the violence. He heard the wind in the prairie grass and it was sighing, as if expressing shame at what he and Black Moon had done to the young Indian women. The rotten episode of stealing the women, and by so doing being the cause of their deaths, had cut a hard groove in his mind, one that would never be eroded away by the passage of time.

A vast clarity came to Ben. God was a joker and had just played a big one. The man who cared the least about living was the one who had survived.

Evan Payson and John Davis entered Monroe, Louisiana, in early afternoon. Planning to catch a train west, they continued on directly across town to the station of the Houston & Texas Central Railroad. When they arrived, a train of four passenger coaches and two flatbed cars sat in front of the station house. The engine was quietly chuffing steam.

A Confederate lieutenant, with his left arm in a sling, was directing a squad of soldiers. He was small and thin and seemed hardly more than a boy. He had six soldiers helping wounded men to climb aboard the coaches. Four soldiers were loading freight, boxes, barrels, and crates onto the flatbed cars.

"The Army has taken over the railroad," John said to Evan, sitting beside him on the seat of the surrey.

"Looks like more wounded from Vicksburg are trying to get home same as we are," Evan said. "Pull up there by the lieutenant and let's talk to him about hitching a ride."

"Right," John said. He pulled the team of horses to a stop with the vehicle close to the lieutenant.

"Lieutenant, do you have room for two more on the train?" Evan called.

The lieutenant looked at Evan. He noted the

slumped shoulders and sallow, bony face of the wounded man. The fellow appeared quite ill. He looked past Evan to John. "I'm taking only wounded soldiers," the lieutenant said.

"We fit that bill," John said.

"You two were at Vicksburg?"

"Yes, sir," John said. "I'm Corporal Davis and my leg's all smashed to hell. And this is Captain Payson, he took a bullet in the lung." *Now don't ask what army he was with.* "We're both from El Paso."

"The train's crowded, but I think you can find space for yourselves someplace." He called out to a soldier near where the wounded were being loaded. "Sergeant, allow these soldiers from Vicksburg to go aboard."

"Yes, sir," replied the sergeant.

"How long before you pull out?" Evan asked the lieutenant.

"Probably half an hour. We're mostly loaded."

"Do you know where we can sell these horses and surrey?"

"See Ed Tomlinson. Three blocks that way." The lieutenant pointed with his good arm. "He's a horse trader. You should get a good price, for horses are scarce with so many being taken east by the soldiers going off to fight. Don't be gone long, for I'll not hold the train for you."

# *Eleven*

Karl Redpath arrived in Shreveport aboard the steamer *Putnam's Pride* after a journey from New Orleans up the Mississippi to the junction with the Red River and then up the Red to the city. When the boat docked, he hoisted his trunk onto a shoulder and left the boat. Moving easily with his load, he walked the six blocks to the station of the Houston & Texas Central Railroad.

Redpath halted when he came within sight of the station. In the long shadows of late evening, some ninety Confederate soldiers, wounded in battles in the east, but able to walk and now bound for home, sat or lay on their bedrolls on the station platform. Several women of the town, carrying baskets of food and buckets of water, moved among the soldiers. To each man, the women offered a sandwich and a drink of water. Redpath noted that every man quickly accepted the sandwich and a dipper of water from the bucket. They gave heartfelt thanks to the women and ravenously tore into the sandwiches.

Redpath selected a location away from the soldiers and placed his trunk down on the ground. He was a large man, well over six feet tall and solidly built. His hair was black, and he sported a heavily waxed mustache that extended outward in thin spikes from each side of his mouth. His clothing was made of excellent material and well tailored to fit his strong body.

He had until recently owned more brothels in New Orleans than all the other whore-masters combined. The brothels had made him very wealthy. Then the damnable Union Navy and Army sailing up the Mississippi with their powerful warships had captured New Orleans. General Butler, the commander of the occupying army, had gradually tightened his control of the businesses of the city. Then he had issued an order making it unlawful to operate a whorehouse. As an example to the other whorehouse owners, he had called Red-path into his office in the Cabildo and told him to close all his establishments, with the threat of being hung if he didn't comply immediately.

Redpath had known he would never per-manently leave New Orleans, for it was too vibrant, too lusty, and its rough, tough under-world fit him exactly. Most importantly, it was a very rich city. New Orleans was often called the Queen City, for it was the financial center of the South. Also, it was a great port city, with the quantity of the ocean shipping passing through its waters, before the war, second only to New York. Even though he loved the city, he had to find a place to wait out the war, a town wide-open to his type of business.

He had chosen El Paso, for he judged it far enough west to escape attack by the Union Army, and also because it was a bustling, growing town at the intersection of the north-south El Camino Real and the much-trav-

76

eled east-west road between Texas and California. He had selected his most lovely women and prized brothel furnishings, and with his man Dubois, had journeyed to El Paso. There he had found, and purchased, the perfect building for his purpose. After designing modifications to the existing structure and a substantial addition, he had set Dubois to work with a construction crew. He had returned to New Orleans to find occupants, with legitimate businesses, for his brothels. He was now on his way back to El Paso. Soon he would have the most luxurious whorehouse in Texas.

The first, faint sound of the train approaching the station came to Redpath.


"More wounded soldiers trying to get home," John said as he looked past Evan and out the window of the passenger coach at the railroad station in Shreveport, Louisiana.

"There's enough of them to form a platoon if they were whole."

Evan's keen surgeon's eyes were, without conscious thought, examining the men on the station platform. The sun was below the horizon and dusk was deepening; still, he saw several men were missing arms and legs, and two men had bad face wounds. A shudder passed through Evan at the recollection of the hundreds of bleeding bodies that had lain on the operating table before him. He had done his best with those mangled bodies, cutting away with sharp steel saw and scalpel those parts beyond repair, and trying his utmost to put back together the less-damaged parts so the soldier could function as nearly like a whole man as possible.

He pulled his mind away from the memory of the heinous butchery of the war. Never again would he take sharp steel to a man's body. His profession as a surgeon was finished for all time.

"Texas is going to have an army of crippled men," John said. He looked at Evan. Though somewhat improved, the man was still very ill. *You and I are going to be part of them*, John thought.

The train was slowing, and Evan braced himself against the coming blast of pain. Always the train came to a halt with a series of sharp jolts as the engine slowed and each car trailing was brought to a stop by collapsing the coupling between it and the one ahead. The jarring made his lung ache painfully.

The train came to a shuddering, jarring stop. Evan clenched his jaws. When the pain had faded from his chest and there was no taste of blood in his mouth, he breathed a sigh of relief.

He poked his head out the open window of the railroad coach. The Confederate lieutenant, who had given John and him permission to ride the train, and his sergeant were coming along the tracks.

The sergeant spoke. "Good God, Lieutenant, we don't have room for that many more wounded."

"I'll not pass them by," the little lieutenant said. He stopped and ran his eyes over the men, estimating their number. "We're going to take every one of them. There's space for twenty or so on the floor of the coaches. The rest will have to ride on one of the flatbed cars. Take all the freight from that first one and double-stack it on the other. What you can't put there, set it off on the station platform. The next train west can pick it up."

"Yes, sir," the sergeant said, and moved off.

Redpath remained sitting on his trunk and evaluated the lieutenant directing a sergeant twice his age. The fellow seemed too young to be an officer. Most likely his father had outfitted the squad of men and thus the son had become an officer. Many of the soldiers fighting for the South were equipped with private money. Redpath lifted his trunk and went toward the train.

"Lieutenant, may I have a word with you?" Redpath called as he drew close to the officer.

The lieutenant turned to Redpath. "Yes, what is it?"

"Is the train going to the end of track at Marshall?"

"Yes."

"I'd like to purchase a ticket." He set the trunk on the ground and pulled a purse bulging with gold coins from his pocket. He bounced the purse on his hand so that the coins jingled. Confederate paper money had little value, but gold should buy him what he wanted.

"This is a military train and not for civilian use," the lieutenant said.

"I'll pay fifty dollars in gold," Redpath said, ignoring the officer's words.

"Maybe you didn't hear me. This is a military train, and I barely have space for the wounded soldiers."

"I'll pay one hundred dollars for a ride."

"Are you trying to bribe an Army officer?" the lieutenant said, bristling.

"Certainly not," Redpath said. He stepped close to the lieutenant and towered over him. "I'm merely trying to get a ride to Marshall."

The smaller man did not budge from his position. He looked up at Redpath with a weary, harried expression. "No civilians will ride when soldiers need all the space. Now I've got to load those men before it gets dark and that's the end of it." He turned away.

Redpath's mud-colored eyes tightened. He reached out and caught the officer by the injured arm and turned him. "Wait. I'll go on board and pay one of the men for letting me have his place. Many of them would be glad to get a hundred dollars in gold for just waiting for the next train." He squeezed the lieutenant's injured arm.

The lieutenant quickly masked the pain that had suddenly ballooned under the man's hard grip. He put his good hand on his pistol. "Get your hands off me before I shoot you."

Redpath's anger soared at the threat. He

would stomp the little bastard and teach him a lesson, and it would take only three or four seconds. He swiftly scanned around to see if anybody was looking and could be a witness against him. A skinny, sallow-faced man was watching him from a window of the railroad coach but a few yards distant. Farther away, the sergeant was looking at him. Even as Redpath's eyes fell upon the sergeant, the man came swiftly forward to stand beside his officer.

With an expression of fury on his face, Redpath gave one quick look at the sergeant and then back at the lieutenant. He released his hold and stepped back.

"Sergeant, if this man tries to board the train, shoot him. That's a direct order."

"Yes, sir," said the soldier. There was a pleased tone in his voice.

The lieutenant turned and walked away.

"You've made a serious mistake," Redpath called after the lieutenant.

"Are you trying to scare the lieutenant?" the sergeant asked. "Hell, he's one of the bravest men I've ever seen. Why, in the fight at Shiloh..."

"Being brave doesn't mean the same as being smart," Redpath growled. He hoisted his trunk up and stalked away.


The sound of a man's loud voice woke Evan from the sleep he had fallen into while he waited for the train to leave Shreveport. He sat up and glanced about to find the source of the voice. The other soldiers in the coach were looking out the windows and through the darkness at the station house. Evan turned his sight in the same direction. The light from several lanterns, carried by a squad of armed soldiers, illuminated the railroad station. The soldiers were being given orders by a captain. It was the captain's full-voiced orders that had awakened Evan. John stood listening on the edge of the station platform.

"John, what's the trouble?" Evan called.

"Somebody killed the lieutenant," John said. He came limping toward the railroad coach. "He was found a few minutes ago behind the station with a broken neck. Those soldiers are from the local garrison."

"Probably that big man who had the argument with the lieutenant did it," Evan said.

"That's what the sergeant told the captain. And that's who the soldiers are going out to search for."

"He didn't seem like a fellow who'd be dumb enough to stick around town after killing an Army officer."

"I feel the same way. And it's dark too. The captain told the sergeant to stay in Shreveport to help identify the man if he's caught. We'll have another officer bossing the train on west. It'll be moving soon."

# Twelve

Rachel Greystone remained in the shade of the porch of the Morgan House Hotel in Marshall, Texas, and out of the sun that was a scorcher.

A block away from Rachel and beyond the brick-paved city that was radiating heat in shimmering waves was the railroad. A train had just arrived from the east and sat steaming in front of the yellow station house. Marshall was the end of line and the train could go no farther to the west. She could see wounded soldiers climbing down from the railroad coaches and one of the flatbed cars of the train. Each soldier carried a bedroll. Some also had small satchels or tied bundles of personal items. Several of the men stopped on the station platform and piled their possessions there. Then they joined with the others coming into the town.

Rachel knew the engine would soon be turned around on the turntable in the switching yard and headed back to the east. The passenger coaches would fill with new recruits for the Confederate Army and the flatbed cars loaded with military supplies. She would be on board the train, for she had made her decision to play a role in that war and not sit safely home in Marshall.

The wounded soldiers, nearly two hundred of them, came straggling along the street from the station. Most of the soldiers were dressed in various degrees of a gray uniform.

All of the uniforms showed hard usage. Here and there a man wore civilian clothing. A few soldiers were using crutches, one because he had but one leg. Three of the soldiers had each lost an arm. Many were limping. In half a dozen instances, one soldier was helping another to walk. Rachel's vision blurred with a mist of tears as a wave of sorrow for the men came over her.

A tall, rail-thin man in civilian clothes and a shorter man in a frayed uniform came parallel to the hotel. The taller man walked hunched forward with his hand pressed to his chest. The other man moved with a limp. The two halted and had a brief conversation. They separated, the shorter man continuing along the street while the other came toward the hotel.

The man moved with a slow pace toward Rachel, standing on the porch and watching him advance. He put each foot down carefully as if walking on ice. His face was gaunt and strained and glistening with sweat. He appeared ready to faint in the heat. He lifted his foot to step upon the wooden decking of the porch. He tripped when his toe snagged the edge and started to fall.

Rachel swiftly stepped close and grabbed the man by the arm.

Evan wanted to hurry and escape the sun that was sucking the moisture out of his weakened body. However, his muscles felt like wet strings and he was having difficulty walking. The final jolting stop of the train had hurt his damaged lung and he was having difficulty breathing. As he stepped upon the hotel porch, he tripped.

A pair of strong hands caught hold of him and stopped his fall. The person pulled strongly upward, and Evan managed to straighten.

"Thank you," Evan said, and turned to look at his savior. A lovely, young woman was watching him with a concerned expression. She had large green eyes, clear as crystal. They were the most beautiful, the most feminine eyes he had ever looked into. For the moment, all he could see were those green eyes.

"May I help you to a seat inside the hotel?" she asked. She still held him by the arm with both hands as if she feared he would fall again. "There are chairs inside the hotel and it's cooler there."

"Yes, please. Seems like I need help to stay on my feet." Evan thought he might be able to navigate the short distance by himself, but he didn't want the pretty woman to leave him. He managed to take his sight from her eyes and see the rest of her. She had long, light brown hair crowned with a bonnet, a delicately carved nose and generous mouth, and a chin perhaps a trifle square. Still, an altogether delightful face. She wore a yellow gingham dress with a row of ruffles down the front and the hem of the skirt brushing the floor. A small purse dangled from an arm.

"Lean on me as much as you need to," she said.

Evan leaned more than he really had to on the woman, and let her guide them through the open door and into the shadow-filled interior of the hotel. On the far side of the lobby, Evan lowered himself onto a leather couch. The woman released his arm and sat down beside him.

"Thanks again," Evan said.

"No thanks are necessary," she said, her green eyes still fixed on him with that expression of worry about his physical condition.

"I'm all right now," Evan assured her. "My name's Evan Payson."

"I'm Rachel Greystone. I saw you come in on the train. Were you at Vicksburg?"

"At Vicksburg, yes. And other places before that." Since they were in Texas, and Texas was aligned with the South, let her think he was fighting for the Confederacy. The fact that he had become a surgeon for the Union Army was purely by chance, since he had come upon their wounded first. He had been unable to pass by the bleeding, dying soldiers without helping them.

"Was the fighting bad?" Rachel asked.

"There were many killed and even more wounded. And not enough surgeons and nurses to tend to them." Evan was experiencing a strange sensation. He was very ill, and they were talking about fighting and dying, yet the world around him had come to feel gentle and safe. Also, the pain of his wound had greatly lessened and he was breathing more easily. All of this had happened but a moment after the woman had touched him. It all was due to the woman's nearness, her obvious kindheartedness, he was certain of that. He basked in the wonderful feeling, but why should she have that effect on him?

"I'm going to be a nurse for our Army," Rachel said.

"Nursing is a difficult task, and a sad one when one of your patients dies."

"But a necessary one," she said, contented with her decision.

"Yes, very necessary."

"Where were you wounded?" she asked with compassion furrowing her brow.

"A bullet hit me here." Evan touched his right breast. "I'm on my way home to El Paso."

"I hope you make it there safely. Are you traveling alone?"

"There's a fellow soldier with me. He's seeing about buying horses for us now. We'll leave tomorrow."

"It's good that you have somebody to travel with you. I hope all the wounded soldiers get home safely. I feel badly that I've waited so long to go and help our soldiers. I'm on my way now."

"Your home is here in Marshall?"

"Not right in town. My parents have a farm a few miles to the south. My father knows the commander of the garrison here in Marshall and he has given me a pass to ride the train east. My two brothers and an uncle are fighting with General Lee in Virginia. I hope to be able to see them."

"Please be careful. It will be difficult to find General Lee and your relatives, for the armies are always marching and maneuvering as they try to get an advantage on the enemy." She was a brave woman to journey more than halfway across the continent in time of war, and then to put herself in danger close to the battle lines.

"I'll find them. Now I must go to the station for I don't want to miss the train." She climbed to her feet.

Evan felt an immediate loss. He wanted to touch this delightful creature. He stood erect and took her hand, enclosing it totally within his. He felt the fine bones within their covering of soft flesh and smooth skin. He continued to hold her hand, not wanting to let go, for he knew he would never see her again. He should say something to prolong her stay, but he was tongue-tied.

"Good-bye," Rachel said. She smiled, seeming to read his thoughts exactly.

"Good-bye and good luck," Evan said hoarsely. His heart was tapping high in his chest and his breath was flowing quickly. It wasn't safe to breathe so fast with his damaged lung, but he couldn't help it.

Rachel pulled lightly on her hand and extracted it from Evan's. She crossed the lobby and picked up her satchel by the door. She turned and fastened Evan with her green eyes.

Evan's pulse hammered. The touch of Rachel's eyes upon him was like a kiss.

Rachel smiled at him and lifted her hand in

a little wave. The smile increased her beauty to a dazzling thing. Then she stepped through the doorway and was gone.

With her going, Evan felt the sensation of a gentle, safe world evaporate. Once again he was a very ill man journeying through a harsh, dangerous land. He marveled at the woman's effect on him. The period of her presence had been short, much too short, but he was thankful that he had been allowed to experience even that brief moment of time.

# *Thirteen*

Rachel fanned her face with a little fan that she carried in her purse, and stared out the window of the railroad coach. Low, wooded hills lay on both sides of the unmoving train. A well-traveled road ran parallel to the railroad tracks. The road lay empty and full of dust.

The train had been on the railroad siding for half an hour as it waited for the westbound train to pass on the single set of tracks. The interior of the coach was sweltering hot and not a breath of air stirred. Every seat was occupied. She was the only woman. The Army recruits, still in civilian dress, sat listless and silent in the heat. Most of them were from farms or ranches and had tanned faces and calloused hands. The men from the towns appeared pale in comparison.

At the beginning of the train ride east out of Texas and into Louisiana, some of the more daring young men tried to strike up a conversation with Rachel. However, the heat, and smoke from the engine, often streaming in through the open windows, soon put a stop to all talk.

The heat had built to a formidable level and Rachel felt suffocated. She rose from her seat and went to the back of the coach, and out onto the little outside platform on the rear to get some air. She had chosen the coach farthest from the engine so as to escape, as much as was possible, the smoke and cinders from the smokestack. She fanned herself and leaned out over the safety chain that enclosed the platform, and looked along the tracks in the direction from which the westbound train would come.

A sense of trepidation at her daring for undertaking a journey that she knew was perilous crept into her mind. Had she made a foolish decision? Should she get off the train at the next station and return to Marshall? She hastily shoved the thought away. The danger to her was as nothing compared to the danger facing the young men inside. They would soon be fighting enemies making every effort to kill them, and they weren't running away.

The whistle of the westbound train sounded shrilly through the woods. She leaned farther out over the safety chain to look for it. The train broke into sight, bore on ahead, came even, and went rumbling past. She watched the train recede along the two glistening rails.

Rachel's train started with a jerk. The sudden movement caught her unexpectedly and she lost her balance. She started to fall and grabbed for the safety chain. Her hand missed the chain and found only air. The chain caught her across the waist and she cartwheeled over it.

Rachel crashed down onto the stone ballast of the railroad bed. Her head struck one of the wooden railroad ties with a sodden thud. Daylight left her with one last blinding flash.

Karl Redpath was two days west of Shreveport and traveling in a Phaeton buggy drawn by a team of black pacing horses. Both the buggy and the horses were stolen.

After killing the Confederate lieutenant, Redpath had hurried west across the town. He had little concern that he would be caught. Most likely the man's body would not be found until daylight the following morning. Still, he knew it was wise to put distance between himself and the soldiers stationed in Shreveport, who would be searching for him.

As he had made his way across the town through the darkness, he had come upon the team and buggy hitched in front of a general store. The buggy was one of Phaeton's largest sizes and had padded leather seats, leather side curtains, and a large rumble seat. The matched pacing horses were of excellent quality. Wanting the vehicle, Redpath looked through the wide front window to the inside of the store for the owner. In the light of two coal-oil lamps, a man and woman were talking and paying no attention to the outside. He had simply dropped his trunk into the rumble seat of the buggy, stepped up into the vehicle, and driven away into the night.

Redpath noted that some distance ahead of him a piece of yellow cloth lay near the railroad track that ran parallel to the road. He thought little about the cloth as the pacers stepped lively along. Just cast-off trash. As he drew ever closer, the amount of cloth visible grew larger. Then it became a woman's dress. Redpath thought he could make out the form of a woman's body within the dress.

He reined the horses off the road and up beside the body and stepped down. The woman lay on her back on the crushed-stone ballast of the railroad tracks. So still and quiet was her body that he thought her dead. He went closer.

The bosom of the woman rose ever so slightly. Then it sank, the smallest of breath taken. Redpath went quickly to her. She lay on her back, and he saw her eyes were half open and staring into the sun. He leaned hastily over her to put her eyes in shadow to protect them from damage by the bright rays of the sun. A huge bruise on her forehead leaked lymph and a little blood.

Redpath knew about broken bones and wounds, for in his business they were often encountered, and he set about examining the woman thoroughly for injuries. He turned to the head wound first. The flesh was badly bruised over an area more than an inch square. He could not detect any damage done to her skull. Most often the seriousness of such a wound could only be determined with time. She had scrapes and cuts from falling onto the stone ballast of the tracks. None of them were of a nature to cause worry.

Though she was bruised, bleeding, and unconscious, the young woman's beauty struck Redpath powerfully. He had owned many women, all of them above the ordinary in prettiness, some exceptional, and he had made love with every one of them before he sent them out to ply their trade of being a whore. But never before had a woman affected him as this one did. He was staggered by the sudden and overwhelming impact of desire for her.

He saw no rings on her fingers and judged she was most likely single. He took the purse off her arm and examined all the contents, discovering her name and address. There was nearly a hundred dollars in gold. She hadn't been robbed and thrown from the train. So what was a single woman doing in this particular place, at this particular time?

From her position on the side of the railroad track, Redpath believed she had fallen from the train. He eliminated the possibility of her being pushed because of the presence of the money. Two trains, one going west and one east, had passed him within the last hour. Which one of them had she been traveling on?

He went to the buggy for a canteen of water from his supplies. On the second day of his journey, he had stopped in a town and bought provisions for a long journey. He returned to the woman and began to bathe her face.

"Wake up, miss," he said.

She gave no indications she felt the water or heard his voice. He shook her, somewhat roughly. Still, there was no response, her body loose and slack as a rag doll. He spread a blanket on the floorboards of the buggy and placed her upon it. The side and rear curtains were dropped to put her totally in the shade. He popped the whip over the ears of the horses, and they quick-stepped with the buggy off along the road.

Now and again he passed people on the road, and each time put a fold of blanket across the woman so she could not be seen. In the evening, he came to a town, but he continued straight through it. The town was large enough to have a doctor, but there was nothing a doctor could do for the woman's wounds that Redpath couldn't do.

He made camp beneath a large tree far enough back from the road that they couldn't be seen by passersby. He tended to the woman first, spreading a blanket on the grass and laying her tenderly down on it. He doctored her head wound and the lesser ones on her body with salve. The one on her head was bandaged.

She must have water, so he turned her head to the side and poured a few teaspoons from the canteen into her mouth. He was pleased when she swallowed the water.

Rachel's eyes opened and she looked up at Redpath. She instantly shrank back from him, and uttered a cry of fright.

"It's all right," Redpath said. "You're safe."

"What happened?" Rachel asked in a scared, bewildered voice. She was totally confused.

"You fell," Redpath replied. "I've doctored your injuries." His mind was racing to conceive how he was going to keep her with him. She was the most desirable woman he had ever met and he meant to possess her. That was so regardless of how much she resisted him.

Rachel touched her bandaged head. "I fell?"

"Yes, from the buggy."

"Where am I?" The fear in her voice was intense.

"With me. How do you feel?"

"I'm sore all over. But there's something wrong."

"In what way?"

The woman appeared baffled by some question she was asking herself. "I don't know who I am. Who you are."

Redpath had his answer. Somehow the blow to the woman's head had damaged her mind to the degree that she had lost her memory.

"Who am I?" Rachel asked, her voice trembling.

"Why, you're Marcella Redpath, my wife."

# Fourteen

The band of six scalp hunters, mounted on strong, long-legged mustangs, crossed the yellow sand hills and halted just below the crest of the hill standing above the San Pedro River in the Arizona Territory.

Tattersall, the leader, swung his wiry frame down from his mount. He stretched once, ruffled his thick, black beard with his hand to brush the dust out of it, then shook himself like a wolf flinging off water. The kinks, bent into his muscles from riding fifty miles since daylight, fell away from his tough body. He checked the sun. There was still an hour of daylight remaining, plenty of time to take these last scalps.

He looked at his riders. They were bandits and ruffians hired by him for their toughness. Adkisson was a short, powerfully built redhead. Oakman, a rail-thin man, had fits now and again; still, he was the best marksman with a rifle of the bunch. Crampton, a mean man who just liked to kill, was almost as skinny as Oakman. Butcher was a blond German who like money and probably had most every penny he had earned killing Apaches. Snyder, a small man, spent all his money on whiskey and whores.

The men stared back at Tattersall from lean, hard faces shaded beneath broad-brimmed hats. Each member of his band wore two Colt .44-caliber pistols. On their ponies they carried two Sharps .52-caliber carbines. All were expert gunmen. They were the finest bunch of fighters Tattersall had ever assembled. He believed the heavily armed band could whip a war party of fifty Apaches.

"Adkisson, come with me," Tattersall said. "The rest of you take care of the horses and keep out of sight while we take a gander down below."

The two men went quietly to the crest of the hill and looked down on the San Pedro River. The mile-wide valley of the river spread itself before them. The meandering river, lying some three hundred yards distant and a hundred feet lower in elevation, flowed north in a slow green current lined with giant cottonwoods and walnut trees.

"There's the Apache camp we came to find," Tattersall said.

Eight tipis were grouped in an open stand of large trees. The skin lodges were heavily stained with the soot of many fires. Up near the smoke holes they were nearly black. Spring storms had damaged the structures, and the patches that had been used to close the rents and tears showed like white scars.

"So they're still here," Adkisson said.

"They had no reason to move," Tattersall said, scanning the encampment. "It's a good place with water, wood, and game. And fish in the river."

The band had spotted the small village during their scalp hunting earlier in the spring, but had passed it by with the intention of hitting it on the way back south into Mexico. They had hunted first to the west, striking the villages in Gila River country, and then had ridden far to the north up the Pecos River Valley. Now it was time to take the last scalps.

In the camp, a group of squaws knelt around a buffalo hide stretched on the ground and worked on it with sharp flint scrapers. The women wouldn't live long enough to finish the hide. A group of laughing children romped and played near the river. Men were gathered around a horse and talking and gesturing, obviously discussing the qualities of the animal.

"I count eight bucks," Adkisson said.

"Best we can come up the river through the trees," Tattersall said. "That way we can hit them without being seen until it's too late for any of them to get away."

"Yeah, should be easy," Adkisson agreed.

Tattersall and Adkisson dropped down from the crown of the hill and returned to the other men. They all climbed to their feet and looked at Tattersall for his orders.

"Check the loads in your guns, then mount up," Tattersall ordered. "We'll take them from horseback in case some try to run."

The band of scalp hunters were gathered in the woods near the river and downstream from the Apache village. The sun had turned red as it floated down to rest on the chain of mountains to the west. The water of the San

Pedro River, bathed in the last light of the sun, had become crimson as blood.

Tattersall knew the outcome of the battle to come wasn't something to worry about. The Apaches, though fierce fighters, had no discipline and fought as individuals. An organized group such as he had would kill every one with ease. In a few days he would be in Chihuahua selling a sack of their scalps to Governor Antonio Beremendes. The savage raids of the Apache into the northern Mexican provinces had so angered the governor that he had placed a bounty of one hundred dollars in gold on every Indian man, and fifty dollars on each woman and child. The coarse, long-haired scalps proved their deaths. Tattersall and his gang would make twelve to thirteen thousand dollars in only a few weeks of hunting. Tattersall's cut would be one quarter.

"We'll use rifles first as we close in on them," Tattersall told his men. "Then pistols to finish the job. Shoot the bucks first. Let nobody escape. Now line up on me and go quiet."

The men rode silently, holding their rifles ready to fire. The trees thinned as they drew nearer the encampment. Then the tipis and the people were in sight hardly more than two hundred yards away. The horse that had been under discussion by the men was being led away by one of them. The other men were dispersing, ambling away among the tipis.

Closest to the scalp hunters was a little boy about seven wading in the edge of the river.

He saw the strange riders and screamed a warning.

"Shoot them," Tattersall shouted.

He raised his rifle to his shoulder and shot a warrior turning to look at them. The Indian was knocked flat by the heavy bullet.

The other Indian men bolted for their weapons hanging on posts near their tipis. As they raced through the village, they shouted shrill orders at the women and children to run and hide.

The women added their cries for the children to flee. Then screaming with fright, every woman and child began to run in frantic haste, scattering up the riverside.

Beside Tattersall, the snarling cracks of his men's heavily charged rifles were deafening. In the Apache camp two braves were hit with deadly blows and fell to the ground. Another was knocked tumbling. He rose to his feet and hobbled toward the thick stand of trees growing along the foot of the bluff. One warrior had been close to reaching his musket. As he reached for it, a bullet broke his spine and he went down with arms flopping. A sixth warrior was running strongly for his weapon. He suddenly fell face-forward as if tripped, slid along to a stop, and did not move again.

"Keep shooting!" Tattersall shouted. He jammed his empty single-shot Sharps into its scabbard and drew his second one. He knew his men were doing the same.

The two remaining Apache warriors had now gained their weapons, both old muskets. They fired at the white men. The bullets missed, whining past the scalp hunters. The warriors were cut down by multiple bullets.

"Snyder, that wounded buck in the woods is nearest to you, so you go get him," Tattersall said to the man on the far right side of the gang.

"Right," Snyder called back.

"Now ride the squaws and kids down," Tattersall shouted. "Catch every one of them."

The scalp hunters pulled their pistols and spurred their horses up the riverside. Five chased after the fleeing women and children. Snyder veered off into the deeper woods.

As Tattersall gouged his horse ahead, an old grandmother jumped up from some bushes. He killed her, a shot from his pistol through the center of her back. A boy of seven or eight came out of the same bushes and tore off at an angle. He leaped over the trunk of a fallen tree and then straightened out in a flat-out run. The little brown bastard sure could travel, Tattersall thought.

Lashing his horse, Tattersall drew close to the boy. He slashed down with the heavy iron barrel of his revolver, clubbing the child to the earth. Tattersall dragged his mount to a halt, whirled it around, and ran it back to the small, still body of the boy.

The firing of his men dwindled and stopped as Tattersall stepped down from his mount. He deftly cut a circle around the top of the boy's head and ripped away a large segment of scalp and hair. He halted at two other bodies, one the old woman, as he returned to the camp, each time cutting away the victim's scalp.

Adkisson, carrying a handful of bloody scalps, came to meet Tattersall. "Mighty fine target practice we all had," he said.

"Stretch and dry these with those you have," Tattersall directed, and handed Adkisson the scalps he carried. "Did anyone get away that you saw?"

"Nope, we got them all," Adkisson said, separating the scalps to see how many had been given to him. "That makes twenty-two of them," he added in a pleased tone.

"Pure gold, just pure gold," Tattersall said with a laugh.

## *Fifteen*

Karl Redpath and Rachel Greystone crossed the Brazos River on a small, steam-driven ferry painted white. It was hardly large enough to stay afloat laden as it was with the team and buggy and heavily loaded freight wagons. Redpath paid the ferryman and climbed into the buggy beside Rachel.

"Ready to travel, Marcella?" Karl asked. The woman had accepted the name and he was pleased at that. With luck, she would never know her real name.

"Yes, I'm ready," Marcella replied.

"Then off we go," Karl said, and smiled at

his good fortune of finding the lovely woman who couldn't remember. He popped the long buggy whip over the ears of the pacers and drove the buggy onto the shore.

Marcella settled herself on the seat of the buggy, glad for the padding in the seat, and prepared for the grueling hours of travel that lay ahead. The morning was barely half spent and already the heat had built to a sweltering temperature.

They climbed up from the river with the iron-rimmed wheels of the buggy grinding and screeching on the gravel and rock of the steep grade. The wheels became quiet as they encountered the clay soil of the forested hills to the west. They traveled swiftly, as they had every day since Marcella had awakened from the unconsciousness of her fall six days before. The days were long from daylight to dark, and many miles had rumbled past beneath the rolling wheels of the buggy.

Karl always drove straight through the small towns widely scattered along the road, refusing her request to stop and find a hotel for the night. When darkness overtook them they simply stopped. Most times they were fortunate enough to find a farmhouse close by the roadside, and Karl would pay for food and a night's lodging for them. Once they had simply spread their blankets on the ground and slept under the open sky.

Marcella had asked Karl about the reason for the rapid, exhausting journey, and he had replied that they must reach El Paso at the earliest possible time so he could launch his new business. She thought it unusual to push so hard even for that reason, but did not voice her thought. When she questioned him as to the type of business, he told her it was a form of entertainment. She had pressed him to describe it more fully, but he had laughed and told her that she must wait for he wanted it to be a surprise.

"You all right?" Karl asked, turning to look at Marcella as he often did.

"Yes, just hot," Marcella replied, not looking at Karl. *And no, I'm not all right. I'm in awful condition for I can't remember one thing from the past.* "I'm thankful for the shade," Marcella added to soften her terse answer.

She stared straight ahead along the road. The woods were dense and the road barely wide enough for two vehicles to pass. The limbs of the trees reached out over the road and met in the center. Driving along the road was like moving down a hot, green tunnel.

To battle the heat, she was dressed in a thin cotton dress and a straw hat. She had other clothing in a trunk in the rumble seat of the carriage. Karl had told her that her suitcases had been stolen shortly before her fall. They had stopped at the first town and purchased several outfits. He had spent lavishly for the new garments.

She felt Karl's eyes still on her, but she did not turn. He had strange, tan-colored eyes; mud-colored always came to her mind. They seemed to have no depth and betrayed nothing of what he was thinking. The nearest thing to emotion she had ever detected was that sometimes when she looked unexpectedly at him, there was a kind of watchful, probing expression. It always quickly vanished when their eyes met.

She knew Karl had a very strong feeling for her. It was apparent in the way he frequently touched her, and every night he came to her and she had to take him into her bed. She did not feel like a married woman; still, she performed all the wifely duties a vow of marriage required. She often wondered why she had chosen Karl for a husband for she felt no love for him. Truthfully, she did not even like him.

There was a nagging feeling that she couldn't shake that something wasn't as it appeared. The feeling was most strong when she would awaken in the darkness of night with a terrible sensation of wrongness, wrongness of where she was, of what was happening to her. She couldn't crystallize the reason for it. She tried to console herself that most probably all of it was rooted in her inability to remember. If she could recall events, the happenings and emotions of the past, the present would be an extension of them and everything would fit into its place. Then she would have no concern.

Karl asked Marcella every morning when they awoke, and sometimes again during the day, if she had remembered anything of her past. She had tried many times to go backward into the past. Oh, how hard she'd tried. There was nothing before her awakening, as if she had been spontaneously created and there she was. The past wasn't a black emptiness, not some dense impenetrable fog. It was just nothing. Yet her mind was starved for memories of things, of places, of people and emotions. The immense hunger for the tiniest memory shook Marcella to the very core.

Marcella had asked Karl to tell her about their life prior to the accident, and about her family. He told her they had been married for two years, that her parents had died of yellow fever the summer before, and that she had no close relatives. They had owned a great house in New Orleans with many servants. Then the Union Army and Navy had captured the city and she and Karl had decided to leave and start a new business in El Paso, a town far beyond the boundaries of the war. They had talked long about the War Between the States. How very strange that a great war was in progress and she knew nothing about it.

His answers always came easily. He would repeat the stories, telling her that he was doing so so she might more quickly break through the block that hid the past.

Knowing she didn't love the man, Marcella had asked him to describe their courtship and marriage. He told her they had met at one of the gala dances the rich of New Orleans frequently held. They had fallen in love almost at once and had married less than a week later.

Marcella again thought of that statement of Karl's, about love and a quick marriage, as they drove through the woods. If she had been so much in love with him before the accident, then why should she not feel some of it now? The chemistry of love should have survived the blow to her head and be present at all times.

At that conclusion, the distasteful feeling of wrongness swept over her more strongly than ever. So powerful was the sensation that Marcella shivered. She controlled the shiver, but there came immediately afterward a dizziness, and a fuzziness to her vision. She felt herself swaying in the seat, and caught hold of the nearest upright iron rod that supported the top of the buggy. She struggled to clear her vision.

Slowly the dizziness left Marcella, and the fuzziness of her vision cleared. However, instead of seeing the road in the forest ahead of her, she was looking along a narrow, dimly lighted channel walled with blackness. At the distant end of the channel was a woman's face. The woman was of middle age and pretty. Marcella felt she should know the woman, but no name would come to mind. The woman didn't speak, or show emotion, merely looking in Marcella's direction.

Even as Marcella studied the face it began to fade. *Hurry,* she told herself, *and identify the woman, for you may never get another chance.* She concentrated upon the picture, desperate to put a name on the woman, to know the relationship between them. She examined in minute details the woman's features, the oval of her face, the curve of her mouth, the shape of her eyes. The powerful focus of her attention held the picture for a tiny moment longer. Then it was gone and a terrible sensation of loss fell upon her.

"What's wrong, Marcella?" Karl asked. He was holding her firmly by the arm. "Are you sick?"

"If not being able to remember the past is being sick, then I'm sick."

"It's more than that. You were shivering."

"I suppose I was. I was trying to remember something, anything, but just can't."

Some instinct told Marcella to keep the vision of the woman's face a secret from Karl.

The woman was haunting Marcella. She should know her. Surely she was someone Marcella once knew, for there was no reason for her injured mind to conjure up a stranger's face. Marcella prayed the woman would appear again and stay long enough to be identified. Perhaps then Marcella could begin to build a past.

"It will all come back to you," Karl said.

He popped the metal tip of the buggy whip over the ears of the horses. They picked up the pace, the buggy rolling easily on its greased axles.

Near noontime, Marcella and Karl came within sight of a two-story log tavern where a north-south road crossed the one they traveled. The tavern sat in a clearing of some four acres in the forest. Several horses were tied to a long hitching rail in front. A skillfully carved wooden sign declared there was food, drink, and lodging to be had. A garden fenced with tall woven wire lay on the right and close by the tavern.

"Are you hungry?" Karl asked.

"Starved," Marcella said. The villages and farms were infrequently encountered now. The last house had been miles behind them. Karl had told her that soon would be only wilderness.

"Then we shall stop and obtain the best food they have," he now said.

As the buggy drew near the tavern, a man came out of the building. He turned to look at the buggy and its occupants as he went toward the tied horses. He had mounted and was riding off to the west as Karl brought his vehicle to a halt in front of the tavern.

Karl helped Marcella down from the buggy and they entered the tavern.


Marcella half dozed as the buggy rolled smoothly along on its flexible iron leaf spring. She had enjoyed the delicious food, especially the blackberry pie. Its taste still lingered in her mouth. The pleasant woman who had served them had told Marcella that she had picked the berries in the edge of the woods that morning. The danger to the friendly people of this isolated place was brought starkly to Marcella by the man who wore a pistol buckled around his waist as he helped his wife to serve the customers.

The road they traveled again ran through the thick forest. It had narrowed to such a small width that had they met another vehicle, it would have been a difficult task to pass each other. The huge trees crowded in close on both sides, and only a stray ray of sunlight here and there penetrated the leafy crowns of the trees to fall upon the ground.

Ahead of them some one hundred feet, a huge mountain of a man came out of the woods and into the road. He carried a length of tree trunk, longer than he was tall and nearly a foot in diameter, on his shoulder. As he moved toward the center of the road, he turned his head and glanced at the occupants of the buggy. The man's head was overly large even for his size and the brows of his forehead bulged over deeply set eyes. He was smiling in a childlike way, a mischievous child who was playing a trick. He dropped the log crosswise on the road, thus blocking it to the passage of the buggy. He continued on to disappear in among the trees on the opposite side.

"What?..." Marcella started to speak.

"Get down!" Karl exclaimed. "It's a holdup!" He caught Marcella by the shoulder and shoved her down onto the floorboards of the buggy.

"Stay there," he ordered, at the same time reining the horses to a fast stop.

He sprang from the buggy, pulling his pistol as he landed. He swiftly pivoted to look around.

Two men had come out of the woods and into the road thirty yards behind the buggy. Both carried rifles raised to their shoulders. One of them opened his mouth to shout at Karl.

Before a sound could come from the man, Karl shot him twice in the chest with his pistol. The man staggered backward. His legs gave way and he fell.

The second man dropped his head to sight along the rifle and fired. Karl was already moving, and the bullet cut the air where he had stood. He swung his pistol and fired at the bandit.

The bullet hit the man and sent him staggering backward. He caught himself, and dropping his single-shot rifle, reached for his pistol.

Karl shot the bandit again, knocking him flat on the ground.

Marcella hadn't been able to see the bandits at the rear of the buggy because the luggage in the rumble seat blocked her view. She did see a man with a pistol come into sight near the log on the road.

"Karl! Behind you!" she screamed.

Karl leapt to the side and spun to the rear in one swift movement. His pistol roared twice, the shots so close together that they seemed to be but one continuous explosion of sound. The range was short and the man went down as if hit by a powerful fist.

"Damn fools," Karl said as he looked about at the corpses.

Trembling, Marcella rose up from the floor

of the buggy. The effortless way Karl had killed three armed men astounded her. Never had she imagined a man could move so swiftly and shoot so accurately.

"Using the halfwit to block the road with the log was a good idea," Karl said, addressing the comment to Marcella. "But then they came out in the open to be shot. That was a dumb thing to do."

He watched Marcella and waited for a response. When she only stared back, he spoke again. "That was quick thinking to call and warn me about the other one. Do you remember seeing him before?"

Marcella shook her head.

"He was that man who rode off from the tavern as we stopped." Karl smiled. "We make a damn fine pair, you and I."

He began to reload his revolver, whistling happily.

A cry erupted in the woods close by Karl. The cry was full of sadness and of rage all mixed together into a frightening sound not quite human. The man Karl had called a halfwit burst from the woods and leapt upon him.

The two men crashed into the side of the buggy and rocked it violently. Karl was driven down hard with the man mountain on top of him. The man began to flail at Karl, striking at him with both fists.

Marcella hurriedly scooted across the seat of the buggy and away from the fighting men. She watched them, mesmerized by the rage on the face of the halfwit and his wildly swinging fists. One of his hands hit the oak spokes of a buggy wheel, but he didn't seem to feel pain from it. The halfwit with his monstrous strength would kill Karl.

Then Marcella saw an astonishing, unexpected thing. Karl, his back pinned to the ground, struck upward with his hand through the fists striking at him. Two fingers of the hand were extended, and they stabbed into the eye sockets beneath the bulging brows of the larger man.

The halfwit's screams instantly became ones of horrendous pain. He ceased the swings of his fists and covered both eyes with his hands.

Karl struck again, a powerful blow of his fist into the man's throat. The screams cut off abruptly. Karl heaved mightily and lifted the man up, and rolled from under him.

Karl rose to his feet and shook himself. Then he stood rubbing at the bruises on his face and watching the halfwit struggle to a sitting position. The giant's chest heaved as he strained to breathe through a crushed throat.

Marcella too was watching the man on the ground, and she saw a clear liquid that was stained with a little blood leaking from both of the man's eye sockets. His eyes were missing.

"Oh, my God!" she exclaimed.

She tore her sight away from the blind man and looked at Karl. "What do we do now?"

Karl was watching her. Now there was depth to his mud-colored eyes, rage so deep, so deadly that it frightened Marcella just to see it.

"I'll show you," Karl said in a grating voice.

He bent, reached under his right pants leg, and extracted a small-caliber pistol from a holster strapped there. He stepped up beside the sitting man, sucking air with a hissing sound. With a movement almost too swift to see, Karl leaned down and shot the halfwit between the eyes.

The giant man went over backward and flopped like a maimed crow, and sprayed blood in the dust of the road. His heels drummed upon the ground and his arms thrashed wildly about.

After a quarter minute, the frenzied motion of the dying halfwit ceased and he lay still. Karl turned away from the dead man and, without looking at Marcella, went to the log blocking the road and moved it aside. He came to the buggy and drove away from the corpses of the robbers.

Marcella was so overwhelmed by the attempted robbery and the killings that she could find nothing to say. She sat with the awful memory of the halfwit dying frozen in her mind.

# Sixteen

Ben forded the slow-flowing Cat Claw Creek, crossed through a hay field of redtop clover, and came onto the southern end of Main Street in Abilene, Texas. He was dusty, sweaty, and stank. He had thirteen horses and eight saddles to sell. None of it rightfully belong to him.

He tilted his head down so that the wide brim of his hat threw his scarred face into shadow and thus made it less visible. He wanted no gawking stares, no expressions of revulsion.

People on the street stopped to look at the long line of horses moving past tied one behind the other with lengths of rope. The horses stretched for nearly half a block behind Ben. He heard a man comment to another on the high quality of the animals.

On a cross street, nearly a dozen boys, all shirtless and shoeless, played ball with a stick bat and a wrapped twine ball. Ben heard their happy laughter as they ran the bases, merely circles drawn in the dust. Four little girls about the same age were on the wooden sidewalk watching the boys. Ben noted that the drivers of the vehicles coming and going on the street pulled to the side so as not to much bother the game.

Three cowboys in leather chaps and big, wide-brimmed hats came racing their horses along the street where the boys played. The pounding hooves of the horses sent geysers of dust pluming into the air. The man in front, wearing a dirty blue shirt, reined his mount to ride directly through the gathering of boys.

"Get off the street, you little bastards," the blue-shirted man shouted.

The boys scattered like a covey of frightened quail to escape the iron-shod feet of the horses. Ben growled under his breath. Had the lads not been so nimble, if one had tripped and fallen, he could have been stepped upon by the horses and seriously hurt, or killed.

Four blocks farther along, Ben halted at a business with a huge sign declaring it to be Thatcher's Livery And Horse Trading. An entire block was taken up by Thatcher's. The front half contained the office building facing the street and more than a score of vehicles of various types and sizes, both new and used. The remaining half block was a log corral holding a few horses. Ben saw the low number of horses. That could mean a scarcity and therefore a high value for the ones he possessed. He dismounted and went toward the office.

A tall, stoop-shouldered man with a handlebar mustache came out from the office as Ben approached. "Howdy, Hawkins," he said, not looking at Ben.

"Howdy, Thatcher. I've got horses and saddles for sale. Are you interested?"

Thatcher sighted along the horses and eyed the saddles. "Did the horses grow those saddles, or were there men sitting them?"

"So you don't get the wrong idea, I'll tell you. Some of the saddles belonged to Mexi-

116

cans who decided to ride double with someone else. The others belonged to men who killed some friends of mine. They won't be needing the saddles."

Thatcher fingered his mustache. "I'll take your word for that. I wouldn't want to buy any animals stole in Texas."

He walked along the horses, examining all of them and the saddles carried by eight of them. He returned to Ben.

"Some Valdes horses, I see. That's okay by me. That saddle with all the silver, you going to keep that one for yourself?"

"Nope. My ass fits the one I've got. I'll take the cash."

"I'll buy the lot, saddles and horses, if we can agree on a price. I'd buy that one you're sitting on too."

"Could never sell Brutus. He'd stomp me in the ground for that. But let's get to dickering for the others."

The two men worked their way along the string of horses and discussed the qualities of the animals and value of the saddles. Agreeing on a price, Thatcher jotted the amount down on a notepad. Finishing with the last horse, Thatcher tallied the figures.

"Come into the office and I'll write you a draft on the bank," he said.


"Yes, Señor Hawkins, your clothes are ready," said the Mexican woman. She kept her eyes on the ground at Ben's feet.

"That's good, Señora Lopez. Would you have Pedro fill the tub with water so that I can bathe?" Pedro was the *señora*'s son. Her husband Jesus worked for Thatcher.

"He is already doing that. I started him at the task when I saw you coming."

"You are very thoughtful," Ben said. He placed several silver dollars in her hand. He had arranged with the Lopez family to provide him with a place to stay in their aged adobe *casa* when he was in Abilene. He slept there in a corner bedroom where the cool breeze blew through, and ate most of his meals in the woman's pleasant kitchen. She kept his clothing clean and ironed. He stabled his horse in a lean-to at the rear of the house. For the privilege he paid them twice what would have been a fair price.

"Thank you for your generosity," said the woman as she counted the coins in her hand without looking at them. "Will you want something to eat?"

"Yes, in about an hour."

"It shall be ready."

Pedro came out from behind the house. He glanced at Ben and then away. "Your water is ready, Señor Hawkins," he said.

"Thank you, Pedro."

Ben bathed in the tub of water in the small bathhouse at the rear of the *casa*. The water was warm, and he knew it had come from the rain barrel that sat in the sun under the south eave of the house. He shaved with a straight-edged razor that he kept among his

118

possessions at the Lopez home. The chore was a difficult one because of the deep crevices and raised scars of his face. Finally finishing and feeling totally clean for the first time in many days, he donned his town clothing—gray trousers, a soft, white shirt, a broad-brimmed hat, and polished boots. How grand it was to feel the fresh clothing against his skin. He knew that within hours, his soiled riding clothing would be in the same condition as the clothing he had just put on.

He buckled his pistol around his waist. It was out of place with the town clothes, for few townsmen carried weapons. However, Ben could not bring himself to leave it behind for he felt only partially dressed without it.

He sat in the kitchen of the *casa* and ate his meal of mutton stew, bean soup, soft cheese, a stack of blue-corn tortillas, and sweet custard. He asked the *señora* for a cup of coffee and a second custard. She brought them promptly.

"Will you want anything else, Señor Hawkins?" she said.

"No, thank you, *señora*." The woman left the kitchen as Ben leaned back to finish his meal leisurely.

Ben left the Lopez *casa* and walked toward the center of the town. He had his hat pulled low; still, he received stares. He would put up with the expression in the eyes of the people for he wasn't going to be a prisoner in the Lopez house. At a tobacconist's shop on the main street, Ben entered and ordered a half-dozen cigars. He hadn't had a smoke in more than two weeks and felt a craving for one. While he waited for the proprietor to roll the fresh smokes, he moved about the small shop, looking at the boxes of cigars and breathing the pungent, delightful aroma of tobacco.

Immediately upon coming out of the shop and onto the sidewalk, Ben halted and lit his first cigar. Then he moved down the sidewalk, not looking at the people he encountered. He came to a little park with a handful of big trees. A Comanche Indian sat on the ground under the tree nearest the sidewalk. He was ancient, with gray hair and his brown face full of wrinkles so deep that they looked like scars. He was stone still with his eyes closed, seemingly only listening to time pass. He wore buckskin pants and jumper, and moccasins with the soles wore through and dirty, brown feet showing. The clothes were frayed, and stained, and hung loosely on his body like a layer of reptilian skin being shedded.

The wind was from Ben to the Comanche, and some of the cigar smoke wafted to the man. He lifted his head and smelled the wind. Like some hunting animal that had caught the scent of its prey, he opened his eyes and twisted around to Ben.

The Comanche smiled, his toothless mouth gaping in a pink-lined pit. He looked Ben straight in the face. He did not turn away from the ugliness, but rather held out his hand as if ready to accept something.

"Old man, if you can stand to look at me, then you deserve a cigar," Ben said, knowing the Indian wanted a smoke.

He squatted beside the old Indian and handed him a cigar. The man put the smoke into his mouth, and then looked inquiringly at Ben.

"No fire, eh?" Ben said. He struck a match against the sole of his shoe and lit the end of the cigar for the man.

The Indian drew a huge breath of cigar smoke deep into his lungs. He smiled, his old cheeks crinkling into a hundred folds of pleasure. He held the smoke locked within his lungs for seconds, then slowly, very slowly, let it out, savoring every curl of it.

"Good, eh?" Ben said.

"Good!" replied the Indian, his black eyes still fastened on Ben.

Ben, smiling at the obvious enjoyment the cigar gave the old Comanche, stood erect and went off on the street.

# Seventeen

Ben drank his first beer in the Mexican *cantina* on the broad plaza in the center of Abilene. The brew had a delicious, tangy flavor, and was cold from the keg having been sunk

121

to the bottom of the deep water well behind the *cantina*. He took another long pull from the mug and let the savory liquid trickle delightfully down his throat.

He sat at a table in the rear of the *cantina*. The building was an old adobe structure, high-ceilinged and with an earthen floor. The furnishings were old and had taken rough usage over the years. He knew there were much fancier saloons elsewhere on the plaza, but he preferred this one.

On his right was a long bar where a handful of men were drinking. In the larger space on the left were two dozen or more tables. Four men were playing poker at one of the tables. A pair of men were drinking and talking at a second table. The remainder were empty.

The evening was growing old and daylight fading. Yet the three coal-oil lamps hanging from the rafters had not been lighted. That was fine by Ben. As he usually did, he had his hat pulled down low. From under the brim he watched the other men in the *cantina*. They were talking, and he listened to the rumble of their voices. The conversations at the bar were too far away to make out. He could plainly hear the men making their bets at the card game. It was good to once again be among men even though he could never have one for a friend, someone to just talk with about unimportant things. Passing time by himself had grown very oppressive after more than a year.

The three cowboys who had run their mustangs through the boys playing ball came through the open doorway. The blue-shirted man was in the lead, and he halted with the others just inside the room to allow their eyes to adapt to the darkened interior. He said something to his comrades and they all laughed loudly. After a few seconds, the cowboys came deeper into the room with a swaggering walk and boots thumping and spurs jingling. They stopped at the middle of the bar and ordered a bottle of tequila. They gulped the first shots, poured a second one for each, and began to talk.

Ben turned away from the cowboys, after noting each man wore a revolver belted to his waist. He held up his mug and caught the bartender's eye.

The man nodded his head, acknowledging the empty mug, and drew and brought a full one to Ben's table. He picked up the empty mug and the silver coin for payment and left.

Two men entered the *cantina*. They paused in the doorway, as the cowboys had done, and peered ahead into the shadows. They looked about for half a minute and then they moved on in. The shorter man walked with a limp, the right leg being the bad one. The second man was quite thin. He had his shoulders hunched forward and appeared exhausted. The men were unshaven and dust-covered.

They took seats at a table not far from Ben and ordered beers. The thin man, the ridges of his bones showing sharply through his skin, sat leaning wearily over the table. *The man needs to gain at least thirty pounds*, Ben thought. The men's brews arrived and they immediately took long drinks. The thin man shivered as the cold beer hit his gullet.

"Damn, now ain't that delicious," John said.

"What's even better is to get out of that saddle and sit in the shade where it's cool," Evan replied.

*They are soldiers from the fighting in the east and both wounded*, Ben thought. *They are like me, damaged, and crippled men.* He knew what they knew, felt what they felt.

The taller of the two men looked at Ben across the tables that separated them. The man's eyes were on Ben for only two or three seconds before he turned away. Still, Ben recognized that the eyes were gentle, and that they had looked through the shadows to the scars on his face.

"Hank, light the damn lamps," one of the cardplayers called out to the bartender. "I'm being robbed here 'cause I can't see my cards."

Hank left the bar and went into a back room. He returned with a short stepladder that he positioned under the lamps, one after another, and lit them. The area around the bar and the card table became illuminated with light, while the remainder of the wide room remained in shadow.

Evan and John ordered two more beers. They drank them slowly as they talked quietly together. Finishing the brews, they rose and started for the door leading onto the street.

The cowboys turned to watch them pass. "Got shot up in the war, eh?" said the blue-shirted man in a mocking voice. "Dumb thing to do for it's not Texas's fight."

Both Evan and John stopped and glanced over their shoulders at the cowboys.

"I thought it was our fight and went," John said.

"Look what it got you," said the blue shirt.

Evan put his hand on John's shoulder. "Our part is over, done with, and not worth arguing about."

"Yeah, you're right," John said.

They again moved, one limping and one with his shoulders hunched, in the direction of the door. The other men at the bar were now watching the wounded soldiers, and so too were the poker players. Ben felt his anger heating at the insulting words of the cowboy.

"There's no argument to be made for fighting in the war," the blue shirt called out in a loud, coarse voice. "We ain't got any slaves."

Ben saw the shorter soldier turn back and start to speak, and again the taller one took hold of him and said something that Ben didn't hear. The shorter man relented to the words of his companion and continued to limp on. Ben's anger was smoking in a corner of his mind. Still, he held himself reined in for he didn't want trouble.

"Any man who went to war was a fool—hell, more than that, just plain stupid," the blue-shirted man called out in a strident voice.

Ben's anger was scorching. He rose, shoving

his chair back with a loud scraping sound. "Say that to me, loudmouth," Ben said in a rough voice.

The sudden challenge froze all movement in the saloon. Then heads swiveled and eyes fastened on the man in the rear corner of the *cantina*. In the shadows, Ben's white shirt stood out like a beacon.

"Tell me I'm a stupid fool," Ben ordered, his words like darts flung through the air at the blue-shirted man. "Tell me what you told those other wounded soldiers."

Ben moved away from his table and into the open space that lay between the tables and the front of the bar. He shoved his hat back to show his face. At the same time he put his hand on the butt of his pistol.

Evan looked into the devil face of the man who had taken insult from the cowboy's words. The flat, deadly way he had spoken and his savage eyes sent a chill along Evan's spine. There was a taut, menacing aura about him, a confident animal ready to fight.

The cowboys saw the readiness of Ben to fight. One spoke hastily to the blue-shirt one. "Better let it go, Rolph," he said.

"Yeah, that's right," added the third man. "I don't want to fight with that fellow. He scares me just looking at him."

"Ugly doesn't mean he's tough," Rolph said.

"He looks tough enough to me," said the third man.

Evan couldn't look away from the scarred man threatening the cowboys. He detected not one ounce of fear in the man, only that willingness to do battle, maybe a desire to start it. He heard two of the cowboys trying to talk the one called Rolph into leaving the *cantina*, and Rolph's words resisting the advice. Then the two cowboys won and all three were moving toward the door.

"You in the blue shirt, apologize to those two wounded soldiers for what you said to them," the devil-faced man ordered.

"Like hell I will," said the blue shirt.

"Do it, you damn coward," Ben said.

The blue-shirt man pivoted around to Ben. "Go to Hell, you ugly bastard." He reached for the pistol in the holster on his side.

*You are the stupid one to draw on a man who already has his hand on his pistol,* Ben thought. He pulled his revolver and shot through the blue cloth covering the man's right shoulder. He knew the .44-caliber bullet would break the bones in the shoulder. Let the man know how it feels to be seriously wounded.

The cowboy was spun to the right by the impact of the large bullet fired from but a few feet away. He crashed into a table, knocked it over, and fell to the floor with it.

His pistol went sliding across the floor. He clutched at his shoulder and began to moan. Ben took a step closer to the two cowboys still on their feet.

"Do you want to try your luck to see if it's better than his?" Ben said.

"It's not our fight," one of the men said quickly. "I tried to get him to let it alone."

"Then sit down there at that table and wait for the sheriff. He'll want to know what happened here. You'd better tell him the straight of it for if you don't, I'll come hunting you."

Ben spoke to the bartender. "Do you know where the doctor's office is?"

"Yes, just a few blocks down the street."

"Go ask him to come here. And bring Sheriff Blackaby back with you so we can settle this matter right now."

"You bet," said the bartender, and hurried from the *cantina*.

All the other men were silent and watching Ben. He didn't see any danger from them. He sat down at a table and laid his gun on top in front of him. Now to see how the sheriff would take the shooting.

Evan and John came across the *cantina* to Ben's table.

Evan spoke to Ben. "May John and I sit with you?"

Ben was surprised at the request, but quickly recovered. "Sure, have a seat," he said.

The two soldiers sat down across the table from Ben.

"We can vouch that he tried to shoot you and you only defended yourself," Evan said.

"That's right," John said. "He had no right to insult us and I'm damn glad you shut him up."

*But I goaded him into pulling a gun,* Ben thought. *So I'm responsible for it coming down to a fight.* He must learn to control his quickness to anger.

# Eighteen

"My name is Evan Payson," Evan said, and put out his hand to Ben.

"Ben Hawkins." Ben shook the offered hand.

"I'm John Davis." He took Ben's hand. "That fellow sure had some mean things to say to us."

"By the expressions of some of the men here, they felt he was right in thinking we had no business in the war," Ben replied.

"It's a divided state on that matter and that's a fact," Evan said. "But he had no right to insult us."

Both Evan and John were looking into Ben's face. They appeared ill at ease at the sight of his mutilated features, but not revolted by them. That was a pleasant thing to Ben. They must have been in the thick of the fighting, and had seen what horrible wounds cannons and mortars and rifles could do to a man. That would account for their willingness to look at him.

The sheriff and doctor, followed by the bartender, came into the *cantina*. The doctor was slender and quite elderly. Sheriff Blackaby was a large, burly man wearing twin revolvers and a belt full of cartridges. He walked with a heavy, no-nonsense step. Both he and the doctor stopped to examine the wounded man.

"How'll he be?" the sheriff asked the doctor.

"He'll live, but may end up having a bad shoulder for there's broken bones."

"Who did the shooting?" said the sheriff, straightening to cast a hard look around.

"I did," Ben said.

The sheriff looked at Ben and at the pistol on the table in front of him. "Put the gun away, Hawkins," he ordered.

Ben picked up the pistol and slid it into its holster. He didn't want any trouble with the lawman. While still a deputy sheriff in El Paso, Ben had met Blackaby. He knew the lawman was tough, but honest and fair in his enforcement of the law. Ben hoped he was lenient with him in this fracas.

The sheriff ran his eyes over the assemblage of men in the cantina. He stopped on a middle-aged man, one of the poker players. "Edgar, you tell the straight of things; did you see all what happened here?" the sheriff asked.

"Yes, Abel, I did."

"Tell me about it."

Edgar related the event, Rolph's words to Evan and John, Ben's challenge, and the shooting.

The sheriff then turned to Ben. "You satisfied that Edgar told it like it happened?" he asked.

"He told it as close as anybody could, so I'll stand by it that way."

The doctor called from where he was treating the wounded man. "Abel, I've done all I can for the man here. Now I need some help to get him to the hospital."

The lawman pointed at a pair of young men standing at the bar. "Would you two help the doc?"

130

"Sure, Sheriff," one of the men said. The other nodded.

The sheriff brought his attention onto Rolph's comrades. "You two run with Rolph, so I'd guess you were with him when this happened. You got anything to say different from what's been said?"

Both men shook their heads in the negative.

"All right then, you can go. Stay out of trouble."

The lawman turned and, including Ben, Evan, and John with a sweep of his eyes, spoke to them. "Edgar said you were insulted for having fought in the war and that led to the shooting. Now I wouldn't like being insulted myself. But I take shootings serious when they happen in my town."

He spoke directly to Ben. "You seem awfully ready to pull a gun. And just a short while ago Thatcher came to see me about buying some horses that you didn't have a bill of sale for. What you do in Mexico is out of my jurisdiction, but selling stolen Valdes horses here in Abilene is my business. Now most people who buy them don't worry about a bill of sale since they once belonged to a Mexican. They remember Goliad and the Alamo. Some of the buyers even fought in the war of '47 and sure don't have any liking for Mexicans. In fact, they're glad to see you doing what you're doing. But I'm bothered by it all. I think it would be best if you left town for a spell, until you change what you do for a living."

Ben rubbed the big scar that ridged down

131

the full left side of his face. He had thought before that the sheriff would sooner or later have a talk with him about the Mexican horses. Now Ben had added to the problem by selling the horses of the men who had killed Black Moon and the two women. The sheriff hadn't mentioned those horses, which meant that he was offering Ben a way out. It would be wise to take it.

"I'm a peaceful man, Sheriff, and want no trouble," Ben said. "I've been planning on visiting El Paso. My mother's buried near there and I should go and put some flowers on her grave."

"Now that sounds like a nice thing for a son to do," said the sheriff.

Ben saw the tenseness leave the sheriff. The man had been prepared to enforce his order, while Ben had absolutely nothing to gain by resisting.

"You'd probably want to leave right away," said the sheriff.

"I was thinking early tomorrow," Ben replied.

"Good," grunted the lawman. He spoke to the bartender. "You can get back to business now." The sheriff hitched up his heavily laden gun belt and strode from the *cantina*.

"Ben, we're going to El Paso," Evan said. "You'd be more than welcome to travel with us. Isn't that right, John?"

"Sure thing," John replied. "There are thieves and Indians between here and there. Another gun could come in handy."

John paused and studied Ben. "I've got a question. There was a deputy sheriff named Ben Hawkins in El Paso a spell back. Are you that deputy?"

"The same," Ben said. He had become deputy sheriff purely by chance. He had won the rifle-shooting contest—the prize was three hundred dollars—that was held yearly in El Paso. He had come in second in the pistol shooting, second to the sheriff of El Paso, Dan Willis. Ben had often wondered how much of his loss at the pistol-shooting contest was due to his final challenger being the sheriff. Anyway, his skill at the match had gotten him the deputy sheriff job, for later that day the sheriff had searched Ben out and offered it. Ben had accepted on the spot. He had already been planning to distance himself from the Mormon community of Canutillo. He had worked as a deputy for but eighteen months before he had gone off on a great adventure to fight for Texas.

"I thought I had the name right," John said. "I remembered it because you were talked about when the sheriff hired you. You know, about a man from Canutillo, and a young one too, becoming a deputy sheriff in El Paso."

"Yes, I was raised in Canutillo." Ben's voice had a flinty tone that said he didn't want any more talk about Canutillo.

Evan spoke quickly to head off any comments John might make about Evan's early life. "We're going to spend the night at the hotel just down the street. Where are you staying?"

"I've got a room in a home off on the edge of town," Ben said.

Evan climbed to his feet. "I'm wore out and need to rest. Stop by in the morning when you get ready to travel and we'll leave together."

"I would like that," Ben said. He meant it. Here were two men who could look him in the face and were willing to travel with him. His lonely, bleak mood was banished, at least for a time.

# Nineteen

Maude knew the other wives of Lester Ivorsen were jealous of her. They tried not to show it, and were succeeding as far as Lester was concerned. However, Maude felt the jealousy as a palpable force filling the big communal room where Lester met with all his wives every evening. Maude was seventeen and the sixth wife.

Lester was seated in a big leather chair positioned with its back against a wall. He was a big-boned, muscular man with sandy-colored hair and gray eyes. His six wives were seated in favorite chairs in a semicircle a dozen feet or so away. Two of the women had babes in arms. The larger of the children of his various wives were seated next to their mothers. The small ones who could walk, regardless of who their mothers were, sat intermingled on the floor at Lester's feet. He was smiling as he talked to the wee ones. He seldom smiled when addressing the wives, or the larger children.

Lester had told Maude that he wanted a child by her. She hoped that never occurred. What little feeling she had held originally for the man had quickly faded during the two months she had been married to him. She knew she had made a terrible mistake in marrying him. *Hurry and end the evening gathering*, she willed silently. *End all the playacting.*

A little blond-headed boy toddled up to Lester's knee and looked up at him. The father lifted the lad and placed him on his lap and held him as he continued to talk with the small children. After a few minutes Lester placed the blond child back on the floor. He pulled his watch and checked the time, as he did every evening when he grew weary of the children.

"Skedaddle to bed," he said to the small ones, and waved them away with his big hand.

Maude watched the children run off laughing. She, same as the other wives and larger children, straightened in her chair and became attentive. Now it was time for Lester to give instructions for tomorrow's operation of his several businesses. Then there would be time for domestic matters, and to settle any disagreements that might have developed between any of his wives.

Lester's rulings were final. Maude recalled

that evening shortly after she had come into the family when Lester had grabbed Alice, wife number five, who was two years older than Maude and had been married to Lester two years, turned her over his knee, and spanked her severely for arguing with him. Maude believed the woman had argued because she was angry with Lester for taking a new and younger wife. The woman had never argued with the man since that day, at least not to Maude's knowledge.

Lester had assigned each wife, with the assistance of her children if they were large enough, the task of operating a specific enterprise. Lester gave overall direction and controlled the flow of money, and banked the profits in his name. Wife number one managed the general store of Canutillo; number two, with her three large sons, operated the cattle ranch in the hills north of town. Then there were the two boardinghouses, and the dress shop to be run. Lester had instructed Maude to work with wife number one, Marie, and learn all the aspects of managing a general store.

Lester completed his instructions for the conduct of the businesses. He again pulled his watch, the signal that he was now going to make his choice of the wife for the night. The procedure for him to do that had been established for years. Maude had learned it the first night of her marriage to Lester. The last one he spoke to in the evening was the one to receive his favors and to prepare herself for him. Lester had chosen Maude practically every night since she had come into the family. She prayed that tonight he would select one of the other wives.

She was certain the other women felt neglected. This evening, as every evening, every one of them had done her best to entice the lusty man to her bed for the night. Each had carefully prepared herself, freshly bathed, hair neatly done, and clothing laundered and ironed. All the children had been presented to their father as well groomed as the mothers.

Maude listened with sinking heart as one after another of the women was dismissed. Lastly Lester looked at her.

"Good night, Maude," Lester said with a penetrating look in his eye.

"Good night," Maude replied.

She left the man standing watching her and went out onto the porch. The building consisted of a large central complex of rooms for communal use and wings extending left and right, each containing three apartments, one for each of the wives. Maude walked toward her newly constructed rooms on the far right end.

The mistake she had made in marrying Lester weighed heavily on her shoulders. Lester was a very handsome man; all of the unmarried girls of Canutillo had spoken among themselves of that. Maude had also thought him handsome. Several of the other men of the town had multiple wives and the young women were used to that, and so Lester's several wives did not seem to concern the girls. He was wealthy, they had said, and a wife of his would never want for anything. They had not recognized the fact that the wives earned their own way by hard work. Maude, once Lester had begun to come to her father's house to court her, had taken special notice of his wives and saw their busy workdays.

She had remained hesitant to accept Lester's proposal of marriage, unsure of her feelings toward him, of how she would fit into the man's large number of wives. However, at the strong urging of her father, a good friend of Lester, she had finally been swayed to accept the man's proposal.

Now she knew that having a handsome husband could never compensate for all the heartaches of being wife number six. Or for even being number two, Maude was certain. She should have defied her father. She wanted out of the marriage. That wasn't easy to do in the small, closed community. She had mentioned to her father that she wanted to leave Lester. Her father had flown into a rage and forbidden it. So Maude had developed a plan. All was in readiness. She just needed a head start.

She entered her apartment, where the odor of the new plaster was still noticeable. There was but a few minutes before Lester would arrive. She gathered her boots, pants, shirt, and hat, and hid them in the chest that sat under the window near the front door.

She had barely closed the chest lid when

Lester shoved open the door and came inside. He immediately took Maude into his arms and crushed her to him. He kissed her roughly.

Maude steeled herself to endure the next hour or so, until Lester tired and went to sleep.


Lester's deep breathing, brought about by his exertion during the lovemaking, had eased and now came slow and regular. Still, Maude lay motionless in the darkness of the bedroom and waited. His arm rested across her breast, and she must be sure he slept before she tried to remove it.

She looked up at the ceiling, invisible in the darkness of the room, and listened carefully to the man. Was he truly asleep, or had he somehow guessed her intention and was now only pretending so as to trick her? Had she unknowingly given herself away by some action? She must not make a mistake for should Lester catch her trying to run away, he would surely hurt her.

Maude cautiously took hold of Lester's arm and lifted it, and slowly began to slide from under. She had moved only inches when the man's breathing halted. She froze. But then after a few beats of her pounding heart, Lester recommenced his regular breathing. She moved on and was clear, and lowered the man's arm to the bed.

She came to her feet and, naked, crept across the room and to the chest near the front door. Careful not to make a sound, she dressed in the riding clothes from the chest. She went out the door and hastened through the light of the three-quarter moon to the rear yard, and onward to the barn and corral behind the communal house. She wanted to be miles away when daylight arrived.

In the corral, Maude whistled softly for the gray mare. The horse came trotting. Maude had been feeding the mare tidbits from the garden and orchard for days so that it would come at her call. She led the mare into the barn, full of the odors of fresh-cut hay, manure, and feed grain, and to the half-dozen bridles and saddles that hung on a long, waist-high rail. With practiced skill she slipped the bridle on the mare's head and fastened the saddle upon her back.

Maude looked out the big double barn door toward the house and watched for movement. Had she been seen or heard? The house loomed dark and foreboding in the night. She saw nothing move around the house or in the yard.

Hurriedly she went into the gloom of the room at the end of the barn and retrieved a blanket roll from where she had hidden it behind the sacks of feed grain. Wrapped inside the blanket were enough provisions for three days and a canteen of water. The blanket roll was tied behind the saddle of the mare.

Maude climbed astride the mare and reined it toward the yard. Freedom lay but seconds away. She pulled a trembling breath of the moonlit air. She was going to make it, make her escape.

She jerked, shocked. The figure of a tall man had stepped into the open doorway. He stretched out his arms to block her way.

"Going somewhere, Maude?" Lester asked.

*Oh, my God,* thought Maude. *I'm so near. So near.* She screamed and kicked the mare with her heels.

The startled horse lunged forward directly at the man in front of it. More swiftly than the horse, the man dodged aside, and at the same time his long arm reached out. Maude leaned far to the side to avoid the extended arm. But she couldn't move far enough and the strong arm hooked her, and raked her from the saddle. She rolled backward across the rump of the animal and tumbled to the hard ground.

Lester was upon Maude instantly. He grabbed her by the shirtfront and the hair of her head and hoisted her to her feet.

Half unconscious and with legs too weak to hold her, Maude started to fall. Lester, his hands tearing at her hair as he lifted, again set her on her feet.

"Stand up, woman. You're not hurt that bad."

The pain from her pulled hair helped Maude to draw back from the partial unconsciousness caused by the fall. She stiffened her legs and stood erect.

"Turn me loose," Maude said. She twisted suddenly and was free.

Lester reached out swiftly and caught her

by both shoulders. He dug his fingers painfully into her flesh. "Now you wouldn't leave your loving husband, would you?" His fingers stabbed more deeply. "None of my wives ever will, unless I want them to."

"Get your hands off me," Maude said, fighting the fear that chilled her.

"Soon," Lester said. He drew Maude closer.

"Don't you dare spank me," Maude said belligerently.

"Why, that's not what I had in mind." He released Maude and slapped her left and right with his large, bony hands. Maude's head snapped back and forth. Immediately he slapped her twice more.

Maude staggered under the onslaught of blows, and a multitude of red stars wheeled and exploded in her brain. Blood from her split lips was suddenly salt and copper in her mouth. She fought not to fall, waiting for the whirling, flaming stars to burn out. Finally she straightened to an upright position.

"See, no spanking," Lester said. "But if you ever try to leave again, I'll beat you black and blue from your ass to the top of your head. Do you hear me?"

Maude heard the threat, but remained mute. The man's blows upon her body had hurt, and for a moment she had been frightened, but in the end they had hardened her determination to escape. This wasn't the last of her attempts to flee. It was only the first.

In the moonlight, Lester saw Maude's cold, defiant stare, and her face with its bloody mouth rigid as stone. The woman was an iron-jawed beauty. He had watched her grow up and had known she would be difficult to control. He had desired her even when she was still a child, a hazel-eyed, silver-blond girl running about the streets of Canutillo. As she grew and rounded into a woman, her hair had darkened to a golden blond. She was more exciting by twofold than any of his other wives. He would never let her go.

"Get back to the house," Lester ordered. "And don't ever come close to one of the horses again." He spun her to the rear. "Move!" he ordered.

"Hurry it," he said, and struck her a stinging blow across the hips with his hand.

# *Twenty*

"Something's rotten here, Tattersall," Adkisson said, a worried frown on his hard face.

"I smell it too," Tattersall replied. "They've never made us wait like this before."

"And we know the colonel's right there inside and could buy the scalps," Snyder added.

"Best we get ready for trouble," Tattersall said. "If they want our guns, don't give them up. If they try to take us prisoner, we'll shoot the bastards that try, and ride like hell out of here."

Tattersall and his band of scalp hunters squatted in the shade under the roofed patio in front of the army commandant's office. Their horses were tied to wooden posts close by. The gang had arrived in Chihuahua in the early morning, and had ridden directly to the large walled military compound with its garrison of soldiers on the south side of the city. A lieutenant had come out of the headquarters building and told them to wait and Colonel Vasquez, the commandant, would see them soon. That had been three hours ago, and Tattersall was becoming ever more worried and angry.

A man never knew what to expect when he rode into Chihuahua. The city officials and the Army officers of the local garrison were changed at the whim of El Presidente in Mexico City. Government policies were changed even more frequently, and Tattersall had heard no news for weeks. Perhaps the governor had revoked his order to pay bounty for Apache scalps. Now the killing of the Indians might be considered murder and the commandant would arrest him and his men. That could only end one way, with a firing squad.

Nothing was permanent in Mexico except the hatred the Mexican people and government felt for Americans. The gringos had beaten their Army in 1836 and taken Texas. Then in 1847 the gringos had again defeated them and stolen all that huge land area of New Mexico, Arizona, California, and part of Colorado. In that eleven-year period of 1836 to 1847,

144

Mexico had lost two thirds of its country to the gringos.

Tattersall watched the squads of soldiers, several hundred in total, drill and sweat on the far end of the broad, dusty parade ground that lay enclosed within the walled compound. Closer to the scalpers, a company of armed cavalrymen was practicing a fast, intricate maneuver with their horses. At a command of the drill captain, a squad of thirty cavalrymen split off from the main body and rode to halt and sit their horses on the edge of the parade ground.

Tattersall saw the position of the men put them between him and the gate that led from the compound. He wondered if that movement of men was just a coincidence. The Mexican cavalrymen were some of the best horsemen in the world, and he didn't want them chasing him.

Tattersall knew that hunting Apaches and selling their scalps was the fastest and easiest way to make big money. For that reason, once each year he rode into the garrison of crack fighting men and placed his head into a trap from which he might not be able to withdraw it. He hoped this wasn't the day the trap closed upon him.

Officers came and went from the commandant's office. Tattersall, wary and his senses whetted, scrutinized the men's faces as they came past, especially the younger ones, for they had less skill at hiding their thoughts. He looked into their dark eyes and saw the old hatred for the Americans, and the desire for revenge against them. The commandant had but to issue the order.

A *caballero* rode up on a beautiful roan horse and dismounted from a saddle that was heavily encrusted with silver. He tied his mount to one of the posts and came toward the commandant's office. He was tall for a Mexican, and dressed all in brown clothing tailored to fit closely to his trim frame. Silver braid adorned his huge sombrero, and the front and sleeves of his short jacket, and down the outside hem of his trousers. The holster of his Colt revolver was heavily inlaid with the bright metal.

As he walked past the Americans squatting in the shade, the *caballero* raked them with piercing black eyes. At the entryway of the commandant's office, the two armed soldiers stiffened to sharp attention. The *caballero* brushed past them without hesitation. Tattersall heard the ringing chime of the Mexican's big silver spurs grow silent deep inside the building.

"He's a walking silver mine," Adkisson said. "And look at that saddle and bridle with all the silver. We could kidnap him and make a fortune in ransom money."

"Shut up," Tattersall hissed. "Don't even joke about that. That's Ramos Valdes. He runs this part of Mexico. You cross him and the whole Mex Army would be after you."

The lieutenant who had told the Americans to wait came and stood in the door leading to the commandant's office. He motioned with his hand. "Señor Tattersall, would you come inside? Your men are to remain where they are."

Tattersall picked up the bag of scalps lying on the ground by his side and rose to his feet. He would soon know what the colonel had planned for him.

"You heard the lieutenant," Tattersall said in a loud voice. Then, in a low voice meant only for his men, he said, "Don't budge from here. And damn sure be ready to shoot and ride."

Tattersall fell in behind the officer. The man had come for him immediately upon the arrival of Valdes. Tattersall knew he had been kept waiting until the important man had ridden in. But what did the rich *caballero* have to do with buying Apache scalps? Perhaps it was something else, something Tattersall might have done against Valdes. He raked his mind, but couldn't recall having ever stolen anything from the man, or in any way crossing him. Still, his nerves tightened.

They went past the sentries and down a long hallway to the commandant's office. The room was large with two desks, a big one behind which Colonel Vasquez was seated, and a smaller one off on the side. The lieutenant proceeded to the second desk and sat down. Two armed soldiers were just inside the door. The moment Tattersall halted in front of the colonel's desk, the soldiers took up positions one on each side of him. They had been given orders and stood vigilant.

Tattersall glanced to the rear of the room, where Valdes was seated by a window where a little breeze was finding its way inside the warm room. The man looked steadily back without expression at the American. The *caballero* was part of whatever was planned, something Tattersall couldn't yet fathom. He was glad for the weight of the two pistols on his sides. He would show them some sharp pistol work if they tried to arrest him. Valdes would be the first to die for he was the most dangerous.

"Good day, Señor Tattersall," Colonel Vasquez said. "I understand you have some business with me."

"Same as last year," Tattersall said. "Some hair trophies to sell you."

"Lieutenant, examine them," the colonel said.

The lieutenant came and took the sack and then returned to his desk. He scowled as he removed the scalps, stiff with dried blood, from the sack. He began to examine each closely for the coarseness of the hair, its length, and the color. Then each was laid aside in one of two piles.

Tattersall knew the officer was looking for scalps that might have come from *mestizos*, people of mixed Indian and Spanish blood, gentle citizens of Mexico. Should he decide there were *mestizos'* scalps in the collection, then Tattersall was in trouble.

The lieutenant glanced at the American scalper. Tattersall stared back confidently. He grinned a crooked, comprehending grin. These were all genuine Apache scalps.

*You're a loathsome son of a whore*, the lieutenant thought. He went back to the grisly task of counting the remnants of once-living, breathing human beings.

The lieutenant finished counting, and made his tally of the bounty. "Colonel, the sum is twelve thousand six hundred pesos."

"Is that amount correct?" the colonel asked Tattersall.

"His count is right." Tattersall hid his relief, for it appeared the sale was going to come off without a fuss.

"Bring the required sum," the colonel directed the lieutenant.

"Yes, sir." The lieutenant went through a door at the rear of the room. Shortly the lieutenant reappeared with a wooden tray of fifty-peso gold pieces and went to his desk. He counted out the gold coins and placed them in neat stacks on the front of his desk.

"There's your pay," the colonel said, chucking a thumb at the gold.

Tattersall pulled a leather pouch from a pocket and moved to the desk. This was the most dangerous time for him. While his hands were busy putting the coins in the pouch, the Mexicans could shoot him. He knew they were not above such a trick.

With quick swipes of his hand, Tattersall raked the coins into the pouch. Instantly he pivoted, bringing his right hand close to his pistol for a fast draw if there was danger. The Mexicans hadn't moved.

A smile of contempt was on the colonel's face.

*To hell with you*, Tattersall thought. "Good day, Colonel, it's been good doing business with you," he said.

The colonel merely nodded in dismissal. He picked up one of the papers from his desk and began to study it.

Tattersall shrugged, turned, and left the room and went down the hallway to the outside. He moved along the patio toward his men. They all came to their feet and waited expectantly.

Behind Tattersall came the thud of boots on the hard ground and the chiming of Ramos Valdes's big silver spurs. *Damn it, I knew Valdes was going to be trouble.*

The *caballero* called out to Tattersall in a flat voice. "Señor Tattersall, I believe you are the man I've been looking for."

Tattersall came to a slow halt, giving himself some time to again try to recall why Valdes would have a grudge against him. Hell, it was too late to worry about that now. He coiled, prepared to draw his pistol and shoot, and turned to face Valdes.

Valdes saw the American tense at his words. The man might have taken the wrong meaning from them. Valdes moved both hands away from his sides and raised them slightly.

"Would you like to earn five thousand dollars in gold?" Valdes asked.

Tattersall, seeing Valdes's hands were not near his holstered pistol, eased his tight muscles. The man didn't want to fight. Tattersall evaluated Valdes. The man was at the most fifty years old, young for what he had accumulated in wealth. He was dark enough to possess some Indian blood, yet he was thin-lipped and had a long, aristocratic Spanish nose. Tattersall had heard a tale that the man had a white gringo woman for a wife. The tale went that as a young man he had made a raid into the States and carried off a beautiful American woman, and kept her locked up in his huge hacienda in the mountains.

"A man can never have too much gold," Tattersall said.

"Then let us find a place to talk where we won't be overheard," Valdes said.


"One thousand in gold now and four thousand when he's dead," Valdes said, taking a purse from a pocket inside his vest and placing it on the table in front of Tattersall.

The scalper never looked away from Valdes's black eyes. The Mexican had become rich and powerful by outmaneuvering his weaker competitors, and ruthlessly destroying the stronger ones. Now he was offering to pay ten times too much for killing a man. Tattersall's spine crawled with the feeling that there was more to this offer than the man said.

Tattersall and Valdes were seated in a *cantina* on the El Camino Real that ran through the center of Chihuahua City. Tattersall's men were at a table nearby.

He didn't trust Valdes, and had ordered the men to drink no more than one *cerveza* each, and not to go off with one of the brown-skinned whores smiling and strutting enticingly about the room.

"It's a matter of honor to kill this hombre Hawkins," Valdes said, reading the American's thoughts. "People know he has successfully stolen from me. Also, he must be stopped from stealing more of my great horses."

"Where can I find this Ben Hawkins?" Tattersall would play along with the Mexican until he gave away more of his game.

"In Abilene or El Paso. He sells the horses in Abilene. He has relatives in El Paso, or rather in Canutillo, which is but a short distance north of there. I suggest you start at El Paso. He has just sold several of my horses and probably has gone home to brag about his success."

"All right, El Paso it is."

"So you agree to hunt and kill him?"

"I'll take the job. We were heading north anyway."

"When can you start?"

"For this kind of money, right now," Tattersall said.

"*Excelente*. But not today. Start tomorrow morning. I will tell Carlos and Leo to prepare to leave with you."

"Who? Why?"

"Carlos and Leo are my sons. If you cannot kill Hawkins, they will."

"We don't need help to kill one man. Hell, I can kill him by my lonesome."

"Do not underestimate this hombre Hawkins. He will not be easy to kill."

"Bullshit!" exclaimed Tattersall. "No man is too tough for me."

"Carlos and Leo will meet you here at daybreak tomorrow," Valdes said, ignoring the scalper's outburst.

"I said I don't want them."

"They go, or we have no agreement. Besides, how will you be paid when Hawkins is dead?"

Tattersall stared across the table at the Mexican. "So your sons will have the money with them, is that it?"

"No." Did the man really think he would send his sons off with him carrying such a large amount of gold? "But they can draw it from the bank in Ciudad Juarez just across the Rio Grande from El Paso."

"All right then. If that's what you want, that's the way it'll be." Tattersall picked up the pouch of gold. "If they're late, we leave without them."

"They will not be late." Valdes rose to his feet and looked down at the scalper. "Be very careful what you say to Carlos and Leo. They anger quickly and will shoot the man who insults them."

Tattersall grinned. "I'm scared already."

"Listen closely to what I'm telling you." Valdes's voice was heavy with a warning. "I want you to kill Hawkins, not fight my sons." On the heel of a boot, Valdes pivoted away from the scalper. The American was suspicious, but that was a long way from knowing. With his silver spurs chiming, a sound that Valdes like to hear, he went across the *cantina* and out the door.

Tattersall was locked in thought as he watched the *caballero* leave the *cantina*. Why had Valdes forced his two sons on him? The reason Valdes had given, that they would draw money from the bank in Ciudad Juarez to pay Tattersall, was logical. Perhaps that was all there was to it.

The two Mexicans rode the most beautiful horses Tattersall had ever seen.

Tattersall and his band of gunmen sat their mounts in front of the *cantina* and watched the armed men draw close. Carlos and Leo were easy to identify for they were close copies of their father Ramos. They even dressed like Ramos. The only difference Tattersall could see was that their skins were much lighter in color and they had blue eyes. Perhaps Ramos did have a gringa for a wife.

Carlos and Leo seemed to swagger even seated upon their horses. Being the sons of a very powerful man, they must believe they owned the world, at least this part of it.

"*Ustedes listos?*" Tattersall said. *Are you ready?*

"We are both ready," Carlos replied. "My father wants this thing done quickly so we should not waste time talking." His English was excellent.

"Well, we don't want to disappoint the great man," Tattersall said. "Let's ride."

The band of gunmen spurred their horses off along the street. Carlos and Leo gently

154

tapped their mounts with spurs, and the animals in half a dozen strides had overtaken the Americans and were running side by side with them.

The band of hunters hurried north on the ancient El Camino Real.

# Twenty-one

The July sun blazed down from a sky bleached to a shimmering gray by the intensity of its rays. The flat Llano Estacado fumed and hot updrafts soared. No bird rode the elevators of wind rushing skyward, nor did any animal of the ground venture out, but instead they hid in their cool burrows, or in the shade cast by the few stunted bushes. Only the five horses moved on all the broad land, and their gait was a slow walk.

Riders were mounted upon three of the horses, and they sat with bodies drooping and shoulders hunched against the scorching heat. The two remaining horses were pack animals. The riders were two days west of Abilene.

"Goddamn, it's hot," John said as he wiped sweat from his face with a bandana.

"Even for Texas," Evan added. "We need to find shade and get out of the sun."

"The Colorado River shouldn't be far ahead, maybe ten miles," Ben said. "There'll be plenty of shade there, and fresh water from the springs along the riverbank.

"You up to it, Evan?"

"Do I have a choice?" Evan said.

The men fell silent, locked within the realm of their own private thoughts.


The bloodred sun was sinking into the bottomless pit behind the rim of the world when the three riders reached the Colorado River. They guided their mounts and the packhorses out onto the bank above the river and surveyed the quarter-mile-wide valley of the river below them.

The Colorado was a blue-green strip of water meandering back and forth as it made its way south down the valley. One loop of the river was but a few hundred feet in front of the men. Several oxbows, abandoned meanders of the river, partially filled with aged, stagnant water, lay here and there on the flat bottomland. Broad expanses of dark green marsh areas of willows, sedges, and tall, rank grass crowded each other for growing room in the low, wet spots. On the edges of the marsh where the sites were slightly drier, large cottonwoods grew. The periphery of the green oasis of the river was dotted with huge walnut trees.

"This Colorado River sure ain't big as the one in the Arizona Territory," John said.

"You've seen that one?" Ben asked.

"Yep. About seven years ago. It's wide and

deep enough for big steamboats to come up from the ocean and the Gulf of California to Arizona City."

"What were you doing there?" Ben asked.

"Another fellow and I went there to work in the silver mines near Arizona City. I want to tell you we saw something strange. The town's ferry slides on a long steel cable that's stretched over the river. The ferry can be made to cross the river just by being angled this way and that way against the current. The river water hitting the slanting side of the ferry just simply pushes it back and forth from one bank to the other."

"I've heard about that ferry," Ben said.

"Let's not sit here in the sun and talk," Evan said. "There's shade under that big walnut tree."

He reined his mount to the side toward the tree. The horse had taken but two steps when one of its front feet broke through the crust of the bank and the animal went to its knees.

The wild boar slept soundly on the cool, damp earth in the shade of the hollow beneath the undercut riverbank. He was big and black, and at the moment his nose was twitching and moving up and down with his dreaming, as if he were rooting for a tasty, buried tidbit.

A piece of dirt broke loose from the roof of the bank overhang above the boar and fell to strike him on the side of the head. He grunted in a coarse bass tone and his ears flared. He jerked to consciousness and his head rose to look at the ceiling. Something large and heavy was shaking the ground directly over his head. More clods showered down upon him from the dirt roof.

The boar came to his feet in one swift movement. He snorted loudly in alarm.

The leg of a horse crashed through the thin, weak top of the bank overhang and landed upon the boar. His snort changed to a shrill squeal and he flung himself into open sunlight. He had no thought of direction or destination. He only knew safety lay elsewhere. With his short, muscular legs driving like pistons, he raced away plowing through the marsh grass of the river bottom.

Ben yanked his rifle from its scabbard and snapped it to his shoulder. He tracked the running hog in the grassy vegetation of the marsh. The front sight settled on the animal and then the rear sight came into alignment. He fired.

The black boar felt the pain from the strike of the bullet and that served to drive him to greater exertion. But something was wrong; the sturdy legs that had never failed him began to fail him now. They swiftly weakened, and instead of tearing through the tough grass, became entangled in it. He went down hard on his stomach.

He tried to rise, but could not. He tried to look around, but could not lift his head. The world around him faded, and then went black forever.

"Fresh ham for supper," John yelled gleefully.

"A damn fine shot, Ben." John uncoiled his lariat. "I'll get him," he said.

He cautiously walked his cayuse out into the mud and grass. With a deft toss of the lariat, he snared the boar's snout just above the tusks, tightened the loop there where it would not slide loose, and dragged the body to the dry land.

"We have a shady camp and fresh meat," Evan said in a pleased voice.

"We're in Comanche territory," Ben said. "That shot could've been heard. I'll find a high spot and keep watch for a while."

"I'll carve out a big piece of ham from that boy and cook up the best feast you fellows ever had," John said.


The lookout point Ben had selected was downwind of the fire John had kindled, and the aroma of the cooking ham came to him. The smell of the food made his mouth water. It also caused a pleasant mood to come over him for soon he would be eating with John and Evan, two men for whom he had a strong feeling of comradeship. It was good that he had found them, soldiers who had been wounded terribly in war like himself and now showed no revulsion at sight of his horrible face.

"Meat's ready," John called.

Ben came down from the raised point of land and joined with Evan, who had lain resting under a tree, and they went together to take seats on the ground where John had spread the food.

"That looks great," Ben said. "And I'm damn hungry."

John had taken provisions from the pack-saddles, and now in addition to a huge chunk of roasted ham steaming and dripping juice, there were hot bread, canned peaches in heavy syrup, cheese, and tins of sardines.

"Hurry up and hand me one of those tin plates," Evan said to John.

The men loaded their plates with thick slices of ham, cut with their belt knives, and sardines, wedges of pan bread, and cheese. The sweet peaches went for dessert. They ate heartily.

"The leg hurts, eh?" Ben said.

"Yeah, now and again," John said as he rubbed his damaged, badly scarred leg. "A cannonball exploded and a piece of it like to rip my leg off here just above the knee."

He looked at Ben. "Godawful thing to see one of your legs just barely hanging on."

The men had swum and bathed, and now sat on flat rocks near the river's edge with their feet in the cool water. Evan had not swum, but only bathed, and now slept on the grass beneath one of the trees growing several yards back from the river.

"You're lucky to still have a leg with that kind of wound," Ben said.

"It was a hell of a bad one, all right, with the

flesh ripped and torn and the broken ends of the bones sticking out, but it wasn't luck that I still have it," John replied, still massaging his leg.

He looked at Evan lying in the grass on a blanket. "Wasn't luck at all. Evan saved it for me."

"How so?"

John turned back to Ben. "Well, several hundred of us tried to break out of Vicksburg through the Yankees' lines when they were shelling the hell out of us. We thought that with all the dust and smoke in the air and the wind blowing it back over their lines, and with all the noise, that we could maybe make it past them. That's when I was hit. Yankees took me prisoner. I come to with a couple of their surgeons having me on a table and getting ready to cut my leg off."

John chucked a thumb in Evan's direction. "Then this other surgeon comes in. He takes a look and says to the others, let's try to save this fellow's leg. That was Evan, the youngest one of them. This head surgeon says that it'll never heal right and that it'll get gangrene. Evan says, if it does, then we'll cut it off. He really said amputate, but that means the same damn thing. I was one sick fellow, but I saw the others didn't like Evan bucking them. They said, you go ahead and try to save it, and they both left. And by God, Evan did save it and I didn't get gangrene."

"Some story. I didn't know Evan was a surgeon."

"The best Grant had in his army. I heard that the general had given orders that if he was ever wounded that only Evan should doctor him."

John extended his leg and looked at it. "With a wooden leg, I'd have a hell of a time getting a woman. Now with this leg, even if I limp, I think one would marry me. Hell, by using my leg I'll probably get to walking even better than I am now."

An embarrassed flush swept over John's features and he looked quickly at Ben's scarred face. "I'm sorry I said that, that about getting a woman."

"It's all right," Ben said, hiding his emotions. "I hope you do get a good woman."

"How'd you get yours?"

"A cannonball saw me as a target and hit me," Ben said shortly. "Do you think Evan would operate on my face?"

John looked doubtful. "He had me give away all his surgical instruments. Damn fine steel set too. Told me he made an oath that never again would he cut on a man. Still, you might ask him. The worst he can say is no. If he did agree, you'd be getting the best there was."

# Twenty-two

Evan lay in the deepening dusk of evening and watched the valley of the Colorado River fill with purple shadows. The breeze moving the leaves of the walnut tree above him was still hot, but the peak of the day's heat was gone with the vanished sun. In the darkening sky, the nighthawks hunted.

The nighthawks were nimble birds, gray in color, with streamlined bodies and narrow tapered wings spanning nearly a foot. At least half a hundred of them hunted within his view along the river. They darted and dove, turning on a wing tip to catch the night insects rising up from the lush vegetation by the water. They called out with shrill shrieks as they chased their evening meal. They snagged the living morsels of meat from the aerial larder with quick mouths and swallowed them whole.

Many times as a boy, Evan had seen the amazingly agile nighthawks feed with their wild acrobatics. He had lain on the ground as he did now and watched them weave about through the evening skies in a feeding frenzy. The sight always brought pleasant memories.

After eating and a nap, he felt stronger. He was healing, with the bullet wound totally closed and only the bright pink scar remaining. The injured lung had regained part of its capacity to draw air. He knew it would never be totally whole. There had been too much damage done to it. He had seen men function with but one lung. He had one lung and half of the other, so eventually he should be able to perform nearly to his previous vigorous level.

Ben and John were within Evan's view sitting near the river's edge. They were talking, and he could hear their voices but could not make out the words. Brutus grazed on the riverbank near Ben. Evan smiled as the thought came to him that the horse acted more like a huge dog than a horse. Brutus never let Ben get far away. Frequently he would raise his head from grazing to check his master's location. If Ben moved beyond fifty yards or so, the horse would close the distance, and then again begin to graze, or stand surveying the land all around.

Evan saw Ben leave John and come toward him through the shadows. He squatted beside Evan.

"Evan, John said you're a surgeon. That so?"

"I was," Evan replied, looking into the man's shattered face. In the gloom of night, the man's appearance was gruesome.

"He said you're the best that ever was. That you saved his leg when other surgeons wanted to amputate it."

"There's some truth to that." Evan was immediately afraid of where the conversation was heading. "I was lucky enough to help, but most healing is done by a person's own body."

164

"Did General Grant appoint you his personal surgeon?"

"He did do that."

"When he had hundreds of them to choose from?"

"Less than one hundred. We were always short of surgeons."

"Still, he chose you." Ben studied Evan, who had now risen to a sitting position. The man had a tense, wary expression, and Ben believed he was thinking of the oath he had made to never perform surgery again.

"I've got a favor to ask you, Evan. I want you to fix my face."

"I can't do that."

"Does that mean you can't or you won't?"

"Both."

"Both? Don't play games with me. Look at me, damn it. I'm a monster."

Evan shuddered, and Ben saw it. Still, Ben drove ahead. "I want to look human again. I think you can do that for me."

"I've cut the flesh of too many men. I can't stand to do it again." He held up his hands and examined them in the half-light. "Do you know how many arms and legs these have severed from men's bodies? Hundreds, Ben, hundreds. And dozens of men have died from the pain while I cut and sawed away on them. I just couldn't save them, no matter how hard I tried."

Evan's whole body was shaking now. "I'll never take a scalpel or saw in my hands again. Not for you, Ben. Not for anybody. I couldn't stand for another man to die with my knife cutting his flesh."

A heartrending moan escaped Evan, and he lowered his hands and clenched them together in his lap to stop their trembling. The thought of cutting into Ben's face made him almost vomit. Never, never would he agree to it. His growing revulsion to performing as a surgeon had begun months ago. The last days as a surgeon with the general's army had been horrible. Yet he was a soldier, and had continued to perform his duty and operate on the wounded. Then at the last, he had made the oath to himself, and with that done he had thought he would have some peace from the heartrending images of men dying under his hands. Instead, with every day that passed, he was repelled more and more from his profession.

"Don't give me a crybaby story," Ben said harshly, boring in. "Your actions didn't kill them. The goddamn war caused the wounds and the pain that killed them."

He caught Evan by the shoulder. "I'm asking you again, help me get shut of this face that scares even grown men."

"I'm not going to operate on you," Evan said, controlling his voice with a determined effort. He pulled loose from Ben's hands. "And anyway, several operations spaced over months would be required. One to do so much, then time to heal, then another operation, and time to heal, and so on. I would have to literally cut your face away from the whole side of your skull and start rebuilding and shaping from the beginning. The pain would kill you, or drive you mad."

Ben threw back his head and laughed, the sound ringing with bitterness and as hard and brittle as the clang of metal upon metal.

"You don't know what real pain is. The pain of being so ugly that it drives you mad." *Or how near I came to killing myself, and only a wolf that was probably as mad as I was stopping me.* "I can take the pain. Whatever amount there is of it."

"It would kill you."

"No, it won't. When we're ready to begin, dose me as best you can with laudanum and cut away."

"I'm not going to do it."

"I've saved eight thousand dollars. It's all yours for helping me to be a man again and not a sideshow freak."

"No amount of money will change my mind. I'm just not going to do it."

"You're a selfish bastard," Ben said with disgust.

"Goddamn you, Ben!" Evan growled, openly angry. "No man can't say that to me." He started to rise to his feet.

"Stay down there, Evan. I don't want you swinging at me. I can whip you with one hand, but I don't want to hit you." Ben knew he had gone too far in calling Evan a selfish bastard. The man had a right to be a surgeon, or not be one.

"I apologize, Evan. I was wrong in saying that to you."

Evan remained there halfway to his feet, staring through the gloom at Ben. Then he dropped back to the ground. "Maybe I am selfish, but that's the way it's going to be."

Without another word, Ben stood erect and went into the night.

For a long time Ben sat morosely on the riverbank and thought of his conversation with Evan. He had so desperately wished Evan would agree to work on his face, to take away some of the ugliness, no matter how little. But between the wish and the thing was a whole world. Life had a bitter taste.

Ben pulled away from his anger at Evan for refusing to help him. He focused on the night, the murmur of the water flowing past at his feet, and the chittering song of the insects of the darkness. The night creatures seemed especially tuneful. The half-moon was overhead and was casting a beautiful silver light down upon the water of the river. There was beauty around him and he could see it, hear it. He was the only ugly thing in all the night.

Ben couldn't continue to travel with the two men after the argument with Evan. His quick temper had robbed him of that pleasant association. He rose and whistled Brutus to him.

He collected his belongings and loaded his packhorse. Without a word to the other two men, he rode into the darkness, and onward through the night and into the next day. At noon, he finally halted in a clump of trees growing in a hidden place. He lay down to rest. Sleep came fitfully, and he dreamed with the image of his face in the water of the spring haunting him.

# Twenty-three

Marcella was exhausted, yet she continued to walk in her endless circling of the camp. She felt her way with her feet for in the deep darkness of the night, the ground beneath her was invisible. The moon had long ago deserted the sky and the faraway stars were mere pinpricks of light and cast no rays down on the prairie. She managed to hold the camp as the center of her circle by viewing the outlines of the buggy and the tethered horses against the sky.

Karl still lay in their blankets. She knew he would be awake and listening to her passage through the tall prairie grass. He was always watching her. His never-ending spying was awfully aggravating.

They had passed through Abilene with but one short halt to replenish their provisions and to have a blacksmith replace a horseshoe that one of the horses had lost. They were now far west of that town. The camp had been made on the open plain when night overran them.

Marcella had slept for a portion of the

night, then had awakened, as she often did, and lay fretting about the lack of memory of her past life. Unable to remain quietly on the blankets with Karl, she had dressed and begun her pacing through the darkness.

The days since coming to consciousness with a strange man as a husband, and the swift, daylight-to-dark journey across the land, had left her bewildered. Her presence in this time and place seemed unreal and she felt lost. Even her husband had an unreal feeling about him. Worse still, each day that passed was adding to her fear that she would never remember her past.

She sensed a great urgency to remember the past. Somehow she knew there was danger in not knowing. She wanted desperately to discover the nature of the danger, and where it would come from so that it could be avoided. Frightened by her certainty that there was danger, Marcella spent most of every day trying to peer backward into that gulf of nothingness and bring forth something of substance, a picture, a word. The return of the woman she had seen that one time before would have been a godsend. To identify one person could perhaps open a door that led to a series of remembrances, to the complete history of her existence.

At the thought of the woman, a thin ghostly whisper of a woman came out of the darkness on the prairie.

"Rachel," the voice said.

Marcella spun to the right from where the

sound had seemed to come. Her eyes stabbed at the darkness. "Who's there!" she whispered.

She waited for a reply, and her eyes battled the darkness lying thick on the land. "Talk to me," Marcella pleaded. "Who are you?"

Marcella caught herself. The voice wasn't real. There was no living woman out there on the black prairie and calling to her. Yet she knew it was real in that it must come from somewhere in her memory. And it sounded so very familiar. She held the voice tightly, concentrating on its timbre, its inflection, striving to remember whose it was.

No answer would come, and she was angry at herself. Why couldn't she make herself remember? Her mind seemed perfectly fine in all other things.

She cried out with frustration. The cry was lost in the murky depths of the plain.

She relented from her effort to discover the owner of the voice. However, she stored it carefully away for later recall and investigation. There was the other question. Who was this Rachel the voice had called out to?

Marcella again took up her pacing. Around and around the camp she went. She saw the gray twilight come creeping in from the far regions of the east. It gave way gradually to the day and the plain became visible, stretching away beyond the limits of her vision. A wind arrived with the morning and the tall, wild grass began to run before it.

Marcella looked out over the prairie with the

waving grass making it appear to be moving. There was not one rise of land to slow the wind, not one animal within sight. The emptiness of the land brought a disconsolate feeling to her of just how insignificant a woman was. She, who had no memory to give life a foundation, was merely a dream woman and did not matter at all.

"Marcella, it's late," Karl called. "I've got the horses harnessed. Let's get on our way."

Karl's voice was sharp, commanding, and Marcella hated the tone. He was becoming ever more domineering the farther west they traveled. The thought of leaving him and striking out on her own was growing strong.

"I'm coming," she called back.

Two hours into the day, Marcella and Karl came to a river. As they approached the ford, she saw two men breaking camp under a big tree down the river a ways. Both men turned to look at the buggy and its occupants. The taller of the two raised his hand in greeting.

The men were too far away for Marcella to see them clearly. Still, the man's gesture seemed friendly and she lifted her hand in reply.

"Don't do that," Karl snapped. "They may be going our way and we don't want strangers tagging along with us."

"Nobody could keep up with us even if they wanted to," Marcella said heatedly.

"Just do as I say," Karl retorted. He struck the horses with the whip and drove the buggy down the last slant of the bank and out onto the rock-ribbed ford. The team splashed their way across.

Marcella looked behind and saw the two men had mounted and were riding toward the river crossing.

# Twenty-four

Maude looked up from hoeing the garden when she caught sight of movement in front of the house. Her father, Simon Bradshaw, was riding up the short lane that led from the main street of Canutillo to Lester's house. He was astride his big sorrel, his prize horse.

Maude dropped her hoe and went to meet her father. This was the first time he had come to visit her since she had told him that she wanted to leave Lester. She was glad that he was no longer angry at her.

"Hello, Father," Maude said happily. She went to be close to him as he tied the horse to the fence that surrounded the yard.

"Hello, Maude," her father replied. "Is Lester home?"

"Yes, Father, he's at Mary's. That's the third door down. She's fixing lunch for him." Lester rotated among his wives for his noontime meal.

"I'm ready to have something to eat," Maude said. "Come in and have a bite with me."

"I don't have time," Simon said shortly. He walked away without a further glance at Maude.

Simon's uncaring attitude hurt Maude. She was lonely for her family, and she wanted her father to sit and talk with her, to show she was his daughter and worth a few minutes of his time. She loved him for he was her father. She had already decided that she did not like him.

The sorrel tossed its head and nickered to Maude. She went to the horse and petted its head and sleek, muscular neck. It smelled Maude and rubbed its head playfully against her shoulder.

"So we're still friends, eh, Red?" she said. She ran his pointed, velvet ears through her hands. Unlike most horses, he had always liked that.

The sorrel was a magnificent horse with deep chest and long legs. Her father had ridden it to win many of the local races. It was nine years old and she and it had grown up together. Due to her small size, she had been the first to ride upon its back when it was still a colt. Even now as a woman, she barely tipped a hundred pounds.

Her breath caught as a wild scheme came to her. She quickly looked along the front of the building that held the apartments of Lester's wives. No adult was in sight. Two boys of three and four, Mary's children, played in the front yard in the shade under a tree.

"Red, let's you and me go for a ride,"

Maude said in a confidential voice. "If we're sneaky about it, maybe for a very long ride."

She hastened into her apartment and stopped by the chest near the front door. Swiftly she dug out the pants, shirt, hat, and boots, and exchanged them for the dress and bonnet she wore. The purse with the 128 dollars was stuffed inside her shirt. She quickly filled a gallon canteen from the water bucket, and carrying it, went to the door and peeked out.

The front yard still held only the two boys. Maude, watching along the front for someone to come outside the home of one of the other wives, hastened down the walk to the sorrel horse. The canteen was tied to the saddle horn, up close and snug so that it wouldn't bounce and flop around when he moved. She swung astride and reined the horse onto the lane to the street.

"Where're you going, Maude?" the larger boy shouted.

At the boy's call, Maude's heart began to hammer. She twisted to look behind, waiting for Lester, or her father, to come and look outside. But no one showed in any of the doorways.

Maude reached the street with no shouts behind her. She reined the horse left.

"Faster, boy," Maude said, and touched the horse with her heels.

The willing beast nickered his understanding and raised his pace to a trot.

Half a block farther along, and out of earshot of the people at Lester's house, Maude spoke again to the horse. "It's time, old friend. Time to leave this town for good."

She touched him twice with her heels. The long-legged steed broke into a swift gallop through the town.

Maude rode south toward El Paso, lying twelve miles away. Andrew Preston and his wife were on the street and she waved at them. Old Man Breslin saw her from where he sat rocking on his porch. Half a score of others noticed her passing. Each one of them would tell Lester the direction she had gone.

Maude would have liked to go to California for she had heard that it was a beautiful place, but there were more than a thousand miles of desert to cross to reach that destination. Not knowing the roads nor the locations of the water holes, she could never make it. She would go east. The escape was the important thing, not the destination.

Canutillo fell away behind. Then it dropped from sight entirely as a hill intervened.

Maude leaned forward close to the sorrel's head, and petting his neck, spoke to him. "Red, we've been friends for years and I've got a favor to ask."

The ears of the big horse angled back to hear Maude's voice.

She continued. "I'm in big trouble now. Don't let Lester catch me. Please, please, don't let him catch me."

Maude took a deep breath. "Let's go," she cried, and slapped the horse a smart blow on the side of the neck.

The horse responded instantly to the command. His ears flicked to the front, and the long legs began to swing fast and far, devouring the ground with great strides.

Maude leaned forward over the powerful front quarters of the running animal, the position that would allow her weight to tire him the least. She felt the powerful muscles of the animal between her legs, bunching and then reaching for distance. The air on the desert was hot, and now made a hot wind as the running horse tore onward. Red was the fastest horse in Canutillo. If he didn't stumble and fall, nothing could catch him.

Maude smiled without humor. Her father had unwittingly provided her with the means to escape from Lester. She couldn't think of a better trick to play on both of them.

Minutes later Maude came to an area of hard, rocky ground and she slowed the horse and guided him off the main road. She had no intention of going to El Paso. She would ride southeast to bypass the town to the north and strike the main road that ran east several miles beyond.

Now off the main road and out of sight of any travelers, Maude let Red move at a trot. She must conserve his strength. Still, even at a trot, give her until dark and she would be forty miles from Canutillo. Allow her the night and tomorrow and she would be a hundred miles away.

★　　　★　　　★

The land slanted upward, climbing toward the Franklin Mountains, a barren, north—south-trending range of peaks. Maude could see the deep notch of McKelligon Canyon that provided passage through the mountains. She dismounted and walked, leading Red. She meant to give the horse as much help as she could to outdistance her pursuers.

Maude reached the summit of the pass with the rocky spire of Comanche Peak towering above her. She had driven herself hard and was pouring sweat. She drank from the canteen as she looked back down the mountainside. She saw no riders.

The horse, smelling the water, came close and nuzzled her for some. "Sorry, Red, none for you just yet." Maude knew she could water the horse at the Rio Grande, which lay some seven to eight miles distant.

She climbed back astride and descended into the desert east of the mountains. El Paso lay off on her right too far away to be seen.

An hour later, she came upon the main road. She took Red down to the Rio Grande, which was close to the road here, and let him drink, but not too much. Then they set out to the east.

In the early night, Maude passed Fort Hancock, sitting on the bank above the Rio Grande. She and her father had stopped and entered the fort once when they had been on a journey to Sierra Blanca to visit relatives. Now she looked at the lights in the fort and identified the barracks of the enlisted men, the row of small homes of the married officers, and the bachelor officers' quarters. The Union soldiers had been forced from the military installation at the beginning of the war, and now a company of Confederate soldiers manned the fort.

Maude was weary, and lowered her head and dozed as the horse carried her on through the darkness. He had been set upon the road, and would follow it until she guided him differently.

She came awake with Red standing motionless and resting in the road. The night was darker and the moon shadows were long and thin, for the celestial body that had been high in the sky was now hardly a hand's width above the horizon. She had slept much longer than she had intended. Maude climbed down from the saddle. She would walk until the moon was completely gone.

Maude lay upon her thin blanket on the ground and rested. The bed was hard, but that was nothing for she was free.

The sound of the horse tearing at the tough desert grass nearby was comforting. She loved the big animal, and was sorry she could not have given him better food. Tomorrow she must find water for the horse and herself.

Her thoughts turned to Lester. He would be looking for her, that was a certainty. She had done her best to mislead him. Perhaps he would be searching for her in El Paso. If not and he guessed she had gone east, how far behind was he?

There was one thing for sure. Lester couldn't track her in the darkness. With that thought in mind, Maude went to sleep.

Daylight found Maude upon Red's back and the steed moving at a trot. In the early dawn, she had veered aside a mile to the Rio Grande and allowed the horse to drink and to graze the lush grass along the riverbank for a quarter hour. They were now traveling east on the main road toward Sierra Blanca some thirty miles distant.

Near noon, sweaty and thirsty, and twenty miles farther along, she came to the Arroyo Calero Ranch. The main house was just off the road, and she saw a cowboy working with horses in the log corral nearby. He gave her permission to use the well. She thanked the man and hurriedly drew water to fill her canteen and water Red. In a few minutes she was back on the road and moving fast with the sun burning down and the deep dust of the road boiling up behind.

She believed she had eluded Lester, and if not, that she had a good lead on him. Still, there was a nagging feeling and she twisted in the saddle to look behind.

In the midday sun and far behind on the road, two plumes of yellow dust rose in the air. At the base of the dust were the dark silhouettes of horsemen. From the size of the dust columns, she knew the riders were running their mounts. It could only be Lester, and her father wanting his horse back. She was shocked. How could they be so close? Surely they had seen her, just as easily as she had seen them.

Maude drummed her heels on Red's flanks. "Now, Red, run like you've never run before. Do it for Maude."

She held the reins lightly, letting Red set his own swift pace. The men could not catch her now that she had seen them, but how had they been able to track her among all the other horse tracks on the road. The answer came to her with a jarring remembrance. Simon valued the horse highly and always feared someone would steal him. One day several years before she had gone with him to the blacksmith to have new shoes put on the horse. To make the tracking of the horse easy in the event he was stolen, the blacksmith had, at her father's direction, made distinctive marks in the iron of the shoes. Her father must have continued the practice. Thus the animal's imprints could be easily identified from all others. She should have thought of that.

Too late now.

She looked behind. To her surprise, the two riders were gaining on her. To overtake Red, they must have fresh, rested horses.

And she knew where they had obtained them, from the Arroyo Calero Ranch only a few miles to the rear. Red had gone many miles, and now would have to run a race like he had never run before.

# Twenty-five

Ben was ten miles west of Sierra Blanca when he saw the apparition coming along the road toward him.

The hot air fuming up from the sunbaked land in quivering waves was distorting a distant horse and rider, creating a spectral creature detached from sound and gravity. The horse had no legs and seemed to be floating in Ben's direction on a shimmering lake of water. The body of the rider was cut into two pieces, a thin middle slice missing, and the remainder bent into a grotesque form.

Ben had journeyed on the main traveled road that led westerly, and was now in the Texas hill country. His way had taken him through the town of Big Springs, then Pecos on the river by the same name, onward past the Apache Mountains, and across the broad valley called Salt Flat.

The land had grown ever drier, becoming almost desertlike. Hills and small mountains jutted up unexpectedly. The grass was shorter and sparse and cactus was intermingled with it. The useless creosote bush was present. Farming had given way to cattle ranching.

The horseman was drawing steadily closer. The distortion of the man and horse caused by the heat waves was less, and now Ben could see the rider was running his mount. Damn fool thing to do on such a scorching day. To Ben's surprise, two additional horsemen became visible on the road far back behind the first one.

The nearer rider halted his horse abruptly as if he had just spotted Ben ahead. He sat his mount for a few seconds staring. Then he looked behind at the two riders closing on him.

He turned quickly back to the front and came on along the road. He was leaning far forward close to the head of the horse as if talking to the animal. Even at the distance of some several hundred yards, Ben could see the horse was laboring heavily with faltering steps. The sad beast was ready to collapse. Ben's anger rose at the cruelty to the animal.

The rider climbed down from the back of the horse. He staggered and caught hold of the stirrup to steady himself. Then he came slowly ahead leading his mount.

The man and horse drew within a few hundred feet of Ben. The rider raised a hand to him as if asking for help. At that moment, Ben saw the rider was a woman dressed as a man.

"Help me!" the woman cried.

"Damnation," Ben said. He sent Brutus running ahead.

The woman and her sweat-lathered mount came to a wobbly halt as Brutus stopped in front of them. The horse splayed its legs to keep from falling and its head sank to almost touch the ground. Blood and froth dripped from his flaring nostrils.

The woman stared at Ben with eyes edged with red and sunk deeply in her dusty, haggard face. Immediately a pleasure-filled flood of recognition swept over her.

"Ben, Ben Hawkins, it's you. Thank God."

"What the hell?" Ben said, disbelieving what he saw. He slid from the saddle and went closer to the woman.

He knew Maude and her family for he had gone to school with her in Canutillo. She had been a few grades behind him, but a boy knew all the pretty girls. Maude had been one of the prettiest with her lovely golden hair. As a woman, even dusty and sweating, she was beautiful.

"Maude, what are you doing here? What's going on?" She was breathing hard, her ribs caving in and out. A pulse throbbed rapidly at the base of her throat, like a tiny trapped animal trying to break free. She caught hold of the saddle horn to steady herself.

"Ben, you've got to help me. They're chasing me and Red can't go any farther. And neither can I."

"What's this all about? Who are they?"

"Ben, they're almost here. Stop them."

Ben pulled his Spencer rifle from its scabbard on the horse. With an almost offhand shot, he sent a bullet whistling between the two approaching riders.

The men yanked their steeds to a halt. They swiftly pulled their rifles. Peering hard ahead along the road at Ben and Maude, they talked back and forth between themselves. Agreeing upon some action, they walked their horses forward.

Ben was surprised at the action of the men. They should have turned tail and run, or at the least have gone into the rocks flanking the road in preparation for a fight. Instead they were riding openly toward him, and they seemed ready to shoot.

"Who are they?" Ben said.

"My father and Lester Ivorsen. Please don't let them force me to go back."

"You're running away?"

"As far away as I can go. Ben, I'm old enough to do what I want, not what someone tells me to do."

Ben was listening and he agreed with Maude. He had left home at fifteen. Maude must be seventeen, maybe even eighteen, and had certainly grown into a mature woman. Another thought was in his mind. Maude had looked directly into his face and hadn't been shocked or repulsed at the sight. He didn't understand that, nor how she knew who he was with his altered appearance. He would like to know more about those things.

"I think so too, Maude. We'll have a talk with them and tell them just that."

"Thanks," Maude said, happy with Ben's

response. "But don't talk with them. Just make them go away."

"Maybe I won't have to fight them if we talk," Ben said as he warily watched the men, who had closed to within a couple hundred feet.

"That you, Hawkins?" Simon shouted out.

"It's me, Bradshaw. Now Maude says she doesn't want to go back with you."

Simon and Lester had continued to advance. They now brought their mounts to a stop a few yards from Ben and Maude. Simon looked at his prize horse. His face reddened with anger. "Damn you, Maude, you've rode him to death."

At Simon's curse of his daughter, Ben's mood turned ugly and his temper flared hot and short. "You ruined him by chasing her," Ben said, his voice rough as if dragged over stones. "Just let her go and be done with it."

"She's going back with me and Lester," Simon said. "She's my daughter and she'll do as I say."

"She's old enough to do what she pleases," Ben countered.

"You're wrong in butting into this." Ivorsen spoke for the first time. "She's going back with us."

"What's your part in this, Ivorsen?"

"Maude's my wife." Ivorsen smiled victoriously.

Ben whirled on Maude. "That the truth?"

Maude nodded dismally. "Yes, Ben. But I'm not a slave. If I'm old enough to marry him, then I'm old enough to leave him. And he's

186

hit me. I want to be free to start a new life!"
A sob escaped Maude. "I don't want to be married. Ben, you know how it is when there are many wives and one man."

Ben knew what Maude meant. His father, Samuel, had had four wives, with his mother the first. Ben was her only child, and the oldest of Samuel's offspring. Samuel had neglected her and she was a sad and brokenhearted woman. When Ben had grown to an age to know which girl was pretty, he had come to understand his mother was a plain woman. Samuel, without regard for his mother's feelings, would choose to spend his nights with one of his pretty and younger wives.

Ben could vividly remember how his mother would primp and dress for the evening gatherings. She kept a tiny glass jar of red mints and each time she thought she would be near Samuel, she would put one in her mouth to make her breath sweet. When she didn't have perfume, she would crush rose petals and spread the fragrance on her skin. During all the years that Ben had been home and old enough to remember events, the evenings that Samuel had accompanied his mother back to her rooms for the night could be counted on his fingers. He hated his father for that cruel neglect of his mother. He believed the neglect had broken his mother's heart and hastened her death.

"I know how it is. Still, I can't help you."

"Ben Hawkins, I never thought you were a coward," Maude said, her eyes cold.

"Coward or not, I can't help you." There was an unwritten code among men that one didn't take the side of a woman against her husband. Maude should get a divorce from Lester.

"I'll never go back with them!" Maude screamed. She snatched up a rock from the ground and hurled it at Lester.

The well-aimed missile struck Lester in the chest. His face became grim. He leapt and caught Maude around the waist and crushed her against him, pinning her arms.

Lester looked past Maude at Ben. "Get on your way, Hawkins," he said roughly. "My wife is none of your business."

"Ben, please don't leave," Maude pleaded. "I didn't mean what I said. Help me."

Ben shook his head. He was saddened by Maude's plight, but not willing to interfere. He went to Brutus, mounted, and rode past the three and off along the road.

He had gone but a short ways when he heard a cry of pain behind him. He whirled to see Maude holding her face and Lester towering over her slight form.

Ben was stricken by the sight. A brutal and grinding thought came that she had been correct. A woman had the right to leave a cruel husband. The old rule among men not to intervene between a husband and his wife was wrong.

He reined Brutus back. He would help Maude to escape from the men. That should have been his decision before. Now most likely one or both of the men would try to prevent him from doing that. If they did fight him, then they would receive the worst of it.

Maude lifted her head and saw Ben returning. His ravaged face was tight and hard with determination, and immensely gruesome. He was coming to help her.

Lester shoved Maude to the side and took his rifle in both hands. Her father moved quickly to stand with Lester. Maude saw the men raise their weapons. They were going to shoot Ben over her.

"Ben, don't!" Maude called hurriedly, frightened for him. "I'm all right. Everything's all right. I'm going back to Canutillo with them."

"You sure, Maude?" Ben said, slowing his advance. "I've changed my mind, and I'll take you wherever you want to go. Those two can't stop me."

"I'll go with them." She wanted to tell him to come and lift her up on his big horse and ride away with her. But she couldn't be the cause of men shooting each other.

"You sure?"

"I'm sure."

Ben knew Maude was lying to him about wanting to return to Canutillo, and he knew why. It was a brave and generous thing for her to do, but a bitter thing for him to go along with it.

He locked his eyes on Lester. "If you ever hit Maude again, I'll beat you within an inch of your life."

With that sure and certain promise, Ben again turned Brutus to the west.

# Twenty-six

The dust, lying thick on the El Paso street, splashed like water from under Brutus's and the packhorse's iron-shod hooves. A yellow tail of the dust, hanging in the air light as smoke, trailed out behind Ben and the horses.

Ben looked about at the town where he had once been deputy sheriff. It was a tough, wide-open place with twenty-five saloons and *cantinas*, and six brothels. The population was about half Anglo and half Mexican. Located on the famous El Camino Real, the town was on the important north—south trade route between cities in Mexico and Santa Fe in the New Mexico Territory. Also, it was on the well traveled east—west road between Texas and California. In spite of the war and many men off fighting, the town was still thriving.

He did notice that most of the pedestrians moving on the wooden sidewalks were women. A large percentage of them would lose a brother, husband, some relative in the distant fighting.

Ben smelled the tantalizing aroma of fresh-baked bread wafting to him from the restaurant just ahead, and his hunger soared. He had been traveling for many days and was looking forward to a cool bath and a good meal. After enjoying both of those things, he would take a midday siesta. In the evening he had a promise to keep.

Brutus's head snapped around as a pigeon dove down from a rooftop and landed in the street beside him. Ignoring the horse, the bird began to peck at something in the dust.

A cat, all teeth and claws, came from under the porch of the restaurant like a gray streak. It launched itself at its prey. The alert bird saw the cat and leapt into flight, fleeing into the sky in a flutter of fear.

The cat landed, its feet puffing the dust up in a yellow cloud. The cat was invisible for a moment. Then it came out of the dust, shook itself, and stalked back in under the porch.

"Gray Cat missed that time," Ben said to Brutus. The cat fed well, for many birds came to scavenge scraps of food dropped in front of the restaurant.

Ben came to the town plaza. There was no dust here, for the ground had been surfaced with gravel from the nearby Rio Grande. A huge Catholic church occupied one full side of the square, and the El Prado hotel, old but well maintained, the distant side. Located on the other two sides were a large general store, a hardware, a *cantina*, a saddlery and boot repair shop, and a few open stalls selling fresh fruits and vegetables. He continued across the plaza and entered Main Street, with its many establishments for buying and selling.

The Hanford Hotel, Ben's goal, was in sight a block distant. However, as Brutus carried him closer, he saw it wasn't the Hanford anymore. The three-story structure was

191

undergoing a major transformation. A new wing, three stories like the main structure, was being added to the building. A slate roof had replaced the tin one and the brick walls had been cleaned and tuck-pointed. Ben could tell the inside of the hotel was also being refurbished, because there was a tall pile of old doors and wainscoting and plasterboard being hauled away by men driving wagons.

A twenty-foot-long sign with bright blue lettering on a snow-white background was being hung across the front of the building. The sign read, "Palace Of Pretty Women." Someone was spending a huge sum of money on a new business, whatever that might be.

Ben was disappointed at not finding the Hanford a suitable place to eat and rest. He could turn back and take a room at the El Prado on the plaza. Instead he rode on across the town and went north.

Ben sat on the large, flat rock on the hill above Canutillo and looked down at the town nestled along the east side of the Rio Grande. He had sat on this very same rock countless times as a boy. Over those years he had seen the town steadily grow, until now it stretched along the river for nearly a mile.

He watched the last of the sunlight desert the valley and dusk rise up out of the cracks and crevices of the earth to fill it with gray. Near the bottom of the hill, a coyote, which had lain hidden in a thicket of mesquite bushes, came into sight stealing toward a band of sheep in a pasture near the town. Delving back into his memories, Ben thought the pasture belonged to Silas Dunlap. *Too bad, Silas, looks like you're going to lose a sheep.*

The dusk condensed to night, and a yellow square of light appeared in one of the houses in the town as somebody lit a lamp. Ben took that as a sign and rose to his feet. He could go the cemetery and not find anyone there to ogle him and then turn away without speaking.

Earlier he had located a patch of the beautiful red Indian paintbrush flowers. Now he picked a handful, and careful not to crush them, mounted Brutus and rode down the slope of the hill.

Ben entered the stone-walled cemetery, well tended by the church elders, and went to the far right side where the Hawkins dead were buried. There he knelt and placed the Indian paintbrush flowers upon his mother's grave.

"I miss you, old gal," he said softly.

He seated himself on the ground and leaned against his mother's headstone. The memories of her and his days as a youth pressed forward wanting to be released. He let them come, one after another unrolling across his inner eye.

There was pleasure in some; others had a sadness that brought mist to his eyes. As time passed, the real world around Ben turned black and the stars and moon became bright shining objects in the high dome of blackness overhead.

The sound of music intruded into Ben's reminiscences and brought him back to the present. He cocked his head and knew instantly the source of the music. It was coming from the People's Hall, the public meeting place for the citizens of the town. Tonight, however, the music told of a dance in progress.

A surge of desire to see Maude brought Ben to his feet. He retrieved Brutus from where he had been left at the cemetery gate. Drawn by the music and the probability that Maude would be at the dance, he walked into the town, going along the street dimly lighted by coal-oil lamps placed at each street intersection. His heart was beating a gentle tempo of anticipation.

Soon Ben could see dozens of vehicles, buggies, surreys, and wagons, with the teams of horses that drew them, lining both sides of the street near the hall. Light streamed from all the windows. A crowd of boys, young and too bashful to go inside and ask a girl to dance, milled about talking and laughing. Ben had once occupied that very same space. Then he had grown and become brave and had always gone inside and danced with the girls in the big hall.

He tied Brutus, went along the side wall to a window, and peered into the hall. He scanned the couples promenading to the music. He saw Lester dancing with one of his wives. Three of his other wives were seated with the men and women on the benches along the walls and calmly waiting their turn to dance with their husband. Maude wasn't in the hall.

Ben continued on to the rear of the building, where there were no windows. He stood in the darkness and listened to the delightful music, dampened by the intervening wall but still easily heard. He could make out the sound of two fiddles and a piano. The piano was part of the furnishings of the hall.

All the musical instruments were being skillfully played, and Ben felt his feet wanting to move to the music, as they had done many times with a girl in his arms. The music was a waltz, a lively one. Without consciously deciding to do so, Ben began to step and swing in rhythm with the music. He held his arms as if clasping a willing girl and whirled about on the hard-packed ground.

Ben stopped, embarrassed by his actions, and backed up to stand against the wall of the hall. He would listen to one more piece of music and then leave.

He saw a shadow move among the trees that grew at the border of the hall's rear yard. The figure hesitated, pressing to the trunk of one of the trees. After a moment the person moved, coming slowly into the yard. It was a woman in a dress and Ben thought he recognized her.

"Maude, is that you?"

"Who's that?

"Cowardly Ben."

Maude came through the night separating

them with quick steps and grabbed Ben by the arm. "Please forgive me for saying that," she whispered huskily.

Astonished at Maude's action to take hold of him, Ben placed his hand lightly on top of hers. The friendliness of her greeting, the touch of her hand, made his blood rush with a joyous thrum. He laughed, something he hadn't done for many a month.

"Tell me that you forgive me," Maude said again.

"There's nothing to forgive. But I'll say it. I forgive you."

"Good. Did I see you dancing a minute ago?"

"You were here? You spied on me."

Maude laughed lightly. "Not spying. I just happened to be there in the trees."

"Why aren't you inside with the music and dancing?"

"I didn't want to go inside. Ben, why didn't you ever ask me to dance? Those last couple of years before you went off to war, I was at the dances and you were too."

"I saw you there. I couldn't help it for you were the prettiest. But you were too young for me."

"I was never too young for you. My mother married at fifteen, and my father was twenty-five at the time."

Maude peered hard through the darkness at Ben. "I wished a thousand times that you would ask me to dance. But you always passed me by and asked one of the other girls."

Ben remained silent, overwhelmed by the discovery of Maude's feelings toward him.

"All you had to do was ask and I would've danced forever with you," Maude said. "Then you left and came back wounded and wouldn't talk with anybody. Just ride that big Brutus through town with your hat pulled down."

Ben was astounded that Maude had not mentioned the ugliness of his wounds. They must frighten her as they did everyone else.

"Listen, Ben, hear the music?"

"Yes."

"Ask me to dance. Like you should've done years ago."

Ben fought through the flurry of emotions Maude had brought to life in him. He stepped back and bowed to her.

"Miss Bradshaw, would you like to dance?"

"It would be a pleasure, Mr. Hawkins."

Ben caught Maude by the waist and the hand and whirled away with her in the night. He felt her easy response to his lead, joining with him, picking up the tempo of the music. They spun about with their steps in perfect synchrony with the beat of the melody.

By the time Ben had made a dozen steps with Maude, he was totally caught up in the music and the nearness of her. He felt her soft breath, light as the fluff of milkweed on his cheek. Her hair glistened gold and silver in the moonlight. He smelled her sweet woman's perfume. Ben smiled in the darkness. The perfection of the night was so great that he wanted it to never end. It was just fine to be alive. How could the touch of a woman change the world so much? Did Maude feel the same way? He wished he could see if Maude was smiling too.

The musicians inside the hall broke into the melody for the *cuna*, the dance of the cradle. To perform the dance, each partner had to circle the other's waist with their arms and swing around and around, leaning back to form the top of the cradle, and at the same time they would move their lower bodies inward to close the bottom. When Ben pulled Maude in close and circled her waist with a firm hold, she cried out with pain.

"What's wrong? Did I hurt you?"

"My ribs are sore."

"Did Lester hit you?"

"No, I fell off a horse. It's nothing, Ben. I just fell."

"Fell?"

Ben took Maude by the hand and led her to the corner of the hall, where there was a little light from the nearest window. He took her face in his hand and turned it so he could see. Several raw, swollen bruises marred her lovely features. Lester had struck her in the face as well as the body. Now Ben knew why Maude hadn't gone inside to dance. She was ashamed of the beating Lester had given her.

Hate for Lester burned across Ben's mind and his fists closed with the need to strike and punish. The man had made a terrible mistake, and he had been warned.

Maude sensed the tension in Ben. "I fell, Ben. Are you listening? I fell. Don't you do something to get in trouble with the law."

"Nothing will happen. You fell, so why should I be mad at anybody?"

"All right then. It's getting late and I had better go."

Maude drew Ben back into the darkness behind the hall. She caught both of his hands in hers. "Ben, it wasn't Lester. I really did fall off a horse. Now promise that you won't do anything foolish."

"All right. I promise not to do anything foolish." Silently he thought, *I'm just going to do something that has to be done.*

"Good." Maude reached up and touched Ben's scarred face. "You're still the same Ben Hawkins under all of that."

She spun about and ran into the night.

# Twenty-seven

Ben watched from the dark street as the dancers filed laughing and talking out of the town hall. Lester and his wives came out, followed by the two fiddlers carrying their cased instruments.

Calling good night to each other, the people began to climb into their vehicles and go off in various directions through Canutillo. Lester helped his wives into his two-seated buggy and

199

drove off toward his home on the south end of the town.

Ben mounted Brutus, and holding a block to the rear, followed Lester. His anger at the man for beating Maude was growing like a great serpent uncoiling in his stomach. Never could he let the man go unpunished for that.

Lester turned off the main street and drove up the lane to his house, where he stopped to let his wives step down from the buggy. He then continued around the end of the house to the barn in the rear.

Ben dismounted from Brutus, hung his hat on the pommel, and shadowed his way through the darkness to the front of the barn. There he waited, listening to Lester unharness the team of horses and put them in their stalls. The man came out of the barn whistling one of the pieces of music that had been played at the dance.

Ben silently approached Lester from behind. He closed the last few feet with a rush, and springing upon Lester, hooked him around the neck with his left arm and bent him far down in front. He struck Lester a savage blow to the ribs. Then slugged him again in the same place, putting all his pent-up rage into the blow. The jarring impact of the blows running up Ben's arms and into his shoulder was a glorious sensation.

Lester went to his knees under the savage onslaught. Then he caught his fall and heaved upward, straining to straighten, and Ben, half lifted off the ground, felt the full strength of the man's muscular body. Ben hung more of his weight on Lester, and tightened his arm into a choking hold and kept the man bent down so he could not see who was attacking him.

Lester spun to the left, trying to dislodge his foe. Ben spun with Lester, maintaining his tight neck-hold and staying on the man's side where he couldn't be hit. He hammered Lester twice more in the ribs with his right fist.

Lester swung his foot out to trip Ben and throw both men to the ground, where he could roll and break free. Ben held them upright, and raised the aim of his fist and rained three fast wallops to the side of Lester's head.

Ben felt Lester weakening under the flood of punishing blows. He gave him three more hard ones to the head. The man's legs gave way and he hung limp in the crook of Ben's arm.

Detesting the touch of the man, Ben flung him down as so much offal and stepped away. Lester lay bloody and moaning on the dirt of the barnyard. Ben's rage wasn't yet cooled. He stepped back close to Lester and stomped him in the ribs. He felt bones break under his boot.

Smiling his satisfaction to the night, Ben turned and walked away.


"Hello, the house. Tom, you there?"

Ben was in the front yard of a two-story house on the east outskirts of Canutillo. The home

201

belonged to his half brother, Tom Hawkins. Tom was the only one of his fourteen half brothers and sisters with whom he had associated. When he had arrived in the town earlier in the day, he had stabled his packhorse in the shed behind the house, and gone off to the hillside above town.

A light came alive in the upstairs and floated down the stairs to the front room. Tom came out onto the porch.

"About time you showed up," Tom said with obvious pleasure at Ben's arrival. "Saw a horse in the shed and figured it was yours."

"Good to see you, Tom."

"You too, Ben. Since you hadn't been around for months, I thought those greasers in Mexico might've shot you. Come on in."

"Sally home?" Ben said, moving up the walk to the porch.

"She's been over to her mom's visiting for the past two days. Seems young wives got to go and see their mom even when they've got a husband to take care of at home." Tom gestured at one of the rocking chairs on the porch. "Sit and tell me what you've been up to."

Ben sat and stretched his legs out on the porch. "Just stealing horses."

Tom chuckled. "I heard that rumor. I wasn't joking about the Mexicans killing you. Someday they'll get lucky."

"Maybe. How's business?" Though a year younger than Ben, his industrious brother owned a wheelwright business. He manufactured the wheels in Canutillo and sold them out of his store in El Paso. The huge traffic of vehicles passing through that town insured a thriving business.

"Better than ever. I'm selling every wheel I can make. I'd like to expand to Abilene and Arizona City. I could use a partner. Especially one with a few thousand dollars. Are you interested?"

A month ago, even a day ago, Ben would have known the answer with certainty. It would have been no. But now? "Maybe so. I'll give it some thought."

"Good. I hope you do come in with me. But that's enough talk about work. What have you been up to so late at night?"

"That's something we need to talk about, in case the sheriff comes around asking 'bout me."

"What happened?"

"I worked Lester Ivorsen over."

Tom peered at Ben in the lamplight coming through the open door. "Lester's a strong man. But I don't see any bruises on you."

"I didn't go to fight him. I went to give him a beating."

"Did you give him a good one?"

"Left him laying flat with broken bones and bleeding."

"Couldn't have happened to a more deserving fellow. He's been needing a thrashing for a long time. Just last month he knocked the hell out of Eddy for simply talking with one of his wives, the one named Alice."

"Hell, if I'd known that, I would've give him even more." Eddy was Tom's younger brother.

"But why did you feel it necessary to fight him?"

"He hit Maude Bradshaw."

"You mean Maude Ivorsen."

"I reckon so, now that she's married to that bastard."

"Lester does rule his covey of hens with a hard hand."

"Too damn hard. She tried to tell me that she fell, but I knew better."

"All of Lester's wives are pretty. But Maude is the prettiest. I remember how she used to look at you when you were around here."

"She is real easy to look at." Ben regretted not knowing Maude's feelings toward him back in those long past days.

"Ben, be careful about Lester for he's a mean one. He probably won't go to the sheriff. He'll come looking for you himself."

"I don't think he ever got a look at my face. But if he does come after me, I hope he comes with a gun."

"I've heard too much already," Tom said. He rose from the rocking chair. "Well, knowing you, you're probably hungry. So come inside and let's see what we can find to eat before we go to bed."

# Twenty-eight

Ben took a room in the El Prado hotel on the plaza in El Paso. He chose one in the oldest section of the hotel, where he had stayed before and knew the foot-thick walls retained the coolness of the night until well into the following day. The old section had its own entrance at the far right end of the hotel's front patio, and he could reach his room without going through the main lobby. He had stabled his horses in stalls provided by the hotel in the rear and carried his belongings into the hotel.

Wearing his money belt, he left the hotel and walked to the Cattleman and Merchant Bank. Keeping three hundred dollars for pocket money, he left the remainder for safekeeping in the bank's steel vault.

Ben drifted through the town with a feeling of being at loose ends. He seemed to be waiting for something to happen, and he had a gut feeling that he wasn't going to like it.

He was glad that he had discovered Maude, but at the same time saddened by finding she was another man's wife. He deeply regretted not helping her escape from Lester and her father that day on the road. By siding with them until it was too late to back out, he had made her a prisoner in Lester's house. How would she react if he rode up on Brutus and carried her off? Even as he considered the idea, he knew

205

the thing could never be. He was just too damn ugly.

He guided his thoughts onto other things. He was surprised at himself for walking so openly on the street. People looked at him and then away as they always had. Still, he did not try to hide his face in any way. The reason was plain to him. Since the night Maude had touched his scars and said, "Ben Hawkins is under all of that," he had felt a lessening of his need to avoid the eyes of others. He knew she had said that because of the darkness that hid his face and because of her memory of him before the injury. In the light of day, would she have touched his face? Still, her action had strengthened him to withstand the expressions of revulsion, sometimes fright, others had when they looked upon him.

He came to Tanner's Gaming and Pool Hall and halted in front. He had often played poker here in the evenings after getting off duty as deputy sheriff, and had found it to be a pleasant experience. He entered the establishment. A game of poker would burn up some time.

In the early afternoon, only one card game was in progress. One of the eight pool tables had shooters knocking the balls around. Ben took a seat at the poker table, where Smiley Tanner, the owner of the hall, was dealing the cards.

There were three other players. Ben spoke to them, recognizing Parsons and Kittridge, but not the last man. None of the men looked at him after the first glance. He handed fifty dollars to Smiley and received chips. Smiley was an honest man, so Ben, knowing he didn't have to watch the dealer, relaxed and played a slow game.

He tossed weak cards in early, and when dealt strong hands, didn't bet as heavily as he might have. Just a friendly game to pass the day.

"What's happening with the Hanford Hotel?" Ben asked Smiley.

"Going to upgrade the hotel and add a gambling hall," Smiley said sadly.

"Local man doing it?" Ben said, knowing Smiley's business would suffer because of the competition.

"No. A man named Redpath from New Orleans. He's said to have a lot of money. He bought the hotel and hired a crew of men. A fellow that came with him named Jean Dubois is overseeing the work. Seems to be good at it."

"I saw the sign, Palace Of Pretty Women. Strange name for a hotel and gambling place."

"I thought so too. I asked Dubois about that and he told me all the games will be run by women. He and Redpath did bring twelve or fifteen women with them when they came. Keeps them in a rented house on the north side of town."

"I heard those women are whores," Kittridge said. "And that Redpath is a tough man and not someone to cross."

"Damn pretty whores, if they are," Parsons said. "I'd give one of them some money for a go."

Smiley spoke. "Dubois said he'll be far enough along with the original hotel part to open it for business in a short while. Then we'll know for sure what Redpath's game really is."

Ben left three hours later and eighty-six dollars richer.

He was just entering the plaza when a spanking pair of matched horses trotted by, drawing one of the larger-size Phaeton buggies with a man and woman riding. The rumble seat behind them was full of luggage. The horses were sweating and the people dusty. They had journeyed a long distance.

The woman, sitting on the side of the buggy toward Ben, turned her head in his direction. He saw her shocked expression as she caught sight of his face. She hastily looked away.

Karl Redpath drove the Phaeton up in front of the El Prado and halted. "We've reached the end of the journey, Marcella," he said. The woman had accepted the name he had given her. After so many days without remembering she was Rachel Greystone, it appeared her amnesia was total and permanent.

"Good," Marcella replied as she examined the well-kept hotel and its walled patio stretching along the entire front and full of shade-giving trees and flower beds in bright colors. She twisted about and looked at the other buildings on the plaza and the people moving about on private errands. "It's pretty here and I've had enough traveling to last for years."

"I could stand a rest too," Karl said.

He stepped down from the buggy and fastened the team to the metal ring of one of the tie posts provided by the hotel. He came to Marcella's side of the vehicle and held out his hand. "Let's go inside and get their best."

Marcella took the man's hand and they went through the large front patio of the hotel and inside. Karl had their luggage brought to their rooms, followed by two portable bathtubs, and lastly buckets of warm water to fill both tubs. They bathed and donned clean clothing.

"You rest while I go and see Dubois," Karl said. "I want to see what he's accomplished while I've been gone. Shouldn't take me long."

Marcella nodded assent. Karl had told her that Dubois was overseeing the construction of some kind of large building. She had no details of its nature.


Marcella sat in one of the comfortable wicker chairs on the front patio of the hotel and watched the long shadows of the evening slip across the plaza. In the lessening heat of the day, more people were on the plaza. Some small boys and girls were running and playing under the big trees. Three women sat and watched and talked among themselves. Two old men played dominoes seated on chairs at a little table, the table and chairs being the fold-up kind they must have brought with them. At the vegetable and fruit stalls, women were making purchases in preparation for the evening meal.

The scene was a peaceful one, yet Marcella did not feel at peace with herself. Everything she had seen since awakening from the unconsciousness of her fall was new to her. At the same time the thoughts that ran through her mind felt familiar, ones she surely must have had in that previous life. The woman who had called "Rachel" to her, and had to be from that same past, had not appeared again after that night on the prairie. There was a growing and frightening belief that with the passage of time with all its new events, broad lands crossed, towns viewed, and people met, the possibly of her recalling her old life was being steadily diminished.

On Marcella's left, the scar-faced man she had seen on the street came out of another entrance of the hotel. He walked with a slow, hesitant step. Yet even as Marcella made that judgment, he straightened and his stride lengthened and he went off with, almost, a jaunty air.

Karl and another man came into the patio. Seeing Marcella, Karl guided their steps toward her. The second man was of medium height and wore a full beard that was trimmed quite short. He had small eyes that shifted from her and off across the plaza and then back to her. Karl and the strange man stopped near Marcella.

"Hello, Mrs. Redpath, it's good to see you again," the man said, and doffed his hat to her. Marcella tried to recall the man, but there was no recollection of having ever seen him before.

"This is Jean Dubois, Marcella," Karl said. "Do you remember him? You've met him many times in New Orleans."

Marcella shook her head and spoke to Dubois. "Good day, Mr. Dubois. Please forgive me for not recognizing you. Karl has probably told you I've had an accident and can't recall things of the past."

"I'm terribly sorry about that, Mrs. Redpath," Dubois said.

Marcella studied the man. By his greeting, he obviously knew her. There was a look in his eyes that she couldn't interpret. Then it came to her. He had the expression of a man lying and not fully able to hide it. If that was so, what was he lying about?

"Mr. Redpath, you'll like what we've already accomplished at the hotel," Dubois said. "The remodeling of the original section is mostly complete and we'll open that part for business in a week."

"Everything is coming along nicely. But, Dubois, don't tell Mrs. Redpath any more, for I want her to see it when it's totally finished."

"Right, Mr. Redpath," Dubois said. He spoke to Marcella. "Mrs. Redpath, I wish to tell you that it's good to see you've made a safe journey to El Paso."

"Thank you." At the man's statement, Marcella saw that liar's look was back in his eyes.

211

Marcella watched Dubois as he hurried away. She thought he seemed very anxious to be gone. It was odd that Karl had brought the man to meet her and then sent him away after little more than a hello. She noted that during the few minutes the man had been here, he had addressed her as Mrs. Redpath several times, even when he had been looking directly at her and there had been no need to.

"I'm sorry you didn't recognize Dubois," Karl said. "I was hoping another familiar face would help your memory to return."

"I had no recollection of having ever met him."

"It will come with time." Karl took her by the arm. "Shall we dine? Dubois has told me of an excellent place and it's not far."

"Yes, for I'm starved."


People on the street turned and stared at the large, handsome man and the beautiful woman moving along the sidewalk. Marcella wore a pale yellow dress with a delicate row of ruffles running from her throat to the tail of the dress. The dress was cut to hang an inch above the ground. Her auburn hair was pulled back to fully show her lovely face, and tied with a ribbon the same color as the dress. The simple clothing and hairstyle had been chosen by Karl. She could not know that he wanted her to be the opposite of the overdressed whores he owned.

They entered the restaurant, and a waiter

hurried to greet them and guide them to a table. As Marcella was helped to be seated by Karl, her eyes fell upon the man with the scarred face she had seen on the street and at the hotel. He sat at a table on the far side of the room. He was looking at her. She wondered how old he might be. With his damaged features, it was impossible to know with any degree of accuracy. However, there was an aura about him that told her he was a young man. How awful for a young person to be so mutilated.

He nodded at Marcella, in a manner that told her he thought she was pretty. She sensed there was more there, a dare for her to acknowledge him in some manner and not look away.

Marcella applauded the bravery of such an ugly man to hold his eyes upon her. She inclined her head in acceptance of the man's appraisal, and kept her eyes on him as she did so.

She thought he smiled. However, it was impossible to tell because of all the terrible scars.

# Twenty-nine

Evan retreated before the squad of approaching soldiers whose eyes were full of death. They were dressed in moldering uniforms and they were crippled and limping, with white skulls showing beneath old flesh. Every one of the soldiers was looking at Evan and calling out

213

to him in weirdly hollow voices, lamenting at having died so young.

Evan knew he must show bravery before these poor fellows. He forced his legs to halt their retreat and struggled to rid his features of the fear he felt. He must meet them and let them have their way with him, for hadn't he killed them with his saw and scalpel?

"I'm ready to stand punishment," Evan called out to the soldiers.

The four soldiers in the first rank surrounded Evan and caught hold of him with skeleton hands. The remainder broke ranks and swarmed upon him.

"Evan, what's wrong?" John said, shaking him.

Evan fought up out of the frightening pit of sleep and came awake with John bent over him in the night. "Okay, John, okay," Evan said.

"You were talking in your sleep," John said, removing his hand from Evan's shoulder. "Something about being punished."

"It was just a dream," Evan said. He rose to a sitting position and looked about him. "I'm all right," he added, glad it was truly only a dream.

"You sure?"

"Yes. Sorry I woke you. Go back to sleep."

"It's almost daylight. What do you say to us getting started now and making it to El Paso today?"

"Fine with me. I couldn't sleep anymore anyway. We could probably make it there by some time in the afternoon."

Tattersall and his band of men, and the two
Valdes brothers, Carlos and Leo, rode into
Ciudad Juarez on the seventh day after leaving
Chihuahua. They halted their mounts on the
high point of the city from where they could
look along El Camino Real and see the Rio
Grande, and beyond the river, the buildings
of El Paso.

Carlos spoke to Tattersall. "Leo and I will
stop here. We have some business to do."

"What kind of business?"

Carlos resented being questioned, but
decided to answer for he needed the Americans. "Our family has a freight station here with
a warehouse, wagons, and horses for our
freight line. We want to talk with the men who
operate that for us. Also, Leo and I shouldn't
ride into El Paso on Valdes horses and in
these clothes. We don't want to be noticed
before we find and kill Hawkins. We will
come across the river later today."

Tattersall nodded, running his eyes over the
men's expensive clothing, the silver-deco-
rated saddles, and the prominent Valdes
brand on their horses. He tried to read more
in Carlos and Leo, but they were as unread-
able as their father.

"Me and my men have talked it over and
we're going to take a couple of days to let loose
and do a little celebrating. Then we'll we go
looking for Hawkins."

Carlos shrugged. "All right. I've been waiting a year to see Hawkins dead, so two more days means nothing."

Marcella moved along the boardwalk on the shady side of the El Paso street. Yesterday Karl and she had arrived late and she had seen little of the town. Today she planned to do considerable exploring.

A scattering of people came and went on the street, some on foot like herself, a few horsemen, some carriages, and half a dozen wagons loaded with freight.

Just ahead of her two young Mexican cowboys were dismounting in front of a *cantina*. They were dressed in worn and faded pants and shirts, and battered, broad-brimmed sombreros. They wore pistols belted to their waists. Both were quite handsome. They turned and looked at Marcella.

To her surprise, they had blue eyes, which quickly ranged over the length of her with a measuring look. In unison, they whipped off their sombreros and bowed with a graceful bending of their upper bodies.

"*Buenos dias, señorita,*" Carlos said. But was she actually a *señorita*? She was very beautiful and he wanted to know for certain. "It is *señorita*, isn't it?"

"*Señorita* will do," Marcella replied, for she certainly didn't feel married.

"*Bueno,*" Carlos said, and gave her another little bow.

Marcella gave both men a little smile and continued on her way.

She had proceeded but a few steps when a man called out from farther along the street. "Rachel. Rachel Greystone."

Marcella glanced in the direction of the call. Two horsemen had stopped on the street. The taller man was smiling and waving his hand. It appeared that he was looking directly at her. She didn't know him, so she cast around to see who might be near her and to whom he was speaking. There was nobody. The man sprang down from his mount, handed the reins to his companion, and came swiftly toward Marcella.

"Rachel, how did you get to El Paso?" Evan asked. She had that same brilliance about her that had so often been in his mind. He gloried in the sight of her.

"Who are you? Why do you call me Rachel?" As she asked the question, she recalled the image of the woman and her saying the name Rachel.

Evan's smile became one of puzzlement. "Why, that's your name. Don't you remember us meeting in Marshall?"

She was dumbfounded, disbelieving what the man was saying. Yet his words had the ring of truth. "You know me? Know me as Rachel Greystone?"

"That's what you told me your name was. Don't you remember me? I'd just got off the train at the station, and when I came into the hotel, you kept me from falling when I tripped."

Rachel caught her head between her hands and closed her eyes. Shadowy figures of wounded soldiers moving on a street were forming. Then she recalled taking hold of the arm of an ill man and helping him into the hotel. "I do seem to remember that. But you look somehow different."

"I've gained some weight as I've healed from my wound. But I'm that same fellow. You were going east to be a nurse for General Lee's army, and to find some of your relatives who were fighting with him."

Rachel stepped and clutched Evan by the arm with a hard grip. "Yes! Yes! It's coming back to me. I did talk with you. And I did get on the train."

Her face creased with a fierce effort to see more in that empty gulf of her previous life. The man was stating the truth, and the truth became the key that unlocked her mind, and the nothingness of the past became suddenly filled with people and events.

Rachel's words came with a rush. "Then later the train pulled onto a siding. I fell off, yes, I fell. Then when I came to, Karl was with me. There was no train. He told me I had fallen from the buggy. He told me I was his wife."

"Married? You said nothing about being married when I saw you in Marshall. In fact, from what you said, I was sure you were single."

Rachel's hands flew up to cover her face. "Oh, my God. That's right. I'm not married. Karl lied to me. I've been living with him as his wife and I'm not." A sob of torment escaped her.

Rachel's hands lowered from her tear-streaked face. "How could he do such a thing to me?"

*Because you are beautiful and he must be a son of a bitch*, Evan thought, but kept silent.

Rachel collected herself and looked more closely at the man who had awakened her memories. He had the most gentle eyes she had ever seen on a man. At the moment they were watching her tenderly and with sorrow. "I seem to recall you said your name was Evan."

"Yes, Evan Payson."

"Thank you, Evan, for not forgetting me. I don't know what might have eventually happened to me if you hadn't come back into my life today."

She smiled at Evan, a frail smile, but a gift of pure gold to Evan. "You seem to be in a bad fix," Evan said. "Is there something I can do to help you?"

"I must get away from Karl," Rachel said. "Go someplace where he can't find me."

"Must you hide from him? We'll tell the sheriff what he has done to you and let the law handle it. What's his name?"

Rachel shook her head, and her hands came up as if to ward off something terrible. "No one must ever know that this has happened to me. No one. Promise me that you won't ever tell."

"I promise." Evan understood the disgrace that Rachel would face from having lived with the man without being married to him. Never had he hated a man like he did this one who had so abused her.

Rachel looked around to see who was close. Two women had stopped on the boardwalk and were looking at them. They were too far away to have heard. Evan's friend and the Mexican cowboys were watching, but at a distance. She looked about in a larger radius for Karl. He wasn't in sight.

"Who is Karl?" Evan asked.

"His last name is Redpath. He owns the Handford Hotel."

"I'll go and have a talk with Redpath. Tell him I know what he's done and that he must never bother you or speak to you again."

Rachel knew Evan, with his youth and slight build, could never stand against Karl Redpath. "He's a dangerous man," she said. "I saw him shoot four men, and he did it easily. He laughed about it afterwards."

"Even so, I should still have a talk with him."

"I don't want to see you hurt."

"All right then," Evan said. He would have that talk with Redpath later. "I'll help you, if you'll let me."

"Would you? I can't pay you for I have no money."

"I don't want payment. My folks own a ranch a few miles west of town. They'd be glad to let you stay with them until you decide what you want to do."

"Thank you. I accept gladly and will always be in your debt. Can we leave right now?"

"Sure."

He took Rachel by the hand and they went quickly to John. "Can I borrow your horse?"

Evan asked John. "Rachel and I want to ride to my parents' place."

"Sure," John said, and swung down to the ground. From the tense expressions on the faces of Evan and the woman, John knew something was wrong. "Is there anything I can do for you?"

"Just let us use your horse," Evan said. He spoke to Rachel. "Give me your foot."

Rachel hoisted her dress to mid-leg and gave Evan her foot. He lifted her astride. She tucked the tail of her dress under her for protection from the saddle, and took the reins John was holding out to her.

"I'll bring your horse back to you later," Evan said to John.

"No hurry. I can walk home from here."

"We mustn't go past the hotel," Rachel said to Evan.

"Won't have to." Evan led off.

Neither Evan nor Rachel saw Carlos and Leo mount their steeds and follow after them.

# Thirty

The laughter of a woman came to Carlos and Leo where they lay hidden and spying on the ranch house. A man's deeper voice joined with the woman's and they laughed happily together.

"The man's sure enjoying himself with the woman," Leo said.

"Who wouldn't with such a pretty one," Carlos replied.

Carlos and Leo had followed Rachel and Evan from El Paso to the ranch house where they had stopped. The house sat at the base of the south end of the Potrillo Mountains. It was a long, rambling structure made of adobe and stone and containing several rooms. The house had a red tile roof and a large patio on the east end where the evening sun could not reach. Rachel and Evan were in the patio. A live stream came down from the mountain, flowed past the house, and onward deeper into the valley. Cottonwoods and willows lined the creek, and the two Mexicans had stolen unseen through the strip of trees until they were now within hearing distance of Rachel and Evan.

"What do you think the man is to her?" Leo asked.

"I've been trying to figure that out," Carlos said. "I'm sure their meeting in El Paso was unexpected."

"Yet they borrowed the other man's horse and left together."

"And very quickly as if maybe trying to not be seen by someone," Carlos said. "I wish I could have heard what they talked about."

"I think Father would approve of her," Leo said.

"I know that I do. She'd make all the other women at the rancho jealous."

"Then you think as I do that we should take her home with us?" Leo said.

"The oldest brother gets first choice," Carlos said. "And I choose this one."

Leo's face became glum. "You always take first choice. I hope we don't have to shoot any of her relatives. That would make her hate us."

"Regardless of how we do it, she'll hate us."

"But perhaps only for a time. If we have a priest perform a wedding ceremony, and then quickly make her pregnant, she will settle down and be a good wife."

"It'll be hard to wait for a priest," Carlos said, thinking pleasant thoughts about the woman.

"Yes, indeed."

"Now's not a good time to take her with it daylight and a man with her. So let's ride to Canutillo and see what that town has to offer us. I've heard the most beautiful women in Texas live there."

"All the men there have several wives, and losing one shouldn't be much of a loss to them."



Rachel basked in the pleasure of Evan's company. He delighted her with his quick, mischievous wit and she laughed often. How grand it was to be whole with all her memories restored, and to be safe from Redpath. She and Evan sat in the patio of his home on a cut-stone bench softened by a stuffed leather cushion. A walnut tree heavily laden with its clusters of green nuts gave them shade. Flowers of a dozen kinds filled the patio, and the wind was drowsy with their perfume.

They had arrived at the ranch to be greeted by a joyful welcome from Evan's parents. The mother had cried and hugged her son back safe from the war. The father had watched and blinked back tears as his wife and only son embraced.

Rachel had stood back, not wanting to interfere with the homecoming. He had told her that he had not seen his parents for nearly two years. How very important an only child, a son, must be to them.

Evan had introduced Rachel to his parents, and she had felt their genuine kindness when they accepted her into their home. The father was tall like Evan, and given to the same boniness. He was deeply tanned and had heavily calloused hands, easily felt when he had taken Rachel's hand into his. Rachel believed Evan would look like this in twenty-five years if he took up ranching. There had to be a toughness in the father to have built such a large ranch in this harsh land. She wondered if Evan had inherited any of the man's toughness.

After a period of light conversation, Evan's mother and father had gracefully left and gone to another part of the house. Rachel thought they had assumed there was a romantic relationship between Evan and her.

"Will you be a rancher like your father?" Rachel asked.

"Most likely. Would you like to live on a ranch?" Evan asked.

"Yes, one as pretty as this one."

Evan's heart beat a tattoo high in his chest at Rachel's answer. He felt the ebb of his life running strong and vital. When just a few days ago he had thought he would die, now he was dreaming of the future like a boy. A thought hit Evan like a rock and his features stiffened and hardened. He would have to kill Redpath for what he had done to Rachel, remove him from the world, before he could ask her to marry him. He turned his face away, afraid Rachel might be able to read his thoughts.

Then he looked back with a feeling of joy at having found her.

Maude was stocking the shelves of Lester's general store when the two young Mexican cowboys came in from the street. Both removed their sombreros as they approached her. The older one smiled at Maude. The younger one silently stared at her.

Two wagons loaded with merchandise had arrived for the store late in the day. Maude had volunteered to unload them and place the items on the shelves. Marie had agreed to the arrangement and left for home. Maude was glad to miss the gathering of Lester and his wives and their children. He wouldn't care that she worked late for he was too sore from the beating—Maude was sure Ben had dealt it out— to want her for the night.

"*Señora*, or is it *señorita*, we are looking for

work," Carlos said. They had seen the pretty, golden-haired girl through the front window and had come inside to get a closer look. "Have you heard anyone speak of needing riders? We are very good with cattle and horses."

"No, I'm sorry but I haven't." It was commonplace to see Mexican cowboys come to Canutillo looking for work, for they were hired to help in the fall cattle roundup. However, that wouldn't occur for another three months or so.

The woman hadn't responded to Carlos's ploy to find out whether or not she was unmarried. He must try again. "That's too bad for we have little money. May we speak to your husband about work?"

"I have no husband," Maude replied. No man who beat her was a husband.

Carlos glanced at Leo. Leo gave a slight nod in the affirmative.

Carlos fished in a pocket and brought out a silver dime. He spoke to Maude. "We are very hungry. Would you sell us some cheese and crackers?" He gestured at the cracker barrel, nearly full, and the rolls of cheese wrapped in cloth on a table.

"I have a better idea," Maude said. "I'll give you some cheese and crackers if you will help me unload the wagons out back."

"That is very kind of you and we accept," Carlos said. "My name is Carlos, and his is Leo."

"My name is Maude. It's already past

closing time, so I'll lock the front door and we won't be bothered. I'd like to get this all done before dark."

"I'll take our horses around behind the store," Carlos said, thinking it was best to get the horses out of sight.

Maude closed the front door behind Carlos. She returned to Leo and guided him from the store and through a storeroom to a loading platform abutting an alley.

The men fell to unloading the boxes, barrels, and crates from the wagons and carrying them into the storeroom. Then with hammers and crowbars, they began to open the containers. Maude resumed stocking the shelves.

"What do you think of this one?" Carlos asked Leo in a low voice.

"She's as pretty as the other one," Leo replied. "Did you ever see such yellow hair?"

"Then you would want her for your woman?"

Leo grinned broadly in anticipation. "I'm glad that you chose the other one."

"All right. Here's how we'll do it. The sun is down and soon it'll be dark. If we went toward the river, there's only one row of houses to pass. With luck, no one will see us leave. We'll stay off the main road and in less than two hours can be in Ciudad Juarez."

Maude came into the storeroom for another load of merchandise and saw the two young cowboys talking and smiling. They were very pleasant fellows and good workers. She would give them a bonus of some canned beef and tomatoes to go with their cheese and crackers.

* * *

"We're all finished," Maude said to Carlos. "I could never have gotten it all unpacked and stocked without the help of you and your friend. Where is he?"

"Outside with the horses."

"Call him in and I'll give you something good to eat."

"Here he is now," Carlos said.

Maude saw Leo, looking tense and nervous, entering from the storeroom.

"The horses are ready," Leo said to Carlos.

"Good," Carlos said. He spoke to Maude. "The cheese now, *señorita*."

"I have a surprise for you," Maude said as she turned.

"And I have one for you," Carlos said, coming up behind Maude.

She heard the threat in the man's voice. Before she could turn or dodge, a hand clamped down on her mouth and a strong arm encircled her waist. "Hurry!" she heard the man call.

A rolled bandana came down over her head, and as the hand was taken away, the cloth was immediately inserted in between her jaws and tied tightly to gag her. She was lifted and carried kicking and struggling through the storeroom and out onto the loading platform.

The younger man hastily mounted the horse directly from the loading platform and took a seat behind the saddle. The man holding

Maude sat her astride in the saddle. The mounted man pulled her firmly against him with one hand and with the other caught hold of the horse's reins.

"Go slow and easy until you're clear of the houses," Carlos directed. "Don't wait for me. I'll not be far behind."

Holding Maude clamped about the body so as to pin her arms to her side, Leo ghosted his horse through the early night. He saw nobody outside the houses that went past left and right of him. Then he was clear of them and free of the town, with the Rio Grande just ahead. He turned south, looking for the ford the ranchers used to cross the river.

The tinkle of a bell sounded ahead, and Leo saw the pale white outlines of a band of sheep grazing in the darkness along the river. The lead sheep saw him and raised her head, and the bell chimed again. Leo looked hurriedly about for the herdsman. He saw no one. Probably the sheep were left by themselves for the night.

He found the well-used road leading west and veered onto it. In but a few minutes, the road led him to the ford and he waded the horse through the slow current. On the opposite shore, he went south toward Mexico.

Carlos closed the rear door of the store and mounted his horse. He wondered how long before the girl would be missed and a search begun. He considered how he could give Leo

229

the best possible chance to escape undetected with the girl. Two horsemen using the same route through the row of houses might draw attention and arouse suspicion when one would not, so Carlos decided to use a different one. The alley was empty, and he rode slowly along it with the hoof falls of his steed barely audible.

At the south border of the Canutillo he struck the road leading west and soon crossed the Rio Grande. He saw the wet tracks of Leo's horse, dark splotches on the sand where he had come out of the river. Everything was working perfectly. Carlos chuckled to himself. His brother had a true beauty. In a couple of hours he would be safely in Mexico with her and lost to any pursuers.

## *Thirty-one*

Dubois entered the restaurant and quickly wound a course among the tables of the several diners. He passed Ben, seated and eating breakfast, and halted at Redpath's table.

"I have news," Dubois said.

Redpath pointed at the chair across from him and Dubois sat down. "Talk," Redpath said curtly.

"I know who has her," Dubois said, pleased with his knowledge. "We can call off the men we have looking for her."

"Not so fast. Who has her?"

"His name's Payson. Evan Payson."

Ben was near enough to hear the man's words, and at the mentioning of Evan's name, focused closely on them. Who was this "her" they were talking about? Had to be a pretty woman to arouse such keen interest in Redpath and Dubois, whom he knew by sight, for they had been pointed out to him when he had gone by the hotel to see the construction. He cocked his ear to hear more.

"How do you know she's with this Payson?" Redpath said.

"Because he was just talking to me and said he wanted to speak with you about a woman. What other woman could it be?"

"Where can I find him?"

"He's at the hotel right now."

Ben glanced at Redpath to see how the man reacted to this information. Redpath showed no emotion except for a hard smile. "That's good news. Saves me from hunting him. Who is he?"

"I knew you would want to know that, so I asked our workers and one of them knew him and told me Payson was a local fellow. That his parents owned a ranch not far from town."

"What kind of a man is he?"

"He's young, kinda tall, and skinny. There's something else. He said for you to bring a gun with you."

"Well, now, that's downright interesting. Anybody else with him?"

"No, just him. And he acted mad."

Ben dropped money on the table to pay for his meal and hastened from the restaurant.

Ben spotted Evan sitting on a pile of lumber in front of the Hanford Hotel and went toward him. He had met Davis the evening before and knew Evan had arrived. Now it seemed Evan had gotten himself into trouble in the first few hours after coming home. Ben halted in front of Evan.

"Hello, Evan," he said.

"Hello, Ben," Evan said, having watched Ben approach. "How are things with you?"

"Ugly as ever. I want to talk with you."

"I don't have much time," Evan replied, looking past Ben and along the street.

"I just heard a man being told you wanted to see him and to come with a gun. That true?"

"I'm going to kill Karl Redpath."

"Why?"

"For what he did to a friend."

"A woman friend, I'm thinking."

"I'm short of time, Ben, and can't talk with you right now."

"I've seen this fellow Redpath you're planning to kill, and I've heard about him. You don't want to fight this man. There's a damn good chance that he'll kill you instead of the other way round."

"So he's tough, and killed men. I've been told that. But he did the woman terribly wrong and he's got to pay."

"Is it a young, green-eyed woman?"

"Yes, how did you know?"

"I saw one with Redpath two nights ago. She's sure pretty enough to get a man to thinking. But not to get himself killed for."

"It's not certain that I'll be killed."

"No, it's not certain. But why not just warn him off? Won't that do?"

"What he did deserves more punishment than that. Haven't you ever felt you had to punish someone for being mean to a friend? Someone who can't fight for themselves?"

"Maybe so. But think hard about this man. Tell him what you have to say. I'll sit here with you and he probably won't start anything."

"But I want him to start a fight so I can kill him."

"Does the woman mean that much to you?"

"Yes," Evan said. He looked directly at Ben for the first time, and Ben saw something in the man he had never expected to see, a huge hatred waiting to lash out at an enemy.

"How do you kill a man who is a better fighter than you are?" Evan asked.

"If you're dead set on doing it, then don't give him an even chance," Ben said. "Do you have a good gun? Do you want to borrow mine?" Ben pulled his pistol from its holster and offered it to Evan.

"I have one," Evan said. "Wait. On second thought, I could use another gun."

Ben handed the weapon to Evan. "It's got a light trigger, so be careful."

"Is it loaded and ready to fire?" Evan asked.

"It's always ready."

"Thanks. Now get away from me, Ben. Goddamn it, get away." Evan's voice trembled.

"All right, Evan." Ben turned and moved away.

Evan called after Ben. "If I fail and Redpath kills me, will you protect Rachel from him? She's at my parents' home. Davis knows where it's at."

"Yeah, I'll do that," Ben replied over his shoulder.

Ben went half the length of the hotel and leaned against the wall to watch the coming battle. He was sorry for Evan. From what had been said about the New Orleans man, Evan had little chance to win.

Evan's muscles were taut as bowstrings as he watched the street for the appearance of Redpath. Never had his senses been more open to the world around him. His eyesight seemed sharper and he saw a little whirlwind far down the street, spinning and spinning. His hearing was more acute and he heard a pigeon cooing on the rooftop of the hotel above him. He knew the impending danger, and most likely his death, had done this to him.

Redpath strode with long strides toward the man sitting on the pile of lumber in front of the hotel. He was looking forward to killing Payson, after Payson told him where Rachel was.

Dubois, by his side, hurried to keep up.

The man had been brought along to serve as a witness for Redpath, to swear the killing had been in self-defense.

Redpath saw Payson remove his hat and wipe his forehead and face with a bandana. *You'd better sweat*, Redpath thought, *for you've not long to live.*

"Wait over there by the side of the hotel," Redpath instructed Dubois.

"Yes, sir," Dubois said, and veered aside to stand near the building.

Redpath walked swiftly on, and came to a stop a couple of body lengths from Payson. He glared down at the seated man.

"So, Payson, you've got my wife Marcella?" Redpath said. The man's face was strained and beaded with sweat. The hand holding the bandana in his lap was trembling.

Evan looked at Redpath. "Her name's Rachel, and she's not your wife. You found her unconscious and lied to her. You're a bastard, Redpath."

Redpath was surprised at the man's harsh words. False courage, that's all it was. Payson's hand with the bandana was shaking strongly now. Redpath almost laughed out loud at the pitiful sight. He glanced to the side at Dubois.

A man horribly scarred was standing close beside Dubois and talking to him. Good, two witnesses were better than one. Now all Redpath had to do was make Payson act first.

"Is that a pistol I see there?" Redpath said, and gestured at the gun in the holster on Evan's side.

"Yes, and it's loaded. Is yours?"

*Damn strange question*, thought Redpath. "Yes, Payson, and one of the bullets is for you."

"I don't believe it's loaded, so how can a bullet be for me?" Evan said.

Again Redpath was surprised at the man's words. He saw Payson's hand, shaking badly, rise holding the red bandana. The man was going to wipe sweat again.

An explosion ripped the bandana from Payson's hand. A powerful blow slammed Redpath in the chest and a terrific pain erupted. He stumbled backward two steps before catching himself. Payson's actions were all a goddamned trick. Redpath reached for his pistol.

Evan jumped to his feet and pointed the weapon that he had kept concealed under the bandana. He fired again straight into the center of Redpath's chest. The man sank to his knees, held there for a moment with an unbelieving expression on his face, and then fell sideways to the street.

Evan sank down on the pile of lumber and stared at Redpath's corpse. He was shaking all over. He put his hands between his legs to quiet them. He did not know Ben had come until he spoke.

"Damn fine job, Evan," Ben said.

"It's hell to kill a man," Evan said, his voice quivering like his body.

"Not if he deserved killing. I guess you figured this one did."

"You were a lawman once," Evan said, looking at Ben, and all the hatred was gone from his eyes. "What will they do to me now?"

"Depends on what story the witnesses tell Sheriff Willis. For me, I saw Redpath reach for a gun and you shot him in self-defense."

"You couldn't have seen that, for he didn't. I tricked him to throw him off guard. Then shot him."

"Don't tell me what I saw," Ben said. "And don't tell Redpath's man, Dubois, standing over there either. He saw what I saw and that was you shot Redpath when he reached for his pistol."

"Knowing you, you probably said something else to Dubois."

"Well, there's a little thievery in every man, so I pointed out to him how, if he thought real hard, he could make money from Redpath's death. And the women they'd brought from New Orleans would be his now and they were very valuable. I think there's more than just a little thievery in Dubois, and he was way ahead of me in just how to take a big chunk of Redpath's wealth."

"You told him nothing else?"

"I did tell him that you were a tough son of a bitch and would kill him if he didn't tell the right story."

"Did he believe you?"

"He just saw what you did to Redpath. So, yeah, he believed."

Rachel whipped her horse at the top of its speed along the road leading to El Paso. She must reach Evan before he was killed by Karl Redpath.

She had slept soundly and awakened tardily. Mrs. Payson had invited her into the kitchen for breakfast and they had sat talking. When Rachel had asked about Evan, she was told he had gone to El Paso. Rachel instantly knew Evan's plan, to meet with Karl Redpath and order him to stay away from her. She had hastily saddled Davis's horse and ridden away.

The road dipped down into the tree-lined valley of the stream that came by the ranch house. Rachel sent the horse splashing across.

The steed took the far bank with long lunges. At the top it shied abruptly as two horsemen raced out of the trees and blocked its way. Rachel was flung to the side by the sudden movement. She grabbed for the pommel, managed to catch hold of it, and stopped her fall hanging half out of the saddle.

One of the riders spurred up close, caught her by the shoulder, and sat her upright in the saddle. Rachel recognized one of the young Mexican cowboys she had seen on the street in El Paso.

"You!" Rachel exclaimed, looking directly at Carlos. "What are you doing here?"

"Looking for you, Rachel." Carlos was savoring his stroke of good fortune.

He and Leo had arrived at daylight and waited for an opportunity to capture the woman. They had seen a man come out of the house and ride off to the north with two cowboys from the bunkhouse. Shortly the man who had brought the woman from El Paso had left and come along the road toward El Paso. The two Mexicans had remained hidden and waiting in the trees to be certain there were no more men at the house. Then, to their surprise, the woman herself came racing past.

"How do you know my name?"

"I heard the man in El Paso say it."

"What do you want?" Rachel said. She wanted to be gone, but the two men blocked her way with their horses.

"I'm going to take you to Chihuahua with me."

"That's crazy. Get out of my way. I must go to El Paso."

"Not today," Carlos replied. "Not tomorrow. Not ever."

Rachel looked at Leo, holding the head of her horse by the bridle. His face was hard and determined. She looked back at Carlos, who was watching her with an expression of such intense desire that it frightened her.

"I'm not going anywhere with you."

"Oh, yes, you are, pretty Rachel," Carlos said. "And you're going with us right now."

"No, I'm not," Rachel cried out. She jerked the reins of the horse to the side to break free of Leo's grip.

Leo easily held the animal. He took hold of

the reins and wrenched them from Rachel's hands.

"You lead and I'll follow," Carlos said to Leo.

Leo nodded, spun his mount, and leading Rachel's horse, went south at a fast gallop.

# *Thirty-two*

"Where's that ugly brother of yours?" Lester Ivorsen shouted out to Tom Hawkins. Lester was standing in the entryway of the building where Tom manufactured wheels.

"Talk polite to me, Lester, or I'll come out there and we'll have some fisticuffs." Tom was enjoying the sight of Lester's bruised face. He was obviously hurting through the ribs from Ben's beating.

"All right, Tom, all right. Do you know where Ben is?"

"He's in El Paso. Staying at the El Prado far as I know. What's your trouble with Ben?"

"That's just between him and me."

"I'll give you a free piece of advice, Lester. You'd better not yell at him like you just did to me. Ben's not easygoing like I am."

"He's got some answering to do," Lester said belligerently.

"I warned you. Don't push Ben."

"We'll see about that," Lester said, and stomped off.

"Have a drink with me," Ben said to Evan as they came out of Sheriff Willis's office.

"I could use one after all this," Evan replied. He was feeling the relief from not being charged with the murder of Redpath. Dubois had told the same eyewitness story as had Ben. After hearing both men, the sheriff had stated that it was probably a good thing that Redpath was dead for he had enough trouble keeping the peace in El Paso without a gambling house, and maybe a whorehouse, starting up in business.

"Let's try the *cantina* on the plaza. It's early but they'll probably be open."

"Okay."

They walked without speaking. Ben had a feeling it was going to be a bad day. It was still early and already there had been a killing. He thought of Tom's offer to become a partner in his wheelwright business. That was the only good thing that had occurred since Ben had returned. No, that wasn't true. The dance in the night with Maude had been wonderful.

They turned into the plaza, and Ben stopped short at the sight of Lester Ivorsen coming out of the hotel. Lester saw Ben and came swiftly at him.

"Trouble and more trouble," Ben said, pointing at Lester.

"He looks big enough to give plenty," Evan said. "And he looks damn mad."

Ben watched Lester's hands and hoped he didn't have a gun and want to fight.

241

"Where's Maude?" Lester called out in a tightly controlled voice.

"Now how the hell would I know that?" Ben replied.

"Because you have her."

"She's your wife so I'd think she'd be in your house with your other wives."

"Silas Dunlap said he was watching his sheep down by the river and saw you ride off with her."

"Silas is wrong." Ben felt his scalp crawl and the hairs rise and twist along his spine. Had something happened to Maude?

"Silas doesn't lie," Lester said, the anger sharp in his voice.

"I know he doesn't, but he's old and half blind. Tell me what he said."

"Just that. That he saw you carrying Maude off on your horse last night."

"Well, he didn't see me last night. In fact, I've been in El Paso for the past day." If Maude had run away from Lester, why hadn't she sent a message to Ben? Then again, maybe Tom had heard from her. "I want to talk with Silas and find out what he really saw," Ben said.

"You're not getting away with that kind of answer," Lester said. He advanced on Ben.

"Hold it right there," Ben ordered. He put his hand on the butt of his pistol. "I'm riding to Canutillo to talk with Silas and I don't have time to argue with you."

Lester halted instantly at the threat. "I know you have something to do with her being gone."

"Think what you want. But I'm going to get my horse and ride to Canutillo, so don't get in my way."

Ben arrived in Canutillo and went past Silas's house, found the old man not there, and continued to the Rio Grande to where Lester said the man had his sheep. As Ben neared the river, he saw Silas rise to his feet from where he had been lying in the shade of a big tree and look in his direction.

"Howdy, young Ben Hawkins," Silas called.

"Howdy, old Silas Dunlap," Ben replied.

The two men's words of greeting were fifteen years old, having begun when Silas had used his when Ben had been just a lad, and Ben, taking affront at being called young, had yelled back his.

Silas laughed in a light, happy way. "It's good to see you, Ben."

"You too, Silas."

Ben had known the old man from the earliest days of his childhood, and liked him very much. He was a kind and gentle fellow who had never married and earned his living with his small band of sheep. Ben noted Silas appeared to have shriveled and grown old since last seen, but then at eighty or so—Ben could only guess his age—changes could occur rapidly.

"What're you doing in Canutillo? I thought you'd be long gone to distant parts with Maude."

"That's what I want to talk to you about. I don't have Maude. Tell me why you told Lester I did."

"Saw you and the pretty lass leavin' last night. Then this morning Lester goes running around town asking about her. Finally he comes to me and I told him what I saw."

"That's my trouble, Silas. Lester's accusing me of taking Maude. But it wasn't me you saw. And I don't know if that was Maude either."

"Well, now, I sure thought it was you and the girl."

"Tell me exactly what you saw."

"Well, this horse carrying two people comes down from the direction of the store and through those houses" Silas pointed up the slope at the town "past me here with my sheep, and then south along the river. The one in the saddle was small like Maude and had long hair. The fellow was riding the rump of the horse behind the saddle and hugging her up close. When Maude was gone this morning, well, I just added one and one and got two, you and Maude. Now you're telling me I was wrong?"

"About the man being me, you were surely wrong. I don't know about the woman being Maude. Tell me more of what you saw."

"Like I said, I'm pretty sure the person in the saddle was a small woman. Men don't go around hugging other men up tight like that. The man, now that I get a fresh look at you up on that horse, was somewhat smaller than you."

"What did he look like?"

"Just a man. Couldn't make out his face. Had a big hat, a sombrero like most of the Mexes wear. Ben, you know there're no secrets in Canutillo. You were seen dancing with Maude behind the town hall and the story's all over town. Then Lester gets stomped real bad. There's few men who can do that to him. And I figure you were the most likely to have done it after dancing with Maude. Like I said before, I just added one and one. Seems I got the wrong two."

"Yes, you did. Maude could be the woman. But who could the man be?"

"Since it wasn't you, I can't guess. I'm sorry I got you in trouble with Lester."

"Don't be concerned about that. Lester doesn't worry me."

"I didn't think he would. You want me to tell him 'twasn't you?"

"Can if you want to. But I doubt he'll believe you with you changing your story."

"Most likely not."

"Gotta go, Silas. I may be back later to have you show me those tracks."

"I'll be here."

Ben reined Brutus toward Tom's place of business. He hoped Maude had left a message there for him. If not, then Ben would have a whole lot of worrying to do as to who really ran off with Maude.

# Thirty-three

Maude paced the small space of her prison and tried to devise a plan to escape. For several hours—she didn't know how long for she had no way to measure time—she had been confined in the room in a warehouse in Ciudad Juarez.

Maude's Mexican captor had not spoken to her as they rode his horse through the night. He had held her against his chest, and at times had fondled her breast. She had made no resistance to his touch, thinking that perhaps he would become careless and she could run into the darkness and hide.

She had studied the stars and knew they were traveling south. Also, she recognized the rough, stream-cut land, with the gullies running from right to left, and knew it lay just west of the Rio Grande. Toward midnight they entered a town and she recognized Ciudad Juarez. They were now in Mexico and her chances of escape had been greatly reduced.

They had crossed through the town and come to the warehouse, where her captor had awakened an old man sleeping in a room on the end of the building. The man had not appeared surprised at seeing Maude. Rather, he had seemed sad.

"Miguel, light our way to the room," Leo had ordered the old man.

"Yes, Señor Valdes," the old man replied.

He took a lighted lantern and guided the way into the depths of the warehouse.

As they moved through the building, with Leo holding Maude firmly by the arm, she surveyed her surroundings, looking for something that might aid her in escaping. The main part of the structure was high-ceilinged and held many piles of freight. In a cleared area near the entrance of the building was a stagecoach, its body painted a deep red and its wheels a bright yellow. Many horses were in stalls on the far left, while on the right side was a row of strongly built freight wagons.

At the rear of the warehouse, the old man entered a small room, lit a coal-oil lamp, and returned to the outside. Maude knew they planned to imprison her in the room, and she tried to draw back. Leo tightened his grip on her arm and propelled her inside.

"You must stay here for a time, Maude," Leo said. "Everything you need is here. Food will be brought to you in the morning."

"Please let me go, Leo," Maude pleaded. "Take me back across the river and I'll never tell anyone what you have done."

"No."

"Why not? I've done nothing to you."

"I'm going to keep you for what you can do for me," Leo said.

"What is that?" Maude asked, but she knew the answer.

"We will talk later," Leo said. He reached out and ran the tips of his fingers along the curve of Maude's chin and across her lips. "Yes, later, but soon."

He left the room and closed the door behind him. Maude heard a heavy bar drop into place to lock her in. A chill ran through her.

She turned to inspect her surroundings, and was surprised at the furnishings of the room and its cleanliness. It was obvious that the space had been prepared for her, or some other woman. A wool carpet of good quality covered the hard-packed dirt floor. A wooden-framed cot had a feather-tick mattress and snow-white sheets freshly washed and ironed. A table held an earthen pitcher full of water, a porcelain cup, a washbasin, and a coal-oil lamp and six matches. A chamber pot sat in a corner.

The room had no windows. The walls were made of thick boards, rough and splintery. The door was of the same material. The room smelled of horses, leather, and saddles. Maude judged it had been used as a tack room prior to being emptied and prepared for a prisoner.

She had listened at the door, and now and again heard movement, as if someone was stationed to prevent her from escaping. Still, even with the presence of a guard who might hear her efforts, she had tried to find an avenue of escape. She had tested every board of the walls, pushing on them with all her strength. Not one had budged the slightest degree. She had considered digging out under one of the walls, but had nothing with which to dig. Dejected, she was resolved to the fact that the only route to freedom lay through the door.

A crack high in a wall began to show a little light, and Maude knew daylight had come. Soon Leo, or somebody, would come to do whatever they planned to do to her. Dreading the future, she sat down on the edge of the bed.

Maude had not waited long when she heard the bar on the door being removed. The door opened, moving outward, and a thin, brown-skinned man wearing a pistol strapped to his waist stepped into the opening. He had jet-black eyes set in a face deeply pockmarked, like brown mud trampled by horses. His sight fell upon Maude sitting quietly on the bed, and he studied her for a moment. Then he motioned at someone Maude could not see to come forward.

The old man who had guided Maude and her captor through the warehouse in the night came into the room with a tray of food. He placed the tray on the table beside the lamp and hastened from the room. The pockmarked man closed the door, and it rattled on its hinges as the bar dropped back into its slot.

She eyed the food, not wanting to eat something her captors had given. Still, she was ravenous, having missed supper, and she would need her strength for the ordeal that lay ahead. She ate, and then lay down on the bed and rested. She had a plan for what she would do the next time the door opened.

*      *      *

Maude heard voices outside in the ware-house, and rose to her feet and took up the earthen pitcher. She had emptied out the water, and now held the heavy pitcher ready to use as a weapon. She would strike her captors and run. If she could reach a horse before they caught her, she would give them a hard chase.

She heard the bar being removed. Then the door began to open. Maude rammed the rough wood with her shoulder, striking it with all her strength, and it flew wide. She charged through, the pitcher held cocked in her right hand and ready to swing.

Maude was startled to find a white-skinned woman standing directly in front of her. Behind the woman were the two men who had kidnapped her. She swerved around the woman and charged on. She hurled the pitcher at the head of the nearer man, Leo, who had carried her into Mexico.

Leo ducked the pitcher, then quickly moved toward Maude as she hurtled past. He hooked her around the waist and stopped her wild flight.

Rachel was frozen in place for an instant when Maude exploded from the room. Then she whirled and dashed across the warehouse. Carlos had anticipated Rachel's attempt to run. He leapt after her and dragged her to a stop.

"None of that, Rachel," Carlos said as he propelled her back.

"They are spirited ones," Leo said, smiling.

"I like that," Carlos said. "They will give spirited colts. Now don't let them out of your sight at any time."

"They won't get away from me."

Maude listened to the two men talking and looked around the warehouse. The old man she had seen before and a younger man were hooking a second team of horses to the stagecoach. It appeared she and the other woman would be hauled away in that vehicle. She had wanted to leave Canutillo and Lester, but not like this. The man with the pockmarked face stood off by himself and watched her and the other woman with his black, coal-chip eyes.

The two kidnappers lapsed into Spanish; however, Maude understood enough of the language to get the gist of what they were saying. She wanted desperately to know what they planned for her.

"Travel as fast as you can," Carlos said to Leo. "Most likely no one will know what has happened to the women. Still, there may be pursuers, and so the farther south you go the safer you will be. Change horses at every one of our stations."

"I'll travel today and through the night, and not rest until dark tomorrow. If I need fresh horses between stations, I'll buy them. Emanuel is our best driver and no one will catch us."

"Leave at once. Guard the women closely for they will try to escape. And watch for bandits."

"Rafael is worth any three other *pistoleros* and will help me keep the girls safe," Leo said, and nodded at the pockmarked man. "What about you?"

"I'll find Tattersall and we'll kill Hawkins. Then I'll follow behind you to stop any gringos who chase us."

Maude heard the name Hawkins. She recalled that the old man had called Leo Señor Valdes, and that Ben had stolen Valdes horses, and the connection came together for her. Carlos and other men planned to kill Ben. He was in danger and she had no way to warn him, nor to tell him she had been taken captive and to come and rescue her.

Carlos spoke. "Arrange for our priest to conduct a wedding as soon as I arrive back at the rancho."

"Two weddings," Leo said.

"Right. Now get the women into the stage-coach and be on your way."

## *Thirty-four*

"Look at the face on that man," Crampton said, peering through the night at the horseman passing by on the street.

"One damn ugly hombre," Butcher replied.

The two scalp hunters had just come out onto the sidewalk in front of La Posada *Cantina* in El Paso when Ben, mounted on Brutus, came past. He was illuminated briefly as he rode through the light shining through the windows of the *cantina*.

"He has to be that Hawkins we've been hired to shoot," Crampton said.

"I think so too, for there couldn't be more than one man that ugly in El Paso."

"Tattersall found out that Hawkins is staying at the El Prado. Let's follow this fellow and see if that's where he's going. If it is him, what do you say to us shooting him and not wait for Tattersall's help?"

"I like the idea, for then we'll get Valdes's money quicker," Butcher said.


Ben rode Brutus into the dark alley behind the hotel. When near the stables, he dismounted and dropped the reins to ground-hitch the horse. He approached the stables warily, for Lester Ivorsen knew where he was staying and just might be mad enough to try to shoot him.

Ben found no enemy lurking in the stables, only the horses of other hotel patrons in some of the stalls. Brutus was brought forward and given a pitchfork of clover hay and a generous ration of shelled corn. The horse went for the grain first. While he crunched away, Ben rubbed him down with one of the brushes supplied by the hotel.

Ben left Brutus eating contentedly and went through the night along the stone-paved walkway to the hotel. He had just arrived from Canutillo. There he had gone to Tom's wheelwright shop to check for a message from Maude, and found none. He had then returned to Silas Dunlap, grazing his sheep by the river, and had had him point out the horse tracks of the rider who had carried off the woman.

The tracks had been easy to follow until they struck the heavily used road leading west toward Silver City. There they had merged with scores of other horse tracks and he had lost them. Ben was frustrated at not being able to follow the tracks further, and deeply worried about what might have happened to Maude. Tomorrow at first light he would continue his search.

He halted at the entryway into the walled courtyard and peered ahead into the partially lighted area. To aid those people arriving after dark to find their way, the manager kept a hurricane lamp lit and hanging on an iron pole in the center of the courtyard where the path from the street met the one coming from the stables. The light only partially lit the large enclosed area, not reaching the darkness under the trees on the perimeter nor the wall of the hotel on the side next to the stables. Still thinking of Lester, Ben stepped sideways to get out of the light coming along the pathway.

Just as Ben moved, a pistol fired with a bright red flash from the deep night shadows beneath a tree on the left side of the patio. Instantly he felt a sting across the outside of his left arm up high near the shoulder. He flinched and moved to the side, and at the same time drew his Colt six-gun.

He fired twice, bracketing the location of the flash, hunting the shooter's chest, and kept moving so as not to give his enemy a stationary target. A man cried out and Ben heard something heavy fall, something that could be a man's body. Damn that Lester for forcing Ben to shoot him.

Red flame blossomed on Ben's right in the blackness by the wall of the hotel. The bullet skimmed past the side of Ben's face with the snarl of a deadly bee.

Ben fired twice again, one shot on each side of the flash, wanting to kill his enemy. Two men shooting at him meant that it wasn't Lester, for the man had no friends who would try to kill Ben. Maude's father was an ornery bastard, and most likely angry at Ben; however, he wouldn't be party to a deliberate night ambush.

A second shot at Ben, poorly aimed, came from farther along the side of the hotel. Then came the pounding thud of feet as a man ran from the patio. The nerve of Ben's second adversary had broken and he was fleeing.

Ben stopped moving. There could be a third man or a fourth and Ben didn't want to blunder into one of them. He crouched and his eyes probed the darkness. He waited, turning his head and listening intently. He saw nothing, and heard nothing, except the moans of the wounded gunman off a ways.

A man shouted from the main entrance of the hotel, "Stop that shooting out there for I've sent for the sheriff."

"Tarlow, stay inside," Ben shouted back. Tarlow was the hotel owner. "It's not safe."

Ben crept soundlessly toward the source of the moaning sound. He held his pistol ready to shoot should the man be only pretending to be injured. The man came into sight, a crumpled form on the flagstones of the courtyard. When closer still, Ben could make out the man's pistol where it had been dropped on the stone-covered ground.

Ben picked up the gun and rolled the man onto his back. The man looked up into Ben's shadowed face.

"That you, Crampton? I can't see good."

"Yeah, it's me," Ben said in a coarse voice.

"Did we get him?"

"He's dead."

"Good," the man said in a weak voice. He felt his bloody chest and found the hole where the bullet had struck him, breaking the thick sternum bone and plowing deep into his body.

"Goddamn, I'm bleeding bad." He inserted his finger into the hole, trying to plug the flow of blood.

Ben wanted to question the man for there was much he needed to know. However, he waited for the man to speak. The most truthful information would be that which came voluntarily while the man thought Ben was his partner.

The man was silent for a time. Then he spoke slowly, with his words slurred. "I'm done for, ain't I? A doctor won't do me any good?"

"That's right," Ben said. The man was

quiet again, considering his plight. Finally his words came, mere whispers.

"I thought so. Tell Tattersall that you get my share of Valdes's money." His voice was faint, sliding down, ever weaker.

"Whose money?" Ben wasn't certain he had correctly heard the last words. The man didn't respond, holding his finger jammed into the hole in his chest and barely breathing.

"Whose money?" Ben said more loudly. The man was dying, and Ben held his thoughts by only a little spider's thread. He slapped the man sharply. "Whose money?"

"Valdes," the man whispered. He went slack, all life gone.

"Valdes," Ben said. So that was what all this was about. He grabbed the man by the collar and dragged him into the light of the hurricane lantern. He knelt beside the man to examine his face. He was a stranger.

Ben rose to his feet. Ramos Valdes had hired men to come to El Paso to kill him because of the horses he had stolen. The gunmen would most likely have succeeded if Ben hadn't been concerned about Lester wanting revenge on him. He had been god-awful lucky.

Ben saw that Tarlow had come forward and now stood in the edge of the light from the hurricane lamp. He called out to the man. "Tell Sheriff Willis that two men tried to shoot me. One got away. This one wasn't lucky. I'll talk to the sheriff, but later. Right now I've got something to do south of the river."

"All right, Ben. I'll tell him what you said."

Ben went to the stables, took Brutus away from his shelled corn, and saddled him. Valdes had a freight station in Ciudad Juarez. Ben knew where it was for he was almost as familiar with that town as he was with El Paso. That was where he would start his search for Valdes.

He rode south the short distance to the Rio Grande, forded the slow-moving water, black as ink in the darkness, and went into Ciudad Juarez. Ben had been careful not to kill any of the Valdes family or their men. However, they considered his theft of their horses to be worth his life, and they had tried to collect it. That added a deadly dimension to the game. He would give them more of a fight than they had bargained for.

## Thirty-five

Miguel sat rocking in his favorite chair—in fact, his only chair—in the darkness in front of his one-room abode in the Valdes warehouse. The room was provided as part of his payment as night watchman for the Valdes Freight Company.

He was thinking of the two American *señoritas* the Valdes brothers had stolen from their homes and carried away. They were very pretty, too pretty for their own good. The *señoritas* had been forced into the stagecoach

258

by Carlos and Leo, and the doors lashed shut with lengths of rope to prevent them from jumping from the vehicle and escaping. The stagecoach had sped off into the night with Emanuel driving the two teams of horses and Leo and the *pistolero* Rafael riding horseback ahead to watch for bandits. Miguel knew the *señoritas* would never be seen north of the Rio Grande again.

Valdes and his sons took whatever they wanted, even the women of the tough Americans.

Miguel didn't like the men from north of the river. He had fought with the Mexican Army against the American invaders at the battle for Mexico City in 1847. The Americans had beaten them, with Miguel being wounded in the leg in the fighting. That defeat was a terrible memory even after all the years that had passed. Yet he was sorry to have been part of keeping the *señoritas* captives.

Miguel felt the presence of something or some person near in the darkness behind him. Before he could turn, a man whispered in Spanish, "Don't move or make a noise and I'll not kill you."

A hand caught Miguel by the shoulder and another clamped him around the neck. He felt the great strength in the hands and his old heart began to pound wildly. He tried to speak, but couldn't find his voice. He did not think this was a thief who had come to rob the warehouse. This was about the American *señoritas*, and the man who held him would be very angry and that made him dangerous. Miguel should have expected someone would come and should have locked himself in his room.

"I'll not make a sound," Miguel said, his voice hoarse because of the pressure on his neck.

"Then you're safe," said the unseen man. The man's hands slid down Miguel's sides, found his pistol, and took it from the holster. "Do you have another gun?"

"Yes, a rifle, but it's in the room." The hands caught Miguel by the neck and shoulder again. "I have questions for you."

"Ask me anything," Miguel said. He was frightened about the hand holding him by the neck. The grip was so tight that he could feel the bones of his spine grinding against each other.

"Has any member of the Valdes family been here recently?" Ben asked.

"Yes."

"When?"

"Early today."

"Who?"

"Carlos and Leo."

"Not Ramos?"

"No."

"Any men with them?"

"No. I didn't see any."

"Did they mention anyone? Any Americans? A man named Tattersall?"

Ben decided obtaining information by asking questions was taking too long. "Tell me everything you know and that they said."

"Carlos told Leo to take the American *señoritas* south. That he was going to stay here and join with this Tattersall to kill a man named Hawkins. Then they both left."

The hand on Miguel's neck clenched down and he gasped at the pain. He was certain that he was going to die. And all because of the Valdes brothers' desire for American women.

After a few seconds, the hand eased its grip and Miguel could breathe again.

"Old man, I think you just lied to me." Ben was surprised at the mentioning of taking the women south. He recalled what Silas had told him about the man he had seen with the woman near the Rio Grande at Canutillo. He had been wearing a large sombrero. What this old man had just said agreed with that. Either Leo or Carlos had been the man with the woman.

"I didn't lie! I didn't!" Miguel exclaimed. "Leo put the *señoritas* into the stagecoach and left with Rafael. Then Carlos left."

"Two *señoritas*?"

"Yes, two."

Ben eased his grip on the man's neck. "When did they bring them here?"

"The smaller one last night. It was dark and I had to light a lantern to show them through the warehouse."

"The second one. When?"

"Early today."

"The names of the *señoritas*, old man? What were their names?"

"I can't remember," Miguel said, wanting the hand to let go of his neck.

"Think fast for I have no time to waste."

Miguel's brain was racing to remember what Leo had called the small *señorita*. The name came to him. "Leo called her Maude. Yes, Maude was the name of the smaller *señorita*, the first one they brought."

"What did she look like? Describe her."

"She was small like I said, and had golden hair, like the sun."

Ben had no doubt that the old man was telling the truth about Maude, for how else could he know her name and the color of her hair? Also, the time was right, enough time for someone to ride from Canutillo to Ciudad Juarez with her.

"Now give me the name of the second one. Be quick about it."

"I don't know it. I never did hear it spoken."

"You lie."

"No, no. The second *señorita* was brought just before they left. I saw her. But Carlos ordered me to help Emanuel harness the horses and I wasn't close enough to hear what they said."

"All right. What did she look like?"

"Taller than the first one and just as pretty."

"What else do you remember about her?"

"She had strange eyes."

"How strange? Describe them."

"They were green eyes, large green eyes."

Carlos and Leo had kidnapped the two women and carried them south, just as their mother had been kidnapped years before.

She had remained with her captor to raise

her two sons. Now those sons were imitating their father, and had assumed these women, just as their mother, would remain with them. Ben had come to fight the Valdes family for trying to kill him, only to discover they had kidnapped two young women, one of them Maude.

His anger rose white hot. About the Valdes family wanting retribution for the horses, Ben could understand. But when it came to stealing Maude, that was a fatal error on their part, and Ben would take terrible vengeance.

"That's all I know about the *señoritas*," Miguel said.

"When did Leo leave?"

"Yesterday morning."

Hours ago, Ben realized. Leo would drive hard, and with frequent changes of horses for the stagecoach, could be deep in Mexico by now.

"What are you going to do if I turn you loose?"

"Whatever you tell me to do."

"You will forget that I was ever here."

"That is what I would choose to do. If the Valdes sons found out that I had told what they had done to the *señoritas*, they would kill me."

"If they didn't, then I would."

The hands released their hold on Miguel. He did not hear the man leave. Yet he knew he was once again alone. He rubbed his sore neck and drew in a deep breath. He shivered at the sweetness of the air.

# Thirty-six

"You're a stupid man," Carlos raged at Crampton. His hand was on the pistol belted to his waist. He wanted the American to fight so that he could kill him.

Crampton recognized the challenge and kept his hand away from his pistol. He had barely escaped from Hawkins's bullets, and didn't want a fight with the angry Mexican.

Crampton still couldn't believe how quickly, or how accurately, Hawkins had returned his shot. The man's bullets had straddled his chest, so close that each had burned his flesh as they drove past. Had Crampton moved either left or right when he fired, he would be dead now.

You found out that fighting Hawkins is more dangerous than killing some Indians from hiding," Carlos said. He shook his head in disgust for he saw Crampton wasn't going to provide him with the opportunity to shoot him.

Tattersall didn't like Carlos's rough words to his man, but he held himself reined in. He would only take Crampton's side if it really came down to a gunfight.

The three men were in the boardinghouse in El Paso where Tattersall and his men had taken lodging. Carlos had arrived a few minutes before to find Crampton telling Tattersall about the attempt to kill Hawkins.

"Was Butcher alive when you left?" Tattersall

said. Crampton had acted like a coward, and Tattersall hadn't expected that.

"I don't know. He shot at Hawkins. He must've missed, or not hit him hard, for Hawkins shot back at him, and at me. I didn't hear anything more from Butcher. He could be alive or dead."

"If he's alive, Hawkins will make him talk," Carlos said. "Now he probably knows that the Valdes family has come north to kill him."

"I'll round up my other men and we'll deal with him tonight," Tattersall said.

"No," Carlos said. "You've never seen what the man can do with a gun, especially a rifle. You don't want to go straight at him when he's ready for you."

"I say there's enough of us to kill him."

"Most likely all of us could. But who wants to die doing it?"

"You're paying the money to kill him, so what do you want to do?"

Carlos understood Hawkins, and was certain he would ride into Mexico to the Valdes rancho and strike at Ramos and Leo. Hawkins might also see the American *señoritas* and try to return them to the States. Both situations must be prevented. Carlos would gather the best *pistoleros* in Mexico and catch and kill Hawkins before he ever reached the rancho.

"Hawkins won't allow Crampton's attack to go unpunished," Carlos said. "So let him come into my country where I have all the advantage."

"What about me and my men?" Tattersall

said. "We made an agreement with your father that for five thousand dollars in gold we would kill Hawkins. We've rode hundreds of miles because of that."

"Come with me and help take his head and you'll be paid as my father said."

"When do you want to leave?"

"This very minute. Gather up your men."


In his room in the El Prado Hotel, Ben quickly packed for his ride into the hostile land south of the Rio Grande. Upon his first arrival in El Paso he had brought his Spencer rifle, bedroll, and the other items of his spartan outfit into the hotel for safekeeping. Now he gathered the outfit up into his arms, left the room, and went to Brutus, tied in front of the hotel.

He attached the scabbard of the Spencer to the right side of the saddle. The saddlebags and bedroll were fastened into their usual places behind the saddle. Then he walked swiftly toward the lobby of the hotel to pay what he owed for his stay and tell Tarlow that he would be gone for several days. He wanted to be gone before other men came to try to shoot him. More importantly, he wanted to catch Leo before he reached the Valdes rancho, which was guarded like a fortress.

"Ben, wait up," a man called from the plaza.

"What do you want?" Ben replied, recognizing Evan's voice.

"I need your help."

"For what?"

"I want you to help me find Rachel."

"What happened to her?"

"That's just it, I don't know," Evan said, drawing closer to Ben. "Early this morning, she left my folks' ranch to catch up with me in town. I never did see her, and she never returned to the ranch."

"Maybe she just up and left you." The words of the old night watchman at the Valdes warehouse came to Ben. The man had said there had been a second woman being taken with Maude into Mexico. That woman had green eyes, and Ben knew Rachel had eyes of that color from having seen her with Redpath in the restaurant.

"She wouldn't do that and I'm sure of it," Evan said. "Something has happened to her. You know what she looks like and I want you to help me find her."

"Evan, I just got back from Ciudad Juarez. While I was there, I talked with an old man and he told me about a pretty green-eyed *señorita* he saw being carried off into Mexico. I didn't know who she might be then. But now you tell me your Rachel's missing. So that must be who it was."

"My God. When did this happen?"

"Early today." Ben felt some guilt at not telling Evan that Maude had also been carried off. But not enough guilt to forestall the plan that was jelling in his mind.

"Who was it that had her? Did he say?"

267

"He told me there were two men. The Valdes brothers."

"Valdes? Isn't that the name of the man that you stole horses from?"

"The same."

"Why would they take her?"

"That's the way their father got his woman, or so I've heard. Now they're doing the same."

"Do you know where they would take her?"

"Most likely to their rancho in the mountains west of Chihuahua."

"You must know where it is."

"Been there a time or three."

"You've got to help me get her back."

"I don't have to do anything of the kind."

"I'll pay you. I can't do it by myself."

"I seem to remember a fellow who had his face all shot to hell and was willing to pay a certain surgeon to fix it for him. Now the surgeon had the skill, but wouldn't do it, said he couldn't stand to operate on a man. Does that sound familiar to you?"

"Yes," Evan said weakly.

"Now that surgeon wants me to ride hundreds of miles into Mexico and get his girl back from one of the most powerful men in that country. Valdes wants me dead and can muster a hundred *pistoleros*, even two hundred, to do it. Hell, the old man can get the Mexican Army after me. Now you want me to ride into that."

"Ben, I can't get Rachel back by myself."

"How much does the woman mean to you?"

"Everything, Ben."

268

"What are you willing to do for me if I would help you? What's the payment?"

Evan studied Ben, standing and facing him in the night in front of the hotel. Ben's face was in deep darkness; however, the massive scars that deformed it were imprinted on Evan's memory. He knew fully the complexity and danger of operating to reshape the man's face. The horrible sensation came to him of holding a scalpel in his hands and cutting living flesh, and seeing the blood flowing, and all the time the man quivering and jerking with pain so intense from a million severed nerve endings that he couldn't control his body to lie still and strong men were required to hold him.

"Help me, Ben, and I'll do my very best to repair your face. But I'm telling you the pain will be so great that you might die."

"It won't kill me," Ben replied. Evan would never know that the pain of being isolated from the world, from all humans, had already killed him. Or would have if it hadn't been for a wolf that acted almost human.

Ben put out his hand. "I want an oath and a handshake on it."

Evan took the hand and gripped it firmly. "You have my word that as soon as we return to El Paso with Rachel, I will do everything I can to restore your face."

Ben retained Evan's hand locked tightly in his. "Not good enough. If by chance Rachel should not return with us, for whatever reason, you will still perform the operation. Say it."

"She must come back with me."

"Say it!"

"Even if Rachel doesn't return, I will still operate on your face. Ben, I want to warn you, you won't look as you did before."

"But I'll look human?"

"Yes, I believe I can do that."

"That will do. Now we'll get you outfitted. And I need more cartridges for my guns. I know a store where the owner sleeps up above. It's late but he'll open up for me."

"Let's hurry."

"Give me a minute to talk with Tarlow and then we'll be on our way."

Ben went into the hotel. He was deeply worried. Valdes, with many tough fighting men, would be waiting somewhere along the route. Ben and Evan would have to shoot their way through them. Then Maude and Rachel had to be taken from them by force, or stealth, or trickery, or all three. If he could succeed in that, he had to keep all three alive during the long journey back to the States. Ben wasn't sure it was possible.

# *Thirty-seven*

In the darkness, Ben slowed Brutus from a gallop to a walk, and guided him off El Camino Real and onto a cross street in Ciudad Juarez. Evan reined his horse to follow.

"Why are we stopping here?" Evan asked.

"We need horses," Ben said. He didn't like being questioned about his actions. "You don't expect to ride that one you have at a run for hundreds of miles, do you?"

"Hadn't thought about that. Just wanted to hurry on after Rachel."

"Start thinking about how we're going to catch up with the Valdes boys," Ben said sharply. "And be ready for anything and everything. Carlos will try to stop us before we get to his family's rancho. Are you ready for a fight?"

"Yes, if there is one."

"You'd better be, for the odds are damn big that we'll have to kill some men before we get Rachel and...Rachel back." He'd almost said, "and Maude." It wasn't time to tell Evan that Maude had also been kidnapped. "For now we need the best mounts we can steal," Ben added.

"You know where some are?"

"Just ahead. I'll need some help getting them."

Ben halted Brutus in front of the Valdes warehouse, and sat listening and watching into the black night. When Evan came up beside him, Ben spoke just loud enough to be heard. "This is one of the stations for the Valdes freight line. There's a watchman here and he'll probably be in that room."

Ben pointed at the door, barely visible in the murk, located to the right of the warehouse's main entrance. "You go up to the door and if

271

he comes outside, you keep him quiet. I'll go around to the other side of the warehouse where the horse corral is. Shouldn't take me long to sort out a couple. He's got a gun, so be careful."

"Right."

"Give me your picket rope."

Evan unfastened the rope from the saddle and handed it to Ben.

"Be back soon," Ben said.

"I'll be here."

Evan swung down to the ground and, leading his horse, went to the door. He pulled his pistol and listened for sound from inside the room.

Ben circled the warehouse to the corral and dismounted. The corral held at least half a hundred dark forms, some standing, others moving slowly about. He knew horses were watching him, and envied them their night-seeing eyes. Carrying Evan's and his picket ropes, he found the corral gate, lifted the latch, and went in among the animals.

Ben knew that two kinds of horses could be mixed in the corral, the more powerfully built draft horses used to pull the heavy freight wagons, and the more slender riding mounts. Valdes bred only riding horses, and purchased the bigger draft animals. The selection of the two horses that Ben needed could be made by feel. The size would be the first cut. Then if the animal had the Valdes brand on its left hip—the scar from the burned skin could be felt—Ben would know he had hold of a riding horse.

It required but the examination of five horses for Ben to choose the animals he wanted and to tie the picket ropes about their necks. Leading the animals, he hastened back to Evan.

"Any sign of the watchman?" Ben said.

"All was quiet."

"Good," Ben said, handing Evan the end of his picket rope. "Let's get away from here."

Back on the street, Ben halted. He jerked the saddle from Brutus's back and carried it to the new horse.

Evan, seeing what Ben was doing, spoke. "Should I change my saddle too?"

"No, leave it on. I've seen your horse and this Valdes one will be better. Ride yours until it can't go any further, then swap your saddle."

"Why are you changing?"

*More damn questions*, Ben thought. "I'm saving Brutus for when I really need a horse that I can trust. He's fast and he'll not stampede when the guns begin to fire, or run off and leave me if I get shot off."

Ben mounted the Valdes horse, rode close to Evan, and looked at him through the murky night. "I'm telling you again to be ready for anything. I'd like both of us to live long enough to get back to El Paso."

"So would I."

"It's time to push hard. We've got a lot of miles to cover before we'll stop to sleep."

Ben and Evan rode at a gallop, the horses' hooves chopping them south on the El Camino Real. It was the last hour of the night and a bright crescent of a moon had sailed up over the rim of the world to the east. It added light to the sky glow of the stars. The contours of the desert terrain had become discernible, and showed the ancient Spanish road lying empty for as far as the men could see ahead.

"I hope the horses hold up and don't go lame on us," Evan called to Ben. He was troubled and afraid that they would fail to free Rachel.

Ben didn't reply. His eyes roamed constantly, scanning the broken, boulder-strewn land through which they were passing. He could make out yucca, agave, and saguaro growing on the hills, while creosote bush occupied the flats in between. He saw no cattle or sheep. There had been no house within sight of the road for many miles.

The night gave way to day and the sun exploded fiery yellow up over the horizon. Inexorably it rolled along its sky path, burning its way across the heavens. The sun passed over its zenith and the shadows twisted around to point to the east.

The two men rode the heat, with the sweat drying quickly on their skins and crusting into a thin film of white crystals.

An hour into the night, Ben and Evan rode into Samalayuca. Ben guided the way, with Evan holding station on his left. Ben had ridden through the town before, and knew the adobe buildings that made up the small village lined both sides of the El Camino Real for less than a quarter mile.

"Stay alert," Ben said.

"Right," Evan said. He sagged with weariness and the journey had hardly begun.

"We need water for the horses," Ben said.

"My canteen's empty too."

"There's a public well in the center of the town and we can get water there."

The two rode on through the town. Here and there light fell out of the window of a house and cast a frail yellow square upon the road, and upon the dust the men stirred to float in the air.

At the well, several women were drawing water with the hand windlass and filling their buckets, all the time talking and laughing. Ben wondered what tale could be so funny. He guessed it would be about men. When the women saw the horsemen, they fell silent and took up their buckets and hastened off.

Ben and Evan stopped at the well, drew buckets of water, and filled the watering trough that was close by. While the horses drank, the men scooped the cool water with their hands, splashed it onto their faces and necks, and washed away the salt and grime. They drew another bucket and one after the other, drank straight from it to slake their thirst.

Ben pulled his bandana from a pocket and wiped at his wet face. As he did so, he turned and looked around them for possible enemies. He did not know why, but he thought danger was not far away. But then every step of the way to the Valdes rancho would be dangerous.

"Evan, get the horses away from the water before they founder themselves," Ben said. "I'll fill our canteens."

"The horses are used up," Evan said as he forced the animals back from the water.

"We'll get fresh ones here."

"How?"

"There's a Valdes freight station here."

"Another one? How close together are they?"

"About every thirty to forty miles. Depends on whether or not there's a town where men can stay permanent. Besides owning a hell of a lot of land, and cattle and horses, Valdes has the contract for hauling the supplies from Mexico City to all the military bases in northern Mexico. He also hauls most of the civilian freight."

"I can see why he's a powerful man. But right now I'm starved. Let's get a bite to eat before we steal the horses."

"We shouldn't be seen here by Valdes men. Carlos might have them on the lookout for me."

"Just a quick bite. And I need a few minutes' rest."

Ben saw Evan was leaning wearily against one of the horses. The man hadn't fully recovered from his serious wound, yet not once had he asked Ben to slow the hard, fast pace he had set.

"All right. We'll take a little time to get some food. That'll also give the people time to get off the street before we go to raid the freight station for horses."

Evan looked about. "I see only one place open, that *cantina* there just across the street. I hope they have food."

"Let's go take a look."

They led their horses to the *cantina* and tied them to the hitch rail in front. Nearly a dozen horses were already tied there. Ben examined each one, running his hand over the left hip and feeling to read the brand.

Evan silently watched Ben. He had heard the dislike in Ben's voice when he had been questioned. Let him volunteer an explanation for his actions.

"There's no Valdes brand on them," Ben said. "We've got to think that every man we meet, every man that looks at us a little cross-eyed, is an enemy, and we shoot him."

"What if we're wrong?"

"As an Indian I once knew would say, that man had bad luck. Now, let's go in and eat."

Ben quickly surveyed the interior of the *cantina*. It was one huge square room with adobe walls and an earthen floor. Two lamps hanging from the ceiling illuminated the place with their yellow flame. The bar was on the right, with a big-bellied fat man behind it. He had turned as the gringos entered and was now looking at them.

Standing in front of the bar were several *vaqueros* in worn, dusty clothing. They were drinking tequila and paid no attention to Ben's and Evan's entrance. A score of men, a mixture of *vaqueros* and townsmen, sat drinking and talking at several tables. Most wore pistols. A few of the men facing the entrance watched the gringos advance into the room. At the far end of the bar was a wide doorway open to the kitchen.

The place was ripe with the stink of spilled tequila and beer, and stale cigarillo smoke, and unwashed bodies. The smoke hung in a thick, gray layer against the ceiling. Even with all the undesirable odors, Ben smelled the delightful piquant aroma of pepper-rich chili, tortillas, and meat frying—he thought it was lamb. There was also the smell of yeast bread baking, somewhat unusual south of the border.

"This is a good one," Ben said, and sat down at a table not far from the door and against the wall directly across from the bar.

The bartender yelled into the kitchen. A moment later a young girl with dark skin and a broad face and large black eyes came into the main part of the *cantina*. The bartender pointed at Ben and Evan and she hurried to them on quiet, moccasined feet. She looked once at Ben as she approached, then looked hastily away and kept her sight on Evan. Both men ordered food, each doing it easily in Spanish.

Ben's attention was totally on the men in the *cantina*. They were surprisingly quiet, with the normal bantering among men being absent. He wondered if the quietness had just begun, and was because of the presence of two *Norte Americanos*. He scrutinized each man's face, evaluating his expression. After the first lock of their eyes with Ben's, every man found something more interesting to look at.

A short, broadly built man wearing a six-gun got up from his table and headed for the door. Ben watched him cross in front of them and leave the *cantina*.

In but a few minutes, the girl came on her quiet feet and served the food. Without a word, she retreated to the kitchen.

"Eat fast," Ben said, still thinking about the man who had left the *cantina*. "I don't like the feel of this place."

"What's wrong?"

"No time to talk. Just eat." Ben cut a large bite of lamb and began to chew.

Ben and Evan had almost finished with their food when four Mexicans—the short man who had been in the *cantina* earlier was one of them—came in from the street. The man in the lead was tall, with narrow shoulders and a long, sharp face. All the men were bearded. The leader was the hairiest of all, his beard like tangled grapevines and hiding that portion of his face below his eyes. He stopped, and as he swept the room with his sight, his comrades came up to stand beside him.

"Evan, shoot that short man on the right side of the tall one," Ben said in a low, tense voice.

Evan looked at Ben, not sure he had heard correctly. Ben's eyes gleamed a feline yellow in the lamplight. Then they narrowed to stitches.

"Shoot!" Ben hissed. He came swiftly to his feet, and his six-gun boomed, exploding the silence in the room.

## Thirty-eight

Ben was on his feet with his pistol pointing and firing, the rapid boom of the shots blending into one continuous roll of thunder.

Evan, startled by the unexpected eruption of violence, was fixed in his chair. His ears rang with the crash of the gun in the confined space of the *cantina*, and the air bucked and heaved around him.

The tall man, the leader of the four Mexicans, staggered back at the punch of the bullet. He caught himself, his face contorted with pain. He began to lean to the side and put out his hand as if trying to get support from the air. He found none and fell full-length to the floor.

The man on the tall one's right was hit by

Ben's second bullet, traveling but a few feet and carrying immense power. He collapsed, his bones seeming to melt. The man beside him was struck, went over backward, and fell hard to the floor of the *cantina*.

The short man Ben had ordered Evan to shoot had his pistol out. His eyes were on Ben and his weapon was coming up. He fired.

Evan sensed Ben flinch. Had he been shot because Evan hadn't joined in the battle? Four men were too many for Ben to kill by himself.

Evan jumped to his feet and snatched his pistol from its holster. He cocked the gun and swung it, trying to bring it into quick alignment on the short man. He had to shoot the man and prevent Ben from being killed.

Before Evan could shoot, Ben fired and the Mexican was hit. He fell heavily. He struggled to sit up, made it halfway erect, and hung there with blood spraying out in a fine mist from a hole in his neck. He sank back down to the floor and began to cry out in an unintelligible sound.

Ben grabbed Evan by the shoulder and turned him to face the rear of the *cantina*. "Goddamn it, Evan, cover those other men back there." Ben's voice came hard and angry. "Keep them off us until I get reloaded."

Evan's face burned at Ben's sharp rebuke. It was fully earned. He pointed his pistol, swinging it over the crowd of men. The ones at the bar were motionless and still held their drinks. The men at the tables were as rigid as the wooden chairs upon which they sat.

He hurriedly checked each man's hands, and found not one touching a weapon. All of the men, just like Evan, had been caught by surprise at the outbreak of shooting.

Ben finished reloading his pistol and snapped it closed. He caught Evan by the shoulder again. "Are you awake now?" Ben's voice still held its harshness.

"Yes."

"Then shoot any man that moves, that even twitches. Can you do that?"

"Yes, damn it," Evan replied, rankled, his own anger rising at Ben's tone.

"Then see that you do. I'll check outside. Maybe I can find us horses."

Ben left quickly.

Evan swept his sight back and forth over the roomful of men. He severely condemned himself for failing to help Ben in the gunfight. He must make up for that. He primed himself to shoot any man who reached for a gun. He stood motionless, not wanting any movement of his to precipitate a battle. If one man started to fight him, he was certain most of the others would join in.

The short Mexican Ben had shot groaned, the sound slicing through the quietness with startling loudness. Evan had forgotten about the man for the moment, and the man was behind him. Evan hastily backed up until the man was in sight. He lay on the floor in blood, whimpering and shuddering. He looked up at Evan with stricken ox eyes. He tried to speak, but no sound came.

As Evan looked down, the jetting blood slowed to a trickle. The man closed his eyes and became very still.

Ben came back into the *cantina* with his pistol drawn. He found Evan threatening the room full of Mexicans with his pistol. Ben recognized that look in Evan's eyes, that he would indeed shoot any man that reached for a weapon. The Mexicans in the *cantina* also believed it, and every one was in the same position as when Ben had gone outside.

Evan and he just might be able to leave the *cantina* without more killing. Ben shed some of his disapproval of Evan's lack of action in the gunfight. He had been caught off guard by the sudden beginning of the gunfight.

"Best we go now," Ben said. "Back slow to the door with me."

Evan began to move backward side by side with Ben.

"Stay inside!" Ben fiercely ordered the Mexicans in Spanish.

Ben and Evan went into the darkness on the street.

"This way. Hurry," Ben said, and led him to four horses tied to the hitch rail directly in front of the *cantina*. "I kept three fresh horses belonging to those fellows inside and ran off all the others so nobody can chase us for a spell," Ben said in explanation.

"Now mount up on that one with the saddle and let's get out of here."

Ben stepped to one of the horses and pulled himself astride.

Evan could make out the shadowy outline of a saddle on one of the horses. He hastily went to the horse and mounted. There was a lead rope to a spare horse tied around the pommel of the saddle.

They left Samalayuca running the horses.


Evan was thinking about the gunfight in the *cantina*. Ben's explosive violence was disturbing. He had drawn his pistol and shot the men before they had given any indication they were there to kill Ben and Evan. The short Mexican had only drawn his gun after Ben had shot his comrades. Perhaps the men had been innocent of intending harm and had come into the *cantina* for a drink or some food.

"Ben, did you get hit when that last fellow shot at you?"

"No, he just came damn close to nailing me."

"Good," Evan said with relief. "Do you think they really meant to shoot us?"

"Yep."

"You sure?"

Ben breathed deeply and let it out, almost sighing. "I'm sure. When that one fellow left the *cantina* and then came back with the other three, I knew. And there were other signs."

"What other signs?"

"I was deputy sheriff in El Paso for a spell. I was damn young then, but the sheriff took me under his wing and taught me how to read the roughnecks, the gunhands, both whites and Mexicans, that came up against

284

me in my work. These fellows in the *cantina* gave signs that told me they were there to shoot us."

"What did you see? I want to learn."

"Beards, eyes, and feet."

"What does that mean?" Evan said.

"Carlos had rightly figured that I might stop at the freight station for fresh horses, or at that *cantina*, for it's the only place to buy a meal for miles along the El Camino Real. So he set an ambush to stop me from chasing him, and he hired Mexicans with Spanish blood for they are the best *pistoleros*, better than mixed Indian and Spanish. Now when I saw all that hair, I was suspicious, for Spanish bloods like to wear beards to show they are above the Indians, who can't grow a face full of hair. Second, that tall fellow set his feet solid for a fight, not to buy a drink. And his eyes—did you see his eyes? they were looking for someone and it wasn't a friend."

"So you're saying Valdes planned ahead and set a trap for you?"

"That's the way I figure it. He's smart, got his father's blood in him."

"But you could still be wrong and killed four men for no reason."

"Maybe. But I don't think so. Would you kill four men to free Rachel?"

"Yes."

"Ten men?"

"Yes."

"Then the next time, help me kill anybody who stands in our way." Ben would, if need be, pave El Camino Real all the way to Chihuahua with dead men to free Maude.

Evan was silent. Ben and he had grown up within a few miles of each other, but their lives had been totally different. Ben had left home and been on his own at an early age. He'd been deputy sheriff in a tough town and had killed men in the line of duty. Then he had gone off to a bloody war and killed. Yes, they had experienced decidedly different lives.


Ben reined his horse in close to Evan's mount and rode beside him. The man was exhausted and slumped forward in sleep, nodding to the step of his horse. Ben feared he would fall from his horse.

Evan gradually leaned ever farther out from his horse. Then he snapped awake and his hand darted out to grab hold of the pommel. He straightened in the saddle and looked at Ben close beside him.

"Almost fell," Evan said.

"Close, all right," Ben said, and reined his horse off a few feet.

Evan understood that Ben had been prepared to catch him should he start to fall. He made a good friend. But a hell of a vicious enemy.

"Ben, I've got to rest."

"Can you hold out until the sun comes up and gets hot? Then we'll find some shade and sleep some."

"How long before daylight?"

Ben looked up at the sky. The thin moon of

286

late night had risen. The moon was like a curved silver sail and seemed to be attached to a small cloud and shoving it across the black ocean of the sky. Ben was quiet, watching the unusual joining of the objects, the cloud just above him and the moon such a great distance away.

"Can you tell how long?" Evan asked again.

"The sun's not more than an hour away. Then another three or four hours to ride. Can you last that long?"

"Not much more than that. I haven't slept or rested for two days. But then neither have you."

"I wasn't lung-shot either," Ben said. Evan had a streak of hard metal in him to have ridden so hard and so long.

Ben came out of his sleep with the sound of a running horse in his ears. He picked up his rifle and spyglass and rolled to look over the boulder behind which he had been sleeping.

"What is it?" Evan asked. Ben's movement had awakened him.

"A rider coming fast south on the road."

The two men had left the El Camino Real at daybreak and hidden their horses behind a rocky hill near the road. They then had crawled back to the crest, from which they could remain out of sight while still being able to see anybody passing by below on the road. There they had spread their blankets for a short rest.

Ben put aside the spyglass for he could see what he needed to with his naked eye. A small rider, a Mexican lad, was bent forward over the neck of his swiftly running horse. He was bareheaded, with his black hair blowing out behind and his shirttail flapping in the wind created by the horse.

Ben raised his rifle and aimed it at the rider.

"You going to shoot the boy?" Evan asked in surprise.

"Yes."

"Why, for God's sake?"

"He's carrying a message to Carlos that their ambush at Samalayuca failed. The Valdes family has a relay system of horses and men, or boys, who ride day and night carrying information up and down their freight line so they can manage their business. They can get a message from one end of their freight line to the other in a couple of days. Carlos would surely use the relay riders to let him know whether or not his men had stopped me."

"You don't know that. You can't shoot him just on suspicion."

Ben lowered the rifle and looked at Evan, and Evan could see the uncertainty in his eyes.

"He could be running the horse for any number of reasons," Evan added.

Ben turned back to look down on the road. The boy on the racing horse passed below him at an easy rifle shot.

"I should've shot him for he was carrying

a message for Carlos Valdes," Ben said matter-of-factly. He lay down on his blanket and looked up at the sky. "Carlos will know we're still coming and that there are two of us. He'll be calculating the best way to stop us along the Real.

"If he's anything as savvy as Ramos, he might succeed. If we get past Carlos, then there's Ramos himself, with his experience at fighting, waiting at the rancho for us. We'd had a much better chance at freeing Rachel if they thought we'd been shot."

Ben closed his eyes. "We'll be riding in an hour," he said.

# Thirty-nine

Maude stood up and craned her neck to see out the window of the stagecoach and past Rafael. The man had dropped back from traveling in front of the stagecoach, and now rode his horse to deliberately block her view. She caught a momentary glance past Rafael, and saw a herd of red cattle and two Mexican cowboys not far off from El Camino Real. The cowboys were watching the stagecoach.

Rafael looked at Maude and saw her standing. He motioned angrily for her to sit down and out of view of the cowboys. She gave him a hard look and shook her head. He had no right to order her to do anything. She continued to stand, holding tightly to the leather hand strap fastened to the side frame of the coach to maintain her footing in the lurching, swaying vehicle.

Rafael reached out and jerked loose the tie strings that held the curtain in front of Maude. The sheet of leather fell, unrolling to obscure her view.

Maude took her seat. She didn't want to show it but she was frightened, for she was a prisoner and being carried to an unknown fate in a foreign land.

She turned away from the window and looked down at Rachel, lying on the pallet of blankets on the narrow space of floor between the two seats, one facing forward and the other to the rear. The two women took turns on the blankets and tried to rest during the endless traveling.

"Rachel, I'm worried that we will never get a chance to escape," Maude said anxiously.

"There hasn't been an opportunity yet," Rachel replied, a deeply troubled expression on her face. "But we must be ready to grab it when it does come."

"If it ever does."

Maude and Rachel had talked often of being rescued. But how could anybody know what had happened to them, or where they were being taken? They were completely on their own and must escape by using their own wits and strength. They knew that to run into the desert without water, without any knowledge of the land at all, was no escape at all. They had to make their break for freedom while passing through a town where there were people who might help them elude their captors. They had been too closely guarded so far for them to make that attempt.

Maude heard Emanuel, the driver of the stagecoach, shout a curse at the horses. His bullwhip cracked as he lashed the horses. He was a cruel man and relentlessly used the whip to drive the animals onward. In those few times when Maude was allowed out of the stagecoach, she had observed the backs of the horses were cut and bleeding from the strike of the iron tip of the whip. Emanuel scared Maude almost as much as did the silent, always watchful Rafael. However, it was Leo Valdes, who commanded the two men, who was Rachel's true enemy.

The iron-rimmed wheels of the stagecoach struck a dusty place on the road and a cloud of brown grit streamed in through the windows. The women's clothing, faces, and hair were covered with the dust that had settled on them during the journey. Maude breathed shallowly until the dust was whipped away by the hot wind.

The evening of the third day was near. Leo had hurried them through the first day, then the night, and until the middle of the following day. Then they had stopped in the shade of some trees set off from the road far enough that passersby couldn't see them. Leo had allowed them out of the stagecoach to walk about a bit to relieve their tired and cramped muscles and to eat. They had spread blankets on the ground and slept through the few hours when the sun was highest in the sky.

During the race down the El Camino Real, they had stopped several times at freight stations and quickly exchanged the exhausted horses for fresh ones. At the stations and during the passage through the towns, Leo always tied the leather curtains down tightly and warned Maude and Rachel not to try to see outside, or to make their presence known in any manner. Rafael stood guard beside the stagecoach at those times to insure they obeyed the order. Twice he had warned off an inquisitive man who had wanted to look inside the curtained vehicle.

Maude heard Leo shout at Emanuel, and the stagecoach began to slow and veer to the side. Maude thrust her head out the window to look ahead.

"What's happening?" Rachel said, rising up from the blankets.

"We're turning off the road and up a lane to a hacienda," Maude said.

As Maude watched, a man came out of the moderate-sized hacienda, made of adobe and whitewashed with lime, and stood and looked in the direction of the approaching stagecoach.

Leo shouted again at Emanuel, and the stagecoach stopped a couple of hundred feet from the man. Leo rode his horse to the window where Maude sat. He gestured for her to lower the curtains. At the same time he ordered brusquely, "Drop the curtains and don't let anyone here see you. I'll tell you when you can come out. Tonight you'll have good food and a soft bed." He smiled, pleased with himself.

Leo spoke to Rafael, who had ridden his mount up and was listening. "See that they do as I said."

"*Sí, patrón.*"

Leo turned and went toward the man waiting at the hacienda.

Rafael reined his horse close to the coach and watched Maude and Rachel untie the curtains and let them unroll to completely cover the windows. Satisfied with their actions, he sat alertly in the saddle, watching Leo and the man from the hacienda.

Maude and Rachel looked at each other. With an unspoken agreement, each woman pulled the edge of a curtain aside a tiny crack and put her eye to it.

"Looks like he's trying to give the man something," Rachel whispered, seeing Leo take an object from his pocket and offer it to the man.

"I'd guess that would be payment for that food and soft bed he promised," Maude whispered back.

Maude saw the man shake his head in obvious rejection of the money. He started to face away. Leo caught him by the shoulder and said a few words and again held out the money.

The man jerked loose from Leo's hold and spoke rapidly. He pointed at the stagecoach and then at El Camino Real. Evan at the distance, Maude saw the man's anger, and knew he was telling Leo to take his stagecoach and leave.

Rafael spurred his horse and sent it bounding ahead. He reined the big animal to a sliding stop barely in time to prevent running over the man confronting Leo. The man sprang back and looked up at Rafael. The *pistolero* put his hand on the butt of his pistol and stared threateningly down.

Leo again offered the money. The man looked at Rafael and then Leo, and seeing the deadly intent in their faces, took the money.

The man pivoted around and went hastily into the hacienda. A moment later Maude heard a woman shouting in a complaining voice, and the man shouting back. Then there was silence. In less than a minute, the man reemerged with a woman and two half-grown girls. The woman stopped and looked angrily at Leo and Rafael, then followed after her husband, who was moving hastily toward the barn and corral located to the right of the hacienda. Shortly the man and his family, riding in a two-seated buggy, went past the stagecoach and off along the lane.

Leo motioned for Emanuel to bring the stagecoach forward. When it stopped, Leo untied the doors and held out his hand to Maude. Maude ignored Leo's offered hand— she didn't want him to touch her—and started to climb down. Leo moved quickly, caught her by the arm, and pressed her flesh as he helped her to the ground.

Rachel stepped down and stood beside Maude. Leo's attention to Maude and his almost total lack of interest in her, except to see that she didn't escape, told her clearly that the brothers had made their choice of women. She was to belong to Carlos.

"This nice hacienda is ours for the night," Leo said. "The Beremendes family was glad to allow us to use it."

He smiled at Maude, glanced at Rachel, and swept his hand in a gesture for the women to enter before him.

"You knew the people and still took their home?" Maude said.

Leo saw Maude's disapproval of his eviction of the man from his home by threatening him. He believed this event would be a fine lesson for her, that he would take what he wanted and when he wanted it. If it wasn't given freely.

"Beremendes owns a store in Ahumada and I have had dealings with him. I've never liked him. So his home was the perfect choice for us to rest. Now let us go in and enjoy its comfort."

Leo turned to Rafael. "Help Emanuel with the horses and then both of you come inside for some food."

Rafael touched the brim of his hat and moved away.

Maude felt the pleasant, shadowy coolness

of the house immediately upon entering. It felt grand after the dusty coach and burning sun. They were in the *sala*, the main gathering room of the hacienda, a room with a carpeted floor and overstuffed sofa. Straight ahead of her through an arched doorway was the dining room. She saw the table had been set for the evening meal, with several dishes of food and a bottle of wine in sight.

"Now wasn't that thoughtful of Beremendes's wife to have done all this for us," Leo said.

"May we bathe before we eat," Maude said, feeling grimy.

"Yes, please," Rachel added.

"Certainly. There will be a bath somewhere. Come with me and we'll find it."

Maude's and Rachel's spirits recovered somewhat as they bathed in the huge tub of water in a room at the rear of the house. They did not speak, trying to find some sense of solace as captives by the simple task of bathing.

At first they had looked at each other with an expression saying that maybe this was the chance they had been waiting for to escape. Then they had heard Leo tell Emanuel to go outside and stand guard under the single window of the bathroom, and Rafael to guard the door.

After a few minutes a knock sounded on the door and Leo spoke. "I have found both of you clean clothing." His arm appeared holding two dresses.

"I don't want stolen clothing," Maude said.

"You *will* wear them," Leo said firmly. He stepped through the door and into the bath. He halted and swept his eyes over the naked women. He smiled, pleased at what he saw. He ran his sight over them for a second time, doing it very slowly. Then smiling more broadly, he hung the clean dresses on hooks fastened on the wall, grabbed up their soiled garments, and left.

Rachel looked at Maude. "Damn him," Maude said.

"Yes, indeed," Rachel said. "But just his looking won't hurt us." She tilted her head at the dresses. "One thing is for certain. We either wear them or go naked. I choose to have clothing on."

"Same here," Maude said reluctantly.

Rachel leaned close to Maude and whispered. "Don't be so belligerent with him. Maybe that way he'll not watch us so carefully and we'll get a chance to run."

"You're right," Maude whispered back. "I'll be sweet to him."

"Don't overdo it, for then he'll be suspicious and watch even more closely."

"I know."

They dressed in the garments of the Beremendes women and left the bath.

Rafael motioned for them to go into the dining room. He followed behind them.

Leo rose from the chair at the head of the table. "You are both very beautiful, even with clothing on." They would give Carlos and him fine sons. He hated the waiting for the love-making to begin, and hoped Carlos would hurry and catch up with them.

"Now let us dine," Leo said.

Maude and Rachel seated themselves on opposite sides of the table at the far end.

"Not there, here near me," Leo said. They were contrary, aggravating women. Once Carlos came and took Rachel off his hands, then he would turn his attention to Maude and teach her the proper respect for a husband's wishes.

Maude rose and moved to sit in the seat on Leo's right. Rachel took the seat on his left.

"Aren't you worried that the owner of this house will bring the sheriff to arrest you?" Maude said.

"Beremendes knows that I'm a Valdes, and that it would be dangerous for him to cause me trouble. And besides, he took my money so how can he complain."

Maude almost burst out to remind Leo that he had forced the man to take the money. However, she caught herself, remembering to be more agreeable during any conversation she held with Leo in hopes he would let down his guard.

"Beremendes is nothing. Let us talk of something else."

"Like setting us free," Rachel said. "Let us go and we won't tell what you did," Maude said. "We'll tell our friends in El Paso that we had gone off together for a visit in Mexico."

Leo's face became stone as he looked at

Maude. "You will have freedom where I'm taking you. But within the bounds that I set. My family is very rich and you will have everything you desire. I will build you a magnificent hacienda all your own. There will be many servants, and money to purchase anything you want."

"A captive bird in a gilded cage," Maude said.

Rachel gave Maude a warning look. Leo did not see Rachel's look for he was staring steadily at Maude. It was not necessary to reply to her barb. She would very soon be trained to do exactly what he wanted, everything he wanted.

They continued the meal with Leo doing the bulk of the talking, and speaking mostly to Maude. The women replied with enough words to keep the conversation moving. Toward the end, Leo called Rafael and Emanuel in and they filled plates and carried them into the kitchen.

"I have a surprise for you, something I found," Leo said to Maude. He rose from the table and left the room. He returned carrying a silver music box about one foot in diameter and half that dimension in thickness. He wound it and sat it on the far end of the table.

"Come and dance with me," Leo said to Maude. He wanted to caress the white skin of this beautiful, golden-haired woman. His woman. *Madre de Dios*, he desired her so much. Her sharp mouth was nothing for soon he would have it trained to speak softly, and gently, and to give loving kisses.

"I don't feel like dancing," Maude said, and remained seated. "I'm too tired."

"We can change that," Leo said. He pressed the release on the music box and a delightful piece of music filled the room. He caught Maude by the hand and drew her to her feet and into his arms.

"Listen to the music and it will take away your weariness," he said. He moved away with her across the room.

Maude was tired and stiff from the long, arduous journey. Still, she knew she must somehow trick this man into making a mistake and allowing Rachel and her to escape. Rachel was correct, belligerence wasn't the way. Sweetness would do it much better. She focused on the music and brought her movement into rhythm, and let Leo guide her around the floor.

She thought of her dance with Ben in the darkness in Canutillo and the pleasure she had felt in his arms. *Just imagine it is Ben who is holding you*, Maude told herself. That did help. How strange it was to prefer Ben's scarred face to be next to hers over that of the handsome Leo. Her heart ached with the thought that she might never see Ben again.

# Forty

"We're in for a bad one," Evan said to Ben.

"Sure looks like it," Ben replied as he watched the billowing, swirling sandstorm roll menacingly toward them. It was a brown monster filling half the western sky and stretching north and south for miles.

"Better get ready for it." He pulled his hat down more tightly and tied a bandana over his nose and mouth.

"Where's your bandana?" Ben asked, noting Evan's lack of something to filter the dust that would soon be filling the air.

"Don't have one. I'll have to use part of my shirttail." With one lung partially defective, he shouldn't be breathing dust. He pulled his shirt from under his belt and sliced off a strip with his jackknife.

"Best we ride on and try to get out of the storm as quick as we can," Ben said.

"Right." Evan quickly fastened the piece of cloth over his nose and mouth and looked at Ben. "Let's hurry."

Ben and Evan were a day south of Moctezuma and crossing a broad expanse of sand dunes. The westerly wind had been whipping in strongly for hours, stirring the sand and sending it streaming in hundreds of ground currents. The sand skittered along the ground, biting at the ankles of the horses and piling onto the lee sides of the long, curving dunes. Some of the dunes, having been blown before the wind for thousands of years, had strayed beyond their birthplace, migrating off to the east to lap against the rock reef of Sierra Los Arados, a chain of steep, barren hills.

The wind increased to a gale as the front of the sandstorm charged ever closer to the two riders. It leapt the last quarter mile with amazing speed and struck them with a roll of churning brown sand and the wind shrieking a wild song. The blizzard of choking sand stung the men's faces and burned like fire. The sand searched for their eyes, and the men squeezed them down to mere slits. Overhead the yellow sun burned scarlet through the dust.

The horses tried to turn their rumps to the brunt of the storm to protect themselves as best they could from the cutting sand. The riders held hard reins and kept the animals headed south.

Some two hours after the sandstorm had struck Ben and Evan, they escaped from its slashing onslaught as El Camino Real climbed into a range of hills on its way to Chihuahua. They halted on the crest in clean, clear air and slapped at the dust on their clothing. They opened their canteens and drank water to wash the dust from their throats.

Evan felt the accumulation of dust that had found its way through the cloth and around its edges and into his nostrils. He took a deep breath of air to blow his nose. At the deep intake of air, a searing pain like a knife thrust struck his wounded lung. He clutched at his chest as a series of harsh, body-shaking coughs erupted.

He knew such deep coughing could reopen his old wound. He breathed shallowly, fighting the urge to cough. He managed to hold the next cough to a weaker one. He stopped the next one that was building. Tears came to his eyes with his efforts to subdue it.

Finally Evan straightened. He hawked and spat on the ground.

Seeing the worried expression in Ben's eyes, Evan spoke. "I'm all right now. No blood. I hope Rachel didn't have to go through one of those."

"Bad one, all right," Ben agreed. Evan looked like hell. Ben considered telling him to turn and ride back to the States. But he knew Evan wouldn't do that.

"I'm ready to travel," Evan said, and pulled himself into the saddle.

"Then let's do it."

They rode off along the scarred, ancient road.

Ben looked out across the hills for any sign of a stagecoach and riders. The hills had been stripped of their flesh of soil by wind and water, with nothing left but worn, gray rock. The gray color of the eroded, raw rock made Ben think of a giant pile of old bones every time he rode through them. The only sign that man had passed this way was the scrape marks left on the rock by the passage of iron wheels and iron-shod hooves.

"The road is solid rock for miles," Ben said. "Let's hope our horses don't throw a shoe. One time I had a couple of horses do just that. I was bringing several north and was in a hurry and couldn't stop. Had to kill the one that would bring the least money and use its hide to protect the hoofs of the two who were barefooted."

"Valdes horses, I reckon? And the Valdes men were chasing you."

"Some of them were. I never came this way a second time."

"Why Valdes horses?"

"They're the best. And the Valdes family can spare them when other people can't."

"That makes stealing right?"

"Maybe not right, but okay, since they got most of their wealth by working poor peons like slaves. At least it's right to my way of thinking." Ben didn't bother to mention the battles of the Alamo or Goliad, for Evan would know about those.

"We need water," Evan said. Ben wasn't going to be changed by anything he said. "Is there a ranch or a town close?"

"None that I know about. But I do know where there's water."


Ben led the way to water at the west base of Gallegos Dos, a dome-shaped hill with a scant growth of desert grass. A third of the way up its flank, one patch of saguaros stood with out-stretched arms like a group of lost desert wanderers. For the past mile or so, the two men had been able to see the spring area and knew it was deserted and safe to approach.

They dismounted and led the lathered and exhausted horses up the short, steep slope to the spring. The animals were left to drink at the lower end of the little stream of water that flowed a few yards from the spring before disappearing into the earth. The men lay down where the water came pure out of the rock of the hill and drank.

Evan finally raised his head from the water. "Better-tasting than I'd expected."

"Lava rock makes for good water," Ben said. "No alkali to spoil it."

"This might be a place where we should rest the horses for a little while."

"I was thinking the same thing, for a couple of hours anyway." Ben knew Evan needed rest more than the horses.

As the men staked out the Valdes horses, with Brutus left free, the last of the day burned down to black ash and it was dark. They spread their blankets in the moonless night and fell wearily upon them. The men lay silent and resting, each thinking his own private thoughts.

"Ben, do you think we'll catch up to them before they reach their rancho?" Evan asked.

"I'd sure like to, for that rancho is like a fortress. But I'm beginning to doubt it, for it's now only a little more than three days away and I don't think we've gained much."

"Do you still think that boy racing past us

just south of Samalayuca carried a message to Carlos?"

"I do, and Carlos sure as hell knows we're still coming. In fact, he'll have people watching for us and with the system of relay riders the Valdes company has in place, he'll be able to keep track of us."

"If so, then why hasn't he tried again to stop us?"

"I don't know why he hasn't hit us before now. But you've got to remember that Carlos knows this land and is picking the best place. Maybe tomorrow will be the day. But there's no way we can know until we see them coming. We got to keep a sharp eye out."

Ben knew it was time to tell Evan about Maude. Though unlikely, the Valdes brothers might have been delayed in their journey south. If so, Evan and Ben just might overtake them. Evan needed to know there were two women to rescue.

"I hope both Maude and Rachel are all right."

"What's that you said? Maude? Maude who?"

"Maude Bradshaw."

"Why do you mention her?"

"She could be with the Valdes brothers. She's missing same as Rachel."

"Some girl you know?"

"She's from Canutillo same as me."

"You knew she was missing and could be with the Valdes when I asked you to help me. Is that right?"

"That's right."

"I remember now. You were all packed when I talked to you at the hotel. You were ready to go south after the Valdes brothers then. You tricked me into promising to operate on your face."

"I didn't trick you. You're the one who asked me to help you. We made a deal. Are you going to back out of it?"

"I don't like what you did."

"Well, hell, now that's too bad. Answer my question. Are you backing out? Is your word any good? We need to settle this right now before we go any further together."

"I shook on it and I'll keep it," Evan retorted.

"Good." Ben had made Evan angry by not telling about Maude at the beginning of their journey into Mexico. Still, he was glad that the man knew Maude was most likely with Rachel. Maybe Evan would soon get over his anger. Now they had to catch up with the Valdes brothers and take the women away from them. And make the kidnappers pay the full price.

"Evan, something's been on my mind. You seemed awfully determined to try to get Rachel back. Do you plan to marry her?"

"I haven't asked her," Evan said.

"Do you aim to?"

"I'm thinking seriously about doing it."

"Is that why you had to kill Redpath? Because he had slept with her and you want her for a wife?"

"I don't want to talk about that bastard Redpath," Evan said tersely.

"Since I'm helping you get her back, then it seems like a fair question."

"What makes you think she slept with Redpath?"

"From what you told me, especially the part that he deserved to die, and I talked with John Davis. I just put what both of you said together and came up with that answer."

"Whether or not she did is none of your business. And further, you have no right to question me because you'd be going after the Valdes brothers for your own reasons."

After a moment of silence, Ben's voice came low and thoughtful in the darkness. "I think it would make a husband feel better if the man his wife had slept with before she came to his bed was wiped off the face of the earth."

"I get it now. You have the same problem. You're interested in Maude and she's slept with another man. Now you're thinking about killing him."

"Maude's married. That makes a difference. You can't just go and kill a man who sleeps with his own wife." Yet the thought of killing a man for a woman, even if she was a married woman, didn't seem all that wrong to Ben while lying in the dangerous darkness of the desert of Mexico.

"Unless you do a good job on my face, no woman's about to marry me," Ben said.

Ben was silent for half a minute, considering whether or not to ask a second question. Then he spoke. "Evan, I've got a serious question to ask you and would like a straight answer. Now that you've killed Redpath, how do you feel about it?"

"I'm glad that I shot him. Now I've got a question for you. Don't the men of Canutillo have more than one wife?"

"Some of them do."

"Most of them, according to what I've heard."

"Maybe most do."

"Well, I've got news for you. While you were stealing horses, did you know that a federal law was passed that makes it illegal for a man to have more than one wife?"

"No, I didn't know that."

"That's a fact. And if Maude's not the man's first wife, then she's not legally married. She can leave him and there's nothing he can do about it."

"Except beat her," Ben said.

"Well, a fellow who cared about her could prevent that. He might even get the chance to shoot him."

Ben realized that it wouldn't bother him to any great degree to kill the wife-beater Lester Ivorsen.

"If that certain fellow needed a witness to help him claim self-defense, I know where he could get one cheap," Evan added.

Ben was surprised by Evan's words, words that meant he would help Ben cover up the killing that had just been in his thoughts. Ben had been sorely disappointed in Evan in Samalayuca when he had failed to help in the gunfight. Now, as he evaluated Evan's promise to help cover up a killing, as Ben had helped with Redpath, and his total commitment to ride into Mexico to get his woman, Ben's opinion of him grew greatly. He was confident that Evan wouldn't fail him in the next battle that was surely coming.

Ben made a decision that if Maude wanted to leave Ivorsen, he would help her even to the point of shooting the man if he tried to stop her. He had killed men for much less than a woman. In the Army, he had killed men for no reason other than that they wore a different-colored uniform. No, it wouldn't bother him at all to shoot Ivorsen.

"We have to get the women back before any of this means a damn," Ben said.

"You're right. I've got to sleep now."

"Same here." Ben was glad Evan was taking more of the lead in deciding what should be done and when in the search for the women. Ben might be killed in the battle with the Valdes brothers and Evan would have to protect and guide the women north of the Rio Grande.

He closed his eyes, begrudging the time he must wait to once again see Maude. As he went to sleep, he recalled the touch of her fingers upon his scars and her words that the Ben Hawkins she had known was under them.

The wild grass scissoring in the wind awoke Ben. He rose up on an elbow and looked around. He hadn't slept long, for he could still smell the lava rock of Gallegos Dos cooling in the night.

The great bulk of the hill obscured the eastern half of the heavens. To the west, the stars were falling down the long, black side of the sky. Brutus had finished grazing and was close by, sleeping standing. The animal's ears were turning just enough to hear danger before it happened. Ben was glad for the faithful horse. With his keen hearing and sense of smell, he made an excellent sentry.

Weariness was pulling on Ben's eyelids and he wanted more sleep. However, Maude and Rachel couldn't wait for that. He roused Evan and they rode into the darkness with the air still heavy with memories of the day's heat.

# Forty-one

"Wait," Evan whispered urgently. "I saw something move."

"What? Where?" Ben said, and instantly halted his reach for the gate of the corral.

"On the roof of the freight station."

Ben looked at the freight station, which was immediately adjacent to the corral. The building was long, with a flat roof that had a low parapet along its edge. The upper quarter of the structure was silhouetted against the star-filled sky. Ben quickly scanned along the top. At midpoint on the length of the parapet, he saw a star vanish and another one come into view. A man had shifted his body as he watched down into the corral.

"I see him. There'll be others with him."

Ben and Evan had warily approached the Valdes freight station in Terrazas to swap their jaded horses for rested ones. They had almost walked into an ambush. The gunmen, from their elevated position and hidden behind the wall, had an excellent location from which they could guard the horses and shoot would-be thieves. With the night brightened by starshine and the light of a moon, Ben and Evan would have been easy targets.

"Carlos almost had us that time," Ben said. "Damn good thing that you got cat eyes and saw the man."

"Close, all right. What now?"

"I think I know where there'll be some horses. Let's get back out of sight."

They drew away into the night and circled the station. Behind a second and smaller building, smelling of the dead ashes and iron of a blacksmith shop, they came to several horses tied to a hitch rail.

"These will do," Ben said.

"How did you know they'd be here?"

"Those fellows on the roof wouldn't walk to the freight station. They'd ride. Since I've been here before, I knew the most likely place where they'd hide their mounts, and that would be right here."

They selected three from the eight and rode the night away, and the sun into the sky, and on into the day until the middle of the afternoon.

Ben halted his small cavalcade on the border of the short-grass plain called Plano de San Augustin. He leaned wearily on the pommel of his saddle and studied the flat expanse of land.

"What are you thinking?" Evan asked. He held his exhausted body in the saddle by willpower alone. His damaged lung ached and felt like lead in his chest. The old gunshot wound had robbed him of the strength and endurance needed to keep up with Ben.

"We're within twenty miles of Chihuahua and thirty miles or thereabouts to the Valdes rancho. Carlos hasn't been able to stop us. I'm thinking he'll try something big any time now."

"He may think they shot us at Terrazas."

"He probably doesn't know about us avoiding his trap there. And I'm betting he wouldn't put all his money on that one hit-or-miss attempt at stopping us."

Ben continued to scan the plain, which was some twelve miles east to west and about an equal distance north to south. On his right the plain lapped against the base of Sierra El Nido, a series of jagged, stony mountain peaks. To his left, it merged into Laguna El Cuervo, a broad and shallow basin that would be a bog hole this time of year. He counted four herds of cattle grouped here and there on

313

the plain and grazing the dry grass. He saw no cowboys.

"Would you expect an ambush out there on the flat land?" Ben said.

"No, I wouldn't. Horsemen could be seen for miles."

"They could stay dismounted and hide behind the herds of cows. If we came upon them, they could ride us down on our worn-out horses."

"So what do you suggest we do? Find another way to the Valdes rancho?"

"We've come straight down El Camino Real because it's the fastest way to overtake Maude and Rachel. We did it even knowing that way made it easier for Carlos to set traps for us. Nothing has changed. We want to get to the girls before they're forced to marry the Valdes brothers."

"So we go straight ahead."

"Right. Keep a sharp eye out. This is Valdes land and he could have an army of *pistoleros* ready to jump us."


"Come out," Leo said firmly as he held the stagecoach door open and offered his hand to Maude. "This is the hacienda of the Valdes family," he said proudly.

Maude stepped down from the coach to the ground. Rachel came to stand beside her. Both looked around at their surroundings. The coach had just arrived at the hacienda and halted in the courtyard.

Ramos Valdes, outfitted in elegant *caballero* clothing, came out of the hacienda and walked toward them across the stone-flagged courtyard. Leo raised his hand in greeting and went to meet him.

"This place is like a fortress," Maude said to Rachel. She spoke quietly so that the stagecoach driver and the *pistolero*, who were close by, couldn't hear.

"More like a prison for us," Rachel said as she surveyed the six-foot-high stone wall that encircled the hacienda and its wide yard.

The house was a huge one-story structure made of adobe and stone with a flat roof. A round, thirty-foot-tall watchtower made of stone rose from the center of the hacienda. The walled compound contained some two acres and sat on the top of a low hill a half mile from the base of Sierra Las Tunas Mountain. The Santa Isabel River flowed past at the bottom of the hill.

"The hacienda must have at least fifteen rooms," Maude said.

"More like twenty," Rachel said. She was still considering how to escape. There had been an armed guard at the gate when they entered. At this very time a man was watching them from the watchtower. Her spirits sank as she realized the steep odds that were against them for slipping away.

A middle-aged woman, fair-skinned, with blond hair and wearing a blue dress, came from the hacienda and joined with Leo and Ramos. She took Ramos's arm and the three moved together toward Maude and Rachel.

315

"That must be Father and Mother," Maude said, nodding at the approaching man and woman. "Why, she's an American," she added with surprise.

"She's beautiful, and her hair is more blond than yours, Maude."

"She's one of us and will help us get out of this place."

"Maybe, but I wouldn't bet on it."

The three were close now and Rachel saw the woman had brilliant blue eyes. That explained the source of Carlos's and Leo's blue eyes.

"Aren't they lovely, Father?" Leo said.

"Most lovely," Ramos responded. They were young and strong and should make fine babies. His sons had done very well in their selection of wives.

"I am Ramos Valdes and I welcome you to our home," Ramos said. "And this is Señora Valdes."

"I too welcome you," said the woman.

Rachel thought the woman's expression showed sadness, even regret, at their presence here. Perhaps Maude was correct, that Señora Valdes might help them. Then the woman smiled and whatever she was feeling was hidden.

Señora Valdes moved forward and hugged Rachel and Maude, an arm about each of them, pressing them tightly to her. Both girls stood rigid in her embrace. They were captives brought to this alien place by force. This was so regardless of the gracious greeting bestowed upon them.

Señora Valdes felt the stiffness and moved back.

"Which one do you claim?" Ramos asked.

"This golden beauty here." Leo took Maude by the arm. He looked at his mother. "Her hair is just like yours, Mother."

Maude pulled free of Leo's hand. "Are we guests or prisoners?" she asked sharply. "If we are guests, then I want to leave."

Ramos's face hardened at the question. Leo looked angry.

"Helena, take them into the hacienda," Ramos said. "Explain how things are to be to them."

"Come with me," Helena said. She gestured at the hacienda and then walked off leading the way.

Rachel and Maude glanced at each other. Rachel shrugged and nodded. Both followed the woman.

Ramos stared after the two young women. Without turning, he spoke to Leo. "Does anyone know that you have them?"

"I don't believe so."

"What about Hawkins?"

"Carlos stayed behind to kill him. He should be here soon."

"Carlos will most likely succeed in slaying him. Even so, I will put two men in the watchtower and start men patrolling the grounds of the hacienda."

"Carlos wants a quick marriage. No banns announced."

"I agree. The sooner the *señoritas* are your

317

wives, the better it will be. I'll send a rider to Chihuahua for our priest."

"I stopped to tell him to come and perform the wedding ceremonies when I passed through Chihuahua. He wasn't there, but his assistant said he was scheduled to be back within two days. So I left a message for him to come here when he returns."

"He will come promptly. Now let's have some wine to celebrate the family's good fortune to find such beautiful wives for you and Carlos."


Once inside the hacienda and out of the men's sight, Rachel caught Helena by the arm and stopped her. "We were kidnapped and brought here as prisoners. You must help us to return to our homes in the States."

Helena removed her arm from Rachel's hold. "I would never do that. My sons have chosen you two and it isn't my place to act against them."

"Kidnapping is a crime, even in Mexico. You would be protecting them by letting us go."

"They are in no danger from the law for my husband is a powerful man with much influence." She looked directly into the eyes of the two young women. "You can find happiness with my sons for they will make good husbands. It will take time and you must search for it, but it is possible."

A sudden understanding came to Rachel. "You were forced to come to Mexico too. And to become a wife against your will."

"What was your original name?" Maude asked.

"That's not important. I have been Señora Valdes for twenty-five years. I will die as Señora Valdes."

Helena looked from Rachel to Maude and back to Rachel. "The Valdes family is very rich. You can have everything you desire. Already Carlos and Leo have their own ranchos, and one day they will inherit great wealth." She paused, looking at them. "You will stay here for a few months and then be taken to your own homes."

"We want to go to our homes in the States," Rachel said.

"And right now, not later," Maude added. She might return to El Paso, but she knew that she would never return to the house of Lester Ivorsen.

"That will never be," Helena said.

"We have friends who will be looking for us," Rachel said.

"Maybe you do," Helena replied. "However, you are many hundreds of miles from the United States and they will not find you. Even if they should, they will not be able to help you for my husband has many *pistoleros*, hard, ruthless men who are loyal to him. It would be better if any friends of yours did not find you, for then they would die."

"You should help us to leave," Rachel said, pressing the woman. "You of all people know what this means to be kidnapped and forced to marry strange men."

"I disapprove of what Carlos and Leo have done. However, they are men and very much like their father."

"And they see how he has gotten away with kidnapping a fair-skinned wife," Rachel said.

"Why don't they get wives like other men do instead of stealing them?" Maude said in frustration at the woman's unwillingness to aid them.

The woman looked stonily at Maude and Rachel. "I tell you again, you must find happiness with my sons for you will never leave Mexico. Now come with me and I will show you the hacienda and your rooms."


*"Un caballero venga mucho rapido,"* shouted the boy Carlos had stationed on the roof of the hacienda.

Carlos stopped pacing the courtyard and looked up at the boy. "How far away?" he called back.

"He's just crossed the arroyo."

"Is he waving his hat?"

"Yes, like a crazy man."

*"Bueno."* The rider was giving the signal that Hawkins had been spotted. It was now time to kill the damn horse thief.

Carlos moved hurriedly across the courtyard. The hacienda and the thousands of acres surrounding it formed a small rancho Ramos Valdes had acquired for the non-payment of a debt. Carlos had chosen it as his head-quarters due to its location on the south end

320

of Plano de Augustin and near El Camino Real. From there he had gathered twenty *pistoleros*, ten from among his own men and another ten from the outlaws and thugs of Chihuahua's underworld, men that his father had used from time to time. He had promised payment of two hundred pesos to each man who rode against Hawkins. In addition, a bounty of one thousand pesos was put on Hawkins's head and five hundred on the head of the man who traveled with him. The bounty would be paid to the man who fired the bullet that killed either one of them. Carlos had put one of his trusted lieutenants in charge of the Chihuahua hard cases to insure they followed his orders.

The message informing Carlos of the failure of his men to kill Hawkins in Samalayuca had caught up to him within a day after the fight. He would have liked to know what had gone wrong that had prevented four men from stopping the horse thief. No word had yet reached him from Terrazas, but Hawkins was now here and so the men he had placed at the freight station had failed.

Carlos had been surprised to learn that there was a second man traveling with Hawkins. His presence worried Carlos. Could it possibly be that it was known Leo and he had stolen the two American girls? That the second man was riding with Hawkins to get them back? The girls were to be the mothers of the next generation of the Valdes family and must not be taken from Leo and him. They would not be, because the large number of men Carlos had assembled would overwhelm Hawkins and his companion.

Carlos entered the hacienda to find Tattersall and his four men playing cards at the table in the *sala*. He didn't like the scalp hunters, but he endured them for they were excellent marksmen. He had seen them practice with their weapons and knew they were better than any of his own men or the men from Chihuahua.

"One of my riders is coming and soon we will know how far away Hawkins is," Carlos said.

"I heard the boy yelling so I guessed Hawkins was close," Tattersall said.

"That's good, for I'm damn tired of waiting," Adkisson added.

"I hope you got your gold handy to pay us," Tattersall said. Carlos's plan was a good one and he was glad he wasn't in Hawkins's boots.

"They're in position. Now we must ride swiftly and trap the horse thief between my *pistoleros* and your men."


"Where did they come from?" Evan said. He had a bad feeling as he looked at the group of horsemen who had come into view to the south down El Camino Real.

"There's low land at the far end of the Plano," Ben replied. "That's about two miles from here." He pulled his spyglass from a saddlebag and focused it on the riders trotting their horses toward them.

"Five of them," Ben said. "All are dressed like Americans. They're too far away to tell much more about them. It could be that Tattersall fellow I was told about. If so, he's got four friends with him. Best we change to our other horses in case we have to make a run for it."

Both men swung down to the ground and hastily swapped their saddles, Ben to Brutus and Evan to the back of his second horse. Ben pulled the bridle into place on Brutus. The big gray horse tossed his head and his big ivory teeth rattled against the iron bit. The horse had covered hundreds of miles during these past days and still he was showing his willingness to run.

"This may be the time when you have to show what you got," Ben said as he petted the animal's muscular shoulder.

He yanked himself astride. Evan mounted and sat his horse beside Ben.

They looked at each other. Then faced south and rode on to meet the band of men.

"What do we do if it is Tattersall?" Evan said.

Ben had turned and was looking to the side and out across the plain. He spoke without turning back. "It's Tattersall, all right, and he's got help. Look." He pointed off to the right and somewhat behind them where a large band of horsemen had come into view from behind a herd of cows. "And over there." He pointed to the left at a second group of riders moving upon them.

Ben checked the new bands of men with his

spyglass. "All Mexicans. They stayed dismounted and hidden until the Americans came into sight."

Evan groaned as he evaluated the position of the riders. "They've got us in the center of a triangle. We're penned in."

"And they're closing on us. Carlos has a damn fine plan." Ben estimated the openings between any two of the three groups to be about a mile and a half long. The gaps were swiftly closing as the horsemen trotted their mounts toward them. "We can't fight Carlos's *pistoleros* out here where there's no place to fort up," he said. "We've got to break out or we're dead men."

"Which way?"

"Toward the mountain between the Americans and that Mexican bunch," Ben said quickly. "If we can get into the rocks, we have a chance to stand them off. First, though, we've got to pass through that gap between them before they get within gun range."

"Looks like the Mexicans are coming at us faster than the Americans," Evan said as he jerked his belt off and held the buckle end in his hand.

"The Americans are holding back so that the Mexes will take our first shots. When our guns are empty, they'll charge in and finish us off. Now we've got to ride like hell. Lay the whip to that horse and keep up for I'm going to let Brutus have his head."

"I'm ready."

"Then let's ride! Ride!" Ben touched Brutus

with his heels and gave a shrill, keening cry. Brutus leapt ahead, his long legs stretching. In three jumps he was in full stride.

Ben saw both groups of foes immediately begin to lay on the whip to cut Evan and him off. Still, he thought they could break free of the closing jaws of Carlos's trap. He bent low and shouted into Brutus's ear. "Run, you big bastard. We can make it."

Ben glanced to the side to check if Evan was keeping up. Evan wasn't there. He looked to the rear. Evan was lashing his mount with the belt. Still, he was two horse lengths behind and falling farther back as Brutus tore ahead.

"Whip that slow son of a bitch," Ben shouted. "Beat him to death! Ride him into the ground!"

"Go on, Ben," Evan shouted. "He can't keep up. Get away if you can."

Ben looked at the Mexicans rushing in on his right. They were closer than the Americans riding in from the left and were almost within rifle range. If he let Brutus run full out, he could make it from between the two bands of men.

He began to rein Brutus in for he couldn't desert Evan. He pulled Brutus down until he was riding side by side with Evan.

"You dumb ass. Save yourself," Evan shouted fiercely.

A searing hot pain ripped across Evan's back. He was hit, a bullet had creased him. He bent forward until the pommel of the saddle was hard against his stomach.

Ben had seen Evan wince as he was struck. He had heard the boom of the gun and knew it was from a .52-caliber Sharps carbine. One of the Americans was very good. He unbuckled his belt and tore it free from around his waist. He struck Evan's horse a half-dozen cutting blows across the rump. The speed of the straining horse increased but little.

A whizzing chunk of lead hit the brim of Ben's hat and partially cut it off, and it drooped and flopped in front of his face. He ripped the piece loose and flung it aside. Another bullet tore past and the top of Brutus's ear disappeared in a bloody explosion of flesh and hair. An instant later, the big horse faltered and broke stride as a bullet plowed through a rib and deep inside. The horse caught himself with great effort and his gait steadied. He ran on, but only for a few strides, when his gait became rough and unstable.

Ben felt the gallant horse striving to maintain his pace. However, he was weakening, and his breath was a hoarse, ragged saw. He slowed more and more, and then came to a staggering walk. He stood swaying and trembling as he fought to hold his feet.

Ben kicked free of the stirrups and jumped clear as Brutus fell.

# Forty-two

Ben quickly knelt beside Brutus and put his hand on the faithful mount's shoulder. The horse laboriously lifted his head and looked at Ben. Its gold-flecked brown eyes seemed to be asking Ben what the problem was. With his eyes clinging to Ben and going soft, the animal lowered his head. The light faded and Brutus died.

"The damn bastards," Ben cursed, and stood erect.

A bullet whined past close beside his head and he jerked back from the deadly sound. No time to think of Brutus now. He wheeled around and found Evan had reined his mount up beside him.

Ben's scurrying thoughts jelled into a strategy for defense. He jumped and caught hold of the bridle of Evan's horse.

"Get Down! Down!" Ben yelled.

Evan sprang from the saddle, thinking Ben wanted him to be less of a target than high on the back of the horse.

"Grab his tail and swing his ass around so that he's parallel with Brutus there," Ben directed, pointing at a position on the ground about five feet from the dead horse.

Evan took hold of his mount's tail and pulled with all his strength. The animal side-stepped under Evan's pressure and came into the alignment that Ben wanted.

Immediately Ben yanked his pistol from

its holster and placed it against the horse's head. He fired, and brains and bone and blood sprayed out on the grass. The horse fell.

"Take cover," Ben said, and dropped to the ground between the carcasses of the two dead horses.

Evan fell down beside Ben and drew his rifle from its scabbard.

Ben pulled his Spencer free and laid it on Brutus's body. He hastily untied the saddlebag with the ammunition for the weapon, and extracted boxes of cartridges and a metal tube some eighteen inches long and slightly more than half an inch in diameter. It was a duplicate to the one that was now inserted inside the Spencer and held the cartridges for injection into the firing chamber.

"Are you good with a rifle?" Ben asked, and nodded at Evan's rifle.

"Just fair," Evan said.

"That's not good enough. Do you know how to load this?" He held the second cartridge tube for the Spencer out to Evan.

"Yes," Evan said, and flung a hurried look at the Mexicans racing down on them.

He ducked as a bullet hit his horse's body not an arm's length away. "They're going to ride straight over us," he told Ben.

"If we don't stop them, they sure as hell will." Ben shoved the tube into Evan's hand. "Load it while I try to slow them down."

Ben seated himself on the ground with his knees raised. He brought the rifle to his shoulder, and rested his elbows on his knees to steady his aim. He looked down the barrel of the Spencer at the Mexicans riding hard upon them. Every rider was bent forward and low over his horse. They had emptied their rifles and now had to depend on their pistols to finish off Evan and Ben. Ben wished he knew which one was the leader so he could shoot him first, for that might weaken the others' appetite for the fight. Perhaps the one in the front was the leader. Even if he wasn't, Ben would shoot him so that the others could see him go down.

Evan was watching his comrade, the scarred face, its features twisted and grotesque with hate for the killing of Brutus. Bullets were striking around Ben, yet Evan sensed no fear in the man, only a readiness, a desire to kill. They had an excellent chance of dying in the next couple of minutes, and Evan wondered about Ben's lack of fear. But could it be only that he was hiding it better than Evan?

He looked at the Mexican horsemen just as Ben fired the Spencer. At the flat crack of the rifle, the rider in the lead threw up his arms and fell from the saddle and rolled and tumbled on the ground. The rider directly behind almost lost his seat when his mount veered abruptly aside to avoid stepping on the fallen man. In what seemed but a tiny fraction of time, Ben fired again. A second man fell from his running horse. The fine Spencer rifle snarled a third time and another man was knocked to the ground.

Ben saw the Mexicans drag their mounts to

a quick halt. He had stopped that bunch and didn't have more time to spend on them. Still seated on the ground, he rotated and looked at the two remaining bands of foes. The Americans were still holding back, trotting toward them at a slow pace. This made the Mexicans coming up from the rear the closer. He brought the rifle up to point at this larger band of riders boring in. They were near enough to make easy targets.

Evan had finished loading the cartridge tube for the rifle, and now looked in the direction Ben was aiming. Ben fired and shot the man riding in front of his comrades. The man was small and the heavy bullet lifted him from the saddle and slammed him backward. Without a pause, and with an accuracy that astounded Evan, Ben shot and knocked three more men from their mounts in rapid succession. The band of Mexicans came to a swift halt.

Ben wheeled about toward the attacking American horsemen. They had seen the slaughter that had been made of the Mexicans, and had stopped and were staring in his direction. They had obviously decided that charging straight at Ben and Evan wasn't a good plan of action.

"Give me the shells," Ben called to Evan, at the same time removing the empty tube from the stock of the rifle. "Hurry."

Evan held out the loaded tube.

Ben took it and shoved it up the tunnel in the stock and into position in the rifle. He levered a cartridge into the firing chamber, raised the weapon, and pointed it at the Americans. The men were sitting their horses and talking among themselves. The range was long, nearly a quarter mile, and they didn't seem too concerned about their safety. They needed a couple of bullets. Ben wished he knew which one was Tattersall, for he would like to try to shoot that man first off.

He elevated the barrel of the rifle and fired at the man sitting most upright and making the biggest target. The man rocked backward at the strike of the bullet. He fought back to an upright position, but then slumped forward onto the neck of his mount.

One of the other men reined his horse in and caught hold of the bridle of the wounded man's mount. Another man called out and the group of men spun their horses about and raced away.

The shot had been a little left, Ben thought. He fired again and the man in the rear slid from the saddle to the ground. The others spurred their mounts hard and drew rapidly off across the plain.

Ben turned back to the first band of Mexicans. They had drawn back a couple hundred yards and stopped, and now were talking and gesturing. They were making the same mistake as the Americans, thinking they were out of gun range.

"They need more convincing," Ben said to himself. He raised the rifle to his shoulder. He knocked two of them from their saddles with deliberate shots. Demoralized by the killing fire, they began to whip the horses back in the direction from where they had come.

Ben lowered his rifle. He breathed deeply, pulling the bitter gunpowder smoke of his rifle into his lungs, watching the bodies lying on the plain. For the time being, their enemies had been stopped.

"My God, Ben, you killed nine, ten men," exclaimed Evan. He could hear the agonizing, pain-filled cries of the wounded and dying men.

"I just did what they wanted to do to us. Too bad I couldn't have shot every one of that bunch for they're the most dangerous," Ben replied as he looked with hooded eyes in the direction of the retreating Americans. "But that'll hold them for a little while," Ben added. He took up his spyglass.

"It sure should," Evan said. "I'd not want to charge into that gun. Not with you shooting it."

"Best rifle ever made. It's a new model and only a few of them around. Makes a man equal to seven who are shooting single-shots."

Ben was studying something with his spyglass. "I bet it surprised Carlos too."

"Carlos? Do you think he saw what happened?"

"That's him over there," Ben said. He pointed at a lone rider sitting his horse off on the plain. "He's watching through a glass same as me. Too bad he's so far off. I'd like to send a bullet in his direction."

"What do you think he'll do now?"

"Talk to everybody to get their courage up. And promise them more money than before to kill us."

"I meant, what kind of attack will he make?"

"They may try to take us when it's dark. Or they might just keep us penned down and starve us for water. But we'll not wait for either one."

"We're on foot now."

"Not for long. There's plenty of horses out there belonging to men who don't need them any longer. We'll see if we can't get a couple when it's good and dark."

Ben leaned against Brutus's back. As he looked out over the plain, he took a handful of the horse's long gray mane and ran it back and forth through his hands.

"I stole Valdes horses," Ben said. "For that they had a right to try and kill me. But they shouldn't have stole Maude and Rachel. For that, I'm going to kill every one of them."

"If we get out of this fix we're in."

"You're right. There's still a lot of them and when it gets dark, they can move in close and throw a tight noose around us."

Ben dug his jackknife from a pocket and cut off a handful of Brutus's mane. He toyed with it for a moment, and then twisted it into a braid and put it into his shirt pocket. He wanted a remembrance of the faithful steed.

Three long-range rifle shots rained down from a high angle. One struck with a thud close by on the plain.

"They're hoping to get lucky," Ben said. He raised his rifle and sent three bullets back in return.

"Best we rest while we can, for it's going to be a long day and night," Ben said. Evan looked ready to keel over. "You go first."

"The horses should give us some protection," Evan said as he lay down close beside the body of his mount. "Wake me when it's your turn."

## Forty-three

A night wind came alive, snuffling along the ground and in between the two dead horses. The air around Ben became heavy with the stink of the bodies. In the sky, dark clouds reached for the nimbus of the half moon. Ben judged it would rain before morning.

"Evan, wake up, it's about time to move out," Ben said in a low voice.

Evan opened his eyes to darkness. He hadn't expected that. He had slept the day away. His sleep had been cruel for he had dreamed that Ben and he had failed to free Rachel and Maude. They had fought their way into the hacienda of the Valdes rancho only to find the girls gone.

"What time is it?" Evan asked, his voice clogged with worry. He looked about them where the moon laid an icy crust of light on the dry grass of the plain.

"Near midnight."

"Midnight?" Evan said, sitting up. "Why didn't you wake me sooner so you could rest?"

"You needed it more than me. And I cat-napped a little while it was still daylight."

Evan saw the black clouds covering more than half the sky. Off to the west, lightning flashed. The rumble of thunder reached them.

"Storm brewing," Evan said.

" 'Pears so, and coming our way." Ben was looking up at the sky. "The moon will be gone in a little while and then we should be leaving."

"If it's going to rain, why not wait for it and then go?" Evan said.

"Any rain that falls might miss us. And we sure don't want to be here when daylight comes."

"So which way do you think is best?"

"Since we don't know where Carlos has his men stationed, why not just continue on south?"

"Sounds right to me." East of the hurrying clouds, cold stars hung in the sky. They could be used to guide them.

"Carlos has had enough time to get more men to replace those he lost," Ben said as he watched and listened into the deepening darkness. "So there'll be a lot of them out there and it's going to be a ticklish job slipping through them."

Evan watched the speeding clouds conquer the moon, and the last of the moonlight left them and ran off to the east. He spoke. "I'm ready to move. If we stay low, the grass will half hide us so maybe we can crawl past them without being seen."

"We take only our guns and shells. And best we go single file. I'll go first, if that's all right with you."

"Lead on."

"I judge Carlos and his men will be out there about a hundred yards or so and ringing us in. We got to see them before they see us."

Ben lay down on his stomach. Cradling his rifle, he crawled off hugging the ground. Evan lay down and snaked his way along behind Ben. A low rasping sound came as they slid through the grass.

They moved the first few yards, and then Ben halted them for a time and both probed the thick darkness, trying to see something that meant danger. Detecting nothing, they went on at a snail's pace, merely inching forward and pressed down into the short grass. The wind increased and the dry grass began to rustle. Good, thought Ben, the sound would help to cover the noise Evan and he were making.

Ben stopped and stared hard into the blackness around them. He saw nothing but the impenetrable murk of the night. Still, he felt the presence of someone or something in front of him. Try as hard as he might, he could not make out a form. Trusting his instincts, he angled off to the side, choosing to go right.

They had gone not more than a few yards when Ben heard a man's voice. He halted instantly and froze. Looking in the direction of the voice, he faintly made out the forms of two men standing on the plain not a long pebble flip distant.

Evan's head bumped into his feet before he too stopped. Ben silently willed Evan not to speak and give them away. Evan remained quiet.

Studying the two men carefully, Ben decided they were facing in the direction from which Evan and he had come. Crawling even more slowly, he led on.

When the men were directly off Ben's left side, one of them spoke. "Fire the grass and give the signal."

Ben recognized Carlos Valdes's voice. The man who had tried to kill him three times was within easy pistol range. Since Carlos had spoken in English, the second man would be Tattersall, or one of his men. Ben felt the hot urge to shoot both men. However, that would give him away to Carlos's men. Maude and Rachel were more important than killing Carlos right now. There would be another time for that, if Evan and he could get away without being spotted.

One of the men bent down and struck a match and lit the grass. Flames leapt, throwing a light over Ben and Evan, penning them with its brightness. They were exposed to their foes should they but only look.

Carlos gave the order for Tattersall to fire the grass as the storm clouds swept across the sky. The clouds held rain and it appeared they would drop it here. Falling rain could provide Hawkins and his comrade with the cover they needed to slip out of the net Carlos had thrown around them. Hawkins must be taken before that.

The crackling sound of the flames consuming the dry grass drew Carlos's eyes back to the earth. The grass burned readily, sending two-foot-high yellow flames flaring brightly in the darkness. A point of fire had appeared nearby on the plain. Another one sprang to life farther off.

As Carlos watched, a dozen more fires showed in the night. Within half a minute more, the plain had come alive with thirty pools of light from burning grass. The fires were spaced in a circle some three hundred yards in diameter, with Hawkins in the center. Everything was progressing as Carlos had planned.

The plan was simple. Illuminate Hawkins and his comrade with fire so that they could be shot. At the same time keep his own men in darkness and thus protected from the deadly rifles of the Americans.

"Help me put out the fire on the back side," Carlos said to Tattersall.

The men began to stomp the flaming grass,

the task easily done for the burning of the fine reeds created mostly light and little heat.

Ben saw the two men begin to extinguish fire on the side opposite to where Evan and he had lain with the horses. With the men's attention on the fire and their boots thudding on the ground, Ben knew it was time to go, and go quickly. He crawled hurriedly off. Evan followed close behind.

Several yards later, Ben whispered to Evan, "I smell horses."

"Yeah, me too," Evan whispered back.

"Let's go get some. We'll come in from the side opposite the fires. There may be a guard, so watch out."

The two men crawled on, pressed as close to the ground as possible. The scent of the horses grew stronger. The sound of a horse moving came to them.

A couple of body lengths farther along, Ben halted and lay, trying to see into the night. Where was the guard?

Carlos and Tattersall controlled the spread of the fire they had set, trampling it out as needed to force it to advance in the direction they wanted. The fire left only short-lived coals behind, and within but a minute the area was cool.

Carlos looked out over the plain. The other fires had grown, broadened. The outlines of the fires were no longer circular in shape; rather, each was a bright yellow crescent of advancing flames. His men were performing their task properly, extinguishing half the circumference of the fire they had started.

The fire Carlos and Tattersall tended joined with the fire of his man on the right. Then the fire on the left merged with theirs. In but a handful of minutes, all the fires on the plain had joined together in one huge ring of bright flames.

Carlos looked at the point where he knew Hawkins and the other man were barricaded. The fire front was marching inexorably upon the men's location from all directions. Carlos's *pistoleros*, hidden in the darkness behind the fire, would be moving in prepared to shoot the moment Hawkins became a visible target.

"Let's go help them kill Hawkins and his friend," Carlos said.

"Once we catch them in the light, it'll be like shooting fish in a barrel," Tattersall said. Hawkins had killed one of his men and wounded another. It was time to make him pay for that.

They moved off in the black ashes left by the quick-burning grass. They held back half a hundred yards to be out of the light of the leaping flames.

# Forty-four

"There's only two horses and no guards," Ben said to Evan. He could see the animals silhouetted against the distant fire. They would belong to Carlos and the American with him. Each of Carlos's men must have chosen to keep his personal mount close by him as he fired the grass of the plain in preparation to fight the two Americans.

"Exactly the number we need," Evan said.

The men rose to their feet. Not wanting the horses to become alarmed at unknown men approaching through the darkness, Ben and Evan went the last short distance walking slowly and talking in low voices to calm them.

"Just a saddle and no bedroll on this one," Evan said.

"Same here, except there's a canteen with some water in it," Ben said. "We'll share that."

They untied the animals from their picket ropes, and mounted. They sat looking at the ring of fire from which they had barely escaped. The fire had perhaps two hundred feet to go to be completely closed in upon itself.

"Carlos will soon know we're not caught in his fire trap," Ben said with a pleased chuckle.

"He's going to be damn mad," Evan said.

"Yeah, and I like that."

To the west along a front, jagged incandescent streaks of lightning punched holes in the night, and thunder rumbled across the plain as the storm struggled at creating itself.

"Best we be moving for Carlos will be riding like hell for his hacienda in but a few minutes," Ben said. "It would be best to get there before he warns the others that he's failed and we're still coming."

They shook out the bridle reins and sent the horses galloping into the darkness. Ben led, holding a course southwest and near the base of Sierra Las Tunas. This course would bypass Chihuahua and shorten the distance to the Valdes hacienda by several miles. If they pressed hard, they could reach their objective by evening of the coming day.

As they passed the edge of the plain, the last piece of the sky vanished and the night deepened to pitch-black and hid the land. As if waiting for that event, a mighty burst of lightning bolts burned the Stygian darkness and the storm fell upon the two riders with a sibilant hiss of falling raindrops. The rain rapidly intensified, and in a moment huge drops were drumming on the horses' heads and rumps and hammering down the brims of the men's hats.

With shoulders hunched against the cold, wet onslaught, the two men traveled on under the leaking heavens. Ben guided them on by using the location of the lightning and the direction of the wind to choose the course.

A weak dawn arrived and the land shaped itself out of the night. The rain slackened to a drizzle and soon ceased altogether. Large clouds of mist drifted down the swales on the side of Sierra Las Tunas two miles off Ben's and Evan's right. Cold and wet from the drenching downpour, the men rode silently on.

The day brightened further, and by mid-morning the sun had burned its way through the clouds and the clothing of the men began to dry. In the early evening, they were hidden on the mountainside a quarter mile away and above the walled hacienda of the Valdes family. Their horses were out of sight in the bottom of a narrow draw a short distance around the side of the mountain.

Ben lay behind a boulder and with his spyglass watched the hacienda and the other buildings that made up the Valdes headquarters. Besides the big main house, there were five smaller homes set off a few hundred feet to the left of the big house. To the right were a corral and two small outbuildings. Ben thought one of the buildings would most likely be a blacksmith shop and the other a place to store harnesses and saddles.

Half a mile farther away, directly in front of the *casa* and near the river, were three large corrals holding many horses, a huge hay barn, and several buildings used for various purposes in connection with the horse-breeding operation. He knew the area by the river well for it was from there that he had stolen the Valdes horses.

"Two men in the watchtower and four men

patrolling the grounds inside the wall," Ben said to Evan.

"That doesn't give us much of a chance of breaking in and getting the girls."

"Do you see those smaller houses near the hacienda?"

"Yes."

"They all have saddled horses tied in front. That means those cowboys haven't gone off to work, but have been kept close to help stop us if we try to break in to take Maude and Rachel. Also, there'll be another half-dozen men down there at the river where the horse breeding takes place."

"Do you think Rachel and Maude are here?"

"They're here. The sons would want to show them off to Ramos and their mother."

"Any idea how we're going to do it?" Evan was worried that even with the best of efforts to rescue the girls, Ben and he would fail.

"Not yet. Let's wait and see what goes on down there. Then maybe we can think of a way to pull it off."

"All ri..." Evan started to cough, harsh expulsions of air sending knifelike pains through his damaged lung. He fought to stifle the coughs, for he didn't want Ben to know how bad off he actually was.

Ben looked anxiously at Evan. "You okay?"

"Yeah," Evan said as he choked off a cough.

Ben didn't think so. The last thing they needed was for Evan to become too ill to travel. Ben shouldn't have allowed Evan to come with him. If Evan had stayed in El Paso, he would have been out of danger and had time to rest and heal. Then he could be in fine condition to operate on Ben's face when he returned with the women. Too late to change anything now. He turned back to glass their enemies.

"Four riders coming," Ben said as he tracked horsemen in the field of the spyglass. "It's Carlos and three Americans. There goes our surprise, if we ever had one." He hoped the two missing Americans had been killed by his rifle shots, for that would serve them right. The men rode inside the compound and Ben could no longer see them.

"With Carlos here now, there'll soon be a wedding," Ben said.

He swept the spyglass over the homes of the cowboys. In front of one was a horse and buggy. He focused there as a woman came out of the house and climbed into the vehicle. In the sunlight, her long golden hair shone bright as flame. For a moment he thought it was Maude. However, that couldn't be for the Valdes men wouldn't allow her that kind of freedom. The woman was most probably Ramos's wife, if the stories were true that he had married a *Norte Americana*. The woman drove the buggy to the hacienda and into the compound.

The blondeness of the woman caused Ben to recall the soft touch of Maude's fingers caressing his scarred face that night in Canutillo. He smiled at the memory, his devil's face twisting ugly and his eyes happy.

"What's so good?" Evan asked, for he was getting better at reading Ben's expressions.

"Just a memory. Just a memory. Let's try to think of a way to get the girls away from the rancho without getting them and us killed."

## Forty-five

"That ugly horse thief has traveled hundreds of miles into our country and in all that time you haven't been able to stop him," Ramos Valdes raged at Carlos. "You had all the fighting men you could ever want and yet you stand there beaten."

Señora Helena Valdes watched the three men of her life, her husband Ramos and sons Carlos and Leo. The four of them were gathered in the big main room of the hacienda. Carlos had finished describing the events of the past several days. Ramos was pacing the floor, his head swiveling as he kept his hard, black eyes on his oldest son. Ramos was a domineering man, quick to anger, and when he rampaged as he did now, he frightened Helena.

Rarely did Helena participate in Ramos's discussions with his sons. She didn't want to know about his methods of doing business, practices that she was certain his sons now followed, for she was afraid of what they were. However, when Leo had returned with the two American girls, and then Carlos had arrived, she had decided to participate. She'd believed the meeting would include much talk about the two girls who were to become her daughters.

"He didn't beat me," Carlos retorted angrily. He began to pace the opposite side of the room. "The four *pistoleros* at Samalayuca weren't as tough as they were said to be, not tough enough to kill Hawkins. So I doubled the number I stationed at Terrazas. Hawkins came and took their horses and they never even saw him."

Carlos ceased pacing and fixed his father with a stare. "He was extremely lucky to have escaped the fire trap on Plano de San Augustin. Like a coyote gets lucky and avoids the traps I've seen you set."

Ramos shook his head disdainfully at Carlos. "A coyote's luck is just dumb luck. A man makes his luck."

Ramos knew there was much more to Hawkins than luck. He was a brazen man and hard enough to carry off what he started. He was clever in that he always took the stolen horses to Abilene. This removed the horses far from Valdes's reach. And importantly for Hawkins's safety, that route avoided El Camino Real and denied Valdes the use of fresh horses at his freight stations with which he could run Hawkins down.

Leo moved to stand beside Carlos and spoke. "Father, you said yourself that this Hawkins is the best horse thief who has ever stolen one of your horses. Then the Americans gave away Carlos's plan when they tried to kill

Hawkins in El Paso and failed. After that he must have been extra cautious."

"Right," Carlos interjected. "Hawkins hasn't really accomplished anything yet."

Ramos looked at his two sons and nodded. He liked the manner in which Leo had come forward to Carlos's defense. They were becoming tough hombres, and with them working together nobody would be able to defeat them.

"What is done, is done," Ramos said in a forgiving tone. "Hawkins will be someplace close by. It's too late in the day to start a search for him now. Tomorrow we will send every available rider we have out scouring the land for him and the other man."

Ramos spoke directly to Carlos. "Do you think they know about the young women?"

"I believe they do, Father. That is why the second man is here."

"I agree, for I don't think Hawkins would ask another man to help him fight his personal battles."

"He has one of those new repeating rifles and he is deadly with it. That is how he stopped the charge of twenty-five men and saved himself."

"How many of our men has Hawkins killed?"

"Twelve, and wounded four badly. Two of them will most likely die."

"Give me their names." Ramos's riders remained loyal to him because of the fact that they knew he would take care of their families should something fatal befall them.

348

Helena had been intently observing her menfolk as they discussed Hawkins. She had previously heard them describe the man and his skill at stealing and pictured him as a horribly gruesome phantom. Now, as Carlos listed the dead, she saw an amazing, frightening thing occur. The light immediately surrounding the three men began to weaken. Not elsewhere in the room, just in an envelope surrounding them. Within but a moment, they were enclosed within a dark umbra. They were ghost men barely seen through a murky, vaporous shroud. At the same time, dizziness seized Helena and she swayed in her chair. A terrifying premonition jarred her to the very core of her being. The murderous Hawkins was going to kill her husband and beloved sons. She believed it with heartrending conviction.

Then abruptly, the darkness around her menfolk lifted and they stood fully illuminated. However, the premonition remained cold and heavy in Helena's bosom. She had had a third son, two years younger than Leo. A similar shadow had fallen over him one day while she was looking at him. She had made little of it, thinking that it was merely a temporary condition of her eyesight. Then the very next day, he had been shot from ambush by one of Ramos's enemies. She would not disregard the omen this time.

"Let the young women return to their homes in the north," Helena cried out in a voice that overrode the men's conversation.

They turned as one to look at Helena.

"What? What did you say?" Ramos could not believe what he had heard.

"Free the women. Give them a horse and buggy and send them away."

"Helena, why would you suggest such a thing?" Ramos said.

"The man Hawkins has killed a dozen men. Now he is here. We must get him to leave before he kills some of you."

"He won't kill us," Ramos said.

"I fear for all of you. Let the two women go."

"Mother, they are to be our wives," Carlos said. "They will give you beautiful grand-children."

"I just now had a horrible feeling come over me that Hawkins would destroy our family if we continue to hold the women pris-oners." Tears came to her eyes. "Please, oh, please, free them so the man will leave us in peace."

"Yes, let us go home and we will find Ben and take him north with us," Maude said from the hallway off the room. She and Rachel had heard the loud voices, left the room where they had been told to remain, and crept close. Her blood strummed with happiness at the knowledge that Ben had come for her.

Surprised at the presence of the girls, Helena and the men wheeled about to face them.

Carlos looked at Rachel, into her green eyes with the brilliant whites. He had not seen her since his arrival, and now swept his sight over her from head to toe, tracing the womanly curves of her. He realized that he had captured a more beautiful jewel than he had remembered. He thought of her sharing his bed and smiled at his good fortune.

"Lovely Rachel, I will never let you go," Carlos said.

"Never is the correct word," Leo said to Maude. "You belong here with me."

"The Valdes men do not give up anything they desire," Ramos said to Helena. He held her eyes, staring at her with a meaning that she fully understood.

## *Forty-six*

Ben and Evan lay on the mountainside and spied on the activity of the people at the Valdes rancho. Four guards patrolled the inside of the walled compound. Two manned the guard tower. All activity at the horse-breeding area had ceased and the workers had ridden away.

When the daylight had boiled down to a crimson brew in the west, Ben closed his spyglass and spoke to Evan. "I can't think of a better plan than what we talked about."

"I've thought it over too and neither can I," Evan replied.

"All right then. First we get two more horses for the girls to ride. Those at the homes of the cowboys are the handiest. They all have saddles on them and that's something we must have. After we get that done, you set fire to the big barn. It'll have tons of hay in it that'll burn fast and make a lot of flames and light."

"And while the Valdes men are all in confusion about the fire, you'll get the girls free," Evan said.

"Just as easy as eating pie," Ben said, not believing a word of it. He was getting to like this man who was very brave and never complained though he was ill and weak from his wound.

"Do you think the Valdes brothers would harm Rachel and Maude if things went wrong while we tried to get them free?" Evan asked.

"I believe they'd kill the girls before they'd lose them," Ben said.

"Then we can't fail," Evan said in a very quiet voice. For an instant he had a black feeling that death was waiting for him down in the valley.

"Right. We won't leave without them. And if I get the chance, I'll shoot the hell out of all the Valdes men."

Ben lay silently beside Evan and watched the last of the daylight drain from the sky, and a dark night arrived. All that could be seen of the hacienda and the *casas* of the cowboys were tiny points of light floating in a lake of blackness below them.

Ben pressed himself against the outside of the wall that surrounded the Valdes compound. In the darkness, Evan and he had stolen two horses from the cowboys without being discovered. Then they had separated, and now he waited for Evan to do his part.

As Ben listened to the sound of the guard patrolling the compound on the opposite side of the wall, he felt growing doubt about the success of the plan to take the girls away. He knew Ramos was much too savvy to be tricked into doing something foolish. Ben's hope was that some of the man's fighters would not be so wise.

"Fire!" came an excited cry from the watchtower. "Fire at the barns!"

The cry was taken up by the guards on patrol and rang loudly throughout the compound. Ben heard the footsteps of the guard nearest to him draw away.

He caught hold of the top of the wall and cautiously hoisted himself up to look over. The guard was trotting toward the front, where he would have a better view of the buildings near the Santa Isabel River.

Ben looked in the same direction. Visible above the wall of the compound was a distant pillar of flame and smoke shooting high into the sky. The burning hay was making a much bigger fire than he had thought. More hay must have been stored in the barn since he had last been there. "Now, Evan, get to the horses at our rendezvous point," Ben said quietly to himself.

He muscled himself up the rest of the way to the top of the wall and jumped down inside the compound. He hunkered low and motionless. Barely making it in time to avoid being seen by the two men who came into sight in front of the *casas*.

"We should go and help the men fight the fire," Carlos said.

"No," Ramos replied. "That fire was set by Hawkins, and that's just what he wants us to do. And anyway, the barn is lost for there's no way to put a fire that size out."

Ramos saw the guards standing near the front wall of the compound and looking at the fire. "Damn those stupid men. Get all of them back on their stations at once. Then go back inside with Leo and guard the two women. I'll go down to the barns and make sure nothing else burns."

Carlos hurried off, shouting at the guards. Ramos struck out for the front gate.

Ben dashed across the open area to the *casa*. A few feet farther along the wall was a window that showed a faint light. He crept to it and found it was open, probably to let in the cool night air. He knelt to peer and listen inside. The room was illuminated by three candles in a silver candelabrum. He could see most of the room and it appeared to be vacant. He swung a leg over the sill and entered. Ben was in a bedroom with a large four-poster bed. He crept over the thick wool carpet to the door and opened it an inch to see out.

To his surprise, the golden-haired woman he had seen in the buggy was coming along the hallway. She surely must be Ramos's wife. A thought came to Ben. Why not take her and trade her for the girls? Even as the thought came to him, he knew it wouldn't work. Where could he hide the woman while he negotiated the trade? And how could he find a place safe from some sort of trickery to swap her for the girls? Worse yet, if by chance the Valdes men agreed to such an arrangement, Carlos and Leo would surely make the two girls their wives before bringing them for the exchange. No, taking the woman wouldn't be a smart action. Another way must be found.

Helena hastened toward her bedroom. The fire at the horse barn meant Hawkins was close. She had a pistol in her bedroom and must arm herself so she could protect her sons. She was still greatly frightened by the black light she had seen fall upon them.

She shoved the door wide and stepped through, thinking at the same time that she was certain she had completely closed it earlier. She stopped, tense and alert. There was someone in the room with her. Her sight darted to the pistol on the nightstand on the far side of the room.

Before Helena could move, a hand came from behind the door and caught her by the face and clamped her mouth shut. An arm encircled her waist and lifted her off her feet. Hanging airborne in the powerful embrace, she was totally helpless. Her heart began to thunder with a sudden rush of fear, for she knew the murderous Hawkins had her captive.

"I don't want to hurt you, but I'll wring your neck if you don't do exactly as I say," Ben whispered into Helena's ear. "Now I'm going to take my hand off your mouth, but don't you make a sound except to whisper your answers to my questions. Do you understand me?"

Helena nodded as best she could within the viselike grip on her face. Anything to gain time to think of a way to break loose.

"That's good." Ben slowly removed his hand, ready to clamp down again should the woman start to cry out. When she remained silent, he set her on her feet. He caught her firmly by the shoulder and turned her to face him.

"Are the two American girls here?"

"Yes," Helena replied, her blue eyes fastened on the man's gruesome face only a hand's width from her own. He was uglier than she had ever imagined.

"Where?"

"Along the hallway to the enclosed patio and then left to the center of the *casa*." The thief watched her with a keen, piercing stare. Would he know if she lied?

As if he was reading her thoughts, the threatening glitter in Hawkins's eyes hardened. "I've no time for tricks. I want the girls. Are they together right now?"

"Yes, and my sons and Ramos are with them. They are expecting me to return and talk with them. You had better leave while you can, or they will kill you."

"You just lied to me," Ben growled. "Ramos

isn't here. He's at the fire. As for your thievin' sons, they're not going to kill me. I'm going to kill them for stealing the girls." He grinned wickedly at Helena for she seemed to be very much afraid of his scarred face.

The ugly man's declaration and the murderous hate in his eyes brought a tremble to Helena. She tried to stop the tremble so he wouldn't know how much she feared him, but she could not for she knew how tough and fearless he must be to have made it to the rancho. And now he had somehow passed through all the fighting men on guard and actually invaded the *casa* of the Valdes family. The premonition that had been born from some instinct deep within her again warned her that this man was very dangerous to her sons. For an instant, a vision of them lying bleeding on the ground and dying came before her inner eye. Her pulse became a mighty drumbeat inside her skull.

Ben felt the woman trembling with fear of him. That bothered him for she was a woman who had done nothing to harm him. Still, her fear was as nothing in comparison to freeing Maude and Rachel. So he would scare her more and make her do what he asked. He gave her a gallows smile, thinking that for the very first time he was gaining something beneficial from his monster's face.

He spoke. "Your sons are in this house with me and I can kill them when I want. And there's absolutely nobody who can stop me."

Helena didn't want to admit to such an awful thing, yet she knew the thief was stating the truth. His eyes, burning with a fury barely controlled, raked her. "Your sons are the worse kind of thieves. I steal only horses, they steal innocent girls from their homes. Both of them deserve to die."

Helena spoke hurriedly. "If I help you free the young women, will you let my sons live?"

"Say that again." Ben's grip on the woman tightened involuntarily.

Helena's blood was running cold and she shivered in the man's hands. "They are my sons and I will do anything to protect them. I know a way to get the women out of the *casa*. I will bring them to you."

Ben searched Helena's face trying to detect the lie, the deception. He had intended to make the woman help him in some manner. However, the extent of her offer, to actually bring them to him, was not believable. Several seconds passed as Ben remained silent, gripping Helena's shoulder as his eyes locked with hers.

Helena saw the disbelief in the thief. "In return, you must promise me that you won't hurt my sons in any way."

"All right," Ben said. He would play along with her and see where she led. "But know this. Any false move on your part and they die."

"No! No! I swear to you that I will do exactly as I say."

"How would you do it, get them out of the *casa* and to me?"

"The wife of one of our riders is close to giving birth. I was there earlier today. Ramos and the others wouldn't think anything out of the ordinary if I went there again tonight. I will bring the girls with me in the buggy."

"I saw you there so I know which house you were at."

Helena was surprised at that fact. "I'll bring them hidden on the floor of the buggy."

"How soon?"

"You have stirred the people up with the fire. All that must quiet down before I can chance coming with the girls. Midnight at least."

"Just you and the girls. No one else."

"You must know that once my sons and Ramos find out what I've done, there's nothing I can do to stop them from searching for you."

"They won't find me. As long as they don't come north of the Rio Grande looking for me, our bargain stands. How long can you keep them from learning the girls are gone?"

"With luck, maybe until morning."

Ben held out his hand to seal the bargain, at the same time wondering what Ramos would do to the woman should she actually carry out the plan she'd proposed.

Helena looked at Ben's hand, but did not take it.

Ben spoke. "When I shake on an agreement it's an oath that I'd not break. I want your hand on it too."

Helena clasped the hand in a tight grip. "You have the word of Helena Valdes that she will keep her bargain. You also have the word of Helena O'Shea."

*So O'Shea was your original name*, Ben thought. "I accept both women's word," Ben said. "Remember this. If you don't bring the girls, I'll come back."

He stepped to the candles and pinched them out. A second later he was at the window. He glanced outside into the dark compound. Saw nobody. He heard the woman moving across the room as he went through the window and into the night.

Behind him Helena was reaching for the pistol on the nightstand. She turned with it in her hand. The man was gone.

# *Forty-seven*

"It's past midnight and the woman hasn't kept her promise to bring the girls," Evan said. "I'm thinking she won't."

"We'll give her some more time," Ben replied. "It could be things haven't quieted down enough for her to get away with them."

"I hope that's it."

The two men, with four horses, were concealed in a patch of brush a hundred yards below the homes of the cowboys. From that location they could see the front of the walled hacienda. No one could be seen near the remains of the barn, now only a large mound of glowing embers.

"She acted damn scared that I would kill her boys," Ben said. "Seems my ugly mug made her think I was a real mean hombre. Evan, there was something really odd about my talk with her. She didn't include Ramos in our bargain."

"Could be she hasn't forgiven him for carrying her off to Mexico."

"What would you think if you were a woman and a strange man of a foreign country kidnapped you and carried you off with just one thing in his mind?"

"I'd be damn mad."

"Right. And the only reason she's stayed was because of her sons."

"Something's happening," Evan said.

"I see it."

A horse-drawn buggy had come out through the gate set in the wall of the compound and turned toward the homes of the cowboys. Two coal-oil lanterns were fastened to the left and right side of the front of the vehicle. They were glowing yellow eyes lighting the way in the darkness. A pair of guards with rifles were visible walking beside the buggy.

"I should have known that Ramos wouldn't let his wife go outside without some of his *pistoleros* going with her," Ben said.

"The woman could use them as an excuse for not bringing the girls." Evan still couldn't believe it would be this easy to free them.

"We'll soon know."

The buggy stopped at the house of the woman nearing her birthing time. Helena climbed down and spoke to the men with her. They extinguished the lanterns and followed the woman into the house.

"Time to see if she brought Maude and Rachel," Ben said. "Stay with the horses and be ready to fight or ride or both, for we don't know what I'll find. Could be something we sure don't want."

"I'll be here and ready."

Ben went quietly through the darkness toward the buggy. As he drew close, he could see the horses watching him. He pulled his pistol, cocking it under his hand to muffle the sound, and went up to the buggy.

He could make out a blanket-covered mound in the rear floor of the vehicle. The form was large enough to be two people. Was it a pair of Ramos's *pistoleros* waiting there to shoot him?

"Maude, Rachel?" Ben whispered. His pistol was aimed to shoot if the wrong response came.

"Ben, is that you?" Maude whispered back.

Immediately the blanket was flung off and the two girls sat up. Their faces burned beautifully white in the darkness.

Maude sprang down from the buggy and into Ben's arms. She hugged him fiercely to her, and whispered into his ear. "I knew that if anybody came to get me, it would be you."

Ben held Maude tightly against him, breathing in the pleasing woman smell of her. Her pleasure at his presence delighted him. She was the only person in his world to act as if the wound to his face was but a minor blemish and he was still the Ben Hawkins as of old. He kissed her on the cheek with his crumpled lips, and she did not flinch at their touch.

"We've got to hurry," Ben said, releasing Maude from his arms. He picked up the blanket and bundled it under his arm. "Follow me close behind," he said, and led them into the darkness.

"Are you by yourself?" Rachel asked as they moved.

"No. A friend of yours is with me."

"Evan?"

"Who but Evan would kill a man for you? Then come chasing into Mexico after you?" Ben intended to make Rachel understand just how much Evan loved her.

"Redpath is dead?" Rachel said in wonder.

"Dead as can be," Ben replied. "There's Evan and the horses," he said as the outlines of the animals with the man holding their reins came into view ahead in the night.

Rachel hastened ahead of Ben and Maude and called out. "Oh, Evan, I'm so glad to see you. Thank you for coming to help me." She had seen Maude's impassioned greeting of Ben. She could do no less for Evan. She clasped her arms around him.

Rachel felt the thinness of Evan's body, his bones sharp against her body. The journey south to rescue her had been hard on him.

Evan returned Rachel's embrace. "I'm glad the Valdes woman kept her promise and brought you to us."

"What did you do to frighten her so much?"

Rachel asked. "She was shaking while she was preparing us to leave."

"Ben did that."

"No time to talk," Ben said. "Evan, help Rachel up on her horse. We've got to be a long ways from here come sunup."

As he guided Maude to her horse, he realized the women were dressed in shirt and trousers. "Where did the clothes come from?" he asked.

"The woman gave us these in place of our dresses for she knew we would have to be riding horseback," Maude said.

"Which way?" Evan asked as he reined his mount close to Ben.

"Ramos will most likely think we'll ride fast as we can for the border. I'd like to fool him if we can. We'll go south for several miles and then west for another day. Then we'll work our way north on the far side of a mountain range called Sierra Las Tunas. It's a much longer route, but should be a hell of a lot safer."

"So you know that country?" Evan said.

"I rode over part of it once. However, most of it will be new to me and we'll just have to take it as it comes."

"How long do you think it'll take us to reach the States?" Rachel asked.

"I don't care how long it takes, not now," Maude said. She reached out through the darkness and touched Ben's arm.

"Several days," Ben said. Maude had voiced his exact thoughts. He sent his horse off.

They forded the black water of the Santa Isabel River. Hours later they passed south of Laguna Bustillos. Just before daylight, they reached the extreme upper headwaters of the Santa Maria River. The first drop of the river came from a spring flowing from a deep cleft in the side of a pine-forested mountain.

Ben called a halt beside the spring. The riders dismounted and stood stiff and weary.

"I'd guess you know where we are since you came straight to the spring," Evan said.

"I found it one day by accident." Ben didn't want to waste words explaining how Ramos had once been hunting him and the horses he had stolen, and cutting him off from a race straight to the border, had forced him into a roundabout route. "We'll stay here tonight. Tomorrow we have to get provisions for a long journey."

Ben spread their only blanket on a mat of pine needles beneath a giant ponderosa. "You three rest on this while I stake out the horses."

"I'll help you," Evan said.

"That's not needed, Evan," Ben said, short-tempered. He instantly regretted his tone. That came from being damn tired after not having slept for two days. "Rest and save your strength for when it's really needed," he said in a kinder voice.

"Like when?" Evan came back, ill-tempered.

"Like tomorrow. We have no food and no bedrolls. There's a town name of Mateo about twelve miles west of here. You'll have to go there and buy a packhorse and the other things we need for a long trip. I can't do that, but you can. Does that answer your question?"

Without a further word, Ben took up the reins of the horses. He led the animals to the small meadow below the spring, where he staked them out to graze.

When he returned, Maude spoke to him. "Ben, there's a little bit of room here on the blanket beside me."

Ben sank down on the edge of the blanket. Maude put her arm across his chest. He felt her hip and shoulder pressing against him. Her touch gave him a grand feeling of being accepted, of belonging. He wanted to say something to her, speak words that told her how much he cared. At the moment, he could think of nothing appropriate to say.

He took her hand in his and went to sleep the happiest he had ever been in all his life.

## Forty-eight

"Ninety pesos," said the horse trader. His sly, black eyes were fastened on Evan.

"That includes the horse and the packsaddle," Evan said, and indicated both with a sweep of his hand. The horse he was buying was of only middling quality and the packsaddle had seen much usage, showing worn leather strapping and splintery wood. Still, both items would serve well enough to get his comrades and him to the States.

"Yes," said the horse trader as his sight drifted away to Evan's mount tied nearby. "Going prospecting for gold?" he asked.

"Yes. Here's your money." The man's interest in Evan's mount, which had the Valdes brand in plain view, worried him.

The horse trader turned back to Evan and held out his hand. Evan counted out all the pesos he had, and finished paying the remainder of the price in dollars. The horse trader pocketed the money, took one last look at Evan's mount, and went inside his office.

Evan buckled the packsaddle on the back of the purchased horse and climbed astride his steed. He took up the lead rope of the second horse and led it off along the street of Mateo. He didn't see the horse trader come to stand in the doorway and stare as he rode away.

Evan had arrived in Mateo a short time before and gone about the town hunting for a dealer in horses. He had searched no further than the first such business he'd encountered because he knew the danger increased with every minute he stayed in the town. Now as he rode to a general store he had seen earlier, his eyes roamed the streets and sidewalks. He was alert for anyone who seamed to pay undue attention to him.

Mateo was a prosperous, bustling silver-mining town. Several of the mines were visible on the forested mountain above town, their locations easily spotted by the large tailing piles of waste rock at each mine mouth. Two- and three-story brick buildings lined the main street, and the homes of the townsfolk were large, all telling of the substantial wealth of Mateo. Many people came and went on the street. He saw no *Norte Americanos*, no one with white skin.

He tied his horses and entered a red-fronted store with a sign stating the business was Rios Tienda. The clerk, a middle-aged woman with very dark skin, was serving two men dressed in miner's clothing. The three looked at Evan and then away and again picked up their conversation.

The store had a wide variety of goods, and Evan began to collect the various items he wanted and to stack them on the unused end of the counter. By the time Evan had made all his purchases, and loaded them on the pack-horse, Mateo had fallen under the shadow of the mountain with the silver mines. He pulled himself astride and rode south. He must hurry and find his way back before darkness hid the trail. Also, he had hungry comrades waiting for something to eat.

He came to a splendid Catholic church painted a brilliant white and with stained-glass windows showing Christ in one big window and scenes from the Bible in three others. A towering steeple rose from the peak of the roof, and a large gold cross from that. The church's double doors were opened wide, and Evan halted and sat his horse and looked inside. A few parishioners could be seen in the pews. Two women were kneeling at the altar, before which stood a priest looking down upon their bowed heads. The priest seemed to be speaking to the women. No words reached Evan. He thoughtfully rubbed his whiskered chin and rode on.

In front of a *cantina*, three coquettish *mujeres*, faces powdered a pale lavender and smoking *seegaritos*, lazed lightly on the sidewalk. One of the languid ladies of the evening stepped out into the street in front of Evan. Her trade was in her eyes as she gave Evan a red-lipped, teasing smile.

Evan touched the brim of his hat and shook his head in the negative. He had a more beautiful woman waiting for him to return.

He left the town traveling south. Frequently he glanced behind to see if he was being followed. When the town had dropped from view and no one was in sight, he turned due east and raised the horses to a lope.

Evan halted on the mountainside to let his horses catch their wind. Dusk was falling, and under the dense stand of tall pines darkness was already gathering. He still had a mile of stiff climbing to make good along a hazardous rocky trail before he reached the camp and his comrades.

He kicked his mount in the ribs and continued the ascent. He was concentrating on finding the trail on the darkening ground when his mount shied abruptly and almost unseated him. Holding to the saddle horn with one hand, he grabbed for his pistol with the other and looked for what had frightened the horse.

Ben stood in the gloom of the pine forest a few paces ahead. He held his rifle and spyglass. Evan knew it was like the man to be on the lookout for possible enemies, and he must have been observing his approach for some time.

"Glad to see you, Evan," Ben said. "Any trouble?"

"Nope. Any here?"

"No," Ben said, running his eye over the loaded packhorse. "Looks like you got enough supplies to last several days."

"I believe so."

"Best we get on to camp before it gets full dark. Here, let me have the packhorse."

Evan handed over the lead rope and then waited for Ben to go first leading the way.

Ben and Evan came to the camp at the spring in the cleft of the mountain. A small fire of dry pine limbs burned in a low place from where the light could not be seen beyond a few yards. A spit had been rigged over the fire, and a piece of meat of at least four pounds sizzled as it cooked.

"I killed a deer earlier this afternoon," Ben said. "Looks like the girls are cooking the tenderloin."

Evan nodded. "Where are they?"

"Playing it safe, I'd guess." Ben whistled a

low tone through his teeth. "Anybody home?" he called.

Rachel and Maude came out from behind trees. Maude held Ben's pistol in her hand. "We heard someone coming and wasn't sure it was you," Rachel explained.

Evan was looking at Rachel. She was in the distant reach of the firelight; however, her face seemed to glow far more brightly than the fire would make it, as if she glowed from an inner light. How he had ever survived before knowing her, he couldn't *imagine*.

"Is the meat done," Ben asked Maude.

"Nearly so but needs salt."

"I've got salt for it," Evan said. "Help me unpack."

The four turned to, and in short order the items Evan had brought were spread on the ground. A meal was prepared of baker's loaf bread, venison hot from the fire, canned corn, and canned pears. The women and men, seated on dry logs the men had dragged up within the light of the fire, began to eat lustily.

As Ben ate, he ran an eye over his comrades. They were far from being out of danger for Ramos Valdes had a long reach. Evan would have been seen by scores of people in Mateo. Any one of them could be in the service of Ramos. A man on a fast horse could ride from Mateo to the Valdes rancho in four hours.

Maude caught and held Ben's eye. She smiled at him. What a glorious thing a woman's smile freely given was, Ben thought.

The group finished eating and Maude and Rachel gathered the tin plates and other utensils that Evan had bought in Mateo. They took them to the spring to be washed.

"How long before we cross the Rio Grande?" Evan asked.

"Three weeks or so. How long do you want it to be?"

Evan grinned at Ben. "I don't care if it takes months. How about you?"

"Same here. I say we take it slow and careful. Go farther west than I first said, say another fifty miles, before we turn north. That would be on the far side of the Sierra La Catrina Mountains. Ramos would never look for us on that roundabout route to El Paso."

Maude and Rachel returned and took seats on the logs. "What were you two talking about?" Maude asked.

"How best to keep Valdes from finding us," Ben said.

"And how is that?"

"Go farther west before heading north," Ben said. "It'll be safer that way. I've never been over the route but that shouldn't be a problem. Just go north until we hit the Rio Grande and then turn east to El Paso."

Maude was watching the flames of the fire play upon Ben's scarred face. The battle wound had done terrible damage to his features. That seemed to have made him stronger, tougher. She admitted to herself that he was horribly disfigured, yet at the same time her mind softened the picture by overshadowing his face with the handsome one he had once possessed. He looked at her and her heart began a little dance.

A thought came to her, but dare she do it? Tense as a hummingbird, Maude climbed to her feet. She knew what she desired. However, she must begin the action for Ben would never do it.

She held out her hand to him. "Ben, I've found a soft bed of pine needles just right for sleeping. If you'd like for me to show you, bring two of those and come with me." She gestured down at the blankets on the ground.

Ben was stunned for a moment, then speedily recovering, came to his feet. What was Maude offering? Could it be what he was thinking? He couldn't tell because her woman's eyes were hiding what she was thinking. He scooped up two blankets and took Maude's hand, still extended toward him.

She led him away from the fire and into the darkness of the forest. Walking slowly hand in hand among the pines, they went a hundred feet. Then Maude stopped them. "Right here," she said. "Feel the softness under your feet?"

"Thick bed of needles, all right."

"I got cold last night," Maude said as she spread the first blanket. She took the second one from Ben and placed it in preparation for a cover. "Tonight that shouldn't happen."

She moved to stand against Ben. She caught his hand and brought it up and pressed it to her bosom.

Ben, his blood a hot, swift tide, began to fondle the warm, soft breast. Maude was offering him everything. He wanted everything.

She took his hand from her breast, and still holding it, drew him down on the blankets with her. Seated there, she began to disrobe, with more and more of her white body becoming visible as first the shirt and then the trousers were removed.

"You too," she said.

Ben hastily undressed and lay back on the blanket. Maude came to him and lay all her naked body along him. Ben folded her into his arms.

As the darkness thickened to deep night in the pine forest, Maude and Ben made their own private world wrapped in a blanket. Afterward, Ben lay holding Maude and studying the big stars studding the ebony sky. They seemed to be murmuring a song down to him. That was impossible, just his imagination. Then, to his amazement, Maude began to hum a soft, melodious tune up into the night sky. Was she as happy as he was and had she also heard the star song?

The joy Ben felt at the sound of Maude's voice was nearly impossible to endure. He rolled onto his side to face her and ran his hand over her smooth, curved body. He basked and reveled in his happiness. She was the right woman for him, and the right woman had an infinite value to a man.

Ben knew one thing for certain. He would have to commit murder, shoot Lester Ivorsen, for the man would never let Maude go, regardless of the new federal law barring multiple wives that Evan had told him about.

# Forty-nine

"Damn it, Evan, you know it's not safe to go back to Mateo," Ben said with a shake of his head. "Ramos might've found out you were there and be searching that area for us."

"I've asked Rachel to marry me and she said yes," Evan replied. "There's a Catholic church in Mateo and I saw a priest. He could perform the ceremony for us."

"He could be gone off on church business and we can't go running around the country looking for him."

"There's a residence beside the church. That must be where the priest lives. The odds are good that since I saw him yesterday late in the day, that he'll be there today if we ride in early."

Ben glanced at Rachel, standing with Maude near the spring and looking in Evan's and his direction. She was a grand sight and he understood why Evan wanted to marry her as soon as possible.

"Do you really have to be married first?" Ben said in a low voice, knowing Evan would understand the full meaning of the question.

"Yes, married first," Evan said sharply.

"She's been through that and I can't ask her to do it again."

Ben faced about to stare down from the mountain and in the direction of Mateo. The sun was up and filled the wide valley. He knew where Mateo lay; however, it was too far away to be seen. He dreaded taking the white women into a town where there were only brown-skin people. They would stand out like jewels, and in minutes the town would be buzzing about their presence. It would require the greatest kind of luck to find the priest and get Evan and Rachel married and then ride away before Ramos found out about their presence in the town. Hell, Ramos practically owned this part of Mexico.

"Did you see other white men in Mateo?"

"No. Still, there could have been others besides me and I just didn't see them." He wouldn't tell Ben how the horse trader had eyed the Valdes brand on his mount.

"It's still a foolish thing to do."

"Ben, I'm going to marry Rachel today with or without your help," Evan said flatly. "But I'd like for you and Maude to be witnesses."

"Does Rachel know how dangerous going into Mateo will be?"

"We talked about it and she knows."

Ben turned to Maude and called out. "What do you think, Maude, about us all going into Mateo so Evan and Rachel can get married?"

"How can we really say no?" She gave Ben a look that told it all, how they had felt during the night in each other's arms.

"All right. The sooner we get it done the better." If Ben's face had been restored, he would at this moment have asked Maude to marry him, make it a double wedding ceremony, for he wanted her permanently in his life. He could not do it for Evan might not be able to perform such a miracle, or he might be killed for there were many hazards to be avoid before reaching El Paso. Ben didn't want Maude to be married to a man with the face of a scarecrow.

*Hurry*, Ben urged the priest silently as the man performed the rite of the wedding ceremony with Evan and Rachel. It was damn risky to be here. Their horses with Valdes brands were on the street, and the front doors of the church were open so that anyone passing on the sidewalk who should happen to glance inside could not fail to see the four *Norte Americanos*.

The sunlight shining through the wide stained-glass windows cast a sparkling, wondrous rainbow of colored light into the place of worship. The priest in his religious vestments was caught in the full splendor. So too were Rachel and Evan, and even their very common clothing was brightened and seemed suitable for a marriage in this religious place.

Ben and Maude stood beside Evan and Rachel. A half score of townswomen were seated in the front pew just beyond Ben. When the four *Norte Americanos* had arrived, the women had been scattered about in the church, no two sitting together as they meditated or said their prayers. Once the women discovered the purpose of the four strangers, they had gathered as near as possible to view the ceremony. A very young woman appeared to be in a trance of wonderment as she gazed at Rachel and Maude.

The four Americans had reached the outskirts of Mateo in early morning. There Ben and the two women had remained while Evan had gone on to find the priest and arrange for the wedding. Luckily, the priest, Father Xavier, had been at home, and readily agreed to the request to perform a marriage. Evan returned to his comrades and they all rode directly to the church.

In spite of Ben's concern with their safety, he was caught up in the brilliantly colored light pouring into the church, in the quiet words and dignity of the priest, and most of all in the joy his friends showed as they were being married. He peered down at Maude, holding his hand. She was absorbed in the ritual. *Pretty gal, maybe someday you and I can do the same.*

The jingle of spurs came to Ben from the rear of the church and he looked over his shoulder. A tall white man stood in the open entryway, eyeing them. He wore dusty clothing and twin pistols and a belt full of cartridges. His face registered obvious recognition. He gave Ben a wolfish grin, and then pivoted about and disappeared from the doorway. Ben focused back to the front in time to hear the priest say, "...kiss the bride."

Evan took Rachel into his arms and kissed her soundly. He looked happily at Ben, and saw worry pulling at his scars. "What's wrong?" Evan asked.

"There was an American in the doorway just now. I could tell he knew who we were. He's on his way to tell Ramos where we are. We've got to leave at once."

Ben caught Maude by the arm and hastened from the church and out onto the sidewalk. He flung a look along the street in both directions. The American wasn't in sight. He would be hiding someplace close to mark the direction of their flight.

"Let's ride," Ben said quickly to Evan, who had followed with Rachel from the church. "Get the girls up."

The presence of the American most probably meant that Evan had been identified the day before and Ramos and his sons were in Mateo. The four of them were in a hell of a fix. Their horses had just covered twelve miles at a fast pace, and now must try to outrun Ramos and his son on fresh ones. It was impossible to do that for the Valdes men would be riding the very fastest of all their horses.

The four mounted hurriedly. With Ben leading the packhorse, they raced from Mateo.

Tattersall came out of the alley and stared after the four riders racing their horses down a street of the town. They were caught and just didn't know it yet. He hastened to his mount and rode swiftly along the street.

Hawkins was a stupid man to have stopped in Mateo, which was only a few hours' ride from the Valdes rancho. Tattersall understood the man's need for provisions, but that surely had been accomplished the day before. Had he remained there for a second day just to get married? And in the meantime allow the horse trader time to ride and give Ramos the information about the presence of a gringo riding a Valdes horse?

Ramos had played it shrewdly upon discovering the two girls had escaped. Carlos and Leo had wanted to mount and race out over the land searching for them. Ramos had corralled them at the hacienda, and in their place had sent a hundred men out to alert the people of the surrounding ranchos and towns that four *Norte Americanos* were wanted by Valdes and that any information as to their whereabouts would be hugely rewarded. Within one day the horse trader had appeared.

Ramos and his sons and Tattersall with Adkisson and Oakman had immediately traveled to Mateo. Ramos had established a temporary headquarters at the home of Juan Bustamente on the edge of the town. Again

Ramos had sent riders out to tell the people of his need to find the four Americans. Tattersall had, with the greatest of good fortune, found the four not a quarter mile from where Ramos waited.

Tattersall entered the Bustamente home and reported his discovery to Ramos.

"Are you certain they were getting married?" Ramos asked.

"They were paired off. The blond woman with Hawkins, I knew him by his face, and the green-eyed woman with the second gringo. The priest was doing the ceremony. They were getting married and that's why they were still in Mateo."

"Are you sure of that?" Leo asked. "Getting married?"

"Sure am," Tattersall answered sourly, not liking being asked the same question twice. He spoke to Ramos. "Hawkins ain't as savvy as you thought he was."

"I'll kill her, I'll kill them all," Carlos raged, no longer able to control his disappointment and anger.

"I don't want to kill Maude," Leo said.

"They've betrayed us, Leo," Carlos said. "They've got to die."

"How could they betray us? They weren't married to us, not yet."

"They knew they would be soon as the priest arrived. They must be punished."

Leo spoke to Ramos. "Father, they shouldn't die for what they did. We'll catch them and go on with what we planned."

"Carlos is correct," Ramos said. "Now that they are married, we can't act as if nothing has happened." Ramos spoke to Tattersall. "Did Hawkins see you?"

"I'm sure he did for they immediately ran from the church and rode off fast."

"How long ago was this? Which direction?"

"To the west and not more than ten minutes ago."

"He'll try to lose us by going into the mountains," Ramos said. "But he won't be able to. The rain has washed out all the old tracks and we'll have fresh ones to follow. We can catch him before dark."

"Don't forget Hawkins's rifle," Carlos said.

"We won't make the mistake you did," Ramos said. "We'll pen them down and hold them until they starve for water and have to give up."

"When they show themselves, we kill them," Carlos said.

"Tattersall, you and your men will come with us," Ramos said. "Now mount up."

# Fifty

"We can't outrun them," Ben said to Evan as he aimed his spyglass back toward Mateo. "We've got to think of something else."

Ben had halted them on the crest of the range of hills west of Mateo. He had to know how many Valdes men were in pursuit. His mind churned, evaluating the possibilities of how to elude his foes, as he focused the glass.

"They're in sight," he said, steadying the glass on the riders streaming like a string of black ants over a ridge top a mile back.

"Six of them," he added as he finished his count. "They'll run us to ground in short order."

He snapped the spyglass closed in his hand, reined his horse around, and sped down the far side of the hill.

"There they are on that next hill," Carlos shouted out above the pounding of the horses' hooves. He pointed across the valley that separated the hill they had just climbed from the one their quarry was climbing.

"I see them," Leo called back. He wished they had not been seen, that they never were found. He didn't want Maude to be killed.

"We'll have them cornered in an hour," Ramos said. He laughed wildly. He had wanted to see Hawkins die for many months, ever since he had stolen those first prized horses.

He looked behind and shouted out to Tattersall, riding directly behind. "You ready to earn your gold?"

"I'm ready," Tattersall shouted back. As he viewed the distant riders, they reached the crown of the hill and vanished from sight beyond. He was surprised at how close they were. He would have thought they had a longer lead than that. He spurred to keep up with the racing Valdes.

Ben felt a sense of abandonment as he watched Evan and Maude and Rachel draw swiftly away. He squashed the feeling for hadn't he ordered Evan, using the threat of a beating to enforce his order, to take the two girls and ride on without him? Ben's scarred face twisted into a savage grimace as he looked in the direction from which his enemies would come. He felt the quickening of a ferocious exhilaration as he anticipated the impending battle with six guns arrayed against his one. Evan and he had taken Maude and Rachel from the Valdes brothers. Now, under Evan's care, they would make it safely north of the Rio Grande. Ben's task was to stop the Valdes men if he could.

He lay in the shallow channel of the dry streambed near the center of the flat valley bottom. Ramos's band of gunmen would soon be riding across the quarter-mile-wide section of land in pursuit of Ben and his comrades. The chase had barely begun, and Ben knew they could have stayed out in front of the men for several more miles. However, for any ambush to succeed it had to be pulled early, close enough that the foxy Ramos could see those he pursued, but not so close that he could see there were only three riders on the five horses. He hoped Carlos and Leo were not with the riders, for he had promised their mother that he wouldn't kill them.

The depression in the land that held him was a foot deep and barely hid his body. He pressed down as low as possible for he must not be seen before his foes were within range of his rifle.

They came swiftly on. Ben heard the growing thunder of the hooves of their steeds. Daring not to look, he cocked his ear trying to estimate their distance from him. He must launch his attack when they were within range, but not so close that they could ride over him before he could get off his rifle shots.

Three hundred yards away? Probably. The six enemies came pounding on. Now two hundred. Yes, surely.

Ben rose to a sitting position with his Spencer rifle at his shoulder. The men were closer than he wanted. He recognized Ramos at once, his brightly colored clothing with its silver decorations standing out like a flag. Carlos and another Mexican, a smaller man, rode with Ramos in front of the Americans. Ben thought the smaller man would most likely be Leo, whom he had never seen. He brought Ramos into the sights of his rifle and fired.

At the sudden appearance of Ben rising up with his rifle, Ramos instantly reined his horse in. But he was far too late. Ben's bullet plowed into him and tore him from the saddle and hurled him to the ground.

Tattersall, who had been directly behind Ramos, ran his horse directly over the corpse. He pulled his pistol and rushed straight at Ben.

Ben fired at Tattersall, catching him dead center and slamming him to the ground. He shot one of the remaining Americans. Before the man could fall to the ground, Ben swiftly rotated the rifle the short arc to the last American. He killed that man too.

Carlos was raking his mount with spurs and rapidly closing on Ben. He fired his pistol.

Ben felt the wind as the bullet fanned his cheek. Carlos fired again and the top of Ben's shoulder began to sting. Carlos was now within easy pistol range and would kill him with the next shot.

Ben shifted the rifle and brought Carlos into the sights. *I'm sorry, Helena, it's either him or me.* Ben fired and saw the bullet knock Carlos from his horse.

Ben swung the rifle farther to the side and caught the third Mexican, who he thought was Leo, in the sights. He moved his point of aim slightly and fired. Leo jerked as the bullet skimmed across his ribs, tearing flesh. He reined his mount away at a steep angle. Ben let him go.

The horses of the downed men ran on ahead, passing Ben with loose reins and flapping stirrups.

Ben climbed to his feet and surveyed the bodies of the men he had shot. They had fallen roughly in a line, with Carlos the nearest, not thirty yards from him. Though confident that his shots had gone true to their mark, Ben cautiously watched them as he approached Leo.

The man was some seventy yards away and

off to the side. He was still mounted, watching Ben and holding his ribs.

Ben eyed Leo warily. He didn't think he had wounded him so severely that he couldn't fight, but hoped he wouldn't continue it. Even as Ben observed Leo, the man slid from his saddle and fell unconscious to the ground.

Ben hastened forward and disarmed Leo. Then he prodded him with the toe of his boot until he came to his senses.

Leo rose to a sitting position. Fighting his pain, he watched the scarred *Norte Americano*.

Ben saw the expectation in the young Mexican's face that he was going to die. However, he showed little fear and that pleased Ben. After half a minute with neither man uttering a word, Leo looked about at the dead men. Tears came into his eyes.

"You killed my father and brother, so what are you waiting for? Kill the last Valdes."

"I can't, but you deserve to die for what you did."

"What's stopping you?"

"Because of a promise, a promise I made to your mother. She loved her sons and because of that helped free Maude and Rachel so I wouldn't kill you. Do you hear me plain? It's because of your mother that you're not laying there dead with the others."

"She betrayed us, and now my father and Carlos are dead." There was a sob in Leo's voice.

"Far from it. She risked your and Carlos's

hate to save you. I would've spared Carlos too if there had been a way to do it."

Again the men fell silent, with Leo staring at the body of his father and brother.

Finally Ben said, "Can you ride?"

"Yes."

"All right. I'll tie Ramos and Carlos on their horses and you can take them back with you."

Ben put the open end of the rifle barrel against Leo's forehead. Leo flinched back at the touch of the hard metal.

"If you ever come north of the Rio Grande, I'll kill you for sure," Ben said in a flat, dead voice. "That's regardless of my promise to your mother. Now go home and thank her for saving your life."

# Fifty-one

Ben, with Maude, Evan, and Rachel, crossed the Rio Grande on the twenty-second day after the battle with the Valdes men near Mateo. Ben had caught one of the slain American's horses and overtaken Evan and the women the evening of the same day. They had traveled leisurely, enjoying their new relationships. Two days after crossing the river, they reached El Paso. Evan and Rachel turned west to Evan's parents' rancho, while Ben and Maude went north to Canutillo.

"Lester's been mad as a hatter ever since Maude disappeared," Tom Hawkins told his brother Ben and Maude.

The three of them, with Tom's wife Sally, holding her child, were seated on the porch of Tom's home. Ben and Maude had come to the house on a route that skirted the town to avoid being seen until they had the latest news about Lester Ivorsen.

"Lester didn't believe Silas's story about a Mexican carrying Maude off," Sally said.

"Silas told the truth for that's what happened to me," Maude said.

"I believed old Silas for I've never heard of him telling a lie," Tom said. "And Ben came looking for you, which he wouldn't do if the two of you had gone off together. But anyway, Lester is so damn jealous of his younger wives that he can't think straight. He's stomped half a dozen men in town because he thought they were flirting with them."

"They'd have a right to flirt with them," Ben said. "There's a new federal law that says a man can have only one wife at a time. So Lester is really married to just his first one."

"You sure about this?" Tom said.

"I was told so by someone who was back East when the law was passed and knows it's a fact."

"Sally, do you hear that?" Tom said.

"Sounds like a fine law to me," Sally replied.

"I thought you'd like it," Tom said with a chuckle. He was evaluating Ben and Maude. "Neither of you seem the worse for the trip to

Mexico. You'll have to tell Sally and me about it."

"We've got a visitor coming and he seems in a hurry," Sally said as she looked down the short lane to the street.

"It's Wade Tidwell," Tom said. He raised his voice and called out. "Wade, what's the big hurry?"

"It's Lester Ivorsen," Wade said as he came to a halt in the yard. "He's set off to kill your brother Eddy." He looked more closely at the people on the porch. "Well, I'll be damned," he said. "Hi there, Ben. Didn't know you were back in town."

"Just got here. What's this about Eddy?" Eddy was Tom's full brother and Ben's half brother.

"Lester came up on Eddy talking with Alice on the street in town. He roughed Eddy up something mean. But that wasn't enough for Lester, and he told Eddy to go get a pistol for he was going to get his and come shoot him."

"Eddy's not good with a gun," Tom said. "He can't hit anything. Lester will kill him."

"That's exactly what I thought and so I came to tell you fast as I could. Just in case you wanted to do something to stop Lester."

"Where is Eddy?" Tom asked.

"Like I said before, Lester walloped him good. He got a bad cut over one eye and a smashed mouth. So he headed for Doc Shelton's office."

"I'd better go and see about Eddy," Tom said, looking at Sally. "There's no time to ride to El Paso to get the sheriff to stop Lester."

"Lester's mean, Tom, so be careful," Sally said with a worried expression.

Ben came to his feet beside Tom. "I'll just walk along with you."

"Glad to have your company."

Ben spoke to Maude. "Will you wait here for me?"

"I want to come too."

"Best that you stay here and let me and Tom handle this alone. Lester might go plumb crazy if he saw you and somehow hurt you before I could stop him."

"All right, Ben. You're coming back, aren't you?" Maude's face was strained with concern.

"I won't be long." All the forces of heaven and hell couldn't prevent him from returning to Maude.


"Lester, you have this all wrong and you've got no reason to be mad at me," Eddy said, his voice thin. Damnation, he hated the big man. The ease with which Lester had beaten him was hellishly humiliating. Adding to the feeling was the damage done to him. The cut over his eye had required four stitches and the stub of a broken tooth had had to be pulled. The taste of blood was heavy in his mouth.

Eddy had just left the doctor, and his lean body was backed up to the fence that ran in front of the office. Lester had come upon him there, and now stood in the street with his hand resting on the butt of a pistol belted to his waist. His face was grim with his intent to shoot Eddy.

"All I did was to pass the time of day with Alice," Eddy said, trying to strengthen his voice. "Just like I would any other woman in town."

A man and woman had halted on the sidewalk halfway down the block and were now watching. A man on horseback sat observing the confrontation. Two men came out of the store across the street and stopped and cast their eyes upon Eddy and Lester.

"You're a liar," Lester shot back. "I saw the look on your face when I came up on you two. Now I'm going to do what any man would do if somebody insulted his wife."

"I didn't insult Alice. Just ask her and she'll tell you that."

"Stop whining and fight," Lester said with a sneer.

"I don't want to fight you, and I don't have a gun."

"You'll have to fight me for I'll make you."

"Lester, Alice isn't your wife," Ben called out in a voice heard throughout the street.

Lester and Eddy had been so focused on each other that they hadn't seen Ben and Tom approach. Now both whirled to look in the direction of the voice.

Ben continued to speak. "She can't be, for there's a new federal law against a man having more than one. So Eddy has a perfect right to talk to Alice. Hell, he can even take her out walking and do a little hugging and kissing."

"Hawkins!" Lester shouted, his surprise complete.

"Yeah, it's me, Lester. I think I'm the fellow you're really mad at."

"God, how I've prayed to see you again and make you pay for running off with Maude."

Ben smiled, pleased at being able to redirect Lester's anger from Eddy to himself. He coiled, ready to draw his pistol and kill Lester. "Like I told you, you can have only one. All the other women you've got can go off with any man they take a fancy to."

"Are you sure about the law?" Eddy asked. "That a man can't have but one wife?"

"Yes, it's a fact. One wife for each man."

"That's a lie," Lester shouted. "I'm going to kill you, you wife-stealing bastard."

"No!" Eddy called out in a strong voice. "Lester, you started with me first. And by God you have to finish with me first."

"Then get yourself a gun," Lester snarled. "Let's get it over with so I can tend to that brother of yours."

Eddy crossed to Ben. "Loan me your pistol, Ben."

"He'll kill you," Ben said in a low tone. "Let me have him. I'll shoot both his eyes out."

"I can't do that. I want Alice for my wife, and I believe she's willing if Lester wasn't around to stop her."

"I've got a woman reason to shoot him too."

"Stop the confab," Lester called out harshly.

Ben and Eddy ignored Lester's shout.

"I know about Maude," Eddy said. "But this is something I've got to do for myself. He's beat me up twice and I can't take that. And he stands in the way of me getting Alice."

"If he kills you, I'm going to kill him."

"I'd want you to," Eddy said with a crooked grin.

Ben pulled his pistol and gave it to Eddy. "The trigger's mighty light, so watch it."

"We do crazy things for a woman," Eddy said.

He whirled and began to walk toward Lester, firing the pistol. The first bullet, fired unintentionally because of the light trigger, went into the ground at Lester's feet.

Lester raised his pistol to return the fire of the man walking with determined steps toward him. As he sighted down the barrel, Eddy's second bullet struck him in the side and spun him partially around. He turned back to the front again and aimed his pistol.

Eddy's third bullet hit Lester in the side of the neck. A fourth stabbed him in the stomach. Eddy was within a very few feet of Lester. He emptied his last two shots into his adversary's collapsing body.

## Fifty-two

Ben's body quivered and quaked with unimaginable pain as the scalpel cut into the flesh of his face. His muscles corded and bulged against the straps that held him to the operating table, and they fought against the strong hands of Talbott, Tom Hawkins, and John Davis, who were holding him down with all their strength.

"Hold him still," Evan said sharply. "I must make this last incision very precisely." The operation had gone on for more than two hours with the shock to Ben's body building relentlessly. Evan must quickly finish before he killed Ben, as he had other men.

The operation had begun when the first sunlight had come streaming in the window and brightly illuminated the operating table within the office of Doctor Talbott in El Paso. The generous doctor had agreed to lend his office and surgical instruments to Evan for the operation. Also, he remained to observe and to help Evan when he could.

Prior to beginning the operation, Evan had heavily dosed Ben with laudanum and whiskey until he was stupefied and finally unconscious. Yet he knew the drugs were only partially effective in alleviating pain and that Ben would suffer horribly from the cutting of the scalpel. Ben had then been strapped to the operating table and the three strong men had taken hold of him. Evan had made his first incision.

Now and again the pain brought Ben up from the stupor caused by the drugs, and his eyes would open and he would seem to be aware of what was happening, and would look at Evan as if trying to see him from some great distance.

At those times, Evan spoke to Ben. "Hold on, my friend, for we are making good progress." And Ben's eyes would close. Each time this occurred, Evan gave thanks that Ben's expressive eyes hadn't been damaged by the cannonball that had struck him.

Evan had cut free, by sections, the flesh that had been damaged and had grown attached to the skull in the wrong place. Then, with his artistic surgeon's hands, he had stretched and shaped the flesh to its original form and sewn it back into place with small, neat stitches.

The operation was turning out more successfully than Evan had dared hope. He had found that some muscles and tendons of the mutilated face were still attached to their proper position on Ben's skull. However, most had been torn completely away from their anchor point. Some of those were ripped and shredded, making their reattachment very difficult.

Finishing the last stitch, Evan spoke to the men holding Ben. "You can release him now."

He turned to Maude, who had sat and watched the operation from the very beginning. He had heard her sob at times, when Ben cried out with pain, and at those times when Evan cut free a section of flesh and blood had poured out and run across the table.

"The operation is complete, Maude," Evan said.

"Thank God," Maude said, looking at Evan through tears. "How is he?"

"This was a very major operation. However, Ben is a stout fellow and has come through it. His face will swell and he will be in great pain for days. Pray that there is no infection."

"Oh, I will pray every minute."

"Ben will need at least one more operation. Nothing nearly as long or as difficult as this one. Just a minor one to put a final smoothness on the scars that remain. In the end, you will have a handsome boyfriend."

"He has been a handsome man to me even during these past months. Now soon he will be my handsome husband."